THE BEAUTIFUL MIND of a Butterfly

Carter Lynn

ISBN: 9780999579954

Library of Congress Number: 2019912708

Publishing Services by Stanton Publishing House

Atlanta, Georgia

THE BEAUTIFUL MIND OF A BUTTERFLY

Carter Lynn

CARTER LYNN

"Every failure is a blessing in disguise, providing it teaches some needed lesson one could not have learned without it. Mostly so-called failures are only temporary defeats."

~Napoleon Hill

DEDICATION

To my sisters, Cookie and Sheila.

CONTENTS

ACKNOWLEDGMENTS

I am very grateful to my mother, Lucille for her continued support and the tenacious hold she has on life. I would like to thank Debra Antney for her encouragement and insight. It has proved to be invaluable. Thank you to Rosa Worth for her advice and editing skills which put me on to a better literary flow. To Arlinda Hawk, who takes care of my aging mother, while I'm working hard to carve my name into the world of suspense writing. What would my family do without you?

To my older sister Cookie, you believed in me when I was finding it hard to believe in myself. I love you! And to my sister Shelia Mack, without you, none of this would be possible. Rest in peace. To my readers, I thank you for taking a chance on me. I promise to provide you with the best that I can. Thank you!!!

PROLOGUE

Brownstown, Michigan was a stone's throw from Detroit. The killer rented a car from the airport yesterday afternoon and an hour ago found that same color, make and model in the parking lot of a low-end gentlemen's club, stole the license plates and using adhesive backing, affixed them to the rental. The killer chose this club because it was small and didn't have any external surveillance cameras. Wearing dark clothing with a dark baseball cap pulled low over their brow, the killer was ready.

The target couple had been out to dinner at Salvadore's, an authentic Central American restaurant in the downtown area. They knew the couple's movements because one of them had bought Karen the iPhone she still carried. Even though the number had changed, she neglected to change the password which logged her or anyone else on to a GPS tracking site for lost or stolen phones. The killer was right now looking at that website on a burner smartphone.

Leaving the restaurant after they pulled away and racing ahead to Brandon Fuller's home where the lovebirds lived together, the shooter parked down the street in front of a large grassy field and waited patiently while listening to smooth jazz on the radio. When Brandon's big Silverado truck passed by and swung into the driveway, the killer pulled up leaving the engine running with the car door open and the interior lights off.

With a large manila envelope in one gloved hand and a Ruger .357 snub-nosed revolver gripped tightly in the right jacket pocket, the killer said, "Process server!"

In one fluid motion, extending the left hand with the envelope letting it drop while pulling the gun, the killer stood on tiptoe and shot Brandon once in his face, and again in the center of his chest. The woman Karen was frozen in shock as a bullet was fired into her face at a downward angle. The first bullet punched out the woman's left eye

while the other tunneled through her brain coming to rest lazily at the back of her skull as she slumped to the driveway's pavement. The killer turned and shot Brandon almost point-blank
in the head twice more and let the empty gun slip from their fingers while rushing back to the car. Game on!

1 CHICAGO

Autumn has always been Chicago's favorite season. She loves everything about it except for the long hours of darkness. It's not that the dark bothered her that much; she just preferred the bright light of day where there were no spooky shadows, dank cubbyholes, or creepy crevices for something or someone to hide in. Light always showed you the perfect imperfections of humanity to be admired, criticized, and rightly or wrongly judged.

Dr. Chicago Daniels often worked late hours because most of her patients held down standard 9 to 5 jobs; which only left their evenings free for the one-on-one sessions they had with her. The late hours were par for the course. She didn't mind them at all; but her husband, Dorian did. He complained about her 80-hour work weeks, them not spending any quality time together, and their recent lack of sexual activity. Chicago realized that of late their marriage was rocky. They argued about everything imaginable; not having children, an abandoned toothbrush on the bathroom vanity, why she used her maiden name and not her married one. A couple of nights before, they even argued about characters in a cable network show. Somehow that ridiculous argument led to snide remarks about Chicago working late, which in turn led to her attacking his ego.

Suffice it to say their home life had been polarized by that rift. He kept to the home office and rooftop patio; she to the kitchen and living room. The master suite was neutral ground only because they both had to sleep. Chicago wanted peace in her household and that could only come from peace in her marriage. As a well-educated and trained behavioral psychologist, she understood the need for peace in her marriage more than most. So, she ended her workday just after six in the evening. If she and Dorian were going to make it, she needed to make a few sacrifices. One sacrifice was to get home early enough to eat dinner with him and maybe have sex.

She'd just left her office and was thinking of her last patient, a mother of three, ages four, seven, and nine who had been in a decadelong affair with her married boss. Two of the three children belonged to her boss; and as is the case in these kinds of relationships, he didn't leave his wife as he had promised her. His reason was that he couldn't trust her because she'd had a child with another man. Oddly enough, Chicago was treating the woman for the resentment she felt toward that particular child and not for her obvious lack of self-worth. Chicago purposed to work that into their future sessions.

This workday hadn't been any different from any other workday that she had seen patients. Nonetheless, her sixth sense was tingling. There wasn't anything, in particular, she could attribute the feeling to, either. Something just felt out of place. She pressed her key fob twice as she walked to her car, glad that it started remotely. She was a bit agitated and jittery. Chicago cautiously looked around the parking lot on Northwestern Highway that she shared with a psychiatrist, two dentists, and a plastic surgeon.

Hurriedly, she slid into the safety of her car and locked the doors. Once ensconced in the cool leather seats, she dismissed her paranoia as undeserved feelings of ill will. Still a bit nervous, she carefully pulled out of the medical building's parking lot and eased into the evening traffic. She fiddled with the radio channels until she heard Adele's strong voice resonate throughout the expensive speaker system soothing her agitated soul. The song ended abruptly and was replaced by a commercial for a "You buy - We fry" restaurant. She was baffled at the thought of anyone buying food from someone sounding like a used car salesman.

When she stopped at a red light, she synched her phone to her car's entertainment system and clicked on the Pandora music app. She heard Jill Scott preaching the beauty and strength of all women in a voice so sultry and audibly inviting that it immediately vanquished her tingles. Chicago sat up in her seat, gripped the steering wheel a little tighter, pressed her Prada boot harder on the accelerator until the Audi's speedometer was 10 miles over the speed limit. It was getting late and there was a stop she needed to make.

The average-looking white man in the dark-colored, panel van kept the lights of the silver, late-model Audi luxury sedan in his sights.

However, he made sure not to increase his speed where he was in Oakland County. Some state troopers or eager beaver sheriff's deputy might have too many questions if they were to pull him over and search his van. He could hear the conversation in his mind:

"Why the handcuffs sir?"

"Well, I've always wanted to be an officer of the law."

"All right; but what's with the rolls of duct tape?"

"It's the epitome of all purpose. Why wouldn't I have a thick roll or two?"

"Okay. That's plausible; but what about this single action .45 caliber Colt with silencer and this here bag of sex toys?"

"To be honest officer, those things along with my 50,000-volt projectile taser are all part of my rape, torture, and murder kit!"

Sanford Smalls didn't think the police would let him talk his way out of going to jail behind that exchange, so he kept his eyes peeled like a good ripe banana for law enforcement and he drove within the legal limit.

The taillights of the Audi were shrinking rapidly, but Sanford didn't have to worry. Looking at the laptop resting in the passenger's seat, Sanford could track her within three miles. My, isn't GPS wonderful! he thought to himself. Fuck what he was instructed to do. Sanford knew what he was going to do. He was going to travel deep inside of Chicago, or was he? This was more of a job for Super Sadist! Dun, dun, dun, dun! The woman who was riding in the car next to him saw Sanford laughing happily and started to laugh to herself while thinking, this guy seems like a joy to be around. An absolute joy!

Chicago flew across three lanes of traffic barely making the Southfield freeway exit south when her phone rang. Thumbing the answer button on the steering wheel she said, "Dr. Chicago Daniels speaking., How may I help you?"

The person on the other end exhaled loudly. "Hello, I'm looking for my wife."

"This is her." He didn't say anything, and she could imagine him brooding. "Hey, Dorian. I'm on my way home as we speak. Do you want me to bring you anything?"

There was a long pause before he responded. "My wife, and maybe some ice cream." To her dismay, the call ended abruptly, and she heard Elton John's voice singing "*Benny and the Jets.*"

At that, she mused that things hadn't been going well for them, lately. Chicago used to think that Dorian was secure enough to handle her success. Not anymore. She even suspected him of infidelity but had no tangible proof. Her practice was thriving and had been consistently for the past few years. Recently, she brought in a friend, Freida Goldberg, from med school to take on her patient overflow. Just the other day, she and Freida discussed bringing someone else in and perhaps purchasing the offices on the third floor to afford them more room.

Dorian, on the other hand, had been hinting at maybe adopting a child; but Chicago had made it quite clear to him before they married that she didn't want kids. It didn't take Sigmund Freud to see what Dorian was trying to do. He wanted to curb her success. But he should know that not every woman was excited by the joys of motherhood. Coming out of her reverie, she turned up the volume and sang along with Elton John. "Benny! Benny! Benny! Benny and the jets!"

Peek-Inns Family Ice Cream Parlor on Woodward Avenue and Peterboro in midtown was open six days a week, Tuesday through Sunday from noon to midnight. Chicago loved their Butter Pecan Peanut Brittle Crunch and Dorian always seemed in a better mood after wolfing down a pint of Roadmaster Rocky Road. It was usually very busy in and around the ice cream parlor, but tonight she found a parking spot less than 50 yards west of the corner of Woodward on Peterboro.

The neighborhood used to be a thriving illegal drug market known as the Cass corridor, but with a new mayor and police chief, some serious changes were made. First, the revitalization of downtown Detroit and now the resurgence of midtown commonly called the Wayne State or University District. The area was experiencing gentrification at a rapid rate. Midtown was already very diverse; and with whites returning in masses, crime plummeted drastically.

Chicago tucked her purse under the driver's seat after getting some money from her wallet. A cautious woman, she checked her surroundings and twisted the four-carat pea-shaped blue diamond on her ring finger to the inside of her hand. She was thinking of being safe as she walked toward the ice cream parlor. She hit the wrong button and instead of arming her car, she set the alarm off. She quickly reset it and looked around. She didn't see anyone, but like Spiderman, her senses were tingling out of control.

Cautiously looking around she took in the empty midtown street. There wasn't anything that looked ominous. The only sounds she heard were the ebb and flow of traffic up ahead on Woodward Avenue and the rustle of trash and leaves propelled along the gutter by the strong autumn wind. Chicago continued walking, and the sound of her heels striking confidently against the concrete, cast away her feelings of something being wrong. She reasoned to herself that the feeling was unfounded, and she convinced herself that the feeling of foreboding was from her getting home and ending up arguing with her husband. Hence, the ice cream peace offering.

Sanford Tolliver Smalls was a man of medium height with thinning brown hair. The only adjective that could accurately describe him was 'bland.' There was nothing at all that stood about him, and that's just how he wanted it. In a major city like Detroit bland was the equivalent of invisible; and being invisible was great unless he wanted to spend the next 25 years playing pick up the soap with a cellmate named Horsemeat Johnson or Elephant Trunk Reams, using his rectum as a parking spot. No, he thought to himself, this invisibly bland white boy has other plans that don't include incarceration. His musings ended as he eased the stolen van, he was driving next to Chicago's Audi.

Inconspicuously, he checked up and down the dark street. His pistol was held snugly in the waistband of his dark blue work pants, while the stun gun rested comfortably in his work jacket. Smoothly, getting out of the van he went around to the passenger side and cracked the sliding panel door just a wee bit. Then he pulled out a small notepad and ink pen pretending to write. This wasn't part of the original plan, but improvisation was definitely his strong suit. It took less than two minutes before he perked up at the sound of the staccato rhythm of his victim's heels drifting on the wind to his ears. Sanford felt himself growing erect and smiled.

As soon as Chicago turned the corner, she saw the panel van parked parallel to her car. She couldn't see much else because of the van's bright headlights. She walked closer and stopped a car length away. Speaking authoritatively, she asked, "Can I help you? What are you doing near my car?"

The man looked up at her. He had been writing something. Even though Chicago couldn't see him clearly, she saw him well enough. He was unremarkable in every way that mattered. Average build, average height, average weight with thinning hair, and a pair of tortoiseshell glasses resting on the bridge of a thin aquiline nose that seemed too feminine for his face.

In a word, he looked harmless.

He quickly explained to her that he was driving up the block when the car in front of him sideswiped hers. "I figured I'd be a good Samaritan and leave a note with what I caught of the other car's license plate and my cellphone number in case a witness was needed." At that explanation, she felt she knew what all the tingling was about.

"I certainly don't need this. I really don't!"

But even as she walked closer to her car to see the extent of the 'damage,' she really sensed that something was wrong. The hairs on the back of her neck stood on end as she suddenly realized that had

9

her car been struck, the alarm would have gone off. And she saw that the side door of the man's van was partially opened. Just as she thought to run, she heard a loud sizzling pop sound just before 50,000 volts of electricity coursed through her body seizing her in an iron vise-like grip of shock. She fell to the ground. Embarrassingly, she felt her bladder empty and a warm gush of urine race from between her thighs then slowed to a trickle. The average looking man was smiling at her right before he plunged a hypodermic needle into her neck. He then picked her up and threw her into the van like a sack of potatoes. He tossed in a bag with something cold in it. "I see you've purchased some ice cream for us. How sweet of you, Dr. Daniels." Just before she lost consciousness, she thought to herself, how does he know my name? Then nothing.

As she drifted back to consciousness, she smelled jasmine and lavender. It smelled just like her bedroom. Thank God, it must have all just been some horrific nightmare, she thought. Chicago started to stretch her limbs in the comfortable bed when the plastic underneath her stuck to her skin. When she tried to feel why there was plastic on her bed, her arms wouldn't move from above her head. She opened her eyes and rolled them back and up as far as she could so that she could see her hands. Her fingers could move and were all present and accounted for. But her wrists were handcuffed to one of the brass bed's decorative bars. When she was able to focus, she realized that she was definitely not in her own bedroom. The room she was being held captive in was three times smaller than hers and covered in wall-to-wall plastic. The ceiling, walls, and floor were all covered in plastic! Chicago dared not even imagine what fate that lunatic had in store for her.

She lay sprawled and naked on the queen-sized brass bed, which was pushed against the wall opposite the room's only door. There was no other furniture in the room except for a high-backed metal chair where the average man from her nightmare sat. Next to him was a tripod with a smartphone positioned atop it, pointed directly at her. She watched fearfully as Sanford took a hefty spoonful of the Roadmaster Rocky Road ice cream that was meant for Dorian. He smiled and gave a gratifying "Mm mph!"

"Now this is really good. I don't think you can find ice cream this good anywhere else. Did you know they make all of their ice cream from scratch?"

She couldn't believe what was happening. He casually stuck his spoon into the pint container before placing it on the floor. Then he picked up what looked like a baton. "Chicago? Do you mind if I call you Chicago instead of Dr. Daniels? It sounds more personable." He waited on her to answer, but she kept her mouth shut. "You and I are going to have so much fun together. First, let me tell you my rules. We don't want to start off on the wrong foot." He pulled a condom out of his pocket and opened it slowly in front of her. She watched in horror as he put it on the baton looking thing he held in his hands. He walked over to her and snatched a piece of precut duct tape from where it was stuck on the wall next to the bed and slapped it roughly over her mouth.

Chicago was completely terrified. He showed her what she at first believed to be a baton. Then when he slid the condom over it, she thought it was some type of grotesque sex toy. It was not! He ran it over her face, between her cleavage to her navel and beyond. "Rule number one: You may scream as loud and as long as you want. In fact, I would prefer it if you did. Rule number two: Whatever I say goes. Sanford says, is more powerful than Simon says. Simon won't kill you, but I most definitely will. Rule number three: My pleasure is paramount to all else. Rule number four: Forget your former life. I am your life and death. Rule five is simple: Any attempt to escape or trying to use your psychobabble on me will result in punishment or death, depending on my mood."

She whimpered as he touched her pubic area. "Do you know what this is? It looks like a vicious phallus doesn't it?" Sanford rubbed it in places her husband hadn't touched in months. "It's a cattle prod." The pain shot through her body causing her to lose control of her bowels. "You filthy little slut!" he shouted at her when she lost her bowels. He zapped her again and she almost swallowed her tongue.

"I'm going to clean you up before we continue." She watched as he went over to a corner next to the door where there was a stack of supplies that she hadn't noticed before. He slipped on a pair of surgical gloves, grabbed some rags and bleach wipes.

After he had cleaned her, he sat a large bucket with a lid on it by the bed. "This is your toilet. When I'm here you will ask my permission to use the facilities or face punishment."

Sanford ripped the tape from her mouth. "Is that fear I see in those gorgeous eyes?" Chicago was definitely afraid, but she was trying hard not to show it. Men like him thrive off of fear. "Why are you doing this to me?" she asked in a calm professional tone reserved for her patients. At that Sanford smiled his crooked smile right before punching her in the stomach. She was clinging to consciousness by a gossamer thread when suddenly, he slapped her across the face. The blow was the equivalent of being hit with a defibrillator.

"You filthy fucking cunt!" Sanford screamed. "I'm not your patient, Bitch!" Her calm slipped away like a child on a playground slide. She watched this man; no, this rabid animal as his eyes went wild and his pale skin turns bright red with fury. Chicago had never seen eyes so black that they shone like liquid pools of oil. She watched in sheer terror while his nose flared, and white foam flecks of spittle flew from his mouth covering her neck and face. "I'm not your patient, you dumb bitch! You belong to me! It is I who decides your fucking fate! I am your god and don't! you! forget it!" He punctuated the words of that last phrase with a series of blows to her body.

Chicago unconsciously nodded her head up and down in agreement while at the same time wondering what sin she'd committed to deserve this level of hell. She didn't have to search her soul long to figure it out. Closing her eyes, she prayed while Sanford Tolliver Smalls preyed upon her. The cattle prod touched her flesh again and she shook uncontrollably, this time biting her tongue in the process. "I'm sorry about that." He pulled a small block of wood from his pocket, which looked as though it could have come from a Jenga game and placed it between her teeth. "Let's start over."

After torturing her for most of the night he tied a rubber tourniquet around her right arm and thumped the crook of her elbow until he found a vein. "This is the good stuff; $200.00 a gram and over

90 percent pure." Sanford shoved the needle in and depressed the plunger. Chicago immediately felt the effects of high-grade heroin. The pain from the devices he used on her started to fade. Thankfully, a sense of peace spread throughout her body. She was free, floating above the clouds of ecstasy looking down at her body trapped in that plastic covered room with her tormentor, but the heroin made her not care; not even a little bit.

She lay there naked. Interestingly, she still had on her boots. Running naked without footwear of some kind was never good. One rusty nail, a piece of glass, or a sharp rock could end an escape before it even got started. The average man had been drugging her with heroin for the past week, between bouts of vaginal and anal rape. Chicago knew how long it had been because he let her keep her watch along with the rest of her jewelry. "It makes the sex seem expensive. Makes me feel rich, bitch!" he said. She tried every trick at her disposal to keep him at bay, but he was relentless. Urination, defecation, it made no difference. Smalls would just clean her up, then begin sexually assaulting her all over again.

At that moment, he sat quietly in what she had come to think of as, "his chair" while staring him down. "I know, I know. If only looks could kill, Dr. Daniels." Smiling, showing dingy, crooked yellow teeth he added, "Unfortunately for you, they don't." He stood and as if by magic a syringe appeared between the forefinger and thumb of his right hand. "Let's see how tough you are without my junk. Get it?" The average man showed up an hour before demanding that she beg him to ravage her. She refused saying, "Why should I beg you when so far you've been taking what you want?" It was important to him that she be thoroughly broken. The heroin filled needle was the carrot. Him leaving it in the seat of his chair was the stick.

When he closed the door, she could hear him sliding home a couple of bolts securing her in the room. Chicago eyed the brass bars attached to the head frame. Specifically, the one holding the chain of the handcuffs manacled to her wrists. It seemed to be weakening from its bottom support. She had been struggling with it every time he left. Just then she felt it loosen a little more. After a few minutes of shaking the bar intensely, her energy was utterly depleted. Her skin, which was filthy from lack of washing felt clammy and hot. Her body odor was atrocious. Just as she gathered her strength for another go at the bar, nausea rolled over her in waves. Chicago's stomach began to rumble, and she became flatulent. She tried to shake the bar loose from its support again when a loud, foul-smelling fart ripped the air. The Average Man, as he had become known to her, only fed her energy drinks with protein bars. This way he didn't have to uncuff her. Tears flowed silently as her stomach started cramping severely. Chicago mistakenly thought that it was the start of her menstrual cycle until she deftly calculated that it was still another week or so away.

She was hit with a gut-wrenching series of cramps and realized that she was becoming sick from her body's need for the high-grade heroin seemingly miles away in his chair. Chicago had to have it if she were going to attempt an escape. She couldn't have her body betray her when she needed it most. "Please God let me get free and far away from this monster!" she prayed aloud. Since taking her, he would leave her alone for hours at a time probably to maintain a sense of normalcy in his real-life while he left her dangling in his fantasy life.

As she continued to struggle with the bar, Chicago wondered absently if Dorian was raising holy hell about her disappearance. Did he have everyone who was available out looking for her? Did her younger sister, Butterfly think she was dead? What about sweet Albany, her nephew? At only five years old, he was probably scared of witnessing the actions of the adults around him. Fuck! she screamed inside her bruised and battered head. The last time that she screamed out loud, the Average Man burst into the room and used the cattle prod on all of her lower orifices. Silence was now her weapon. Even when the hateful bastard did his sadistic best to break her, she grunted and moaned in pain but otherwise kept her mouth shut. It made him so upset that he would shrivel up inside of her like a wet noodle, and that made him even more furious. She saw it as a win until he would start beating her. That act of violence always brought his erection back. Each session was more vicious than the last. Any day now he would tire of her. Boredom for a sociopathic sexual sadist of this caliber meant death for his victim. She had to escape. For all she knew about the human psyche, Chicago was an emotional wreck. What she needed was some rest, but she couldn't sleep because of the pain in her abdomen along with the nagging thought of how good that heroin in his chair would be at that exact moment.

Sanford arrived in his dark blue Ford F-150 pickup truck. It was one of the most common vehicle brands in the country, especially Detroit. The street he parked on was in the Black Bottom section of the lower eastside. There were only about five houses on blocks where at one time there were 50. The area looked more like rural farmland. Urban blight had set up residence in the neighborhood and seemed prepared to stay. The destruction left behind by the 80s crack era, along with the vanishing act by the Big Three auto industry perpetrated on the blue-collar workers in the metro Detroit areas, was the equivalent of detonating a small yield nuclear bomb. It always tickled Sanford when he saw deer or coyote alongside pimps, whores, and drug dealers.

The particular street he was parked on was quiet, but if interrupted by the police, he and his partners would claim they were scouting properties to purchase. At that moment, his partners or truthfully his employers pulled up right behind him.

Sanford was unafraid of the majority of things on earth. His employers were an exception to that rule. They made his hairs stand on end; but if push came to shove, he would deal with them also. One of his employers got out of his vehicle and slid into Sanford's passenger seat shutting the door quickly.

"Why do you have your dome light on? Cut it off." He did as he was told. "Do you realize the situation you've put us all in? We no longer need your services. Tell me where she is, and it will be handled."

Sanford acted insulted. He already had his lie structured so that the delivery was as smooth as a newborn baby's ass. "It's been handled. I just thought nobody, no proof." The employer looked at him, doubtfully. "She's dead? Where's the body? Had you followed our instructions and made it look like a carjacking gone wrong, we wouldn't be having this conversation." The employer stared hard at his profile while he pretended to casually check all of the truck's mirrors eyeing their immediate surroundings.

"So, where's the bitch's body? It needs to be found to stop the police from looking in places they shouldn't. Where'd you dump it?" Sanford had anticipated that question. "That could be a problem. See, I drove deep into Macomb County and dropped it into a well on an abandoned farm. An archaeologist might find her in 500 years if he's lucky." His employer seemed outwardly impressed with that recent deception. "Okay, Sanford." He flinched at how his name sounded coming out of his employer's mouth. "You'll get the rest of your money within the next day or two. Be patient until I contact you." His employer got out of the truck without another word. When he did, Sanford expelled the breath he'd been holding. His employer could be pretty scary at times. Sanford waited until they pulled off in the direction of the river before he made a U-turn. As he headed back to Chicago, he thought to himself, all great love affairs must come to an end.

Driving away, the employer mused about Sanford Tolliver Smalls. How dimwitted could that little nothing of a man be? He thought they were some type of partners. That's like having the guy who cuts your lawn think he owns a piece of your home. Sanford Tolliver Smalls is just like any other hired hand - expendable. He was contracted to do a job and instead allowed his base desires to get in the way. His employer could smell the stink of unwashed sex all over him. Running off playing hide the sausage with Chicago when he should have killed her on the spot was disappointing. Smalls had to get the ax and who better to give it to him than his employer.

It was obvious when the asshole disappeared that something was wrong. He should have killed her a week ago. The litany of excuses and deviations from the original plan set off alarm bells in the employer's head. They expected an unforeseen problem or two, but nothing of this magnitude. It was okay though. The key to survival is the ability to adapt and overcome on the fly.

Staring at the newly purchased smartphone's screen as the little dot scurried across the map of the Detroit area, the employer thought how stupid Sanford was to think that those bullshit answers given in his truck were satisfactory. Maybe to an average person, but certainly not to someone as extraordinary as the employer. The global positioning transponder attached to the underside of his truck's passenger side rear wheel weld allowed for Sanford to be tracked the same as he tracked Chicago; with undetectable ease.

Sanford drove up to the decrepit four-story apartment building on Church Street and John R. Avenue in the city of Highland Park right on the border of Detroit. If Detroit is the skeletal shell of its former self, then Highland Park would be its anal cavity. Simply a shitty place. It was a perfect spot for Sanford to play with Chicago. No neighbors and little foot traffic. The walls were thick enough to limit sound from reaching out on the street. Before bringing Chicago there, he had tested that by using a boom box on high volume. It couldn't be heard outside on the street. Besides, the lesson with the cattle prod was enough to keep the doctor in check.

Sanford built his lair by covering the room in painter's plastic for easy cleanup. Then he found an old brass bed with a comfortable mattress at a garage sale in Grosse Pointe Woods and trucked it to the building. Next, he made his perch using a metal high backed chair with a black comfortable seat cushion positioned kitty-corner to the bed. After surveying his domain, he strategically placed a tripod with an iPhone attached to it so that it would film all of the action that was going to take place on the bed. After sprinkling a few battery-operated camping lights around the room, the scene was set.

So much work and subterfuge for so little time. Even though his employer seemed satisfied the deed was done, Sanford had a sneaky suspicion that he was working on borrowed time. He opened the door to Chicago's deep moans. "Did you miss me sugarplum?" Sanford asked in a syrupy, fatherly tone. The bitch was sweating profusely and had peed the bed.

"Fuck you asshole!" Chicago spat out at him. He smiled crazily. "That can be arranged. You did say, fuck your asshole, didn't you?" He walked back towards the door in the corner where a couple of buckets and cleaning supplies sat. "You ungrateful slut! If it weren't for me, do you think you would be down two dress sizes! Let's get you cleaned up, doll. Afterward, we'll get you all dirty again."

Chicago's stomach was all twisted in tight throbbing knots. "Please make the pain stop!" Her pleas were uttered through clenched teeth. Sanford just smiled at her. She watched in agonizing fear while he stripped naked, then quickly started cleaning the soiled plastic sheets. When he was done with them, he started in on her. Gently, with a tenderness belying his sadistic nature he wiped her body clean while lingering in delicate places more than was necessary. The entire time ignoring Chicago's pleas for the heroin. He knew the withdrawal was excruciatingly painful for her while for him, the rhythm of her pain was poetry in motion. Only when he was ready and not a moment before would he relieve her pain.

When he walked over to his chair and picked up the syringe, her heart skipped a beat. Sanford could see the hope in her eyes. "God grant me the serenity to accept the things I cannot change . . . Blah, blah, blah, blah, blah! Just kidding doll face. Tell me what you really want?" Chicago grappled with her pride and the pain for all of two seconds. Her pride had been shattered for days and the pain was a black belt that repeatedly kept kicking her ass. Steadying the shaking in her voice she said as sweetly as possible, "I wanna ride your junk. Can I ride the white horse?" He twisted a piece of rubber around her thigh and slapped at it until a vein popped up like a turtle peeking from its shell. "This is your femoral artery. Saddle up for the last ride of your life." She felt the prick of the needle then the numbing glow like a total body orgasm.

She hated herself for the gratitude she felt towards him as the heroin traveled through her bloodstream. The Average Man witnessed the relaxing transformation take place in her facial features as he spread open her thighs. "No condom; this is special. You'll remember me throughout eternity as not only your last but the best fuck you ever had." Chicago knew that she would see his face forever and a day. "You ride the white horse and I'll ride you!" Sanford entered her roughly, but she didn't even care. She just hoped that she stayed high long enough to escape.

Sanford's employer thought this man was definitely not all that bright. He concluded that about Sanford when he followed him to the neighborhood where he had Chicago captive and saw his late-model truck parked adjacent to the decrepit building. It stood out like a naked woman covered in Christmas lights, casually walking up Seven Mile Road. It was just stupid. Three blocks north of the abandoned apartment building on East McNichols sat a liquor store and cellphone shop. After parking at the far end of the lot, the employer searched for surveillance cameras and found several; avoiding them as best as possible.

Hurriedly walking up the deserted stretch of John R Avenue, the employer pulled a pair of earphones from the pocket of his expensive athletic suit putting them on. The employer and one of his guards who were with him, looked carefully around then broke into a jog. The employer thought to himself, nothing to look at here, officer. Just a couple of late-night runners. Within a couple of minutes, the running had brought them next to Sanford's vehicle. Bending low under the guise of tying a shoe the employer made sure the coast was clear then plucked the GPS transponder from that idiot's truck. It was the same model they suggested he use to track Chicago. Cautiously eyeing everything while carefully moving into the building heel to toe, they coiled the earphones into a ball in exchange for a small, but lethal Smith & Wesson .380 caliber pistol. "Let's see if Sanford's loafing on the job," the employer whispered to the other man.

The building they were at was truly dilapidated. There was no rear door and almost every window was busted out leaving the interior open to the elements. Using a small penlight with a green bulb they navigated their way through used condoms, dirty syringes, empty crack vials, and broken malt liquor bottles. When the employer reached the stairwell, Sanford seemed a little smarter than previously thought. Small clusters of broken glass along with thin plastic balls a little bigger than a marble littered every stair. They were the kind kids played with popping them between their fingers or stepping on them because they sounded like tiny firecrackers. It was an effective low budget early warning system. The employer took to the edge of each step where it was less likely to be weakened by overuse and squeaking, then headed up.

A man like Sanford wouldn't be caught dead on the ground level or first floor. The little self-important coward would be on the third or fourth floor to give himself enough time to escape in case something went wrong. On the second-floor landing, they stood statue-still while listening for sounds of life. Nothing! On the third floor, the employer paused with an ear cocked like a satellite dish seeking a signal. Still nothing! It was just as silent as the second floor. But the fourth floor was different. A quadriplegic could feel the energy of another's presence coursing through the air. They delved deeper into a further level of stealth mode.

The doors to the left and right hung open askew on their hinges. To the employer it felt like, Let's Make A Deal. What door should be chosen? His natural inclination screamed right; but Sanford's truck was parked to the left and could easily have been seen from any of the fourth-floor windows on that side, except for the far-left rear windows because they were boarded up. Left it is! The employer thought.

Running the dim green light around the floor and doorframe it was easy to see the razor-thin filament wire stretched across its opening. "Sanford, Sanford, Sanford." The employer exclaimed in a whisper. They made sure it wasn't a dummy wire then stepped cautiously over it; all the while listening for the slightest sound or any change in atmosphere. Quiet!

The employer could see a stream of light crawling beneath the seal of the door. This had to be the place, the employer thought. The frame was solid with two slide bolts and a deadbolt lock. It would be foolish to barge in. He may have safeguards that could forewarn him. Suddenly, it came to the employer. In between the room and the tripwire was a closet with no door. The employer tripped the alarm wire then eased back up into the closet. It didn't take long for Sanford to come creeping pass. He glanced inside, but the closet was deep with shadows. The employer and his guard closed their eyes. When they opened them, they could make out Sanford's silhouette, specifically the back of his head and the large-caliber handgun hanging from his wrist.

Chicago laid there in emotional turmoil. She was battered and abused, but far from beaten. Despite the violent continuous sexual assault perpetrated on her, Chicago was basking in physical bliss. She could hardly feel where his teeth ruptured the skin around her areola on one of her nipples thanks to the numbing effects of the heroin flooding her system. This average, nothing of a man mistakenly thought he'd won; but their battle was far from over. She was just biding her time, waiting for the right moment to strike.

The brass bar securing the chain of the handcuffs was broken. Chicago did it as he savagely pumped into her. While the bed was banging against the wall, she saw her opportunity and seized it. Gripping the frame, she pulled every time he pumped. When it broke, she had the foresight to put it back in its place. Chicago stared between her breast down to the juncture of her thighs where Sanford's tears mingled with his filthy semen. Up until now he always wore condoms. Not tonight. Tonight, he claimed was special. He kept babbling incoherently obviously lost in his delusional fantasies.

Chicago knew he was almost done with her and that she had to do something. She was no longer afraid of him. She felt dangerous, more dangerous than the city she was named after. The Average Man spoke of her giving birth to his child in the afterlife. If there is an afterlife, they would be sharing it together. She had a plan or at least the makings of one. The drugs would slow her down, so she was mentally hyping herself up to move fast when the time came. Beep, beep, beep, beep. What the hell was happening? With a speed that could only be called freakish, Sanford pulled on his pants and slipped into his shoes then grabbed his gun.

"What's happening? Where's that beeping noise coming from?" She asked him frantically. Chicago watched him tiptoe to the door with his gun arm raised and ready while his other hand rested on the knob. Looking back at her he threatened, "Make a fucking peep bitch, and you're dead!"

He cracked the door and looked back at her. The fear etched into his facial features shocked her. It was now or never. Her eyes stayed locked on him as he slithered silently out into the hallway. Desperately Chicago pushed the brass bar out of its bottom support slipping the chain of the handcuffs free. Her bleeding wrists were still manacled but now she was freed from the bed. Quickly she stood up and was struck with a wave of dizziness and almost fainted. Steadying herself she hurried to his chair and drug it over to the door wedging it underneath the knob so no one could get in. The next part of her plan was crucial. Chicago went for the phone attached to the tripod. The heroin made her feel super sluggish even though she was moving speedily around the room. It seemed as though it was taking forever to switch from video mode to the keypad. Chicago pressed 911 and spoke as soon as the connection was made. The operator tried calming her down, but in her mind she was calm. "Listen to me! My name is Dr. Chicago Daniels! I've been kidnapped and held hostage, but I don't know where I am. Please trace this call, it's only a matter of time before he comes back!" Her mind was sharp as Damascus steel, but her words were slurred. The operator started asking questions, which she purposely ignored. "Trace the fucking call before he comes back and kills me! Send help! Trace the fucking call!" Chicago tossed the phone on the bed and searched through her captor's jacket that was hanging on the brass frame.

Finally, a blessing, she thought as her fingers grazed a ring of metal. There amongst several other keys was a very small handcuff key. She unlocked her wrists quickly and pulled on the lightweight jacket belonging to the asshole who abducted her. With her nakedness covered she looked for a weapon. Nothing was visibly handy until she spotted a large flathead screwdriver in the corner where the supplies were. Picking it up, she hefted it in her hand and made a few practice stabbing motions then stood next to the door with it hoisted over her head prepared to kill the monster as soon as he showed his face. He had a gun, but she had her faith and a tremendous will to live. Chicago was ready. Then two successive shots shattered the air and the faith she had tenaciously clung to started to wane.

Sanford checked around but found nothing. The early warning system he had set up wasn't fooled proof. The tripwire was positioned 10 inches from the floor so that a rat wouldn't mistakenly set it off. It could've been a cat or a possum. There have been plenty of those little ugly bastards around, he thought while sensing movement to his left as he passed the closet. The click of the hammer cocking signaled his end. "All you had to do was kill her. Was the pussy worth dying for?" Before he could utter a syllable in response, a bullet impacted his brain at almost 1,200 miles per second followed by its twin. The employer watched as the muzzle flash illuminated Sanford's brain matter decorating the hallway. Watching Sanford's brains splatter the walls turned the employer on. He thought to himself, now it's time to finish the job.

2 THE PRESENT

It was two in the morning on a Saturday. The runner didn't care. The time didn't matter. To this runner time was inconsequential. Speed, distance, sweat, and adrenaline were the only important things. The only things that mattered. Nothing else mattered; nothing at all as the Friday night leftovers poured from the local midtown bars and restaurants openly staring at the beautiful woman. Just looking at Dr. Chicago Daniels in bright, tight fluorescent spandex made them feel a twinge of guilt from their excesses.

Chicago ran with her long jet-black ponytail braid bobbing like a thoroughbred mare's tail with each footfall of her green and orange Nike running shoes. Appearing a decade younger than her actual age and definitely more athletically fit than someone half her age, no one staring could see the ugliness underneath the beauty. Chicago exercised twice daily and ran every other day. The endorphins generated from her workouts and running quenched a forbidden thirst. Her long strides carried her up Third Street to Calumet where she headed east a half block to her apartment. Actually, her apartment building, because she did own it.

Punching in a six-digit code on an alarm panel next to the entrance Chicago hit the enter button, waited for the click, and grabbed the handle. The five-story walkup built in the early 20th century sat on a beautiful tree-lined street in the midst of late 19th and early 20thcentury Victorian homes in various states of repair. Some of the homes looked battered and weather abused, while others were undergoing varying degrees of restoration. The area surrounding her building was once predominantly African American. With the expansion of Wayne State University's campus and real estate incentives given by certain major business concerns, the midtown neighborhood was a multicultural hodgepodge.

Chicago took the stairs two at a time to the top fifth floor of the building. The fifth floor was nothing like the other floors. There was a thick covering of bulletproof glass stretching wall to wall, left to right with a seemingly ordinary oak door in its center. It was actually oak veneer with a steel core. She punched in another numerical code, waited for the click then pushed it open. Stepping into a vestibule that had an identical door facing her, she reached into her fanny pack pulled out her house keys and unlocked several locks before gaining entry.

The entire top floor had been converted into one luxurious apartment with cathedral ceilings throughout several thousand square feet of space. There were six skylights interspersed throughout the living, dining, and kitchen areas. To the left of the door was a beautiful dining area with an oblong cherry wood table that could seat 20 people. The dining room walls were decorated with paintings depicting famous and, in some cases, infamous meals. To the right sat a gourmet chef's culinary fantasy. A Viking range with two ovens, two broilers, and a topside grill with ducts to carry the smoke to the roof. There was a Sub-Zero refrigerator and a walk-in freezer along with a sizeable pantry for dry goods. Inside of the pantry was a hidden temperature controlled wine cellar, which could only be accessed through a secret door.

The kitchen floor was done in grey porcelain tile, a perfect match for the grey trimmed glass-fronted cabinets. An industrial stainless steel butcher's block, standing four feet wide and eight feet long with its Italian marble top doubling as an island with seating for six was the centerpiece. Above that hung a large rack of copper pots and pans with other kitchen utensils. Chicago snagged a bottle of water from the fridge turning it up and swallowing half its contents before taking a breath.

Walking out of the kitchen area her shoes made a soft, slap-tap against the original teak floors that ran throughout most of the apartment. She passed the first of five bathrooms gliding into the family room where to her extreme left windows were lined up like sentinels retreating to the front door. The wall facing her held a 72' flat-screen television. It was linked to a closed-circuit surveillance system and bracketed by floor to ceiling bookcases with two antique ladders. The window configuration was the same to her right. A large suede sectional wrapped itself in sort of a 180° arc separating the dining and living spaces. There were beautiful wood tables inlaid with

25

beveled glass and soft leather chairs strategically placed on expensive Persian and Oriental rugs to give it that Home & Garden lived-in look.

She would spend a fortune on curtains if the apartment had any. Instead, the glass was pixelated like a computer screen and worked by a remote. Picking up the remote and clicking it, mirrored the outside of the windows. She could see out, but no one could see inside. She grabbed the television remote and clicked on CNN. She kept the volume down low as she walked to double doors along the same wall as the television. When she opened the doors there a long hallway with several rooms. To the right was a jacuzzi room, sauna, fully equipped gym with universal and free weights, and a bedroom. To the left was a home office replete with separate phone lines and an updated computer system along with three more bedrooms. The first and second rooms shared a Jack & Jill bathroom. The third had its own en suite as did the one across from it.

She paused at another set of doors, pushed them open, and walked into her bedroom. A California king-sized bed rested in front of her. The same window configuration was carried into her bedroom except when turning left one had to look through a glass-enclosed In suite that was almost the size of most people's apartments. There were his and hers cedar-lined walk-in closets. Finishing off the bottle of water, Chicago went to her closet, stripped naked, and walked into the bathroom.

The bathroom was equipped with two deep claw foot his and hers tubs. (Now they were all hers). There were two free-standing porcelain sinks with gilt-framed mirrors hanging from suspension wire over them. The his and hers toilets hidden behind frosted glass stall doors were definitely all hers. Kitty-corner to them was a huge rainforest shower. All mine! Chicago thought to herself as she stepped in cutting on the water. Jets of ice-cold water hit her body from almost every angle simultaneously.

She screamed at the top of her lungs for over two minutes, until her throat was raw. She let hot tears mingle with the ice water to purge some of the pain. Chicago took several deep calming breaths then began to recite a poem she had memorized. It wasn't the cold water that made her scream. It was the cold fury encasing her heart. The fairytale she had been living from the time she met Dorian in college had come to an end. She had been living the American dream until three years ago when that maniac, Sanford Tolliver Smalls forced his way into her life. Now she was trapped in what seemed like a perpetual nightmare.

Every day since Smalls had entered her life, she felt a pain slicing deep into the marrow of her bones. A pain so intense that it bruised her soul; yet, Chicago was still standing. She was fractured but whole. A well-manicured but shaky hand twisted the dial turning the water as hot as her skin could take it. By the time she stepped from the shower, her nerves had calmed. As she walked naked through her bedroom allowing her body to air dry, she thought about how unfair life actually is. Dorian was dead while his killer and the accomplice of that lunatic who kidnapped her, still roamed free amongst the masses. Life is so unfair, she thought.

The shirt was too big and faded in spots. But she didn't wear it as a fashion statement. Chicago wore it to remember. After pulling on a pair of yoga pants, she donned the very old, too big, and faded Wayne State University tee shirt that still smelled of her late husband. Chicago Alexandria Daniels padded barefoot into the kitchen where she grabbed a thick-handled wooden spoon along with a half-pint of Peek Inns, Butter Pecan Peanut Brittle Crunch, then plopped down on the couch in front of the television to watch CNN.

The latest word was an asshole in North Korea was taunting the latest presidential asshole of the United States. She sat half-listening to the reporters, political pundits, and other assholes offering their opinions on the state of the world. The current president called it fake news. A fake president condemning fake news? Shoving the spoon into the container she set the ice cream aside and reached for the remote surfing through the channels.

In the past three years, Chicago had watched more television than all of her prior adult life combined. Scandal, Power, Billions, Game of Thrones, Blacklist, it didn't matter. She knew the cast and characters almost intimately. Well, as close as one can get in high definition.

27

Television had become her therapy. In some ways, it was her escape. She went past a familiar face then went back. Ben Kingsley was playing the role of an FBI trained behavioral analyst who, ironically, finds and kills serial killers. She watched the movie intently as the plot thickened then unfolded. Ben Kingsley's character did some bad shit to catch an even worse monster who was a normal unassuming truck driver. An average man. She fell asleep underneath a comfortable Afghan blanket around five in the morning. That's when she started to dream about the Average Man.

Like a horror movie viewed too many times the scenes of her abduction and sexual assault no longer held the same frightening effects. Those scenes no longer terrified or spooked her. They didn't instill fear in her anymore, either. They were things that happened to her once upon a time. The two loud thumps that she heard were gunshots. Chicago held the screwdriver tighter in her fist while watching the doorknob turn. At that point, she was usually scared to death, but no more. The person on the other side kicked at the door, but the chair wedged against it prevented it from opening. They were enraged at not being able to gain entry.

The vulgar expletives would make a hardened sailor blush. It wasn't him! Could it be another monster? Back then she was terrified. Not anymore. She just observed everything with clinical detachment. Her senses were heightened like never before. Chicago could smell her own body odor, her funky vagina, bad breath, and her fear then. She could hear the accelerated beating of her heart sounding like a primitive kettle drum as she prepared to fight for her life.

When the first bullets crashed through the door throwing chunks of wood and paint into the room, she shrieked involuntarily while flattening herself further against the wall. Without warning something fast, hard, and hot punched through and into her shoulder. Animal screams tore through the air as another bullet found its way through the maze of wood, plaster, paint, and drywall. One grazed the back of her leg as she ran to nowhere, tripping and falling in the process. Several more bullets crashed through the wall and door, missing her only by the grace of God. Somehow, she still gripped the screwdriver. Chicago tried pushing herself up off the floor only to fall face first, smashing her forehead against the plastic-covered concrete and blacking out.

She woke up to the incessant ringing of her cellphone. It was on the other side of the apartment still nestled in her fanny pack on the kitchen counter. Unwrapping herself from her Afghan cocoon, she ignored the phone and headed to the bathroom. Yanking down her yoga pants she peed, wiped, then washed her hands. She stopped and looked into the mirror at her red-rimmed eyes and sad face. Chicago thought the broad in the mirror needed to smile. So, she tried a few variations of smiling: tight, full-lipped. She tried the top teeth only smile, and a full wattage thirty-two teeth smile. None of them seemed to fit, but she had taught herself to wear them well. Still looking in the mirror she addressed herself as though her reflection was a stranger who needed to know something very important.

OUT OF THE NIGHT THAT COVERS ME BLACK AS THE PIT FROM POLE TO POLE I, CHICAGO ALEXANDRIA DANIELS THANK WHATEVER GODS MAY BE FOR MY UNCONQUERABLE SOUL.

She continued and finished with the other three verses. It was like receiving an infusion of positive energy. The poem was her empowerment, helping her through another day. She recited it every morning from the time she left the hospital after her ordeal. In the kitchen, Chicago checked her caller ID and saw her younger sister's number. The phone belonged to Butterfly, but it was probably her nephew, Albany calling. It didn't matter who it was; she needed caffeine fortification before morning conversation.

IN THE FELL CLUTCH OF CIRCUMSTANCE, I HAVE NOT WINCED OR CRIED ALOUD UNDER THE BLUDGEONINGS OF CHANCE MY HEAD IS BLOODY BUT UNBOWED.

She dropped a coffee pack into the Keurig and cut a grapefruit in half. Lastly, she popped a slice of raisin bread into the toaster. She chewed slowly while cradling her cup of coffee. Was it Albany or

Butterfly calling? Unlike most eight-year-olds, he had yet to have his own phone; so, he often used his mom's phone to call his Auntie Chi. Finishing off her grapefruit she made another cup of coffee. Picking up both cup and phone Chicago made her way back to the couch while dialing. Albany answered on the first ring. "Auntie Chi, what took you so long to call back? We were just about to leave!" She spoke to her precious nephew for almost ten minutes reassuring him of the big adventure for his upcoming birthday." Where's your mom? she asked. "Waiting for me to get ready. I told you, Auntie Chi, she's making me go to this kid's party I don't even like anymore."

"Why don't you like him, Albany?" He stated bluntly as only a child can, "He's a thief and a liar! He stole my Transformer's watch." Chicago offered her nephew a bit of advice. "Don't let his flaws stop your joy. Go to the party and have a good time. Now, let me speak to your mom."

BEYOND THIS PLACE OF WRATH AND TEARS LOOMS BUT THE HORROR OF THE SHADE, AND YET THE MENACE OF THE YEARS FINDS AND SHALL FIND ME UNAFRAID.

IT MATTERS NOT HOW STRAIT THE GATE HOW CHARGED WITH PUNISHMENT THE SCROLL I AM THE MASTER OF MY FATE I AM THE CAPTAIN OF MY SOUL.

Eagle's Landing Country Club in Stockbridge, Georgia north of Atlanta houses an ultra-exclusive enclave of the rich, wealthy, and super-rich. Bankers, financiers, actors, musicians, athletes, and other celebrities all call it home. Mrs. Butterfly Baxter wasn't born rich nor did she build all of her wealth on her own. Butterfly just happened to marry well. Her husband, Morgan Baxter is one of the South's premier real estate moguls. He has degrees in business and architecture with licenses to practice the sale of real estate in Georgia, Florida, Alabama, and Tennessee. Morgan has an uncanny knack for not only buying, selling, and building new developments but also the remodeling and refurbishing of old houses in urban neighborhoods. He's been called the gentrification genius; a name he hates. Morgan made his millions by turning decaying urban areas into epicenters of growth.

The couple had been married for four years. As far as both were concerned, they were still on their honeymoon. Was it love? For him, yes! For her, she wasn't sure about that, but it felt good. It felt really, really good! He was extremely generous in all areas that mattered most. Bed, bank, and beyond.

On this particular day, Morgan the Mogul was golfing at a private course outside of Savanna, Georgia and wasn't due home until the following evening. Butterfly quickly glanced at her Pasha Cartier wristwatch. "Albany, Sweetheart, we're going to be late for Benton's party! We still have to pick up his gift, then drive all the way out there to that place! Please, hurry up, and bring Mommy's phone!" When she stopped yelling, she could hear him running down the stairs. "No running!" Albany ignored her while skidding into the kitchen holding her cellphone out to her. "How can I hurry up without running?" Albany asked with a smile on his face. Before she could respond, he said, "It's Auntie Chi. She told me that she can't wait to see me!"

Albany loved his aunt with all of his heart. Butterfly was once jealous of their love, but after all that happened, she felt foolish to feel like that. Butterfly took her phone while shooing him away. "Go get your jacket, babe." Grabbing her purse while walking to the front door she said, "Windy City, what's up girl? Is everything all right?" There was a pause as if Chicago were swallowing something. "Yeah, I'm fine Caterpillar. My handsome nephew called to remind me of his upcoming birthday."

"He's going to make me strangle his little butt if he doesn't hurry up. We're supposed to be going to a birthday party of one of his schoolmates. Coincidentally, the boy's mother is in business with Morgan." Pressing the phone to her breast she yelled, "Hurry up slowpoke! The last one to the car is a rotten egg!" Placing the phone back to her ear again, "Sorry about that Sis." Chicago gulped down the last of her coffee then asked, "Is the Mogul coming with you guys?" Butterfly watched as Albany zoomed by her out the front door and hopped into the backseat of her BMW SUV. "Who knows with Morgan. As long as there's no business crisis demanding his immediate attention the three of us will be there."

The two sisters had never been close growing up. The 13-year age difference was a big deal to them as adolescents and teenagers. But as adults looking back, it was a stone's throw versus a lifetime. Since Chicago's abduction, they had grown much closer. They spoke almost daily and visited one another whenever possible. "Let's hope you all can make it. I've got everything planned. Remember, don't rent a car I'll pick you guys up from the airport. "Butterfly wondered how they would all fit comfortably in her sister's sports coup and told her as much. "Don't worry, I'll take care of everything. Besides, we won't be in Detroit long after I pick you up from the airport."

"Does this have something to do with Albany's birthday?" Hearing his name Albany piped in from the backseat where he was playing a video game on his tablet. "It's not just a birthday Mom, it's a birthday adventure!"

"You hear that Windy City?"

She had heard it. Albany's birthday will certainly be one to remember, Chicago thought to herself. The two sisters spoke for another five minutes. Chicago had a support group meeting to attend so, they agreed to speak later that night. Butterfly turned the radio up a little allowing herself to think about how close she and Windy City had become in the past few years. She started thinking of the past and how it should remain buried because to go digging back there could cause one to get dirty. As a matter of fact, downright filthy!

3 THE RECENT PAST

For almost a week every major network was asking a single question: WHERE IS DR. CHICAGO DANIELS? News trucks were camped outside of Wayne State University's administrative offices trying to catch friends and colleagues of her husband, Dr. Dorian Brooks, who held dual doctorates in criminology and psychology. They were hoping to capture the next tantalizing sound bite for the evening news. Other media were in the University District outside of the apartment building where the missing woman lived with her husband.

All eyes were on the husband, even though he was the one who reported her missing after she never made it home while allegedly stopping to pick up ice cream. Investigative reporters found that the couple had few friends and even fewer family members. The wife's car, an expensive luxury sedan was found off the iconic Woodward Avenue on Peterboro Street. Scenes of the vehicle were shown so much during news cycles that the manufacturer considered paying advertising fees. Police canvassed the area and found a surveillance camera showing the woman leaving a popular ice cream shop, then nothing. The beautiful, successful behavioral psychologist had vanished. Her neighbors and colleagues were interviewed by law enforcement and the media. No one had anything negative to say really, except for one comment by a neighbor. When asked by a local news reporter what the woman thought about her neighbor, Dr. Daniels being missing she replied, "That white man probably disappeared that pretty wife of his for the insurance. White man always has to make a profit, no matter what he was doing."

Butterfly wasn't in Atlanta when she received the news of Chicago's disappearance. She was out of town. Morgan and she had only been married a year, but the situation made it feel like they'd been married forever. The newlyweds met in Detroit and holed up with Dorian at the apartment. By the fifth day, all three had cabin fever.

Morgan was ultra-supportive, but he had a business to run, certain aspects of which required a personal touch. If things continued the way they were, he would have to return to Georgia, his base of operations. Butterfly would be left with her distraught brother-in-law who was seemingly inconsolable. Morgan didn't want to leave his wife with her sister missing; but what else could he do? Then on the night of day six, while she was out clearing her head, they got the call. Chicago had been found - alive!

She met up with Morgan outside of Detroit Receiving Hospital's emergency entrance. Her husband was a big man, standing 6'4 tall. He was a muscular 220 pounds, with a burnished mahogany complexion. He resembled more of the college football player he once was rather than the real estate mogul he had turned into. She rushed into his strong arms where he cradled her close while speaking. "They found her alive, but she was drugged out of her mind." The EMTs told the nurses that she kept saying, "Butterfly." She was calling for you, honey. She's been shot and badly beaten, among other things." He held her at arm's length and Butterfly could see her reflection in his glasses. What she saw was a nervous wreck. "Dorian is in the surgical department lounge. We should hurry and get back there. The detective in charge of her case told me, because of the high-profile nature of Chicago's disappearance that someone will eventually leak her presence here at the hospital. Any minute now and we could be overrun by the media." Butterfly allowed her husband to be supportive and take charge. She followed his lead.

Morgan pulled his wife along into the hospital, winding through the cold corridors and polite security checks, beyond the public waiting room to a private lounge for immediate family members only. Dorian sat there with his elbows planted firmly on his knees and his face pressed firmly into the palms of his hands. Butterfly looked around seeing a man and woman dressed in cheap pantsuits with even cheaper shoes. They stood deep in a back corner of the room drinking from paper cups as they whispered to each other. She touched her grieving brother-in-law, startling him. "Have you heard anything?" Instead of answering her, he stood up and hugged her. "Has anyone told you anything yet?" Slumping back down hard on the small waiting room couch, he ran 10 well-manicured fingers through his curly, blue black hair. "Nothing! I haven't heard anything after getting the call that she'd been found. The detectives only told me they were bringing her here."

Butterfly sat beside him rubbing his back while trying to comfort him when a doctor with a surgical nurse stepped into the room. A small Asian man wearing scrubs with running shoes on his feet came in, looked around, then walked directly up to Morgan, and started talking. "We were able to stop the bleeding and successfully repair the tendons in your wife's shoulder in the process." Morgan was at a loss as to how he should respond. He looked over at his wife and Dorian seated on the couch. Butterfly spoke as she stood and moved towards the two men.

"That's my husband, Mr. Baxter. He's my sister, Dr. Daniels 'brother-in-law." She pointed to an obviously shaken Dorian and said, "This is my sister's husband. You should be addressing him. Because of Chicago's race you've made an incorrect assumption. I hope you haven't done the same with her medical care."

The doctor was contrite in his apologies to all of them. "Please allow me to begin again. My name is Dr. Shea. I am Dr. Daniels' surgeon. Currently, she's in critical though stable condition with nurses monitoring her progress in the recovery ward. Within a couple of hours maybe less, we'll move her into a private room. You'll be able to see her for a short time, providing the authorities have no objections."

His last statement was made while eyeing the cheap suits in the corner. Dorian thanked the doctor then began pacing back and forth. Morgan hugged Butterfly closely, rocking her body against his chest when his cellphone rang. Sadly, he apologized to his lovely wife and eased out into the hallway. She discreetly eyed the cop couple in the corner. It only took a few seconds to size them up. They couldn't catch cold walking around naked in the Arctic. Cautiously she signaled for Dorian to meet her on the other side of the room away from the ears of the police. "How ya holding up, Loverboy?" Glancing nervously around he whispered, "Are you insane! Don't call me that! The police have been up my ass like a rectal thermometer since this all started." His sister-in-law leaned in close enough for him to smell her tangerine scented breath. "The spouse is always the first suspect." Dorian's nerves were frayed enough without her playing her little mind-fuck games. "Don't forget a close runner up is always family," he responded. Butterfly lowered her voice even more so that he had to strain in order to hear her. "I'm rich and have no motive, unless . . ."

"Unless what?" He asked. "Unless you count fucking and sucking you, Loverboy." His face paled visibly. "Stop it! Chicago needs us both right now."

"You don't have to act for me. Save your role-playing for the authorities." Butterfly raised her voice a little higher when she said the word authorities. Dorian glanced suspiciously over his shoulder towards the two plainclothes police across the room in the opposite corner. They seemed acutely zeroed into their conversation."

"If any of our secrets were to come to light right now, we would both become prime suspects." Her brow creased, "Of what?" Dorian led her further into the corner and quickly explained to her in hushed tones what the police had told him thus far. The man believed responsible for kidnapping Chicago was found dead outside the room where she was held captive. The police had to break down the door to rescue her. "I overheard some other officers talking when I first arrived. They doubt it was a suicide because the back of his head was blown open. We have to be careful." A cloud of confusion shaded her beautiful features. "Is it that you don't get it, or you don't care?" She shook her head slightly from side to side. "They know that worthless son-of-a-bitch had a partner who's still out there. Until he or she is caught, captured, or killed, the suspect pool is deep and we're swimming in it." Butterfly took it all in then replied, "In that case, you keep my secrets and I'll keep yours."

Morgan walked in with an attractive Latino woman. It was close to midnight, but she looked fresh and alert. The woman was tall for a female, especially a Latino woman. She wore a brown waist-length leather bomber jacket, Detroit Tigers tee, blue jeans, and Air Jordan gym shoes. Her detective's badge hung about her neck like a rap star's necklace. She was endowed with full breasts, a pretty face, and a generous ass. She seemed to be in her mid-thirties with no children.

Her stomach was too flat; plus, she didn't have that look a mother carries with her when she has to leave a child in the middle of the night. Butterfly checked the policewoman out from head to toe and thought, Definitely the A-team. She pushed her hair back from her face while giving an almost imperceptible nod to the two members of the cheap suit B-team, motioning for them to do like Michael and beat it. She approached Dorian with her hand extended. "Dr. Brooks, my name is Detective Sargent Jasenya Jimenez from the Detroit Police Homicide Task Force. I'm the primary or rather lead detective. That simply means I'll be in charge of investigating your wife's case." Butterfly quickly interjected.

"Why is someone from homicide handling my sister's kidnapping?"

Sargent Jimenez gave her the same tolerant smile Butterfly gives to her son Albany when he asks her questions where the answers are obvious to her. But she has to remind herself to be patient because he's only a child. "Well, a man was killed. Whenever a shooting, homicide, or kidnapping occurs it falls under the preview of DTF. We handle all major violent cases, Mrs. Baxter." Just then Morgan walked up with three cups of coffee. He gave them to Jimenez, his wife, and Dorian. Both men looked like panting puppies as the detective pursed her lips blowing on the hot liquid.

Brooding, Butterfly said to herself, I don't like this bitch, not one bit. She seems more than smart. She seems determined. Sipping the awful coffee, she concluded that she didn't like the south of the border bimbo at all. Looking over the rim of her cup, Butterfly looked her over again. Athletically fit with short, no-nonsense fingernails. No wedding band. Again, the detective's badge caught her eye and she thought to herself, that's because Miss J-Lo wannabe is married to her job. If it's a good marriage, Butterfly thought, it could be a problem. She decided to probe a little. "Dorian told me my sister's kidnapper was found dead at the scene. Who was he? Was he one of her patients?"

The detective replied, "I'm sorry but I can't discuss the case. Not only would it be premature, but whether intentional or not a leak of any kind could damage this investigation."

Morgan wondered aloud, almost absently to himself, "Why did that monster pick Chicago or was it random?" Jimenez took a sip of her coffee before saying, "Don't quote me, but I think that this wasn't a random abduction. Thank God, something went wrong with his plan and it turned out right for Dr. Daniels. Let's thank the Man Upstairs that she's still alive." Dorian spoke up then. "I should be able to see my wife soon, right? She will be coming out of recovery shortly." Jimenez gave the three a tight-lipped smile before saying, "I'm terribly sorry, Dr. Brooks, Mr. and Mrs. Baxter, but I've got two uniforms on your wife with very detailed instructions that no one be allowed to speak with her except for God and me. Your wife's first words could be the key to solving this thing." Dorian was livid. "The hell you say! First, your department questions me as a person of interest, then you search my home and now you're forbidding me from seeing my wife!" The veins in his neck were stretched taught with anger as he pointed a rigid index finger at Jimenez's ample cleavage.

"Fuck your department! When Chicago's eyes open, she's going to see family. God only knows what she's been through. Otherwise, I'll have so many lawyers down here it'll look like shark week on the Discovery Channel. And if that doesn't move you, my family and I will hold a press conference and let the court of public opinion weigh in." Jimenez didn't want any publicity. "Dr. Brooks, please calm down. We're all on the same team." She placed a placating hand on his arm.

The detective knew this pretty boy prick was loaded financially, plus he had a few heavyweight connections, which could impede her investigation. She couldn't treat him like a repeat offender. If she played hardball with this jerk, there was no doubt in her mind that he'd have half the Michigan Bar Association breathing down her neck. This situation would require the ballerina in the China shop and not the bull. She knew that she had to apply a little diplomacy and tact for now. Hardball would come later. Jimenez let her hand slip from Dorian's arm after giving it a gentle squeeze. "I can see you love your wife. A man of your stature is used to taking control, but this is not something you can take control of. Would you want me to teach your students? I don't think so. Let me do my job and procure justice for your wife. It may be the only peace of mind she'll get for some time." Dorian deflated some, but was still puffed up when she quickly told him, "How about you guys visit with her as a group for 10 minutes and don't talk about anything pertaining to the case?" Jimenez glanced at her watch then said, "Go home and get some sleep. By this afternoon you guys will be able to visit at your discretion. Besides, after her ordeal, I'm sure Dr. Daniels can use the rest."

Morgan threw in his two cents and it dissipated Dorian's anger, further. "That sounds like a winner. You don't want to seem as though you're at cross purposes with the police investigating your wife's kidnapping and assault. The goal is to catch the other persons involved. That can't be done if you're making this about you instead of Chicago." His look held more importance than his words. Observing his brother-in-law's face, Dorian could easily interpret the look: You don't want to become their focus.

Just then, a nurse pushed open the waiting room door announcing that Chicago was out of recovery sooner than expected and had been moved into a private room. The detective observed closely as husband and brother-in-law flanked Butterfly on the left and right. What sparked Jimenez's interest was how Dr. Brooks and Mrs. Baxter's fingers grazed in an intimate caress. Maybe it was nothing; but call it a hunch, the detective figured the Professor was poking Mrs. Baxter in the study with his candlestick. Was Sanford Smalls their Colonel Mustard? If so, how are they all connected? She would follow each clue to its source, just like the board game.

Lieutenant Roderick Templeton believed in the Montessori method when building a skilled homicide detective. He let those under his command come to learn their strengths by recognizing their weaknesses. Detective Sargent Jimenez was of a different breed. She was a natural investigator. On the force for 12 years, three in uniform on street patrol, six years undercover bouncing from narcotics to vice, and the last almost four years in homicide. For the past year, she'd been working without a designated partner. Sandoval Curtis, her former partner with 30 years on the force retired the previous October.

A huge baseball fan, everyone in the section chipped in and sent him and his wife to the major league baseball World Series. Since then, Jasenya has been a true maverick, working alone. Detroit's Homicide Task Force was comprised of well over 20 members with liaisons from Michigan State Police, ATF, DEA, and the Wayne County Sheriff's Department. She was able to pull support from them when and if needed. Normally, there was no way a detective would be working alone; but Templeton gave her more leeway than others under his command because she produced results. Her closure rate was over 87 percent. It was by far the best in the section.

Templeton watched her from across his desk, as she chewed on bubblegum and stared over his shoulder as if her focus was miles away. Most detectives dressed in professional attire. Not Jimenez. She dressed as though she were still in vice. The one time he ordered her to wear professional attire, she told him that all her clothes were made for undercover. Templeton didn't care, she'd better dress up. Jimenez came in dressed all right. She looked like a $2,000.00 a night call girl. He ignored it for three days then finally called her into his office and told her to go back to her former way of dressing.

"All right Jimenez, tell me the short version of where you're at with the Daniels' investigation?" It was winter, so she was wearing thick-soled boots. She stood up and began pacing up and down. Her boots made a nerve-wracking thump against the tiled floor. "Stop pacing and give it to me," he ordered.

Jimenez stood still. "Lieu, whoever was in on it with that sick Sanford Smalls, is a ghost. Forensics couldn't come up with anything. Absolutely no physical evidence linking anyone else to our case except our dead kidnapping, rapist. The phone used by our vic to dial 911 only held video of that bastard sexually assaulting the vic. We recovered a burner phone from Smalls' truck.
It had been preprogrammed to dial only one number."

Lieutenant Templeton listened intently while she explained how the tech boys tried tracing the number but to no avail. They pinged it, triangulated its location and found it outside a rest stop in Tennessee. Actually, it was found in the spare tire of a motorhome owned and operated by Nico Williams, a 60- something-year-old retiree from Ypsilanti, Michigan. "The Tennessee State Police put the old guy on the phone with me for a little Q & A session. I learned that he stopped in the Detroit area to visit his daughter who lives in Highland Park on Elmhurst and Hamilton Streets. As you know, that's a few miles southwest of where we found Dr. Daniels and that piece of shit, Smalls. Lieu, anyone could've tossed that burner into the spare tire of that motorhome."

Up until that point, Templeton sat silently in thought with his fingers steepled as if meditating. "Do you have a working theory?" She sat back down and scooted her chair closer to her boss' desk. "Hell yeah, I got a theory. It was Professor Plum with the aid of a Butterfly." Templeton was at a loss for words, but his facial expression said it all. "For Christ's sake, she blurted out. Have you ever heard of the board game called Clue? Colonel Mustard, Professor Plum, the rope, candlestick, etc.? It's why I love detective work. His brow relaxed as recognition dawned on him.

"Continue," he said. Jimenez explained her theory of Dr. Brooks bending over Mrs. Baxter, his sister-in-law. One or both of them wanted the wife dead; only they chose the wrong asshole for the job. "I think Smalls was infatuated with Dr. Daniels. You're a man, you've seen her. Both she and her sister could slip their photographs inside a prescription bottle and outsell Viagra." Templeton laughed out loud at that remark. "What if Sanford Smalls was supposed to kill her, but decided to have a little fun first?"

"We know he has priors for rape and unlawful detainment," the Lieutenant said. "Why the kidnapping and attempted murder? Was he evolving, escalating to greater levels of violence?"

Jimenez looked at her boss. "Who gives a crap? I want to know who he was involved with. The night our Vic was rescued, she said Smalls acted as if he'd been forced to get rid of her. We know from the bullet holes in Smalls' head there is someone else out there connected to this." The detective stood and started pacing again. "Uniforms found over six grand at Sanford's mother's house. All crisp hundreds, fifties, and twenties were stuffed in the back of an old television in the basement."

41

"What's with these sick bastards living in Mommy's basement or attic?" Temple asked. It was a rhetorical question, but Jimenez had an answer. "Makes them feel like they're still in the womb."

Lieutenant Templeton swiveled in his chair looking out the window at the dreary overcast sky. "Tell me why you believe Smalls' accomplice killed him?" She stopped pacing and stared at the back of her boss's head. The kidnapping of adults almost always involves multiple perps. This wasn't a kidnapping though. I mean, there was no ransom and if it was just about sex, Dr. Daniels didn't fit Smalls' normal profile. His previous victims were white middle-aged women with large breasts and bottle blonde dye jobs. They all resembled his mother. Now he deviates from what he obviously desires for a black woman. I'm thinking of murder for hire gone wrong. Just think, if it was a murder for hire then Sanford Smalls screwed up big time. The media attention alone was motive enough to kill him."

Templeton spun back around facing Jimenez. "Let me get this straight. Smalls allows his twisted desires to overcome his contractual obligations and gets a double-tap to his dome for his trouble? You believe the sister and husband are or at the very least were bed buddies. If Smalls was no more than a hired hand, then we need to answer two questions: Who hired him? Who else did they hire? But my question to you is this: Do you have any proof to substantiate any of this?" Jimenez slumped further into her chair. "When you put it like that, it sounds wrong. So damn wrong!"

"Sargent, you are by far the best closer I've seen in my eight-year command of homicide; but until something breaks, or you bring me actionable intel on any of the parties involved I'm going to need you working on current cases."

Standing, she shoved her hands in her pockets, a sign of obvious capitulation. "Copy that Lieu. Although, I have been working on current cases."

"I'm aware of that, but I need you to reverse things. Instead of working on current cases in your spare time and the Daniels' case fulltime, reverse it."

Jimenez left his office feeling like a loser, but still grateful that Templeton didn't take her off the case altogether. Even if he had she wouldn't drop it. She was like a pit bull with a bloody rabbit. Jimenez would keep shaking until she got lucky.

4 PRESENT

Chicago finished her meeting but sat in the back of the church basement listening to a mother of four speak about how she viewed her alcoholism as a curse handed down to her through Irish and Native American genes. "My father was Irish; my mother is a Chippewa Indian. I was practically doing shots out of an Evenflo baby bottle before I could talk. "Chicago was only half-listening to the woman whose name she thought was Natalie or Nicole when her friend Billy slid into the seat behind her laying a friendly hand on her shoulder. She smiled while covering his hand with her own.

"What's up Lakeshore?" he whispered in her ear. "The sun, moon, and of course, the stars Kidd," she replied. Billy leaned his gaunt face over her seat, pressing his dry lips to the soft skin of her cheek.

"How are you feeling?" she asked. Stifling a cough, he swallowed hard then said, "Between the disease and the cure I think I'm dying a little faster every day."

Chicago got up and pulled Billy into the empty hallway leading upstairs. Before she could speak, he gave her a serious look and asked, "What are we doing Lakeshore?" She touched the stubble on his face noticing how thin he'd gotten in the last month. "Let's go get drunk." He looked at her as though she were crazy. "Come on Kidd, I know the perfect place." Billy took a deep breath and sighed heavily. "What the hell; it's on my list of things to do."

A half-hour later the two friends arrived at their destination in their own cars. Chicago stepped from her Mercedes Benz S65 coup with a fifth of 1738 Remy Martin cognac and two glass snifters. "Hell, I don't know if I can drink this without plastic." She laughed, "This is the good stuff. No plastic." They had driven across East Jefferson Avenue to the shoreline of the Detroit River. The area where they parked was practically abandoned. With Billy's Toyota Camry and her Benz, they might be mistaken for drug dealers, but they didn't care.

The two friends sat on the Camry's trunk sipping the amber liquor slowly while reminiscing about the last few years. "How are Sandy and Jack Jr.?"

Billy coughed up some phlegm mixed with blood and spat into some weeds next to his car. "They're doing fine just waiting on me. Jack is growing fast. I'm going to miss him the most."

She took a sip of cognac letting it warm her throat before speaking. "I, for one, am going to miss you dearly."

He downed the liquor in his glass like a thirsty man does water." I would tell you to come with me but it's a one-way trip." Billy nodded toward the bottle clenched between her thighs. "Hit me again Lakeshore."

After pouring him another drink she said, "Take it easy, we don't need you catching a DUI. This and your meds could make you feel woozy. Matter fact, let's just talk and watch the sunset." After putting the rest of the bottle in the trunk she turned to him, "This is the last time we'll be spending together."

The deep sadness in her voice hurt him more than his disease." All right Lakeshore, let's talk and watch the setting of the sun." Chicago scooted back up on the trunk of Billy's Toyota Camry and watched several cargo ships cruise downriver. "Are you ready for what comes next? Are you ready for the endgame?"

She inhaled the smell of the water along with the diesel fumes of the passing ships then said, "I should be asking you that, seeing as how you're faced with the ultimate.

Looking at Chicago, Billy simply said, I'm inspired, or I should say galvanized to see this through." The two friends hugged each other then clicked their glasses together in a toast. "Here's to paying it forward." Chicago added, "And to paying it back!" They both started laughing, which made her think of the old adage, "She who laughs last, laughs best."

Albany was fast asleep in his stepfather's arms as they all trooped up the five stories to Chicago's apartment. She and Butterfly were loaded down with luggage. Chicago also lugged a huge bear that she won on the Bullseye shooting game at Cedar Point Amusement Park. She had excellent hand to eye coordination. There was plenty of room in the Sprinter van for the bear. After picking them up from Metropolitan Airport in Romulus, southwest of Detroit, she told them to sit back and relax. Then she drove to Ohio where they spent three nights and three days at Kalahari Resort and Water Park to begin Albany's birthday adventure. On the fourth day, they hopped over to Cedar Point where her nephew went wild on every rollercoaster and ride, he was permitted to get on. The entire day he gorged himself on cotton candy, corn dogs, ice cream, and everything else with sugar in it, plus everything that had been deep-fried. But now the little guy was out like a light.

Morgan placed him in the second to last guest room, then went back down to the van for the rest of their luggage. The two sisters plopped down on the couch in the living area. It was almost midnight and it had been a long day. Butterfly asked Chicago, "Do you remember when Momma would bake us her deep dark double chocolate cake? That delicious cake, $20.00, and a card with one of her wonderfully wise sayings."

Chicago chimed in, "Put time and prayer on a problem and it will solve itself. And what about this one: Don't let your friends fall behind you. They may be tempted to stick a knife in your back."

"What does that even mean?" Butterfly asked. Chicago turned her head to look Butterfly in the eyes. "It means your friends should be on the same level as you in all aspects lest they become jealous or resentful towards you."

Butterfly could sense a sudden change in her sister. "What's wrong, Windy City?"

"Birthdays were the only thing worth celebrating in that house. Thankfully each year got me closer to adulthood."

Butterfly caught the disgruntled tone in her older sister's voice. "Big Shirley wasn't all that bad."

Chicago seemed lost for a moment before replying, "You're absolutely right. She loved us and taught us how to survive and overcome. I'm thankful for that and much more."

Morgan came into the room just as Chicago turned on the stereo. "Brother, last room on your right. Hell, who am I talking to? You know your way."

She tossed the stereo remote, kicked off her Gucci sandals, and padded softly to the door where she checked the locks and set the alarm. The entire building was replete with over two dozen surveillance cameras, most of them hidden from sight. All Chicago had to do was put any television in the apartment on channel three and 26 separate displays would appear on the screen. When the man who had installed her entire security system had finished he told her "There are great dangers on the other side of your doors; though after two decades in this business I've learned that sometimes evil lurks closer to us on the inside." Chicago thought to herself, that's true.

Aretha Franklin's, *"Ain't No Way"* came on the stereo and Butterfly asked her, "Do you remember this song, Windy City?" How could she forget, it was their mother's favorite. The doctors told the sisters that Shirley Marie Daniels died from a cardiac event at 50 years old. Tragic! What was even more tragic was the truth that Big Shirley died from a broken heart. When she lost her husband, Martin Daniels, or rather when she was robbed by the reality of the idea of him, the woman was never the same. The couple was married when they were both 18 years old in Cook County in Chicago, Illinois. Big Shirley was pregnant when they married. And because Marty D had a wandering eye, a lying tongue, and thieving hands, the newlyweds had to leave Chicago.

Detroit was thriving at the time with the metro area boasting a population of over two million. Marty D bought them a house and checked out; then in. and then out again. It all depended on his mood. Chicago only knew him in passing; while Butterfly never knew him at all. For years the couple fought and made up. The story goes that during one of those makeup sessions, Butterfly was conceived. The only thing he ever gave the girls were their names. Chicago after the city he loved and left. Butterfly, because when she was born, she was a wrinkled, ugly little thing who would have to blossom into her beauty. Just like a Butterfly.

Big Shirley was a small woman who stood 5'4 tall and maxed out at 120 pounds. She was beautiful with silky skin and large doe eyes. Everyone called her Big Shirley because she had a big heart. She loved Marty and her girls fiercely. People say after he was shot to death for sleeping with a friend's wife, she never let the girls or anyone else for that matter speak badly about him. Ask anyone who was around, and they'd tell you that her will to live seemed to have vanished after his death. It was almost as if she blamed herself. After Butterfly graduated high school, Big Shirley simply let go of the chords that held her to this life.

Chicago watched the beautiful Butterfly as she sang along with the Queen of Soul. The two women had their father's height and green flecked hazel eyes but shared a mixture of both parents' complexions. One had a light complexion and the other a dark one, making for a sweet honey hue. Both women possessed stunning figures, but whereas Chicago has athletic curves and runway model sophistication, Butterfly has a 'come sex me or I you' voluptuousness. She boasted fuller breasts with a high, round well-sculpted ass. Neither woman had any excess weight.

The song ended and Chicago clapped for her. "Bravo! I see or rather hear you still have a beautiful voice." Her little sister bowed at the waist. "Thank you! Thank you! Thank you very much!" Chicago laughed while going to snag a bottle of wine. She came back with two glasses. Butterfly asked, "This won't have you relapsing will it?"

"Only if there's heroin in it," she replied simply.

"Sorry, just looking out for you." Morgan came through the hallway door in his pajamas and robe. When he spied the wine, he pulled his glasses down the bridge of his nose, looked pointedly at Chicago than his wife. "I'm going to bed ladies. Goodnight!" Quickly turning on his heels he threw his hands in the air while hurrying away. They laughed as he retreated.

After pouring them each a glass, Chicago gently took her sister's hand in hers. "Tell me your secrets and I'll tell you my truth." Butterfly squeezed Chicago's fingers while saying to her, "If I told you my secrets, they would no longer be mine, they'd be ours. And being a behavioral psychologist, you should know better than anyone that a shared secret isn't a secret at all. It becomes something you fear someone telling someone else."

"Okay," Chicago said. "I see your point. Let's talk about something other than secrets. How's married life treating you?"

Sipping her wine, Butterfly seemed thoughtful before answering. "Morgan is great. Any woman would want him, and I have him. Big in the bank and long in the tank." She grabbed playfully at her crotch.

"But do you love him?" Chicago asked, pouring more wine into her glass.

Butterfly's disposition seemed to change. To Chicago's learned eye, she grew serious. "Windy City, love is what love does."

"Is that how you quantify love in your life?"

"That's how I quantify love with a man in my life. What's the alternative? Me being caught in a shit storm accepting what a man dishes out under the umbrella of love and proclaiming that our love will see me through? No, I'm much more comfortable being the author of my own tail…" She rubbed her buttock, "… even if it's a tale of woe."

"Are you that cynical because of Todd?" Chicago asked her sister. A look of surprise shadowed by fear registered on Butterfly's face. "I know you don't like talking about Albany's father and I don't want to upset you. But my nephew asked me if he looks like him and have, I ever seen him. He's at that age where he's going to ask questions about his biological father. I have deflected his inquiries for now, but he won't be denied the answers he seeks. You know how persistent your child is."

Butterfly relaxed visibly and told Chicago, "Todd is dead to me and Albany. He didn't want to man up and be present in his son's life, so fuck him!" Chicago had never laid eyes on Todd, no last name. Butterfly met him when she moved down to Atlanta after college. Less than a year later, Albany was born. Chicago wanted to meet the SOB who fathered her nephew, but Butterfly said he was married with children and wanted nothing to do with either of them. For almost a decade she believed the story her sister had given her. Now she wasn't so sure anymore.

Butterfly reached for the bottle of wine and emptied the contents into both their glasses. "Morgan is Albany's father and that's that. Since we're talking about the men in my life, let's discuss the men in yours."

At that, Chicago clutched one of the couch pillows to her breasts as if it was a shield, then quietly she said, "I have no men in my life."

Butterfly asked, "What about the man of your dreams?"

Chicago guffawed. "The man of my dreams kidnapped me, screwed me with a cattle prod, and shot me full of heroin. I see his face four out of seven nights in a week. Even if I wanted to make things work," she said sarcastically, "He's dead, just like Dorian."

Butterfly couldn't recall the last time they'd spoken like this. "Dorian loved you." Chicago drained her glass of wine then folded her arms around the pillow clutching it tighter to her chest. "I'm not so sure. I think he was unfaithful for most of, if not all of our marriage."

Her sister seemed genuinely shocked at this admission. "Windy City, I just can't imagine him cheating on you. You're smart, successful, and gorgeous with a banging body. You're everything a man wants."

"Unless a man wants more than what anyone woman can give him. I guess with him dead it's a moot point," she retorted. "Looking back on it now, there was a great deal of tension in our marriage right before my abduction. Then after I was rescued it was as though we were newlyweds again. Dorian was attentive and caring, but it felt wrong. Almost like he was playing a part."

Butterfly put her glass down and drew Chicago close, hugging her. "Momma would tell you, ain't no going back in time, so concentrate on moving forward."

The two hugged a while longer. Chicago looked her sister deep in the eyes, which mirrored hers, and said, "I love you more than you'll ever know."

That admission made Butterfly uncomfortable. Before hurrying off to bed she uttered a hushed, "Me too!"

Watching her sister walk down the hallway Chicago thought, lies travel around the world before the truth has even taken its morning pee.

Normally, Chicago would've slept curled up on the couch under the watchful eye of CNN; but since she had guests, her bedroom would have to do. Even though there was a California king-sized bed in front of her, she preferred the small loveseat in the lounge area next to it. Besides, the bed held too many awful memories for her. Memories of her late husband, Dorian, and his spectacular brand of bullshit. Stripping down to her panties she pulled on an old tee shirt and grabbed a tattered blue comforter from the closet, then balled up on the loveseat. Staring at the empty bed triggered her memory of the last time she saw the lying, cheating bastard breathing. It made her smile.

51

5 DORIAN'S DEMISE

The apartment was cold even though the entire heating and cooling system had been modernized. "Is something wrong with the heat?" Dorian asked while effecting a trembling body shiver. "No. It was hotter than Hades, so I turned the thermostat down a little." She pointed to the steaming plates of food on the dining room table. "I saw you coming. Veal Parmesan will warm you up in no time at all." Throwing his overcoat onto the couch, Dorian took his briefcase and laptop into their home office. Before returning he stopped in the main bathroom to quickly freshen up and yelled through the open door for her to pick out a nice red wine. "Nothing too dark please!" When he made it to the table, she held up the bottle for his approval which he gave with a shrug and a nod. Dorian didn't wait for Chicago to finish blessing the food before digging in hungrily.

"How was your day Dorian?" He sliced off a small piece of veal pausing, "It was going well until the end of my last class. That's when my teaching assistant, Sheldon Grosby, told me that he was quitting because of some family emergency. I need more time in a day, Dr. Brooks." he mimicked in a whiny singsong voice. Chicago toyed with her food as she listened to the inconsiderate, selfish man she married. "Is something wrong with your food?" She picked up her plate, "I'm not really hungry, I'll save it for later." After wrapping and storing her uneaten food in the fridge, she sat back down and picked up her wineglass.

He felt her gaze on him and looked up from the table. "Something on your mind sweetheart?" Chicago leaned her forearms on the dining table bringing herself closer to Dorian. "Are you seeing someone?" He dropped his fork, wiped his mouth with his napkin, then took a hefty swallow of wine. "Jesus Christ! Where is this coming from?" Her full lips curved into a smile. "I'll take that as a yes. How many have you been with since our marriage?" Dorian ignored her while picking up his plate and glass. He was in the kitchen rinsing his dishes when he asked her, "What's this really about?"

"It's about you and me," she shouted. "I've been with you for the better part of my life. Do you think I don't know you? You have a healthy libido. You enjoy sex! Even when we were upset with one another, we still had sex, Dr. Brooks. You know —Fuck!" Chicago spat the profanity out like a bullet.

Dorian turned from the sink facing her anger head-on. "Chicago, why are you trying to destroy what little we have left?"

Laughing derisively, she mocked him, "What little we have left? Are you kidding me! We have nothing!" The more she spoke, the angrier she became. "How many of those starry-eyed impressionable young students have bounced up and down in Professor Brooks' lap for a passing grade?" Chicago had gotten up and moved into his personal space.

Disgusted at her, he yelled. "You're obviously delusional!"

Chicago walked over to the wet bar in the living area with her empty wine glass and filled it to almost overflowing with Cîroc Vodka. "Why are you doing this? Stop it before you can't turn back."

"I'm only finishing what you started, stud!" He kept talking but she fazed him out like useless background noise. Tipping her head back she swallowed half of her glass. "I'm not going to stay here and watch you self-destruct!"

Chicago's focus returned. "For two years we have not had sex, screwed, fucked or heaven forbid, made love! Tell me, husband, have you been masturbating for these past two years? Is that what you want me to believe?"

"I don't give a damn what you believe!" Chicago started crying. "I've always loved you. I was never unfaithful. I need you to know that. Why won't you give me some honest answers about your infidelity? Tell me Dorian, how many women have shared your mediocre penis?"

The trap had been set. The bait dangling bloody in waiting. The ego, raw and exposed.

"Mediocre! Mediocre? You must mean magnificent! You never had any complaints!" She laughed hysterically. "That's only because I've had nothing to compare it to! I can tell you that the bastard who kidnapped me made me orgasm more in a week than you did in 10 years." Dorian stopped cold. His concerned husband facade instantly shattered. "Maybe you can only get off when you're playing the role of victim."

The empty glass sailed an inch past the left side of his face breaking into countless shards against the backsplash of the sink. "As I recall my mediocre penis kept you on your knees throughout our courtship and the majority of our marriage. If you've forgotten you can get on them now and take a refresher course or ask some of the younger, prettier freshmen class females who can remind you of my sexual gifts."

Chicago walked closer to him, but he made sure they stayed separated by the butcher block. "When I started standing up for myself, building my practice along with my financial individuality and not being led around by your leash, your ego and erection shrunk a little more each day."

She watched his nose flare in anger as a crimson tint crept up his neck discoloring his facial features. "Bitch! You'd be nothing without me!" She waved her hands in dismissal.

"Asshole! You're probably arrogant enough to think that. Please tell me you're not foolish enough to believe it! Do you know why I kept my maiden name? It wasn't so people wouldn't confuse us if there were two Dr. Brooks in the home. It was because I knew I could easily allow myself to become lost in you and as a consequence forsake my own identity." She walked to where his scarf and overcoat lay across the back of the couch and picked them up tossing them at his feet. "I'm still my own woman. Get the fuck out! Take a walk, cool off or whatever, I don't care. Just leave!"

He looked at her as though she were speaking gibberish. "You must be crazy if you think I'm walking around in that weather!" Chicago picked up her cellphone and pressed 9 then 1. "If you want, I can press this other 1 and see how fast the police can remove your verbally and physically abuse self from this apartment."

"I haven't touched you!" he yelled.

"And again, you never will. Tomorrow's Detroit Free Press will read; 'WAYNE STATE PROFESSOR ARRESTED FOR PUNCHING WIFE." "How will your colleagues respond to that?"

At that remark, Dorian picked up his coat and scarf, slowly slipping into it formulating his next move. Chicago interrupted his thoughts. "I know, I know. Bitch comes to mind doesn't it?"

"I'm leaving but I'll be back after you've calmed down. We'll talk about how to proceed with our divorce. Hopefully, you'll be rational by the time I return."

"Get out!" She watched him stomp out like a petulant child, then spent the next ten minutes changing the alarm codes. That was the last time she saw him alive. Ironically, he made the papers all on his own: 'WAYNE STATE PROFESSOR KILLED IN CARJACKING.'

Detective Sargent Jimenez had partnered up with Detective Donald Gleason over a year ago. She had no desire to link up with another detective; but Gleason was methodical, quick-witted, and didn't know the word, 'Uncle'. The man just refused to ever give up. A couple of inches shorter than Jimenez and bald with a light olive complexion compliments of his Chaldean mother, while his cleanshaven head could be attributed to his receding hairline handed down from his Polish father. When he complained last Thanksgiving about his lack of hair, Harold Gleason told him, "Grass doesn't grow on a busy street. You should be grateful that your grandfather, God bless him, changed Glenkowski to Gleason, otherwise you'd be a bald Pollack camel jockey and the butt of many jokes." In hindsight he was thankful.

Donald Gleason was the detective investigating the carjacking homicide of Dr. Dorian Brooks. When Jimenez found out that bit of news, she made sure they became fast friends. Her gut was telling her that the two cases were connected. It only took him all of 10 minutes to figure out Jimenez's sudden interest in being partners. On the surface, these two cases have a central common denominator. Both husband and wife were victims of violent crimes, and their perpetrators are presently unknown to us. "So now," Gleason blurted out, "…you go from Chuck Norris to team player."

"I don't get the Chuck Norris reference," Jimenez said.

"It means lone wolf," Gleason explained. "Why the sudden interest in my case?" She hesitantly shared her theory of how the cases were connected. "Your Vic was murdered after leaving the home of one of his students, a senior named Georgina Flynn. The wife, Dr. Daniels, told us that her husband came in from work, ate dinner then left their apartment sometime after she laid down for a nap." Jimenez checked the file in front of her. "Their alarm systems digital log has him leaving at 8:17 p.m., but he was murdered after 2:00 a.m. We know he was screwing Ms. Flynn. What we don't know is why Mrs. Brooks, aka Dr. Daniels, never called to see where her hubby had gotten himself to when she woke up and he was nowhere to be found. I wake up and find my husband gone, I'm calling to see where he is. I ran her phone, she never called him."

"So, you think the wife knew he was having an affair and had him bumped off?"

"I don't know about that. It just seems strange that someone carjacks and kills a man for an expensive SUV only to dump it without even taking the radio. It's all a little too suspect for my taste. I'll bet my stripes and a year's salary they're connected. What if the husband was responsible for his wife's kidnapping, which I believe was a murder for hire gone wrong and his accomplice is doing some house cleaning?" It was right after that discussion with Gleason that she humbled herself and asked if they could work together. Technically, Jimenez was his direct superior, but you can catch more flies with honey than you can with vinegar.

Little good their union did. She had been working on the case for two years, and one of the years was with Gleason. The two had been working hard together but they had nothing. Jimenez had just brought in a suspect earlier on second-degree murder charges. He'd beaten his girlfriend to death but claimed it was an accident. She passed him off to an officer for transport to the Wayne County Jail. She was looking for Gleason, but everyone was busy sorting through violence and death. No one seemed to know where he was. She texted him a message: "WHERE R U?" He texted back: CON ROOM 3. She headed to conference room three wondering what he was up to. She was angry when she initially found out what he was up to. But that anger quickly turned to gratefulness because they finally had a clue.

The box was addressed to Detective Gleason and had been delivered via UPS. He opened it and read the accompanying letter, then rushed into the conference room shutting the door. When Jimenez found him, he was sitting in a chair with his hands behind his head staring at a laptop screen. "What's going on? Why are you hiding back here?" Looking up at her Gleason replied, "I received a package in the mail today. I thought it was some type of hoax at first. Now, I don't know what to believe."

He spun the computer around so that she could see the screen. "Who's this guy?" Instead of answering, he picked up a box from the floor next to his chair and shoved it across the table. She was speechless. Inside was a .357 snub-nosed revolver and some photographs. "The DVD on the laptop also came with the box. Have a look. I've already watched it twice. It's the mother of all confessions. It has always been said that the third time's a charm."

Jimenez pulled Detective Trooper Shackleford from his cubicle into the conference room where she and Gleason were still watching the confession video. Shackleford worked for the Michigan State Police but was attached to HTF. Because of rampant corruption in the DPD under the previous administration and shoddy work by the crime lab, the state police stepped in to pick up the slack. With the DPD crime lab now under the purview of the MSP, all evidence gathered by DPD was analyzed by MSP except for some firearm's evidence which was sent to the Oakland County's sheriff's department to their Firearms & Tool Marks Division. This is where the slugs, or rather spent bullets, that were recovered from Dr. Dorian Brooks' body were sent.

After hearing and seeing the confession, Jimenez and Gleason wanted to know if Shackleford could pave the way and get a rush job on the bullets from their Vic matched to the gun in the box. If so, they would be well on their way to solving the case. They just needed the man in the video to corroborate on the stand what was said in his confession or deepen their investigation to find independent proof of the man's claims.

During the two weeks that they waited on ballistics and latent fingerprinting to come back, the two detectives dug deep into the background of all the players except for the Confessor. That's what they called the man in the video. There was nothing in their database on the Confessor. They even went old school, back to physical mugshot albums, but still found no match for the man in the video. Lo and behold, the dots were always present, but the lines were either missing or obscured.

This case wasn't like a Hollywood movie where the director cuts right to the captured scene. The majority of their cases required grunt work, going through reams of paper, and knocking on doors. Jimenez and Gleason were making things clearer. They were filling in those lines and connecting the dots. Still, it was a process. When they received that box, they backtracked over the times, places, and financials that they had for this case. They looked at things with fresh eyes. Hence the meeting of the minds. Jimenez pulled together some of the HTF members.

Lieutenant Templeton sat at the head of the main conference room's table along with detectives Wilkerson, Hodgkins, and Corporal Simmons from the computer intelligence division or CID. All listened intently as Gleason and Jimenez explained how their cases were going nowhere fast; but it was Jimenez's belief that the two were connected, so she partnered up with Gleason and voila`, in comes a box of evidence.

Ted Wilkerson, a big bear of a man who sported a kind grandfatherly face with a salt and pepper military buzz cut asked, "Why are we here, Jimmy?" Wilkerson had been calling her that ever since she mistakenly laid an arrest report on his desk and he asked, "Who is Jim Enez and why is his report on my desk?" She didn't take offense. Jimenez knew the error was due to her sloppy handwriting. The two had been friends from then on. He's a whiz at crafting affidavits for arrest and search warrants.

Alma Hodgkins, a petite Jewish woman who grew up near Gross Pointe on the east side during the gang-related 70s and crack epidemic 1980s, was a numbers genius. Both parents wanted her to join the family accounting business, but she joined DPD instead. With a degree in Forensic Accounting, she could follow the money better than anyone, wherever it led.

Simmons was a kid. He was an arrogant computer geek who was great with cracking computer encryption and bringing back to life data that people deleted. A tall gangly African American with glasses, a bright smile, and a pinched face. CID lent him to HTF for the duration. Jimenez and Gleason brought together people in the squad whom they trusted and knew would get the job done. Corporal Simmons was unknown to Jimenez though Gleason worked with him before and vouched for his integrity.

Detective Sargent Jimenez observed her audience, intentionally drawing their attention to her. "This video is the jaw-dropping missing link. I should've brought popcorn so you guys would have something to put in your mouths while they're hanging open. By far, it's the most interesting confession I've ever heard." She nodded for Gleason to hit the lights just as Shackleford slid into the room. He wore the look of the cat who finally shitted out the canary. "What's up Shack?" Jimenez asked in a whisper. He leaned into her ear, "We better move our asses; our suspect is about to leave our jurisdiction in a matter of hours." Gleason pushed play on the remote and all eyes focused on the large television hanging on the wall.

The screen popped on showing a man sitting on an old wooden barstool in what appeared to be a single car garage. A bare dingy yellow bulb hung from the ceiling by an electrical cord, slightly behind and over an emaciated man's bald head. He looked frail though it was hard to say for sure because the coveralls he wore swallowed his body disguising his shape. The man brought a cigarette to his lips then cupped it with a pair of roughly calloused hands and lit it. The flame highlighted his gaunt, haggard facial features, sunken eye sockets, lips which seemed too full for such a small face, and a prominent forehead.

The confessor took a long, deep drag on the cigarette allowing the nicotine to fill his lungs. Everyone watching sat waiting on the man to stop staring into the flame of his Zippo lighter and start speaking. He exhaled snapping it shut to a metallic clink and with a flourish put it in his pocket. Jimenez likened his skin to parchment paper. Every detective in the conference room was hard-pressed to give an accurate estimation of the Confessor's true age. He could be anywhere from 40 to knocking on death's door 80. A blue plume of cigarette smoke drifted like a lazy cloud into the camera's lens as the man seemed to be building up his nerve by puffing harder on the cancer stick. When the smoke cleared, they heard his voice.

"I ain't never killed nobody before. Don't get me wrong, I've done a lot of bad shit just never that." The spectators all watched as he appeared to gather his thoughts before he continued. "Over a year ago, I met a woman through a mutual friend who wanted her boyfriend dead." He thumped a long ash from his cigarette, inhaled deeply, then continued speaking while smoke streamed from his nostrils like an old weary dragon. "Paid me fifteen grand in cash up-front and gave me a pistol, too. You should have it already if you're looking at this. Anyway, never would've done it if her story wasn't so convincing and I didn't need the money."

The man tossed the butt to the ground then screwed his fist into his bloodshot eyes as if he could push the memories from his brain with the action. "Lies! All fucking lies! The woman played me like a fiddle. She's a master of manipulation and deception. Bitch told me that her boyfriend was abusing her and their son." The Confessor's eyes glazed over while his face seemed to tighten in anger. From a breast pocket, he produced a prescription pill bottle. After dry swallowing a couple of pills, he slipped the bottle back into his coveralls. "I followed this guy from his apartment in midtown to a townhouse on West Harper Avenue. The woman told me it was where his mistress lived — at least one of them. Him and her came out and took her car to a bar in Redford, then back to her place. The way they were pawing each other, I thought he was gonna poke her right there in the snow. Son of a bitch must have had Bugs Bunny for a daddy. He stayed in there for more than a couple of hours. Keep in mind it was December and cold as a witch's tit. Even though I was dressed warm, I didn't like being out in the open like that. So, I walked back and forth until the lights in the townhouse came back on. It didn't take long after that."

The Confessor extended his left arm while fashioning his thumb and forefinger into the shape of a gun. "Ran up on him with my ski mask on. I was wearing boots with my jeans sagging and a red and black winter coat with a black hoodie. Look just like one of them rowdy thugs accosting law-abiding citizens outside of gas stations and stores all over the city." Gleason paused the disc. "I checked Georgina Washington's statement. Her description almost matches this guy to a T." He started the video back up.

"You can tell my voice is gravelly with a southern twang. When I deepen it a little and speak slower, I sound like one of those young thugs. The ones who address everybody as nigga regardless of race. Nigga! Give me yo' motherfucking wallet and car keys! Anyway, I popped him four times in the midsection then put the money shot in his dome for good measure. I left the wallet, snatched the key fob, jumped in his car, and took off. I dumped it by West Outer Drive and Evergreen."

Everyone's eyes in the conference room were glued to the screen as the man lit another cigarette, blew a few clouds of smoke, cleared his throat then continued speaking. "Next day I'm watching the local news and see that this boyfriend is actually a doctor whose wife was kidnapped by that Smalls fella a couple of years before. They're rich people. I see a picture of the guy I killed wife, a pretty black woman. She looks a lot like the woman who hired me just not as sexual. Know what I mean?" At that statement by the Confessor, there were a few loud gasps from some of those in the room as the puzzle pieces started fitting into place.

"I could've let it go, but something gets to gnawing at me and I need to find out why. Plus, since the woman lied to me, I was gonna need more money." He thumped the cigarette butt and stretched his arms over his head. "More than what I got for killing the good Dr. Brooks. See the woman is really rich. I Googled her and her husband. They got that F. U. money. You know, Fuck your money. Tried to get me some of that but it didn't work out as I planned."

The man continued talking. He talked about how he did some amateur investigating and surveillance. He even attended Dr. Brooks' funeral. "A wig, little theatrical makeup, and I was in." Laughing he said, "Who's looking for a white guy? Nobody, that's who! I see the woman that hired me with her husband and a little boy. The child resembled the man I murdered except he had a way better tan if you get my drift." The Confessor pulled a piece of paper from his coveralls. "They are Mr. Morgan Baxter and his wife, Mrs. Butterfly Baxter. After doing my homework I came to figure it was mighty odd her boy looks like the dead doctor and he's her brother-in-law. I spend some time on a computer and this kid has no father listed on his birth certificate. I get to thinking how the local news says the dead guy's wife was kidnapped a couple of years ago. I come to the conclusion that there's too much going on with this one family, so I play a hunch." The room is deathly quiet. You could hear a field mouse pissing on a grain of wheat. Every detective was glued to the screen. A phone rang somewhere far off as the man dubbed the Confessor described how he tried to blackmail Mrs. Baxter.

"I made it a point to bump into the woman and played my hunch. I told her that I knew who she was and had irrefutable proof that she and her late lover were behind the attempted murder of her sister, Dr. Daniels. When it failed, they had a falling out and she had me kill him." The room exploded into a cacophony of 'Oh my Gods' and 'Oh shits!' "At first, she denied any involvement, but I could see the lie in those pretty eyes. I tell her to get me $100,000.00 cash or go directly to jail. She tries to tell me I'll go to and I tell her, for a lot less than her. She tried to play the old Mexican standoff card, but yours truly wasn't buying it." Another cigarette was lit and puffed on furiously before he continued. "Thought we had an agreement until Mrs. Baxter showed up to our next meeting with pictures of my kid and grandson. Bitch said she found a guy who would kill both of them for a quarter of the money that I wanted."

The anger was visibly etched into the man's worn face. He continued speaking of how he hid his daughter and grandchild then decided to snitch the woman out. Everyone watched as he burst into laughter until his eyes teared up. "In the box is some interesting photos. One, in particular, I had a friend take of her paying me for the murder. Then there's the gun itself."

"Well, go get her coppers. By the time you identify me, I'll be in a faraway place." Standing, he inhaled deeply on his cigarette before tossing it. "My suggestion is you take a crack at the missus and forget about me. Truthfully, my money is on her. She has elephant balls, is tungsten steel tough, and can act better than anyone in Hollywood, California. That evil bitch can charm the slither from a snake and the growl from a Gorilla. Good luck!" The video showed him walking out of frame. A second later the screen went blank then turned to static snow.

Everyone in the room erupted at once. Lieutenant Templeton stood stretching his arms out, "People, people, people! Let's take it down a notch! Detective Gleason, Sargent Jimenez tell us your game plan." Gleason looked at Jimenez who yielded the floor to him with the wave of an open palm. "Right before we began viewing that video, Shackleford relayed some good news. Our suspect is in Detroit." He held up a state of Georgia DMV photo. "This is Mrs. Butterfly Octavia Baxter. Her maiden name is Daniels. She was born and raised in Detroit, attended Northwestern University where she graduated with honors. Mrs. Baxter is also the younger sister of Dr. Chicago Daniels, the woman who three years ago was abducted, sexually assaulted, and tortured for a week by Sanford Tolliver Smalls.

Somehow, Dr. Daniels got free and dialed, 911. Before first responders reached the scene, an unknown assailant murdered Smalls and shot Dr. Daniels. The bullets recovered from both victims matched; so, we're working on the premise that it's only one shooter." Gleason gave the floor to his partner.

"When I first started investigating this case, I believed Butterfly Baxter and the now-deceased Dr. Brooks were having an affair. However, there was no proof. To me, his murder suggests that he was in league with his sister-in-law to get rid of his wife. We now believe Dr. Daniels' survival caused a rift between the co-conspirators, which led to her hiring the man in the video to kill him." At that Templeton asked about their next move. "We'll need Ted to draft the affidavits for a search of Dr. Daniels' apartment and an arrest warrant for our suspect, Butterfly Baxter."

"Why are we searching there again?" Templeton asked.

"Because maybe we missed something before. Last time we were looking for a body or signs of foul play. This time we're looking for any link between the husband and sister. E-mails, phone records, credit card receipts, etc. Also, I'd like to see if we can obtain a warrant for some buccal swabs from Baxter's son, Albany Daniels. A positive DNA result could go a long way to prove a motive."

Gleason interjected. "Hodgkins will take care of the financials while Corporal Simmons will dredge up any information, he can from the electronic devices listed in the warrant."

The Lieutenant stood up. "I'll get in contact with the authorities in Georgia and see if we can get them to execute a search warrant on the Baxter home. Good job Jimenez, Gleason. Now the real work begins. Let's bring this case to a close." Jimenez was the last to leave. Templeton stopped her, issuing a word of warning. "These aren't street thugs with an overworked court-appointed lawyer. These are educated folk with plenty of coins. Cross your T's and dot your I's."

6 TO CATCH A BUTTERFLY

Jimenez sat in the passenger's seat of the stakeout van parked on Calumet off of Second Street. The luxury StarCraft van manufactured by GMC was confiscated in a drug raid and now used as an undercover vehicle. Shackleford was lounging behind the steering wheel playing Candy Crush on his smartphone, while Gleason sat in the back in one of two captain's chairs. Last night after watching the confession video for the fifth time, Jimenez put an unmarked scout car on Dr. Daniels' apartment building with specific instructions to follow Butterfly Baxter if she left the apartment, but do not approach.

This morning before Wilkerson finished drafting warrants, the entire family trooped out climbing into a Mercedes Benz Sprinter van and had breakfast at Southfield's Original Pancake House. The detectives who followed them into the suburb northwest of Detroit knew how to do undercover work. Jameson and Thaddeus often worked as a couple because people overlooked them. A little after 11:00 a.m. the family returned to the apartment. Jimenez had been on the scene since before noon. It was a joint decision to keep the arrest team small. No one thought Mrs. Baxter would pull an Uzi from her designer bag and start spraying bullets. It would be a soccer mom takedown.

The Sargent placed a radio patrol car up ahead on Third Street. Someone had the good sense to run the plates on the Sprinter van. It was a rental due to being returned that day. Gleason found out the Baxter's had three first-class return trip tickets on Delta Airlines from Detroit to Atlanta. Their plane was scheduled to leave in three hours. That meant they would be leaving the apartment soon. The rental van was parked facing west, so the team figured when the Baxter's left, they would travel towards Third Street where the uniform patrol would execute a routine traffic stop. Once the family was pulled over and Butterfly Baxter secured, Jimenez's team would then swoop in and make the arrest placing the Butterfly in a jar.

"HTF 2-3 to tac support 6-1-2?" There was a short burst of static then a voice said, "Copy! This is 6-1-2." "Look alert and alive, this show should be getting started pretty soon" Jimenez spoke into the radio.

Yolanda Jameson, one of the undercover detectives came on the air. "I hope so Sarge. Thaddeus is gnawing my ear off about politics." Her partner, Darren Thaddeus took his politics seriously. He keyed his radio, "No one seems to appreciate that one bad decision by this clown could have us all glowing orange like him for the next hundred years." Jimenez and Shackleford laughed. But Gleason asked, "Shouldn't we be maintaining radio silence?" Jimenez agreed. "All right! Let's focus on people and maintain radio silence except for relevant issues."

Normally, she would've taken a crew and hit Dr. Daniels' apartment, but she had been there several times over the years and saw that it was a fortress. Not only would it be tough to get in without someone's cooperation on the inside, but it would take a small army to cover every exit. No, Jimenez didn't want a barricaded killer splashed across the local news media. She also didn't want Butterfly Baxter to hole up long enough to understand the gravity of her situation and lawyer up.

She went over things again in her head. The patrol car would pull them over under the guise of a routine traffic stop. The officers would identify Mrs. Baxter and pull her out of the van, separating her from the family. Once arrested and transported to homicide she'd be thoroughly interrogated. When faced with the evidence of her crimes the woman will fold, begging the prosecutor for a plea deal. Gleason interrupted her train of thought. "They should be coming out soon. Between baggage check-in and TSA security screening, you damn near have to show up a day early to be on time for your flight." Shackleford looked up from his game. "Patience young grasshopper. What will happen, will happen because it could not have happened any other way." Gleason and Jimenez looked at each other than at Shack. "If I didn't need you right now, I would shoot you for mixing television and movie lines. You're too dark to be Cain from Kung Fu and way too slow to be Morpheus from the Matrix."

They were all still laughing when Morgan Baxter exited the building loaded down with luggage. "Uniform Patrol 6-1-2, this is HTF 2-3." The scout car responded, "6-1-2 Copy!"

"Target should be in route momentarily. Look alert!" Gleason slipped his wingtips back on and sat up a little straighter. Shackleford placed his phone casually in his pocket keeping an eye on the Sprinter van and Morgan Baxter. Jimenez was already envisioning the man's wife sitting across from her in Church. That's what the members of HTF nicknamed the interrogation room. Jimenez thought to herself, Time to confess your sins, Mrs. Baxter.

Officer Bryce Wilson sat comfortably in the driver's seat of his patrol car running the name of a young woman with the ass of a beach ball whom he had met at Flood's nightclub a couple of days before. The popular club on Lafayette Avenue across from the Greektown Casino Hotel in the heart of downtown Detroit is a top-five destination for singles to hookup in the metropolitan area. His partner, Officer Gerard Feeps, nicknamed Jeepers, looked at the computer monitor.

"Yeah, she's pretty but I don't think it was your charm that snagged her. Ms. Angela Hull owes hundreds of dollars in traffic tickets. How much you wanna bet that as soon as you're done tossing that ass like a beach ball you'll hear, "Big Daddy Bryce, can you make my tickets disappear?" Wilson clicked off the woman's DMV photo. "Unh, Unh! I'm not fixing squat. By the time I tap that, and she asks me for the favor, I'll be in plain clothes."

Jeepers looked at his young arrogant partner as though he were crazy. "How are you supposed to make the leap from uniform to plain clothes? Every good cop knows you don't choose it; it chooses you."

Wilson gave him a sideways glance. "This isn't the 90s Jeep. In the 21st century, we don't wait for life to happen. We make it happen." He was about to check the young buck when Sargent Jimenez radioed in. Wilson snatched the mic before his partner could. After receiving their orders, he said, "Now that's a fantabulous piece of ass. Muy Caliente! I could do the sexual salsa with Sarge." Jeepers shook his head. "There's no such word as fantabulous. Just like there's no such thing as you being with a woman like Detective Sargent Jimenez." Officer Feeps had been on patrol for 16 years and went through two fists full of partners in that time. None were as arrogant, high strung, and narcissistic as this one. "Just follow orders and don't do anything stupid." Wilson smiled, "Champions take chances." People who didn't know any better assumed Officer Feeps got his nickname Jeepers because of his thyroid problem that caused his eyes to bulge. In truth, he got it because he could always spot the creeps.

Chicago locked up her apartment then walked hand in hand with her nephew, Albany, down to the van where Morgan and Butterfly were.

Her sister slid from the passenger seat to behind the steering wheel. "What are you doing?" Chicago asked. "I'm driving, you're not on the rental agreement." Butterfly looked at her older sister through the open window. "Cop a squat in the back with your nephew, Windy City and relax."

She started to protest but Butterfly said, "You drove us down to Ohio and back. The least I can do is make the drive to the airport."

Morgan acted as valet holding the side panel door open while Albany climbed in letting his Auntie Chi fasten his seatbelt. He slid the door closed as Chicago was strapping herself in. Butterfly asked for them to check and make sure they had everything before pulling off. Everyone said they were ready. Butterfly shifted the vehicle into gear and drove off. Looking in the rearview mirror, she saw a gold van and a late model sedan pull out behind them. Butterfly turned off of Calumet traveling northbound on Third Street heading towards Forest Avenue so that she could crossover to the John C. Lodge Expressway. Checking the rearview mirror, she saw a marked police cruiser. Glancing down at the speedometer Butterfly realized that she was five miles over the legal limit, but before she could blink, the police's red and blue lights were oscillating, and their sirens were on. Morgan looked into his side mirror, "Aww come on! Are they pulling us over?" Instead of answering, Butterfly eased the van to the curb right in front of the Artist Stop Bar & Grill. It was an old Wayne State University haunt. "Let's just hope it's quick and you guys can make your flight," Chicago said.

The two police exited their vehicle. Wilson waited for his partner to position himself on the sidewalk near the passenger side of the van before rapping his knuckles on the driver's window. Butterfly pressed the button until the glass rolled down about five inches. "Can I help you, officer?"

The patrolman was all business. "You were going over thirty miles in a twenty-five mile an hour zone. Roll your window down all the way."

Butterfly didn't move. "I can hear you just fine."

"I'm going to need you to step out of the vehicle!" His tone was loud and too aggressive for a traffic violation.

"This is about a speeding ticket? I have my license, vehicle registration ..."

"Get out of the fucking van!" The officer unsnapped the catch on his holster, then looked to his left. She followed his gaze and saw the gold van up ahead. When she looked into the driver's side mirror, the dark sedan was idling behind her at the corner of Calumet. Something was definitely wrong.

Smiling sweetly, she turned to Morgan who was upset at the officer's disrespectful language and brusque manner.

Her husband told her, "Just cooperate for now. I promise he'll be dealt with." Butterfly fingered the automatic start, slapped the gearshift into drive, slammed her foot down on the accelerator, and zoomed off!

Several shots rang out. Chicago and Albany screamed as bullets punched into the Sprinter van's shell. "What in God's name are you doing?" Morgan yelled in panic as Butterfly blew carelessly through a red light on Forest, hooking a wide left turn heading for the freeway. "Butterfly! Stop! Stop this right now! What in the hell are you doing?

You have to stop!"

Albany was shocked into silence. He was half-covered, and half cradled in Chicago's arms. She was screaming to the top of her lungs, "Butterfly, pull over before you crash! Please just stop!" She looked down at her nephew taking his hand in hers and winced as he squeezed with all his fearful strength.

The van careened northbound onto the service drive on two wheels barely missing a Mustang GT. Butterfly took the ramp onto the expressway at 70 miles an hour and kept speeding up. Chicago and Morgan were hollering for her to stop and pull over.

"Shut the fuck up!" She yelled at them. "Something was wrong back there. That wasn't a traffic stop. Just be quiet and let me think!" Looking in the rearview mirror she could see her pursuers, the police cruiser that stopped her, the gold van, and the dark sedan still behind her. She took the exit ramp at West Grand Boulevard doing over 100 miles an hour. She slowed considerably, then turned east.

Morgan found his voice again. "Are you out of your damn mind?" He unbuckled his seatbelt and turned in his seat preparing to do only God knew what. "Butterfly, you need to stop this right now!" She ignored him taking a tight right turn, stomped hard on the brakes, slammed the gearshift into park, and jumped out before anyone in the van could fathom what was going on. She clutched her purse as she moved quickly across the sidewalk disappearing through the west entrance of the Cadillac Building.

Morgan, Albany, and Chicago scrambled out of the van, dazed by what just happened. They stood huddled together on the opposite sidewalk from the Cadillac Building that Butterfly disappeared into. All three of them looked dumbfounded and scared as police leaped from their cars with guns drawn looking for their mother, sister, and wife. Passersby's scurried away while others stood to gawk with phones out filming the action.

Chicago immediately recognized Detective Sargent Jimenez. She had her weapon out and was barking orders. A few patrol officers checked the van as Jimenez approached them, holstering her gun. "Which direction did she go?"

Morgan pointed to the doors of the Cadillac Building. She issued a flurry of commands into the radio she held then said, "Dr. Daniels, Mr. Baxter, I'm sorry for all the drama. Let's all pile into that gold van over there and go to my office where I'll explain what's going on to you guys. I'm sure the two of you have lots of questions."

Morgan and Albany both seemed to be in a mild state of shock. Chicago just seemed perplexed. All three walked robotically behind Jimenez as she led the way. Jimenez thought to herself, Butterfly Baxter is flying free instead of a prisoner in the detective's jar. She'll be caught soon enough, or will she? Summing up what had happened, Jimenez thought again, my suspect appears to have more layers than an onion and we don't know any of them. When they reached homicide, she called a uniform over to watch Albany. Then she took Morgan and Dr. Daniels to church.

Lieutenant Templeton and Gleason were waiting in the lieutenant's office staring at patrolmen Wilson and Feeps. After telling Templeton that she had Mrs. Baxter's sister and husband in the interrogation room, Officer Feeps quickly explained what happened in vague, sometimes convoluted sentences. Jimenez gave him a tightlipped smile before telling him, "You're a good cop to try and protect your partner. I'm sure everyone here can appreciate your sense of loyalty. That's why I am going to allow you to walk away. Go write up your report for Internal Affairs and make sure you tell the truth."

Feeps looked at her then at his soon to be ex-partner, Wilson. Lieutenant Templeton told him, "You're excused, officer. Finish your report then clock out. Make sure you report to this office at 7:00 a.m. sharp tomorrow morning. Jimenez glared heatedly at Wilson who was showing nothing of his earlier bravado, but spoke to his partner, "You can leave now." The steel laced in her voice sent Feeps scurrying out of the office without a backward glance. She turned her penetrating gaze on Wilson. "What in the hell possessed you to open fire on a family?" Nervously, the young officer said, "I thought the suspect was attempting to use the vehicle as a weapon."

Stunned, Jimenez shouted, "Don't you fucking give me that shit! Look at the optics! A blond, blue-eyed, Ken doll wannabe shooting into a van full of seven-figure prominent, African Americans is not something this department needs!" She lowered her voice a few octaves before asking, "Are you crazy or just a fucking idiot?"

Wilson jumped to his feet. "Lieu, she's out of line talking down to me like this!" Jimenez got right in his face. She was so close she could see the open pores on his skin. "Sit down Officer Wilson or do you want to add insubordination to your growing list of dumb things cops do?"

She moved to within a hair of his face. "And don't you ever skip the chain of command. You will address me if there's a problem!"

The lieutenant saw the fire in her eyes brimming over and interceded. "Back off Sargent!" She didn't move until Wilson backed away and sat down; then she retreated slowly to a spot next to the door. Templeton lowered his voice establishing a more professional tone. "Officer Wilson, you know the drill. You'll be off until I.A. wraps up their investigation. Contact your Union Rep and pray that the passengers in that van aren't feeling litigious." He waved him out. "That'll be all."

Wilson walked past Jimenez and mumbled something under his breath.
"What was that, asshole?" Jimenez was ready to fight. Templeton yelled, "That's enough Sargent! Get outta my office, Wilson!"

Gleason who had been silent during the entire exchange went over and closed the door shutting out the questioning eyes of the squad room. He stood with his back against it as Jimenez paced violently back and forth cursing to herself. "Rein it in partner. You and I have an interrogation to do and you can't step into church with that anger of yours."

She turned on him with her brown eyes blazing. "That arrogant asshole screwed up a textbook takedown trying to be a cowboy!"

Templeton motioned for them to have a seat. "Where are we with finding Mrs. Baxter?"

Gleason spoke first. "It seems she walked through the west side doors and out of the east doors of the Cadillac Building. We're talking about a building that houses the Secretary of State, charter schools, and countless businesses. We sealed off the building but obviously, she wasn't in it. A witness saw her getting into a convertible, probably a Corvette with an Arabic looking guy. To be on the safe side, I left four units at the building, but the witness's description was dead on. Butterfly Baxter is in the wind."

Jimenez put in, "I have a team checking surveillance cameras on every business for a quarter square mile. If there's nothing viable by the evening news cycle tomorrow, I want to splash her photograph everywhere making it impossible for her to hide." The lieutenant leaned back in his chair eyeing his detectives discernibly. "This arrest was supposed to close a couple of major cases, not open up Pandora's Box with a fugitive on the run. Do I need to tell you two that I'm not liking this one damn bit?!" He paused contemplatively. "Let's bring an end to this as soon as possible. Before spreading Baxter's face all over the news, contact the U.S. Marshal's service and the Georgia Bureau of Investigations. Let the latter know what the deal is. Send them everything we have and see if GBI can get search warrants for the Baxter home. Tell the former that we have a runner. That'll be all people." Gleason was out the door when Templeton called Jimenez back for a parting word. "You're an exceptional investigator, but you need to reign in your temper. Any other superior would take you to task for it. Be careful Jasenya and remember; 'On what slender threads do life and fortune hang?' Do you know the difference between cops and criminals?"

She hung her head answering in almost a whisper, "One bad decision."

"It's good that you know because most people don't. Now go find our fugitive and bring her back." Jimenez pulled the lieutenant's door shut behind her without another word. She walked by Gleason as if he were invisible, but then she stopped and said, "We're late for church. Let's go see what we can get out of the sister and husband."

Big Shirley didn't raise a fool. As she watched television in Chicago's apartment, Butterfly checked the surveillance feds periodically out of boredom. The street was teeming with people. It was a beautiful summer day and the area had quite a few restaurants and retail shops. So, a lot of foot traffic on the street wasn't out of the norm. She loved watching, especially when no one had any idea she was watching. It was while she observed the people walking on the street that she noticed a gold-colored van along with a Dodge Charger sedan with people parked in both of them. It seemed suspicious on a hot summer's day. Maybe they were waiting for someone? Maybe not. Her better sense told her to keep watching and also to be the one to drive out to the airport. Thank goodness that she did. As soon as she pulled out, so did the van and sedan. Then that bullshit traffic stops with the cocky young officer acting as though she had a dismembered body in the back of the van instead of her family.

Butterfly loved German engineering. Just thinking about the high-speed chase made her giddy until she thought about poor Albany. Morgan and Windy City must be a mess. She had never known her big sister to handle pressure all that well. Butterfly didn't have any idea what the police wanted. Considering her crimes went back to her college years, it could be just about anything. And although Butterfly couldn't be sure what they wanted her for, knowing they wanted her was enough.

When she leaped from the Sprinter van her brain synapses were firing rapidly. It was like an interactive chess game where pieces had to be sacrificed in order for the queen to survive. Through one door and out of the next. She felt like Robert DeNiro in the action movie "Heat." You had to be able to leave everything behind in 30 seconds or less because the heat or police would be becoming. That's exactly what she had done. Soon as Butterfly stepped off the curb, she came bumper to hip with a handsome middle eastern man in an electric blue late-model Corvette. Kismet? He smiled and blew at her. She quickly admonished him for tooting his own horn while slipping into the soft leather seat beside him. Butterfly smiled seductively, "I need a good, hard ride. Can you help me?"

"My name is Saif, and I will let you ride me or with me until you can't walk."

She thrust her breasts forward. "I'm Octavia Winters from Laurel, Virginia. Pleased to meet you Saif." He turned left on West Grand Boulevard. Butterfly pulled her Coco Chanel shades from her Chanel bag and slipped them on as they passed the throng of police and spectators. "I wonder what has happened," Saif said. "There's no telling sweetheart. This is, after all, Detroit."

Her hand fell on his thigh giving it a gentle squeeze. Ignoring the sight of Albany being helped into the gold van by that Latino bitch detective, Butterfly leaned into Saif and said, "I see you like fast cars? I warn you; I like mine big and powerful." Laughing, he replied, "A good driver knows when to slow it down for his passenger allowing them to enjoy the ride regardless of the vehicle. But worry not Octavia, you have come upon a man who has something big and very powerful for you to ride." "I do hope we aren't talking about cars anymore." Saif gunned the engine making her swoon. Butterfly just loved adventurous men. Where would she be without the fools?

Jimenez sat across from Morgan Baxter and his sister-in-law, Dr. Daniels, in Interrogation Room Two. Albany was sitting at Detective Hodgkins' desk playing a videogame on her personal laptop. "I'm terribly sorry for having you both here for so long without an explanation, but I was hoping to apprehend your wife." She turned to Chicago, "And your sister, so that you could hear the truth from her."

Morgan folded his arms defiantly across his broad chest. "The truth about what?" Dr. Daniels must have thought it a worthy question because she leaned forward a bit awaiting the detective's answer. Jimenez rested her forearms on the table while clasping her hands together as if in prayer. She almost turned around to see if she could see Gleason, knowing she would only glimpse her reflection in the two-way mirror. Telling a family member or friend that the person they trust, or love has killed someone or is suspected of trying to kill them is always difficult. It was the hardest part of the job.

"Exactly what is my sister accused of having done?"

Jimenez ran a hand through her curly locks and cut straight to the chase. "We believe she's murdered, two men. One of them being your late husband."

Morgan erupted, "The hell you say! My wife is no murderer!" Jimenez looked at him empathetically. Her silence took the wind out of his sails. "Please Mr. Baxter, there's something that you and Dr. Daniels both need to see."

"You can't show me anything. The police are not above manufacturing evidence. Look at Desmond Ricks!" The detective couldn't argue with him about that. There were several cases of police fabricating evidence, most notably Desmond Ricks who spent 25 years in prison because the police handling his case swapped out the ballistic reports to frame him for the murder of his best friend.

Chicago placed a calming hand on his shoulder. "Let's hear what she has to say."

"It's not so much as what I have to say, as to what I have to show you." With a click of the remote, the television in the corner sprang to life.

Butterfly was sprawled naked across a bed at the MGM Grand Hotel Casino in downtown Detroit where Saif was already a guest with a deluxe suite. The man was handsome if you like the whole olive skin, hawk nose, chiseled eight pack thing. There was one small drawback though. He was only an inch taller than 'Octavia.' Any man that she could look at eye to eye was a problem, but he was a generous man of means, so it evened out. After a few hours inside of Somerset Collection in Troy, where he purchased a few much-needed items for a girl like her on the go, they ate a delicious late lunch at Morton's Steakhouse. After that, she gave him an evening blow job with the top down.

At her urging, she and Saif visited two other Detroit area casinos. While at Greektown and Motor City, she was able to get several cash advances on her credit cards totaling $35,000,00. Before leaving Motor City, she made her transition from Butterfly to Octavia completely by slipping her legitimate credit cards and identification into a woman's bag who was her approximate age, weight, and height. The woman had the demeanor of a born loser. With any luck, she would be tempted to commit a little identity theft. It wouldn't be long before the police would start tracking her credit cards. If the born loser did what she hoped that she would, the police would be thrown way off her scent. But, for the present, her focus was on her sugar daddy. How sweet he would turn out to be, depending on how well she played her part.

Saif was originally from the Detroit area, but lived in the Chicago suburb of Riverside, currently. He was married with three children. A girl and two boys. He was arrogant, intelligent, and funny with a biting sarcastic wit. He was also sexually insatiable, which suited her at the moment. The sex helped to relieve her of the stress she had been feeling. Saif was supposed to return home that very night on Southwest Airlines, but Octavia convinced him to drive with her to Chicago instead. It was only a four-hour trip and that way they could spend another night together.

"Octavia, maybe you could teach my wife to be a cowgirl. I would never again stray from her bed if she was as skilled as you in the art of fornication."

Smiling with her tongue lolling lazily around her full lips while stretching languidly like a contented cat, she pulled her ankles to her ears and held them there. "Talking about your wife's lack of sexual skills is far from a turn on. If you want to show me your true gratitude sweet prince, do it orally, but silently."

He let the towel fall from his waist, "Not another syllable, I promise." Octavia looked down as his mouth made contact with her flesh and thought how powerfully arousing the top of a man's head could be if seen in the right position.

When they were both satisfied, Octavia and Saif showered together then got dressed. She wore a pair of robin's egg blue Gucci capri pants, a man's red silk button-up shirt with collar and cuffs matching her pants. The red Tom Ford espadrilles completed her wardrobe ensemble. Octavia's black curly hair hung far below her shoulders. After tossing her locks in the mirror and arranging them to shield most of her face, she tried on her shades. The new look would have to do. Sugar daddy Saif spent a small fortune on several new outfits, shoes, and a Louis Vuitton hard shell duffle to carry it all in. How endearingly sweet of him. She snapped the band of her platinum Cartier wristwatch in place then put her wedding ring back on her right hand where it had been since getting into the car with Saif. Her black Chanel bag with its false bottom sat on the bathroom vanity. Listening cautiously for her little sheik, she secured the bathroom door then unscrewed the four studs on the bottom of the expensive purse exposing a hidden compartment. Inside was a birth certificate, social security card, license, credit cards, and passport in the name of Octavia Winters. She removed them along with $10,000.00. The rest of her money and two small prescription pill bottles were left hidden as she replaced the studs.

When she was done dividing the money between her ample cleavage, panties, and the inside of her purse, Octavia unlocked the door stepping from the bathroom presenting herself for Saif's viewing pleasure. He hung up his cellphone and opened his arms wide. Instead of accepting his embrace, she turned her back showing him her perfectly sculpted ass. "Be a dear sweet prince and take care of the bags. It's time for us to be going. The last one to the lobby doesn't get any sex." Saif scrambled hurriedly to catch up to her.

By the time he gathered their things reaching the hallway, Octavia was swinging her hourglass hips like a pendulum almost at the elevator. "Hurry, hurry! You don't want to be last to the lobby." She was so alluring at that moment that he contemplated leaving his wife and kids for her.

Jimenez studied the husband and sister as they watched the video. Both seemed genuinely shocked especially the part about Mrs. Baxter's son being fathered by the deceased Dr. Brooks. Once they made it through the quagmire of emotional turmoil, Jimenez started interrogating them. The detective came across as trustworthy, empathetic, and a good listener. She answered a few of their questions to gain their confidence while deftly dodging others under the guise of it being an active investigation.

Morgan leaned into the corner by the door. Utter defeat and betrayal seemed to drape his entire person. At that moment he resembled a frightened child and not the confident man of wealth that he actually was. The tears shimmering in his eye sockets were held there by the force of sheer willpower. Morgan refused to cry. Finding out the woman you love is an adulterer, murderer, and all-around diabolical deceiver is not only embarrassing but a shock of epic proportions. To cry in front of these women because of it would be the ultimate in emasculation, adding further insult to an already grievous injury.

Chicago sat with one hand covering her mouth and the other clenched into a tight fist buried in her lap. She didn't hold her tears back like her brother-in-law. No. Chicago's tears flowed openly like the Mississippi River. "We have no direct evidence that your sister orchestrated your attempted murder that led to your abduction by Sanford Smalls. We don't have anything concrete that says she and your late husband had someone kill Smalls either. Though it's likely they did once their plan fell apart." Chicago blanched at the mention of her tormentor's name. "What we have is an abundance of circumstantial evidence."

Chicago's hand moved from her mouth to her breast. "I don't believe it! Who is this person in that horrible video? Why aren't you questioning him? How do you know he is, in fact, telling the truth? Surely if he will murder, this man will lie!"

Jimenez went over to Morgan and led him back to his seat. "This is why it's so important for us to speak to your sister. Surely, a woman of your intelligence can see the urgency in resolving this matter as soon as possible. My superiors are inclined to believe the man in the video, especially when your sister has fled."

Morgan huffed, "I don't believe any of it. My wife probably ran because she was scared. After all, it's not every day that a police officer opens fire on a van full of unarmed people. With her condition, there's no telling what she was thinking."

The detective sat up straighter. "What condition is that?" No one answered as the silence grew thick. Chicago glanced at her brother-in-law then said, "My sister is bipolar with a mild personality disorder, but as long as she's taking her medication properly there isn't a problem."

"Has there ever been a problem, Dr. Daniels?" Chicago looked at Morgan then answered, "Not to my knowledge there hasn't."

Jimenez doubted that was true but decided to let it go for the present. "There is one thing we can prove beyond a shadow of any doubt."

Chicago and Morgan asked almost simultaneously, "What's that?"
"I have a sample of your husband's DNA from evidence storage in his murder case. All we need is for you to pave the way with your nephew and we can clear up paternity." Stepfather and aunt both exploded with objections. The detective remained silent until their voices died down.

"We don't want to traumatize the boy but know that my asking is a courtesy and not a request. I already have a warrant for the collection of his DNA by buccal swab." She watched as they exchanged consent between each other almost telepathically. "A few swipes with a Q-tip on the inside of his cheeks and we're good. The lab is on standby, so the results will be almost immediate. I'm sure that both of you would like to know the truth."

Morgan leaned into Chicago's ear whispering something then turned to Jimenez. "We've had a long day. Take your samples from Albany so that we can go."

Detective Sargent Jimenez hated to further spoil their day but, "I'm sorry. I know it's been a long day so far but it's going to get longer. I need to interview you separately and I'd like to speak with Albany."

Morgan spoke up sounding more like himself before the morning's ordeal. "No, you may not speak with my stepson. However, Dr. Daniels and I will be available to speak with you tomorrow. Like you've said, it has been a long day. After you retrieve my stepson's DNA, we'll be leaving." Jimenez started to object, "No one's going …"

"Detective, you obviously have me confused with the poor, ignorant, illiterate masses who troop through this room. I'm worth over fifteen million dollars liquid and twice that in assets. Would you like to see what kind of lawyers my type of money can buy, or should we ask the news media to get involved and inquire why a multimillionaire real estate developer and his family were shot at by a Detroit police officer? Would you rather remain in our good graces or involve attorneys and the media?"

Jimenez knew when to forge ahead. More importantly, she knew when to back off. "All right. Let's go see Albany."

Navy Pier, Sears Tower, da Bulls, da Cubs, Grant Park with its annual Taste Festival, and deep-dish pizza; it was all Chicago baby! Octavia thought back to a time when she was a caterpillar inside of Butterfly. Back when she taught Butterfly to hate Chicago with childish passion her sister, not the city. All she ever heard was, "Listen to Chicago; and follow Chicago's example." Fucking give me a break! Octavia thought. A therapist she saw after Big Shirley died suggested that her jealousy towards her big sister caused her to have an unhealthy case of sibling rivalry. The therapist also surmised that Butterfly's feelings towards her sister bordered on pure undeserved hatred. Musing to herself again she thought, Good thing that bitch is a therapist and not Border Patrol, because I crossed over into the land of hatred a long time ago. Back when I was a sweet sixteen.

Octavia remembered everything as though it just happened. But she had to refresh Butterfly's mind from time to time otherwise she would go soft on Chicago. Again, the woman not the city.

It was late September when Chicago showed up unexpectedly in the early afternoon. Butterfly had forgotten that Big Shirley and her weren't the only ones with keys to their house. Chicago had a set, though up until that day she couldn't recall her older sister ever using them, unannounced. Of all the days to use them, she chose the day when Butterfly was with handsome David Howard. Tall, strong, compassionate David Howard. With eight sisters and one brother, he knew a lot about girls. David had black wavy hair, a smooth butternut complexion with a brilliant smile as bright as Arctic snow. He looked like a model. Octavia grew moist just thinking of him.

Chicago crept into the house and found them making love all tangled together like spaghetti with nothing to see but ass, elbows, hands, and knees. David, at 18, was so sweet. But that meddling bitch, Chicago, treated him like a criminal threatening to call the police. It was Butterfly's idea to skip school and do it. For three months she begged him to come over and pop her cherry. He finally agreed and after the initial pain and discomfort, Butterfly fell into sex like a fish to water. They'd been at it for several hours before big sis ran him out of the house half-naked. Then she proceeded to harangue Butterfly about the ills of unprotected sex, teenage pregnancy, and sexually transmitted diseases. It was her and David's first time. They were virgins. Handsome David Howard was her first love.

Big Shirley got on her case, too. When she asked her mother, what gave her sister the right to come in their house and throw her boyfriend out, her mother responded calmly, "Here you are Caterpillar on your first box of tampons with your first man thinking you're a woman. What job do you have? What bills do you pay in this house? Chicago has every right to keep you on the straight and narrow. It's you who don't have any rights. You forfeited them when you allowed more than air up your skirt." Big Shirley grounded her for three months and to add insult to injury, Chicago went over on Indiana Avenue to the Howard home and spoke with David's mother, Mrs. Lucy Howard. She forbade him from having any contact with Butterfly.

They still tried to make it work, but it wasn't the same. Less than two years later, right before she was to attend college, David fell prey to leukemia and in an instant was gone. Her dreams of getting married and having a family bigger than the Howard clan were destroyed and it was all Chicago's fault! Octavia made sure Butterfly knew who to blame, and over the years she fanned the flames of hatred with a little action here or there. As the years went by, the hatred burning in Butterfly's heart dimmed to glowing embers. Then, Dorian Brooks came into their lives. At first, Octavia convinced Butterfly that it was just a little revenge, pure and simple. Fuck her sister's husband and make him fall in love with them. Then one day the unexpected happened. They fell for him. He was cool and amoral. It wasn't loved as much as it was an addiction to living life on the edge. Dorian was up for anything Octavia could think of and she dragged Butterfly along for the ride.

Pretty soon the tables were turned, and Dorian was manipulating them into submission. He kept raising the adventure bar until they couldn't surpass it without him. Then came the baby. Octavia suggested an abortion, but Butterfly freaked out. She threatened to tell Chicago everything. Dorian and Octavia relented letting her keep the bastard.

For years, everything was fine. Morgan came into their lives and their relationship with Dorian was over. Then Octavia threatened to tell Morgan all about their sordid affair if she couldn't start up with Dorian again. But the sex just wasn't enough that time around. You could only do a ménage à trois or an orgy so many times before it became boring. It was time to up the ante and play for higher stakes. What's greater than life or death stakes? Not a damn thing.

Octavia disguised herself as Butterfly and forced Dorian's hand. He was apprehensive about killing his wife, but who wouldn't be? Get rid of her and they would divorce Morgan. It had to look normal and what was more normal in Detroit than a carjacking turned deadly? Dorian claimed to know the perfect guy to do the deed. Some loser named Sanford Tolliver Smalls whom he saw as a patient when he was working part-time for Macomb County Circuit Court as a therapist. There could be no loose ends, especially with a third party. Octavia volunteered to get rid of Mr. Smalls when he successfully carjacked Chicago. Then she would dominate Butterfly and reveal herself to Dorian. After a few years of laying low, they would reinvent themselves. She might even keep Albany and maybe even grow their family. It would just depend on how things turned out. Obviously, they didn't turn out too well. Octavia thought she should've handled everything herself. Leave it to a man to mess up.

Shit would've gone according to plan if that nut job Sanford Smalls knew the difference between a carjacking and a kidnapping. Dorian believed that the authorities would go through his life with a fine-tooth comb once Chicago was murdered; so, he allowed Butterfly to be the conduit between him and Smalls. What he didn't know was that Octavia was running the show. After giving her careful instructions Octavia and Smalls arranged to meet. She never liked him and spent hours fantasizing about how to kill him. When he screwed up the simple task of eliminating his target, he put a bullseye on his own back.

When Smalls neglected his task of murdering Chicago, Butterfly got cold feet. She knew that the man was a sexual predator and was probably torturing her flesh and blood. Octavia grew tired of Butterfly's whining, but in a way she was right. How hard was it to just shoot someone and steal their car, making them another inner-city fatality? Instead, Sanford allowed his penis to override his professionalism.

And even though Octavia admired Chicago's intelligence, tenacity, and remarkable will to live, and regardless of Butterfly's whining, Octavia had made up her mind to kill Chicago anyway. She just couldn't get into that damn room! Shooting blindly through walls isn't a good way of insuring someone's death. If all had gone well, after a brief though necessary intermission Octavia and Dorian would have been together in their new life. Neither could have known that the fickle bitch 'Fate' would slip her cruel hand into the mix and pull Chicago back from the brink of death.

Ironically, the same scenario the two adulterers devised to kill Chicago is exactly how Dorian was murdered. Octavia thought Butterfly made the right decision by moving on in her marriage to Morgan. Dorian had grown timid, shying away from making another attempt at taking his wife's life. He had become a scared little boy. Octavia knew that Butterfly didn't even miss him and since his death, she no longer felt that immense hatred towards Chicago. Dorian's demise seemed to have squashed the grudge she held for all these years.

Still, Octavia realized that there was another problem looming. She found that it was becoming harder to control Butterfly. Octavia thought to herself, were it not for the police looking for them, Butterfly would be down in Georgia at her country club estate baking cookies and attending PTA meetings. Now that the heat is on, the bitch shows her true cowardice leaving her to take care of business because she doesn't have the stomach for the rough stuff. What a cunt! The police just want to arrest them for their recent criminal misadventures. Since college, they've been towing a fine line between normalized citizenry and outlaw. Hell, things have a way of working themselves out given a little time and a different locale.

Octavia was doing the thinking now; so, going forward things should be a lot smoother unless someone does something disrespectful, if that happens, Octavia thought, all bets are off. For instance, Mr. Saif Mahmoud would be dead if he were anything other than a super respectful sugar daddy. Sometimes Octavia's sexual habits mirrored those of the female praying mantis. If Butterfly were running the show she would've fucked and sucked Saif dry, then clung to him like cat hair on cashmere. Octavia would have done the former then like the female praying mantis, did away with him.

Butterfly broke through and convinced Octavia to spare the sweet prince. So, she crushed a few of her sleeping pills into his champagne and left him in dreamland at the Marriott on Michigan Avenue minus his cash and Royal Oak Audemars Piguet watch. Smiling to herself she thought, plenty of pawnbrokers in Chi-town will ignore the watch's providence for 60 percent off the retail ticket. That's why Octavia was standing on the corner of 79th and Halstead Streets where Google determined there were no less than three pawnshops within walking distance. The cheap smartphone she bought outside of Kalamazoo was not as sleek or gifted as her former phone, but it served its purpose.

The first pawnshop on her list was almost directly across the street to her left. Almost every vehicle with a male occupant and even a couple with only women in them slowed down to stare at Octavia as she stood waiting on the traffic light to change. She wore a dress that left very little to the imagination and a pair of heels that any woman would kill for. Just as the light changed to green a young man pulled up to the crosswalk on a crotch rocket motorcycle. Lifting the visor of his helmet he asked if she needed a ride. "Much too, dangerous!" she yelled over the rumbling of his engine. "Motorcycles are just as safe as cars!" He told her. She had crossed to the other side of the street and the light had changed back, but the motorcyclist was still trying to convince her to ride. "No, silly! The bike isn't too dangerous for me. I'm too dangerous for you." Still, he watched her walking away opposite the direction he was traveling amid blaring horns and profanity urging him to stop blocking traffic. He checked out her butt one last time thinking to himself, She's probably way too dangerous for me.

The day after Mrs. Baxter fled and eluded the long arm of the law, Jimenez sat at her desk talking to Terry O'Sullivan of the U.S. Marshal Service's fugitive recovery team. "The car is a rental. A surveillance camera on a Kinko's yielded a plate number along with a nice profile shot of Butterfly Baxter." She flipped attentively through the notes on her desk. "Ahh, here it is. Saif Mahmoud, formerly of Dearborn, now a resident of Riverside, Illinois. He rented the vehicle after flying into Metro from Chicago's Midway Airport. Our Mr. Mahmoud was supposed to return the car before his flight back home but decided to keep it another day."

O'Sullivan was a veteran with the Marshal service. After he served three tours of duty with the Marines in the Middle East fighting in places most people found hard to pronounce, he joined one of America's oldest law enforcement agencies. A big man by any standard at 6'2 tall and 250 pounds, the frosty grey-eyed, red head's presence screamed semper fi. "How do we get in contact with this Ma-mood character? Was its happenstance that brought them together or did they have a prior relationship? Is he harboring her, or did he unwittingly aid in her escape?"

"I don't think he knew her before she got into his car." Jimenez glanced at the time on her cellphone. "Two hours ago, I spoke to his wife, Kheila Mahmoud, pretending to be a business associate of his and obtained his cell number. He answered after the fifth try." She explained the conversation to O'Sullivan. "At first speaking with Saif Mahmoud was like taking a molly trip on a merry-go-round. Once I explained that he wasn't the subject of my investigation but could be and that acting an asshole would only get him screwed, he began to cooperate. I asked what happened to the woman he picked up in Detroit? That question led to a rapid stream of what I believed was Farsi, interspersed with a lot of profanity." After he calmed down, Saif Mahmoud told me everything.

"Let me guess? As long as you kept his wife out of it. Right?"

The detective shook her head. "Fuck no! He could care less about me telling his wife anything. He only cared about his watch." Jimenez could see the mounting curiosity in O'Sullivan's face. Butterfly Baxter stole a $122,000.00 limited edition Audemars timepiece. Evidently, a woman matching Baxter's description got into his Corvette looking for a ride to anywhere. One thing led to another and I quote, "She rode me better and longer than a Bedouin rides a camel across the desert. Long, hard and rough. End quote." For another night with her, he swears he would've given her the damn watch. He said she's using the name Octavia, which is her actual middle name. He doesn't recall her giving any last name, but says she has plenty of cash."

Jimenez told O'Sullivan that she thought Mahmoud could've probably been a little more helpful, but he was obviously infatuated with Butterfly Baxter even after she stole from him. Whatever she does, she does it very well.

Jimenez answered a few pointed questions that O'Sullivan asked, then continued. She'd had Hodgkins run Baxter's financials and found out that she made several large cash advances against her credit cards. There were other strange charges across the metro Detroit area, some of which came within minutes of the others but were miles away at different stores. Hodgkins figured the credit cards were circulating like that because Baxter had ditched them. "If she can sell the watch for a third of its value, she'll have close to a hundred grand. That'll give her plenty of traveling money."

"What was her last known location?" O'Sullivan asked. In a matter-of-fact tone, Jimenez said, "Mahmoud last saw Butterfly Baxter literally on top of him in his suite at the Chicago Marriott."

The marshal thought for a minute before saying, "This lady seems pretty calculated. From everything you've told me about her I don't think she makes wasted moves. Why not head for the two fugitive favorites, Canada or Mexico? And if you think a big city can lose you, why not New York or L.A.?"

Jimenez had already contemplated those things. "If you would've given the file more than a cursory look you might have noticed that our fugitive graduated from Northwestern University. She has ties to the Chicago area. All we need to do is find one and it will lead us right to her."

"So, a friend, lover, or an old college bud in the city? Cool beans! My team and I will get right on it."

She knew that the marshals had way more resources than DPD and appreciated any help she could get, but this was one case Jimenez wasn't ready to relinquish just yet. "The husband gave us access to their landline phone bills and her cell, which is on a friends-and-family plan that he pays for. My partner, Gleason is running a reverse trace on the phone numbers. We found her cellphone inside of a garbage receptacle in the Cadillac building. Just like a pro, she tossed it immediately as she made her escape."

O'Sullivan rubbed his head before responding. "Are we sure this chick is just a Georgia soccer mom who tried to kill off her competition? She seems to have some skills. Anyway, I don't want to put boots on the ground in Chicago unless we have a solid lead. The current administration has us tightening our belts till it hurts." He stood up stretching his huge frame signaling their meeting was over.

"I'm going to take another run at the sister and husband later today. I'll call you."

"All right J. Dick. Keep me informed." She looked at him in disbelief.

"You throbbing red hemorrhoid! Didn't I tell you not to call me that?"

He threw up his hands in mock surrender. "Don't kill me, I'm just kidding around. Why are you so mad? J. Dick is short for Jimenez-detective."

She flipped him her middle finger. "It's short for go fuck yourself." He left laughing.

Gleason, with Jimenez riding shotgun, pulled up to Dr. Daniels' apartment building. They saw Morgan Baxter climbing into Chicago's S65 Mercedes Benz sports coup. He recognized the detectives and stepped out leaning against the car. "How are you doing, Mr. Baxter? Sorry to trouble you." Gleason said. "Mind if we talk?"

He looked suspiciously at him, and Jimenez who waved a hand in greeting. "I was just going for ice cream and pizza."

"Do you mind if I join you?" Gleason asked. Morgan eyed the car then Jimenez, who said, "If you guys are going, then I'll just go see your sister-in-law." The two men slid into the expensive car and drove away.

Jimenez was thankful that she would have some alone time with Dr. Daniels. With them gone maybe, she'd be able to coax some useful information out of her concerning her sister. By the time she reached the top floor, the detective had a little burn in her quadriceps. She made a mental note to get back to the gym. The good doctor was at the door in sweats, ankle socks, and a Detroit Lions' football jersey waiting for Jimenez. Her long dark hair was pulled into a single French braid. Chicago could see the questions in the other woman's eyes just as Jimenez could see the pain in hers. "Hello, Dr. Daniels. I'll try not to take up too much of your time." Jimenez hiked a thumb over her shoulder. "My partner is with your brother-in-law."

Chicago stepped aside fully opening the door. "Please come in, Sargent Jimenez."

Every time she came to the doctor's apartment, she marveled at its opulence. To be located in midtown and not Los Angeles or Manhattan made it, even more, a thing of beauty. It was like finding a rose among daisies. Chicago saw the look of awe on her face. "Haven't you been here before?"

"Yes. When you were abducted, I came here after the initial search of the premises. Your late husband felt so violated by the experience that this is as far as I have ever made it."

Chicago closed then carefully locked the door. "Then let me give you the ten-cent tour."

Jimenez stood in the entryway and did a complete 360° circuit letting her eyes soak it all in. "If you don't mind my asking, what's the rent like?"

Chicago gave her a self-deprecating smile." I own the building, so for me, it's rather cheap. As for the rest of the units, it depends." Jimenez was stunned. "My husband thought we should buy a house. I, on the other hand, wanted to live in an apartment, but paying rent for an indeterminate amount of time would've been a bad investment. So, I bought the building then told him about it."

"The building is pre-World War II with mostly all original fixtures and no elevator. It took three years to remodel the lower 32 units, eight units on each of the four floors beneath them. And it took an additional two years to convert the entire fifth floor to a single apartment. The patio rooftop took another year. The first two floors were all original in keeping with the time when it was built. Of course, the kitchen, plumbing, and electrical had all been upgraded. There are open floor plans on the third and fourth floors; with bigger bedrooms and their own en suites. The bottom two floors run about $1,800.00 monthly and the others are $2,600.00 a month."

The detective did some quick calculations and figured the doc was making over $400,000.00 a year in rent alone.

"Do you own any other properties?" Jimenez ventured. In a toneless voice, Chicago answered, "A few here and there."

"This seems like a pretty nice investment," the sergeant remarked.
In that same toneless voice, Chicago said, "I won't be standing in the soup line anytime soon. Come on, follow me, and get your dime's worth." Jimenez knew that the doc was like that famous sculpture by Rodin, Self-Made.

After she was kidnapped, she sold her share of her practice to her partner, Frieda Goldberg. How can you fix others when you're broken yourself? Hodgkins ran the numbers, Dr. Daniels is rich. She had a burgeoning stock portfolio, earning three times the money her husband did and that was after taxes. The insurance payout for her husband's death netted a million and a half due to a double indemnity clause so, she was flush with cash.

They walked through the open area viewing the kitchen, dining, and living areas. Beyond those areas was a set of double doors that opened into a long hallway. The hallway walls held precious artwork as well as black and white photographs of her and her late husband in happier times. To the left was an office bigger than the detective's living room and two guest bedrooms next to that. On the right was a sauna, gym, and jacuzzi room that Jimenez would barter her soul for. Next to that was a second master suite. Albany, Dr. Daniels' nephew barely looked up from his videogame when she opened the bedroom door. "Is the pizza here yet?" Chicago smiled at him.

"Not yet," and pulled the door shut. At the end of the hallway was another set of double doors. When Chicago opened those doors, Jimenez almost fainted. Talk about heaven! The glass-enclosed bathroom with it's his and hers theme was awesome. There was a beautiful glazed subway tile on the floor and at certain places on the walls. Jimenez jokingly asked if she could take a bath.

"Come, let me show you the roof." In the far-left corner of the master was a decorative wrought iron spiral staircase.

"This is one of three entrances, four if you count the fire escape." Jimenez's brow furrowed in thought. "Right now, you're probably asking yourself where, because you didn't see them. Well, there's one in the pantry and one in the in suite of the second master. The fire inspector insisted on it because the place is so big you could burn before you made it out. But if you count, there are no less than 12 fire extinguishers throughout.

The detective's mind wandered a bit. She was thinking that those minor details could've wreaked havoc if they would have made a tactical entry to arrest her sister. Instead of mentioning it, she said, "Dr. Daniels you have a beautiful home."

The spiral staircase ended at a raised steel, cellar type door. Next, to the door, Chicago punched a numerical code into a keypad and waited. There was a click then a LED display showed the word OPEN and the steel cellar-styled door parted in the middle. From where they were on the stairs all they could see was the blue sky.

"Come on, let me show you where I go to relax." There were bright flowers arrayed in decorative wooden beds and others in colorful designer clay pots. The back half of the roof was covered in lush artificial grass while the front half was a recreational area. There was a fire pit and even a large waterproof flat-screen television that raised up out of a half wall separating the patio lounge area from the gaming area. There was a billiard table covered with a plastic tarp, a ping pong table, two sand-filled horseshoe pits with a shuffleboard grid painted in primary colors against a blacktop. Looking at the wrought iron patio furniture, Jimenez knew that it cost a fortune. She sat down facing a beautiful outdoor kitchenette, expecting Martha Stewart to start cooking at any moment.

"Can I get you a beverage, Sargent?" Chicago went over to a small but well-stocked refrigerator. "I have grape, orange, apple, and lemon tea."

"I'll take a grape, thanks." Chicago twisted off the tops wrapping napkins around the bottles then handed one to Jimenez before sitting down. After she sat down, candidly she asked, "What would you like to ask me?"

With the same frankness as Chicago, Jimenez rebutted, "What would you like to tell me?"

As if that was all the coaxing she needed, Chicago began. "You probably think I'm a fool. How does a woman not know that her sister and husband have a child together? Butterfly told me that Albany's father was a married man named Todd who didn't want to acknowledge his biracial son. I am not stupid, Detective, nor am I blind. Busy, self-absorbed, and inattentive, yes! Stupid or blind, never!" Jimenez didn't say a word. Sometimes there's value in silence. "I knew my husband had been increasingly dissatisfied with our marriage, even possibly to the point of unfaithfulness.

There was never any hard evidence, but intuitively I knew in my heart that he strayed. To be honest, I just didn't care. Though never in a million years did I think he was screwing my sister."

Jimenez thought Chicago was not at all the woman she at first imagined. "Dr. Daniels tell me about your sister. She has no criminal record but seems to have a true criminal nature. Forgive me for saying so, but your sister appears to be Bonnie and Clyde all rolled into one." Chicago took a small sip of her juice.

"My sister is a genius. I mean she literally has a genius-level IQ. Sadly, she also has some mental issues; and with her echelon of intelligence she doesn't believe the rules of a normalized society apply to her."

"What kind of issues does your sister really have?" Sighing, Chicago said, "I've told you already."

The sergeant replied, "No, you told me what your sister is diagnosed with having. Now share with me the truth."

Chicago leaned back in her chair and stared at the clear baby blue sky. "The truth is my sister is an immovable object. She's also an unstoppable force. Butterfly is her own ally and enemy, equally. She is anything and everything to anyone and everyone. You'll never find any record of her being seen by a doctor. Blame me for that. I used favors from colleagues to have her treated. That's all I can really tell you." The sergeant inquired, "Do you know if she's been treated for anything recently?"

Chicago slowly moved her head from side to side. "She's an adult. I'm no longer privy to her medical files. At one point in time, it would've been possible to peek into her life. My mother made me Butterfly's guardian in case something happened to her. With me being so much older than her and my mother always working it was just practical. In essence, I guess that I raised her. Didn't do a good job, did I?"

"You sound like you still love your sister a great deal, in spite of what she's accused of."

A single tear rolled down Chicago's cheek. She wiped it away with a casual flick of her finger. The women grew quiet for a brief time, each seemed to be having a moment of inner reflection. "Why does your sister hate you?"

Chicago looked the detective straight in the eyes and sounded a bit perturbed, "Hate is a strong word, detective."

"Okay then. Why does she dislike you enough to sleep with your husband, bear his child, and try to kill you?"

Chicago glared at Jimenez for a split second. "You don't pull any punches, do you?"

The detective gave a halfhearted shrug. "I can't afford to. I'm a homicide detective. That means that I fight for life and the loss of it as vigorously as the law will allow."

Chicago took a deep breath before speaking. "To answer your question, I don't know why. The only real blow up that I recall she and I ever had was a long time ago. I was a second-year resident at DMC when this huge woman who was diagnosed as being a paranoid schizophrenic attacked me and, in the process, ripped my shirt and brassiere. I had an extra shirt but no bra. At the time, Dorian and I were living in an apartment complex out in West Bloomfield. It was quicker to stop by my mother's and borrow a bra rather than drive all the way home from downtown Detroit."

"So, what happened?" Jimenez asked.

"I walked in on my 16-year-old little sister having unprotected sex with a young man. He was 18 and knew better than to be skipping school having sex with a minor. I spoke with the young man's parents and made it clear that if he attempted to see her again there would be consequences of the institutional variety. Our relationship was bad for a little while after that but grew worse when the young man died."

"How'd he die?"

"Cancer."

The sergeant contemplated her next move. "Let's set aside your sister's hat and put on your hat as Dr. Daniels, a behavioral psychologist. In your professional opinion, is that one situation reason enough to want you dead?"

Chicago took a healthy swallow of her grape juice giving the question considerable thought. Finally, she said, "Cain killed Abel because he felt slighted, so anything is possible."

"What about your husband? Besides the affair with your sister, what other reason would he have to want you dead?" Chicago leaned forward with her elbows resting on her knees. She was holding the grape juice bottle between thumb and forefinger swinging it slightly back and forth. Jimenez felt the silence stretching into awkwardness and was about to speak when Chicago said, "My husband was a brilliant man. Like all people of great intelligence, he had his flaws to balance him out. Pride, arrogance, selfishness, and the inability to recognize his own limits. On top of all that, Dorian could never reach his potential because he was envious of the other people's progress. He could have wanted me gone for my money, but I don't think so. If anything, he would want me gone for two reasons: Jealousy and control."

"Please explain." Jimenez urged.

"My husband grew jealous of my success as a doctor and a businesswoman. He couldn't control me the way he wanted to. Keep in mind this is in hindsight, but I believe I was a long-term project for my late husband. I think he sought to control me through mental manipulation.

When it became evident that I was not susceptible, I became a thing to be discarded and nothing more." She finished her juice, picked up Jimenez's empty bottle, and dropped them both in the trash. While the detective was mulling over what she just heard, Dr. Daniels' cellphone rang. She excused herself, spoke for a minute then started dialing a number then stopped.

"Morgan and your partner are back."

Jimenez pointed to the phone in her hand. "Do you need to make a call?" flipped through her thoughts quickly. She liked to think of it as mental gymnastics. "It's not uncommon for a busy woman to miss certain clues of infidelity from her spouse. I'm curious though about something else." They were at the bottom of the spiral staircase in the master suite.

"And what is that something detective?"

"How you went from denying that your sister and husband have a child to speaking with me and sounding sure of it?"

The detective watched as the doctor slipped into her walk-in closet returning with a flash drive and a bundle of letters tied together with a garter belt.

"I've forgiven my sister and husband for their indiscretion and deception. After you showed me that video, I didn't want to believe it, but little things were nagging me; so, I searched my apartment thoroughly and found these."

"What are those?" Jimenez asked.

"I read two of the letters before it became too much for me. The flash drive contains pictures and videos of a pornographic nature starring guess who? I couldn't tear my eyes away from it but trust me when I tell you that I haven't slept well since seeing it." Chicago handed the items to her and they felt heavy like some type of deadly weapon.

"When did you find these?"

"The day after being at your office. And please, don't say anything in front of Morgan. I haven't built up the nerve to tell him yet."

Inwardly, the detective was ecstatic with this find. She did, however, remain calm outwardly. "Thank you for bringing these items forth. I know this wasn't easy for you."

Chicago tilted her head while extending her arms out to her side with her palms facing up in a gesture that was meant to say, "What else could I do."

Jimenez tucked the flash drive and bundle of letters away in her jacket's inside pocket just as Albany ran into the room. "Auntie Chi! `scuse me, the pizza is here!" He waved at Jimenez and rushed back out before she could respond.

"Thank you, Dr. Daniels. I'm sure this will be a great help. Let me just ask you one more question. Does your sister have any friends?" Without precursor, Chicago said, "Butterfly has zero friends. She only has pawns that she moves for her own benefit or advancement, like any other queen."

The detective told Chicago they believed her sister was in of all places, Chicago, Illinois. The police knew that the Daniels family was from there originally, but they also knew they had no extended family there anymore. "Are you sure there's no one your sister could be holed up with? A distant relative, old boyfriend, college buddy? Anyone?"

Chicago seemed to give her questions some serious thought before she replied. "Butterfly was born in Detroit and has never met any of our extended family. However, there was an acquaintance from college. If I recall correctly, her name was Pamela. If you watch the videos on the flash drive, I think you'll see her."

Jimenez almost choked on her saliva. Finally, she asked, "Do you have any other information about this Pamela person? Last name, phone number, anything?"

"I think she's in finance, a venture capitalist or investment banker. Outside of that, I have nothing else for you. Now if you'll excuse me, I need to sit down with my nephew for some pizza. You're welcome to join us."

Detective Sargent Jimenez declined. She was chomping at the bit and couldn't wait to follow up on the leads she accumulated. No way did she have time to eat. Fuck, she could hardly breathe. "Thank you for your time and help. I have to get back to work."

Leading the way out of her bedroom Chicago thought, I'm sure you do. Once more, Jimenez turned in a complete circle soaking in the aesthetics of the room.

7 YESTERYEAR

Pamela Nothnagel has been married to her wife Sommar for almost three years. Sommar, pronounced 'summer' like the season was the partial cause of divorce from starter wife number one, Porsha. She was glad to have traded that bitch in for a newer more improved model. Her first wife turned out to be a monumental mess. Twenty years older than Pamela, the Northside debutant was more Rosie O'Donnell than Portia de Rossi, which was never a problem for Pamela. She saw where Porsha's true beauty lied her bank account and family connections. An opportunist of the worst kind, she couldn't care less what other people thought. It was the way of the world: Use or be misused.

Pamela, never Pammy or Pam, resembled the full-figured supermodel Ashley Graham. People she knew would see them out together and think her mother had flown in from Connecticut. Coming out of grad school she needed a stake if she was going to survive those first few lean years in investment banking. Porsha was her willing benefactor. Things were a little rough starting out, but Porsha provided a wonderful financial cushion while introducing her to the right people. Pretty soon her star rose, and Pamela's name became synonymous with financial growth. Porsha became jealous and controlling. That's when the starter wife was finished. There was only room for one alpha bitch in their marriage. Unfortunately, in her confusion, Porsha thought it was her.

Sommar held no illusions about her position in their marriage. At 26 years young, the new Mrs. Nothnagel accepted her role as a submissive trophy wife with relish. She quit her job as a regional manager for a national hotel chain because Pamela made it clear that she only has two jobs, enjoying life and seeing to Pamela's needs. So far, she was exceeding all expectations and excelling at both. However, Sommar's real test is if she can survive Butterfly's visit.

Pamela received a call. "I'll be at your place in a few hours. I need somewhere to rest for a day or two. My name is Octavia Winters. Be sure and keep up, we don't want to confuse wife number two." Pamela offered to put her up in one of the city's many hotels, but Butterfly just laughed and hung up. At that, Pamela thought to herself, she could be very obstinate and extremely vindictive if she doesn't get her way. "Sommar!" The young woman came to Pamela's open home office doorway. "Hey, babe! Wassup?" Sommar asked.

"My old college roommate is coming into town for a short stay. Please get one of the guestrooms ready." Turning around Sommar peered over her shoulder looking down at a perfect heart-shaped ass. "Do you like my jeans? I bought them at that boutique on Roosevelt." Pamela looked up at her wife from a portfolio that she was reading just as Sommar bent over at the waist. "Well, do you like it?"

"Honey put on a nice skirt or dress."

Pouting, Sommar said, "I thought you liked my butt."

Smiling at Sommar Pamela said, "I love your tight ass honey, but please just do as I ask, my friend will be here soon. Hurry, we don't want to appear as bad hosts."

After Sommar left, Pamela poured herself some scotch to wash the word 'friend' out of her mouth. Butterfly was no one's friend. She either controlled you or handled you. To refuse any request from her who was presently going by the name of Octavia Winters could cause trouble especially when she was adopting the persona of her alter ego. She liked to put screws in people and then turn them at her leisure. Since graduating college Pamela had seen her on average, maybe three times a year. Each time they saw one another Butterfly sank her claws in deeper than the year before. Pamela couldn't quite quantify her feelings for Butterfly. Love, hate, resentment? One thing she knew for sure was that she was going to give the evil bitch whatever she wanted and be rid of her as soon as possible.

Octavia loved the Gold Coast, Lakeshore Drive, Chicago's magnificent mile, and the raw smell of wealth that it all represented. Pammy was doing well for herself living in a 3.5-million-dollar penthouse apartment. You can walk out of her building and into Lake

Michigan. Octavia wasn't easily impressed like most country girls. But she admired the lifestyle Pammy led if you were turned on by that whole captain industry thing.

The doorman let her in while appraising her with a practiced eye. The width of his smile let her know he thought she belonged. She approached the security desk and told the man in the cheap blazer who she was there to see. Octavia had been to the Winthrop building several times before with Butterfly and didn't recognize this particular guard. Security was pretty tight. She didn't know the exact number of guards per shift, but she knew there were a lot of them, and they all were well trained. The man whose name tag read Burton-directed her to a bank of elevators on the left. They serviced the 20th to the 24th floors only. Each floor above 20 had four penthouses, two with lakeside views, and two with downtown views. Everyone living there got a piece of breathtaking scenery.

Octavia pressed the bell and almost immediately the door was opened by a stunning blond in a well-fitted primrose colored sleeveless dress. This must be wife number two, she thought. Wow! What an improvement from the old broad. This one has a sunny disposition, nice hair styled in a short pageboy, an engaging smile, and full natural tits. You go, Pammy! "Hello, you must be Sommar. I'm Octavia Winters. How lovely it is to finally meet you after being separated so long by those needy bitches, autumn and spring." Sommar laughed enchantingly. Pamela's wife leaned in for a polite hug and thought nothing untoward when Octavia pulled her closer gently squeezing her firm ass. "It's nice to meet you too," Sommar said enthusiastically while stepping back." Please come in. Come in. Pamela's in the kitchen." Sommar's great ass led the way.

In the kitchen, Sommar went over and stood behind Pamela who sat in a chair made of tarnished copper with decorative branches and leaves across its back; at a large Cherrywood island shaped like the trunk of a tree. Octavia waved for her not to get up, but she ignored her, giving her guest a warm embrace. "Well hello, gorgeous. Thanks for allowing me to stay at your humble abode." Everyone laughed. "Where's your luggage?" Pamela asked. The fugitive raised her Chanel bag in the air. "I'm traveling light with only a duffel, sort of like a vagabond. "Pamela looked back at her wife, who then left for a brief minute and returned holding a Louis Vuitton carry-all. Sommar remarked, "I'll put it in the guest room facing the lake. You'll love the view. It's spectacular." Excitedly, Octavia replied, "I've heard. Another college buddy of ours, Butterfly, wouldn't shut up about it." The young wife smiled brightly then walked off.

Pamela went over to watch Sommar, making sure that she was out of earshot. Then she whirled around at her guest; "Butterfly, you can't…" A perfectly delivered slap interrupted the rest of her words. Octavia's palm met flush with Pamela's ear throwing her equilibrium off and rendering her speechless.

She leaned into Pamela's opposite ear and said in a hushed tone, "My name is Octavia! Who in the fuck are you to tell me I can't?" Pamela's ear was still ringing like church bells. "Keep my cover tight and I won't have to tell your deliciously lovely wife how well we really know one another."

Pamela sat back down rubbing her ear. "I was saying that you can't stay here long." Pamela couldn't hear her tormentor with the persistent ringing in her head. She more or less had to read her lips. "I'll be gone by late tomorrow or the day after. I just need to get my bearings."

Pamela's hearing and equilibrium righted themselves just before Sommar reentered the room. "Babe, are you okay? You look a little flushed." Smiling up at Sommar, Pamela said, "I'm fine, maybe it's the excitement of seeing Octavia."

That made the young wife wonder. "How did the two of you meet? I know it was in college, but exactly how?" Sommar was facing Octavia otherwise she would have seen the horror on her wife's face." What an interesting question my Viking goddess. Let's go somewhere more comfortable. One should always be at ease during the telling of secrets." The pretty wife laughed gaily while being led from the kitchen.

Pamela had never thought about actually killing another human being, except for Butterfly. She followed close behind Sommar and

Octavia; all the while imagining herself thrashing the bitch to death. She did, however, know that in her heart of hearts she never would. But the thought was extremely calming.

Why did this have to happen to her! She finished her first year of college with a 3.8 GPA. An exotic brunette with a killer body who was smart enough to avoid gaining the 'freshman fifteen.' Pamela was considered full figured already. Fifteen pounds would have her tipping the scales making her a fatty. She didn't want that at all. Her roommate, Butterfly Daniels, was in another league altogether. She effortlessly maintained a 4.0 GPA, was a runway model gorgeous in the face with a video vixen body. Pamela thought she was probably born into money. She never needed or wanted for anything. She looked over at the pretty woman in the bed across the room listening to her iPod and began crying uncontrollably. Instead of rushing to console her, Butterfly stared at her with the curiosity that the spider reserves for the doomed fly.

When the distraught freshman was all cried out, she pulled out the earphones and moved quietly over to her asking, "What did all of that woe is me shit accomplish? Let me guess. Not one damn thing!" Grabbing some tissues, Pamela blew her nose loudly then wiped at her green, red-rimmed eyes until they were dry. "Okay, I'll bite. Why are you crying, Connecticut? Pamela's tone was harsher than she intended. "Not everyone has a rich sister who pays their tuition!"

Butterfly cocked her head to the side as though she were wondering what's gotten into little miss east coast. "I got a full academic ride. My sister just thinks she paid for my four years of tuition. Now are you going to answer my question, or can I go back to my music?"

Pamela stood up and started babbling at the speed of light and pacing back and forth. "Slow down and speak as though you have some sense, Connecticut."

She stopped and faced Butterfly who was relaxing on Pamela's bed. "My parents want me to sit out a year. My dad has made some bad investments and needs all the cash he can lay his hands on. It just so happens that my college fund is within arm's reach."

Looking up at her blandly Butterfly said, "So you sit out a year. What's the big deal?"

Young Pamela became almost hysterical. "I have my life planned out! I can't sit out a fucking year! Four years undergraduate degree, two years in business school at Stanford or Wharton for my MBA, then off to New York or staying here playing with other people's money like my dad, only better!"

"So, what do you need?"

Pamela turned and gave Butterfly a confused look at that question. "I need money. It's the only solution to my problem. Without it, I won't be coming back in the fall."

An enterprising young businesswoman, Butterfly saw an opportunity waiting to be seized. "Connecticut, you are rich. What you need is for someone to show you how to convert your riches over to monetary currency."

Pamela turned and looked at Butterfly with a blank expression. "What in the hell are you talking about Daniels?"

It was Butterfly's turn to look confused as if Pamela should already know. "I'm talking about you being in a position to not only pay your tuition but acquire six figures by this time next year without chipping a fingernail."

That statement made Pamela perk up and listen intently. "How do you suppose I do that?"

"Stand up and turn around in a circle", Butterfly said.

"What?" Pam asked. The look on her roommate's face sent her spinning 360°.

"You're big-boned, but there's not an ounce of fat on your curvaceous frame. Nice lips, tits, and ass. You're Jewish, but you could pass as Italian, Greek, or Arabian. How tall are you?"

"I'm 5'9" tall barefoot. Why?"

Butterfly didn't answer her. She asked her another question. "Can you walk in 6" heels?" Pamela gave her a quizzical look. "Well, can you?"

"The highest I've ever walked in was 4" tall. Why are you asking me all of these questions?"

Butterfly gave her a smile that could only be termed, wolfish." I know a guy named Dick who'll be happy to give you the money you need."

Shock, disrespect. She had no idea what she felt. If she could believe her ears, Daniels was talking about prostitution. If Dick's last name was penis, she was way out of the running. Pamela held a secret that no one knew. Her parents and friends back home were clueless as to her true sexual orientation. Pamela was attracted to girls. But the small town where she lived outside of New Haven, CT, was as conservative as it gets, and no one knew it. She had a bit of trouble during high school when some rumors arose concerning her sexuality. To combat those rumors, she picked up a boyfriend, Aaron Cohenberg. She had sex with him a few times knowing he would brag to his buddies on the football team. Aaron was a jerk, but his constant bragging about his sexual exploits with Pamela put the rumors to rest. Shortly after that, she broke up with him. She had sacrificed her body with the whole fake boyfriend experience and promised to never do it again. There's no way that she would sell herself for money. "Just what exactly are you suggesting Daniels?"

Candidly and unashamedly she said, "That you open your mind and your legs. You'll thank me for it later."

Pamela was positive that her roommate had lost her freaking mind. There's no way Pamela was going to be a prostitute. Still, as crazy as she thought the whole thing was, she didn't actually tell Butterfly no. She kept listening. The seemingly street-smart freshman always had an answer or logical point better than Pamela's. Butterfly let her know that she wouldn't be alone in it. She reasoned that there were plenty of girls doing it and that these girls remained anonymous. "It's happening Connecticut. Several girls are already doing it. They're mostly seniors, though there are some freshmen and sophomores. Those that are mature enough to handle it, that is."

For months Butterfly had been arranging high paying rendezvous on www.Snatchme.com. The other girls, their schedules permitting were flown all over the country for these trysts. All bookings were done two days in advance as was the payment. Pamela didn't care, she wasn't going to do it. Their discussion went on for a few hours. Butterfly could see the obstinance in those big emerald eyes. She grabbed her book bag and removed a small metallic case thinking, always save your best punch for last. Inside of the case were twenty debit cards totaling one hundred thousand dollars. "See Connecticut, you think the world turns on ideas when it doesn't. Ideas are the engine, money is the fuel and power is the guiding force that makes it spin. You, being an aspiring financier, should know this."

Pamela was floored. She couldn't believe what she was hearing. "How long did it take you to make that?"

Smiling and with a hint of pride in her voice Butterfly said, "Eight months; but this is only a fraction of what the dedicated girls make. I only have a few clients. How much you could make would depend on your menu." Pamela didn't understand and told her so. With a tolerant tone of voice Butterfly explained, "My menu is, Master P; meaning I don't have a limit." Butterfly saw the dumbfounded look on her roommate's face and said, "After the rapper who owns No Limit Records? Duh!"

"I thought you came from wealth. Is this how you get your money?" Patting the book bag where she returned the debit cards, "Some of it, though most of it comes from pretty young things like you. I make 25 percent off every date. I arrange client introductions, and in some cases, I provide security and make sure that all potential clients are screened. That's what the 48-hour advance is for. It allows me to provide an extra layer of safety between the girls and any crazy shit."

Wide-eyed and wanting to know more, Pamela watched silently as Butterfly booted up her laptop. Her fingers danced rapidly over the keyboard, beating out a machine gun staccato rhythm until a website popped up. After punching in her password, she spun it around and let Pamela see it. Her hand flew to her mouth so fast that her gasp was trapped in her throat almost choking her. "This beautiful seductress is Asia Menage, but you know her as our resident floor manager Miss Amy Nguyen. What you see listed to the right of her picture is her menu. This is a secure site and can only be used by members. You have to understand that 90 percent of our clients are married; 8 percent are female, and 100 percent are rich. We operate off of referrals only and we follow the M.A.D. principal."

"What's that?" Pamela asked.

"It means," Butterfly quipped, "Mutually Assured Destruction. If a client gets out of line or decides he wants to cooperate with law enforcement he gets a gentle reminder that if we go down, he's going down. No pun intended."

Pamela was taken aback as she read the bold red letters, NO with several exclamation points. After that was typed: BONDAGE, NO GREEK
FUDGE and each had a red X through them. Underneath that was, I ENJOY ANAL, ORAL, WATERSPORTS, THREESOMES, AND ROLEPLAYING. I SPECIALIZE IN NAUGHTY NURSE AND SEXY ASIAN EXCHANGE STUDENT! Beneath that was an asterisk then the phrase DEEP THROAT SPECIALIST. Pamela blurted out, "What's Greek Fudge?"

"I love it! The only thing greener than your mind are those pretty eyes. Greek Fudge is when a client wants to shit on you, or you to shit on them."

Pamela's eyes rolled skyward. "Ewwww! That's so, fucking gross! Yuck!"

Butterfly waited and watched her roommate's face closely when she told her, "It's six to receive and four to do what you do every day anyway."

"How can you even think of letting someone shit on you for $600.00?" Pamela genuinely inquired.

"Six hundred dollars can buy a lot of toilet paper and soap. But I told you a client doesn't slip on a condom for less than $1,000.00. It's $6,000.00, not $600.00." Pamela couldn't help but calculate a month's worth of her bowel movements. She felt ashamed but still couldn't help thinking of all she could do with a little shit.

"Listen Connecticut, I've been rooming with you for almost a year. You think that I don't know you'd rather munch on carpet pie than ride a hard one?"

Pamela acted confused. "What are you talking about? Are you crazy!"

Butterfly was wearing gym shorts and a tank top. The shorts came off exposing her nakedness. Do you think I don't see how you look at me when I'm getting undressed? Your pretty little mouth waters. I'm not fooled by all the guys you date. Word on campus is that your hand jobs are better than most girl's blow jobs. The guys you go out with are called the Smurf Squad because they have blue balls. Did you know that?"

She opened her thighs wider. "Look at you, you can't tear your eyes away from my beautiful flower, can you? My poor destitute Dyke in distress." Butterfly turned around to slip her shorts back on giving Pamela a good long look at her ass. "I'll give you 24 hours to accept my offer. Since we're roomies, I'm only going to take 15 percent of your earnings and I'm going to personally take you under my wing and show you the ropes."

Pamela looked Butterfly straight in the eyes. "I'm not a prostitute." "How about I out you to your parents and all those people in your little town? Then get that professor you're screwing fired. What's her name? Mrs. Berloff isn't it? I'm sure her husband and the Dean would like to know."

Pamela's eyes got big as saucers. "How do you know that?"

"The problem for you isn't how I know sweetheart. Your problem is that I know." Pamela didn't know what to do so, she did and said nothing. "It's all an act. You're either being paid for your performance or just an extra. Who are you? You're worried about having a penis inside you when you walk around with a tampon inside of you for days. Trust me, it's no different. Think about your plan, Pamela."

There's was no way in hell that she would prostitute herself, but she told Butterfly, "Please just let me think about it, okay?" But in her mind, there was no way, none whatsoever. Being a whore wasn't part of the plan. There was no way that she would become a whore. She thought and thought and kept thinking for most of the night. She stayed up during the night crunching numbers, too. If Daniels made that much money in eight months, then she would need only a few months to make next year's tuition. Pamela didn't factor in any legal ramifications at all. Her reasoning was based solely on her need to stay in college and fulfill her plans.

Butterfly fell asleep knowing full well that Pamela was thinking hard trying to convince herself not to do it; because her need or greed had already said 'yes.' Of course, she could do it for a few months and no one would be the wiser.

Pamela reflected on those few times with Aaron. Then she started switching his face with other men of different ages and races. Aaron Cohenberg would feel her up, pull her panties aside, and enter her. It was almost like when she fingered herself. He'd thrust and pump vigorously for a few minutes and orgasm. She could let a man do that for the type of money they were paying. She needed the money. At 2:00 a.m. she called over to Butterfly.

Butterfly stretched, yawning with the back of her hand covering her mouth. "Connecticut, do you have any idea what time it is?"

Pamela didn't answer. Instead, she said, "I think I can do it."

Butterfly yawned again, loudly this time. "You think you can! Are you the little engine that could or are you a fierce, powerful young woman who knows her value? Sometimes I think I'm someone else. But, so fucking what! That has nothing to do with the price of tea in China. You need to know that you're capable of doing it."

"I can do it. I know I can do this." Pamela asked timidly, "When do I start?"

"Tomorrow. "We'll go over the basics then when I think you're ready you'll start seeing clients. Until then Connecticut, you're on probation."

Nervous and curious Pamela asked, "What does probation entail and how long does it last?"

"It entails whatever I say and lasts until I say it doesn't. Now go to sleep."

"But I need to know." Butterfly hated to be awakened and this bitch was becoming annoying.

"Pamela, do you remember Emily Deighton?" Practically everyone on campus, at least those in the dorms knew who she was. A junior majoring in mechanical engineering who swallowed a handful of oxytocin like they were Skittles candy. "What about her?" Butterfly curled back up under the sheets, but not before saying, "Emily was on probation just like you are. Thankfully, you're a lot smarter than her. I'm sure you won't screw up like she did."

Pamela was super curious. "What did she do wrong?" "Goodnight!" The tone of Butterfly's voice made it clear they were done. Pamela knew right then and there that she should try to back out, but a small voice told her there was no going back. Truthfully, she didn't know if it was fear or need that kept her mouth shut. After some deep contemplation, she came to the woeful conclusion that it was both.

She sipped slowly at her scotch while watching her wife and Octavia. Their guest spun a tale so believable sprinkled with elements of the truth about how they met in college that Sommar hung on her every word. After dinner, Pamela retired to her study with Octavia in tow. Within a few minutes, Sommar came in with a couple of cups and a steaming carafe of coffee. "There's sugar and creamer on the tray if either of you need it. I'm off to meet the Sandman. Goodnight ladies." Octavia watched as the wives kissed, then she said goodnight to the beautiful Sommar.

Pamela was pouring coffee when she heard the snap of the study's lock engaging. "Finally, we're all alone, Pammy."

"Please don't call me that. One would think you'd show a modicum of respect after I've opened my home to you on such short notice."

Octavia ignored her as she looked around at the vast collection of leather-bound books. She pulled the Count of Monte Cristo by Alexandre Dumas off a bookshelf and smiled. "The candy-ass movies they've made don't even scratch the surface of Edmond Dante's revenge." She returned the book to its place, still looking around. The study was immaculate. "I see you still love the outward appearance of organized control, while inside you're all chaos and confusion." Pamela handed her a cup of coffee and sat down. "You're not joining me?" Octavia asked seductively.

"I have to be up by five and out a little after six. I'm going to sleep." Octavia set her coffee cup next to the tray it was carried in on and reached underneath her Emilio Zenegra skirt pulling down her underwear. She stepped out of them and dropped the gauzy silk thong in Pamela's lap. "I'm a little tense after all of the recent drama in my life. Be a dear and do that thing you do so well with your tongue."

Instead of responding, Pamela closed her eyes tight while hoping that the evil thing in front of her was an apparition that would fade away by the time, she opened them again. No such luck, she thought, as Octavia stood there waiting. Pamela tossed the panties in her lap to the floor at her guest's feet. "You should put those back on before you catch a cold."

Octavia sat across from Pamela in a comfortable leather chair folding her panties. "Over the years you've grown to hate me more and more. I recall a time when you would never refuse me. Do you remember that time? More beautiful now than you were then. Persephone, Butterfly's bottom bitch. It was I who taught you the art of fellatio. I'm the same one who taught you how to block out the faces, have fun, and make your money. You're the reason for all that you have achieved while I'm the cause. When you and I were together I felt invincible and so did you. Persephone and Butterfly up high in a tree, K-I-S-S-I-N-G. We were a team and now you hate me."

Tears rolled slowly down Octavia's face. Pamela marveled at the woman's ability to cry on cue. "Save your bullshit Butterfly. I'm not buying any of it!" Butterfly gave her hostess a look that almost withered her resolve to stand up to her. "My name is Octavia. Don't act like you don't know what I'm capable of."

Pamela stood moving to the study door. "I'm aware of who and what you are. You taught me well. What was it you use to tell us, girls? Fear nothing in this world, you are a WOMAN! No other animal on earth can bleed continuously for almost a week and walk away from it. Oh! and my favorite one was every woman can fuck, but not all of us can act. Your performance isn't as good as it used to be." Pamela laughed scornfully. "Now that the tears aren't working, what next? Let me guess, threats."

Octavia was getting angry. "You walk out that door and you'll regret it. Besides, you know you want to. I'll bet a million dollars that little Miss Sunshine doesn't make you feel the way I do."

At one time, Pamela was infatuated with Butterfly and her alter ego Octavia. But as time passed, she grew to despise them both. "You're absolutely right. You repulse me and Sommar's never done that."

At that remark, Butterfly grew angry. but tried not to show it as she moved within striking distance of Pamela. "I heard you on the phone before dinner," Pamela said. The police are looking for you, which doesn't surprise me. Rich, beautiful, and more intelligent than any person I've ever encountered; yet you crave danger and excitement like a stunt woman. Maybe you should tread lightly."

Octavia stopped short of smacking some sense into her. "In spite of your lack of feelings for me, I still love you. Come on Pamela, do me for old time's sake?"

"You know nothing of love. You only know pain, pleasure, and what you want or think you need. Nothing else!"

"Pamela, stop this. I'm not your enemy. Right now, I'm going through a lot and I need you to be Persephone. I need you to have my back and make love to me the way you used to."

Anytime Butterfly called her Pamela and not Pammy or Connecticut, was always a bad sign. "When you call me Pamela it always leads to your wanting something from me, other than me, which leads to trouble. I'm tired of being your footstool. Expose my secrets to the world. I don't care anymore because I'll survive. Octavia, Butterfly, or whoever the hell you think you are, I'll need you gone by tomorrow."

Octavia started clapping. "Look who's grown a set of balls. I'm proud of you, Connecticut. If you don't want me as your guest, I won't impose upon you any further. Thanks for standing up to me. I guess I needed it to gain some perspective." She leaned in quickly kissing the other woman on the lips. "You do know that I was going to do you next, right?"

Pamela unlocked the door and opened it wide.

She gave a barely audible goodnight then said, "By tomorrow." On the way to sleep, she should have felt strong, empowered, but all she felt while scooting up next to Sommar was afraid.

Jimenez and Gleason sat parked on Belle Isle, an island park off of Jefferson Avenue sitting in the Detroit River. They had just finished watching a litany of videos and viewing hundreds of digital photographs that their carjacking victim collected of his sexual conquests over the years. From the style of dress and hairstyles of the women, the pictures went back over two decades. With the use of technology, the late Dr. Brooks was able to place his collection on a flash drive. They could have done what they were doing back at homicide, but they both knew the constant interruptions would slow their progress.

Most of the photos were lewd and all of the videos were pornographic in nature. Gleason had to get out of the squad car when they watched a video of their suspect dressed up as a naughty stripper. If Butterfly Baxter and the deceased went into the porn business, the boys and girls in Van Nuys, California would have some very stiff competition. There were two main players for the most part in the videos contained on the flash drive. They were Butterfly Baxter and Dr. Dorian Brooks. But there was a third. A full-figured brunette with exotic features and sad green eyes. During most of the sex acts, she looked as though she'd rather be tossing hand grenades in a minefield in hell.

Gleason spoke, "This case has turned out to be an onion. It stinks, makes you want to cry, and just when you think that's it, another layer appears."

"Let me see the names from Baxter's home phone?" Jimenez asked. The detective scanned the list finding several numbers with Chicago area codes. "Where's the list of college buddies?" He handed it to her. "See this name right here registered to this number? Pamela Nothnagel. She graduated the same year as our fugitive. In fact, they were roommates."

Gleason looked at her as though she had horns. "How do you know
    that?"

Jimenez looked at him with an exaggerated pained expression. "ay, Dios Mio! Are you serious? I am a trained detective!" She rolled her eyes then burst into laughter. "Dr. Daniels gave me the lead. I just followed it up. The woman's name is Pamela Nothnagel. She was our fugitive's roommate for four years of college."

Gleason punched the name into the computer and waited. Illinois DMV kicked out nine matches. Only two were in their thirties, but only one looked identical to the woman in the videos. Gleason pressed a few keys and the woman's picture enlarged, filling the screen." Check out our porn star," he said turning the computer towards Jimenez. "Do you think Baxter is in Chicago with this Nothnagel woman?"

His partner grabbed at her crotch "I'll bet my cojones on it! After we read these letters, we're going to contact that loveable prick O'Sullivan and trap our Butterfly.

After dividing them, they began reading. The letters were stretched out over an almost seven-year period. Some of the letters were missing. In lieu of a formal signature, they were all signed, FOREVER YOURS. Both detectives came to the same conclusion after reading through most of the material. The last one they read was written before Dr. Brooks' murder.

There in the bottom right corner of the page was a pair of full lip prints tattooed on the paper in the brightest shade of red lipstick Jimenez had ever seen, and it still reeked of expensive perfume. While most of the correspondence was erotic, there were a few which stood out.

One, in particular, was head and shoulders above the rest.

{Dear Dorian,

She's my sister in name only. We share nothing in common except the vaginal sheath we came out of and you. Remember, it was you who suggested we undertake our current course of action now your backpedaling. I've seen and even held your balls in my hand, so I know you have some. I'm only wondering why you refuse to use them. Sweetie, the die has been cast! We move forward.

FOREVER YOURS}

Gleason held another letter up, "I believe this one here is in reference to you. Listen to this; 'Asshole, don't fucking do anything besides care for your wife! That puta is no dummy! The slightest misstep or misspoken word will land you in hot water with Miss Mexico fanning the flames. For all your supposed intelligence, don't be stupid!' and it's signed like the others. They're referring to you Jimenez or should I say, Miz May-E-Co?"

Jimenez rolled her brown eyes and almost told him to go screw himself but flashed him her middle finger Instead. He burst into uncontrolled laughter. She waited until Gleason caught his breath before admonishing him, "Let's get serious arid focus. These people are worse than the Borgia's or Kennedys."

"Like one of those telenovelas on Univision," Gleason offered. Jimenez was quick to correct him. "A telenovela consists of love and honor. The sick characters in this drama know nothing of either."

Staring through the unmarked squad car's windshield over the murky waters of the Detroit River to Windsor she was muttering, "Cemmerdon En Inferno! May they burn in hell!" Gleason looked over at her. "We need to be in on the arrest. O'Sullivan is great at what he does, but I need to be there to interrogate Butterfly Baxter as soon as she's caught. She needs to be taken apart with surgical precision." He didn't respond or interrupt because he knew from prior experience, she wasn't talking to him. She went on to wonder why, after three years of graveyard silence, is this case just now starting to turn? Why is it begging to be solved now?

"We need to find the old guy in the confession video. He's the key to this entire investigation. A mysterious man in the middle of a mystery. That just won't do, we need to find him. Take us off the isle detective Gleason ... and do it slowly, I need to think."

She lapsed silently into her own thoughts. Usually, when a case grows cold it rarely heats up again. Who lit the match under this one? Catching their fugitive closes the case, but that doesn't mean it's solved. Something about this case was gnawing at her nerves.

It started after that damn confession video. A thousand-piece jigsaw puzzle and she only has nine hundred ninety pieces. Although the big picture is clear, it always bothered her when every I wasn't dotted and each T wasn't crossed. Those missing ten pieces are the same as missing details, and that's where the devil is. Always right there hidden amongst the details. Every question has an answer, so where are they in this case? Now that's a question deserving of the detective sergeant's full attention.

Lt. Templeton listened intently to Jimenez and Gleason as they recounted where they were in the Daniels' case. "You guys think the Nothnagel woman is possibly harboring the sister, this Butterfly Baxter?" Jimenez shifted uneasily in her seat. "Yeah, the two of us are about to hook up with O'Sullivan and see if we can pick her up." Templeton stood from his desk fanning his arms out wide with an index finger leveled at each of them. "Two of you?" The detectives looked uncomfortably at the ceiling and floor. "I don't think so! One of you can tag along with the Marshals but I got a supposed suicide that's probably a homicide, a triple on the west side and a double in the red zone on the east side with these street gangs using civilians for target practice." The partners looked at one another wondering who the lieutenant was going to let go when he said, "I'll let the two of you decide which one of you goes, but only one of you will." He started shuffling papers on his desk. "Now if you don't mind, some of us have work to do." He shooed them out and told Gleason to close the door behind them.

Back at their own desks in the squad room, Jimenez turned her chair toward Gleason. "You wanna call O'Sullivan and give'em the lead we got on this Nothnagel woman?" The junior detective who was rubbing his bald pate held up his free hand to stop her. "Look, you're the Lone Ranger. I'm just Tonto along for the ride. This is your baby, just bring me back a souvenir." Jimenez was already dialing when she told him, "I'll do better than that, I'll bring you back a talking Butterfly Baxter."

Marshal O'Sullivan was glad to hear that DPD had a solid lead. It made his job a whole lot easier. Jimenez had met up with the U.S. Marshal's fugitive recovery team after her informative phone call. After laying out some minor operating protocols and making sure she knew that he was in charge, O'Sullivan welcomed Jimenez aboard. She stared out the window from the backseat of the lead SUV at the passing scenery as they traveled along westbound Interstate 94 towards Chicago. It didn't take long to get the federal arrest warrants signed considering their fugitive's making all the local news channels with her fleeing and alluding. The long arm of the law takes great offense when a suspect makes themselves shy of its reach.

O'Sullivan was driving while humming along to a country song. Next to him, Marshal Eugenia "Genie" Proctor was scrolling through messages on her phone. The young buxom, perky blond with her wide hips and even wider smile was definitely the team's lure. Her full heartshaped ass was responsible for catching more fugitives than John Walsh. The four other team members were trailing in a tricked-out Sprinter van loaded with communications gear. Jimenez saw the signs indicating they were almost at the Indiana border.

"I just received a text from the Ferret. Security at the Winthrop building sent a screenshot of some CCTV feed of an African American female who's visiting the Nothnagel penthouse." Genie passed the phone back to the detective. "It's not a good pic, but it resembles the file photos." Jimenez handed the phone back. "It's grainy, though if I had to wager, I'd bet my money it's her. Let's see if we can get building security to keep their mouths shut and let us know if she gets on the move." The blond looked at her boss who gave a slight nod. "I'm sure that the Ferret is already on it, but a gentle reminder never hurts."

Upon meeting the team Jimenez marveled at their easy exchange. They all had nicknames, but O'Sullivan's was the best. "So, what's the plan, Hooch? Are we going in hard, soft, or what?" He caught her eye in the rearview mirror. 'Well J Dick, I don't know about DPD, but we at the service start our mornings with the rooster. Considering we won't reach our destination until a little after 2300 hours, that's almost eighteen hours of uptime. When we arrive in the Windy City, we'll slide into a motel, get some rest and when the rooster rouses us, we'll set up on the Winthrop building and snatch our fugitive." He stuck out his tongue like a know-it-all fifth grader. She gave him her middle finger before pulling her earbuds out of her bag.

Genie watched the entire exchange then asked curiously, "Were you guys ever a couple because the sexual tension between you two is pornographic." The dashboard lights caught O'Sullivan blushing when Jimenez said. "The big red dog wishes!" He mumbled something about suspending Genie for insolence and she laughed.

Within forty-five minutes, they rolled into a downtown motel parking lot whose location put them less than twelve minutes out from where they believed their fugitive to be taking harbor. U.S. Marshals Samantha "Sammy" Burman, Barclay "Ferret" Fahret. Marcus "Mac" McAbee, and Jonathan "Jon Jon" Johnson were casually huddled next to the vehicles with their bags waiting on their boss. Jimenez heard his baritone voice way before actually seeing him. When they came into view, Genie was trying to calm him down. "What's the deal?" O'Sullivan looked at her as if he wanted to bite her head off. "Fucking scrawny dip shit hipster taking me around the rosies about the government credit card. I show the little twat every fucking piece of ID and he asks for a fingerprint. He goes, 'Can't be too careful with Identity theft. You wouldn't believe the types we get.' I started to shove my badge up his wazoo! Fucking asshole!" Everyone laughed until he passed out the room assignments.

The women were in room 107, while Mac, Ferret, and O'Sullivan were in 105. Jon Jon piped in, "What about me?" O'Sullivan pointed towards the Sprinter van. "Hooch, you gotta be fucking kidding me!"

The team leader wasn't kidding at all. After a fugitive recovery team lost a shitload of tactical equipment to car theft in Houston, the heat was turned on by the higher-ups. "That van alone is worth a small fortune. With the comms gear, it's worth a pretty big one. You can come in and shower in the morning."

O'Sullivan checked his watch, "I'll relieve you a quarter to 0600 hours." Jon Jon knew from the man's tone that his decision was final.

Turning to Jimenez he said, "Rest up, I'll see you in the A.M."

She shifted her chin in the direction of Marshal Johnson. "What did he do to end up in the shithouse?"

The team leader ignored the homicide detective. "In the morning," he said before hoisting his duffel bag onto a beefy shoulder and sauntering off to his room like John Wayne with a stick up his ass.

Sammy nudged her as they fell in step behind Genie. "Jon Jon shot and killed a fugitive on a recovery. Creep broke into an apartment on Detroit's worst side raping three generations. The oldest was over sixty, the youngest just nine. We caught up with him outside of Raleigh, North Carolina. He turned into a dark alley and Jon Jon was waiting. Dumbass brought a knife to the O.K. Corral and ended up auditioning for Cyclops the movie."

Jimenez recalled the brutal sexual assaults and couldn't find a single problem with the outcome. Genie threw in her two cents. "Hooch only had a problem with his state-of-the-art body camera mysteriously going offline right before the shoot. Jon Jon's explanation was very plausible. He said he mistook the night vision switch for the off switch. The BCs were new, we had only used them once before. The boss is clear about following the team's motto."

Genie and Sammy recited it together; "We're not judge, we're not Jury, we just capture." The short brunette shrugged, "He's lucky that Hooch is loyal as they come. In recent years, I've seen careers lost over less."

Jimenez knew that was the truth.

Inside the room were two double beds. Genie said that she'd share with
Sammy as long as she showered first. The woman tossed down her bag, "You're going to keep bringing up Pittsburgh? I was practically on seventy two-hour surveillance!"

Genie pinched her nose. "There's no excuse for poor hygiene."

Sammy snatched her bag back up and stomped into the bathroom. "You don't have to be such a bitch in front of company."

Thirty minutes later, Jimenez was lying in bed listening to the other two women fart and snore. Something was needling her about this case. It wasn't just the mystery man in the video, there were other loose ends which were slapping her subconscious, but she just couldn't connect the strands. She drifted off thinking there was someone else pulling strings behind the scene.

Strings that were sure to entangle her too.

8 CIAO BELLA

Pamela woke up to the beeping of her alarm clock. She didn't get much sleep with Butterfly right down the hall from them. Cutting off the alarm, she tossed the sheets back before looking over at Sommar. She needed to make sure her young wife would be safe. After all. it was her fault for letting the danger in. The only way to ensure this was to get that evil bitch Butterfly slash Octavia, slash Satan's mistress, out of their penthouse and far away from them.

Sommar stirred just as Pamela pulled the covers back up kissing her shoulder. After taking a second to capture a mental snapshot of her young beautiful wife sleeping peacefully, she walked into their en suite. Three minutes under a hot shower with another two under a freezing cold spray awakening every nerve fiber in her body, Pamela stepped from her bathroom into a spacious walk-in closet where she air-dried while picking out a black pencil skirt with a dark creme colored silk blouse along with a matching pair of Balmain demi boots. A burnt orange single-breasted distressed leather suit jacket and a burnt orange crocodile Birkin bag completed the ensemble.

While getting dressed, her focus remained on one thing. That "thing" was right down the hallway. Pamela walked to a wall covered with racks of expensive footwear from floor to ceiling. She went to a chest-high rack with two pair of limited-edition Louis Vuitton's and removed them, depressing a notch in the cedar. The secret panel popped open with a slight hiss exposing a small titanium safe, and she punched in the date that she officially stopped whoring for Butterfly. Grabbing an empty rectangular accordion file folder, she loaded it with five bundles of cash, secured the clasp, then closed the safe replacing the shoes as an afterthought.

Octavia could hear the soft tap of high heels approaching outside of the bedroom door. There was a sharp knock before the knob twisted and Pamela's head peeked in. Even in the semi-darkness, what she saw was typical of Butterfly. "Have you changed your mind, Pammy? Because my finger is a poor substitute for your talented tongue." She stepped into the room averting her gaze while pressing her back against the wall next to the open door.

"No, I haven't changed my mind." She said tossing the small file folder on the bed next to the naked woman. "That's fifty K, I can get you more later if you need it." Less confidently she added, "I'd prefer you to be gone before my wife wakes up in a couple of hours."

Octavia slid seductively out of bed before walking over to the other woman. Pamela saw the hand coming up and flinched, but Octavia was only cutting the light on. "Don't be afraid sweetheart." She eyed her suspiciously. "Why are you up this early?" Pamela avoided the woman's nakedness by looking all around the guestroom. "I have an important meeting scheduled this morning."

Pointing to the money on the bed she told her that a little change could get her moving in the right direction, but a lot of sexual healing could get her gone. The wife nervously twisted her wedding ring. "I just want you gone as soon as possible. How long before the authorities track you here? Come on Butterfly, be smart!" With lightning speed, Pamela felt fingers coiling themselves in her hair before snatching her head sideways. "Octavia, bitch! How many times do I have to tell you!" Reflexively, Pamela put her hands up to ward off the crazy woman and succeeded only in covering a naked breast. Octavia seized the opportunity, "So you do want me? How about a quick munch before your workday? Breakfast is the most important meal."

Pamela pushed the woman with the double identity away stepping back into the hall almost tripping over her own briefcase and purse. In a hushed hurried whisper, she spoke with as much confidence as she could muster. "Don't underestimate my desire to have you out of my life. I'll be calling my wife per usual around noon. You better be nothing more than a fading memory by that time." Octavia watched as the woman gathered her things and hurried to the waiting car and driver. Damn, what can a woman take that would grow her a set of balls overnight thought Octavia. Who does this cunt think she is? Hell, who does she think I am? Octavia leaned against the doorframe while considering going back to sleep when another thought took hold. There's some fun to be had right down the hall.

Sommar Nothnagel was curled up like a snail beneath the high thread count breathable sheets snoring softly when Octavia and Butterfly slithered silently into the master suite cutting on the light. Look at that! Sommar's blond hair was splayed across her pillow like fresh-cut wheat. This was going to be absolutely awesome Octavia was musing when Butterfly butted in. "This is definitely wrong. You shouldn't do what you're planning ..." Octavia reached up pinching one of their nipples between thumb and forefinger then twisted painfully until Butterfly shut up agreeing to get on board. "Enjoy the show!"

Sommar stretched onto her back when the sheets were gently pulled away. The baby doll nightgown the young Mrs. Nothnagel wore had ridden up her spread taut thighs exposing her sex. Octavia looked at the ridiculous sleep mask with its pair of large open cartoon eyes printed on it as she climbed onto the bed licking her lips and giggling. Within a few minutes, the only parts of Sommar touching the mattress were her toes and the crown of her head. During the encounter, she had at least three body wracking orgasms. "Did you enjoy it?" Octavia had to ask twice before the other woman hesitantly pulled off her mask. "My God! Oh, my God! What're you doing? Why are you in here?" She asked frantically while her houseguest audaciously stroked her manicured nails over her still damp thighs causing her to recoil scrambling backward to the headboard, seeking safety that would never be found.

Sommar looked horrified as she started yelling. "Pamela! Pamela!" Laughing, Octavia wiped her lips with the back of her hand. "Your wife, my whore, has gone off to play the captain of industry or something. It's just you and me babe." Sommar tried getting out of bed when a strong hand gripped an ankle. "Unh, unh, unh! It's time for you to reciprocate Mrs. Nothnagel." The younger woman snatched her leg free. "I thought you were my wife. I'm not about to do that to you!"

Octavia stood up displaying her nakedness. "Come on, I've experienced your wife countless times, so I know that she doesn't possess my skill set. I taught her almost everything I know. Almost. Do me and we'll call it even." Sommar was shocked and asked if Octavia was serious or just insane.

The blow came with the speed and efficiency of someone accustomed to violence. The young wife had no time to react. The fist smashed into the other woman's temple causing immediate dizziness. Before she could even think to recover, her hair was being pulled and her body followed suit until she was on the floor. A vicious kick to Sommar's midsection sent jolting waves of pain throughout her frame. When she was able to focus and catch a breath, she started begging for Octavia to just leave.

"I promise I won't call the police! Please just leave!" A flurry of punches quickly followed her pleas. "I've dealt with stuck up whores like you before. Selfish cunts who want to receive but are too stingy to give. You stupid, stupid girl." Octavia snapped off a short-left jab, stunning the woman into near unconsciousness then circled, grabbing her into a vicious chokehold that would've made any big-city police department proud. Sommar slipped into darkness just as her bladder released.

O'Sullivan carried two steaming large cups of black coffee as he walked across the motel parking lot in the early morning darkness towards the Sprinter van. Jon Jon was just stepping out of its sliding side door when he saw the big redheaded man the team unanimously nicknamed Hooch, after the big red mastiff that was Tom Hanks' partner in the movie *Turner & Hooch*. Jon Jon looked at the time on his phone and saw it was 0530 hours. "What's up?" O'Sullivan asked as he extended the second cup of coffee. "Did you sleep well?" Jon Jon rolled his bunched shoulders and cracked his neck. "I thought I was getting an early start, but I guess not." He took a sip from the cup. "My back's a little tight, other than that I'm fine Hooch."

They grew quiet as both sipped at their cups while watching the oncoming sunset. The men turned at the sound of multiple voices. Sammy, Jimenez, and Genie were walking their way. Jimenez was attired in her standard uniform of jeans and gym shoes, but the marshals were wearing jogging suits with reflective stripes. They greeted the men just as O'Sullivan was handing Jon Jon his room key and telling him to hurry up and shower. "Good morning, there's a nice Joint a half-block east of here. We can all get a bite to eat there and map out our strategy."

At the very moment they were finishing their breakfast, Octavia was teaching Sommar how to be a better hostess. By 0700 hours, Jimenez and O'Sullivan were parked a quarter block south of the

Winthrop building's main entrance while Sammy and Genie powerwalked around the block. They fit right in with the early morning joggers, runners, and dog walkers. Mac went in and spoke to the building's head of security, then donned a grey blazer manning the desk. It was decided a loose surveillance net would be best. If Butterfly Baxter made an appearance in the lobby, she would be taken into custody. But if she didn't make one by noon, the team would discreetly breach the penthouse. If they wore on the southside instead of near Lakeshore Drive it wouldn't be a problem, but the Winthrop building's occupancy held multiple persons with eight-digit bank accounts who contribute heavily to the two biggest gangs in America- Democrats and Republicans. As much as O'Sullivan's team consider themselves outlaws in the field of law enforcement, they were not stupid enough to ruffle the feathers of the rich and powerful. At least, not without a great deal of cause.

It was around 0900 hours when Sammy and Genie started alternating half-hour shifts around the building's perimeter. It wasn't like their fugitive could spy on the ants with badges from the penthouse. Jimenez was in the backseat of the SUV playing Candy Crush while listening to Lizzo. O'Sullivan sat upfront monitoring communication traffic between team members. He glanced at his watch. If the fugitive didn't stick her head up soon, they'd have to go in. Though before that happened, he had a trick up his sleeve.

When Sommar came to she found herself in her walk-in closet tied to the leg of a heavy baroque chaise lounge with a pair of Vondera Bleau designer stockings that Pamela had given her as a gift upon returning from a European business trip. Her living nightmare was standing over her with a thick leather belt. "I found this in Pammy's closet. A man's belt, kind of butch don't you think?" Octavia looked around. "Love how you guys have separate walk-ins. Hers and hers, how cute is that!" She reached down viciously ripping the baby doll nightgown off the woman. "I'm going to get you in the mood, then you're going to do me and I mean, like I've never been done before or you're gonna get a lot more of this." Before Sommar could ask what "this" was, Octavia stuffed a piece of the torn, gown in her mouth. Many years ago, Octavia learned from Butterfly how to inflict maximum pain with minimal bruising.

Several hours later, a bloody and slightly bruised Sommar lay still, sprawled naked on the floor of her closet while her dearly insane houseguest tried on her clothes. "My breasts are a little bigger than yours, but you definitely have a nice ass like mine." Octavia could tell by her eyes that Sommar didn't understand. "Sweetie we're the same size." She was holding up a fitted silver Zenegda dress in one hand and a yellow Alexander McQueen with a flared skirt and light bodice in the other. "Sunshine, in memory of you and our wonderful time together, I think I'll wear the McQueen. Whadda ya think?" Seemingly in shock Sommar nodded in agreement. Any defiance had been squeezed from the young wife's soul within the first hour. She was now thoroughly compliant.

"How about this nice wide patent leather bell and those black patent leather Gucci stilettos I saw in Pammy's closet?" She spun towards Sommar and spied a yellow Marc Jacobs tote with black trim. "Yes, yes, yes darling! Ab-so-fucking-lute-ly divine." A half-hour later, Octavia was dressed and speaking to Sommar. "We're Just waiting on wifey to do an E.T. and phone home. After that. I'll be out of your pretty blonde hair."

The distraught young woman who was tied up and gagged just continued to nod glassy-eyed. Octavia hated to have to tie her up again, but she couldn't have her alerting the authorities. Especially after they've grown so close. The ringing cellphone startled them both. "Oh look! My whore and your wife." She placed the call on speaker. "Hi sugah, Sommar and I were just saying our goodbyes." Pamela could hear the sadistic glee in Butterfly's voice. "Let me speak to my wife." Octavia applied a streak of color to her bottom lip and checked it in the mirror. "Pamela, dear sweet Pamela, in due time. Let's not make demands of me. You know how much I loathe that. Besides, she's a little tied up right now." Pamela's voice lowered to almost a whisper. "Is she alive?"

"Is she lively you ask? Well, she was a little tight at first, but once I applied sufficient lubrication, we got along very well." The maniacal laughter on the other end of the phone shook Pamela to her core. Octavia modeled the Marc Jacobs tote then decided it was too much yellow and tossed it aside casually.

"You know Connecticut, you should have treated me better. Your abominable hospitality last night was shamefully atrocious. No bottle or oral service, and on top of that you're making me seek lodging elsewhere. How dare you! Thankfully your beautiful wife

recognized the slight and apologized profusely. I mean, over and over and over, until I was drained and dripping with gratitude from her gracious generosity."

"You fucking bitch! Crazy, twisted, unhinged bitch!" Octavia grew serious. "Don't interrupt me, Pamela. If you do, I'll have to address my grievance with your wife." "I'm sorry, please forgive me. Can I speak with Sommar?" Octavia checked her hair in the dressing mirror while smoothing a hand over the fabric of her taught stomach. "I told you she's busy. Now I have to go. You'll find your wife working out some things in the closet. Why hasn't she come out yet? That's a question for another day." She pressed END.

Turning to Sommar who was curled up on the floor with tears welling in her eyes Octavia said, "Sweetie, momma has to go. Even though our tryst has been short, I'll cherish it for eternity." Sommar's eyes grew wider as they followed the insane woman's movements. A warm hand touched her cheek just as a tear fell. Octavia caught it on her index finger and brought it to her lips. "Precious. Precious and sweet." The young wife continued watching until the woman's footfalls faded. That's when she realized she'd been holding her breath and exhaled thinking, she never wanted to meet another friend of Pamela's as long as she lived.

Ten minutes to 1200 hours, the team was gathered around the Winthrop's security desk staring at the CCTV monitors that showed the lobby, inside the elevators, rooftop, and all other exits. What they didn't show were the individual floors. Pamela Nothnagel stood nervously in the midst of them. O'Sullivan and Jimenez had driven to the woman's office and explained the gravity of her situation. She claimed to have no idea that Butterfly Octavia Baxter was a fugitive from justice and agreed to cooperate fully.

The plan was for Mrs. Nothnagel to ring the penthouse bell under the guise of having lost her keys. Seeing as how Butterfly Baxter was a guest and a fugitive, it was unlikely that she would be the one opening the door. With a high probability of certainty, they expected for the other Mrs. Nothnagel to answer. When that happened, team members would pull her out into the hall, execute a search, and apprehend their fugitive. They were just about to head up when Pamela recounted to them that she was supposed to call at noon and Butterfly knew this.

Jimenez had her place the call on speaker. They heard every word. When Butterfly hung up, Jimenez was the first to speak. "She's a sociopath. We're not just dealing with some soccer mom who went sideways. This woman is seriously bent." They headed for the elevator. O'Sullivan issued orders with military precision. Pointing to the surveillance cameras he exclaimed, "Watch those cameras. Mac, Jon Jon, take the other elevator! Sammy, Genie, hit the stairwells." By the time the elevator doors opened on the penthouse floor, Jimenez and O'Sullivan had their weapons out leading the way.

When they arrived at Pamela's door they found it partially open. The detective nudged it with her toe, her gun at the ready. The big marshal gave Jimenez the point while scanning left and right for any signs of their fugitive. They cleared rooms quickly until they reached the master suite. The two found Sommar Nothnagel tied up and sobbing softly.

The detective snatched the gag from the woman's mouth. "She's gone," Sommar stammered. "What is she wearing?" O'Sullivan asked. The young woman was obviously in semi shock and slow to answer, but the big man didn't have the luxury of time. "Focus Mrs. Nothnagel! What is she wearing?" She stared up into his eyes and told him. Jimenez was linked to their comms and relayed the info. "Our fugitive, African American female Butterfly Baxter is wearing a yellow dress. She has to be close by. I repeat, she's wearing a yellow dress!"

Jimenez heard Jon Jon and Mac announcing themselves. "U.S. Marshals!" The men stated this several times while clearing the other end of the penthouse. The detective left O'Sullivan with the woman and loudly declared who she was as she ran through the spacious apartment passing Mac and into the hall where she saw Sammy and Genie moving rapidly towards her with a questioning look on their faces that immediately gave her an answer. "Call CPD in and let's get a floor to floor search going!" Where was this crazy bitch!

Outside in the van, Ferret was taking in all of the communications traffic when he caught a flash of yellow in his peripheral. Looking out the windshield he saw a black woman wearing a yellow dress walking hurriedly away from the Winthrop. "Listen, I've got a possible on our fugitive. African American female wearing a yellow dress heading west. O'Sullivan caught the dispatch. There was no way he was going to ride the bench for this takedown. He ordered Jon Jon to stay with Mrs. Nothnagel while the rest of them took the elevator downstairs with Jimenez.

In the lobby, Jimenez only paused long enough to whisper into Pamela Nothnagel's ear, "Go be with your wife. She needs you." Outside she climbed into the driver's seat of the SUV. O'Sullivan glared at her until she wordlessly slid into the passenger seat. Mac jumped in the backseat with his head on a swivel.

The Ferret was driving the van with the other two female marshals riding shotgun. At the moment, they were driving parallel to each other on different westbound streets but neither saw any signs of their fugitive. "Get me the location of the nearest L train station." Mac hollered at his boss over the roar of the engine. "There's one two blocks south of our current position." He pointed to their left, "If she cut through the park, we could've missed her. The station's on the other side!"

"Call Jon Jon and see if either of them has a number on Baxter!" O'Sullivan was definitely off his game. That should've been the first thing he asked the wife.

It took a couple of minutes, but Jon Jon recited the number out loud that Pamela Nothnagel had. It was from the cellphone Butterfly called from when she first showed on the Magnificent Mlle. O'Sullivan told the Ferret to ping the phone and get them a concrete GPS, but he was driving the Sprinter van. Before any adjustments could be made. Genie had a visual on that yellow dress moving fast out of the park and heading for the L platform. O'Sullivan and Jimenez had just turned onto the avenue when they both saw a flash of yellow streaking up the station's stairs.

They all knew that the train would be moving away from the stop before they could put feet on the ground. The team leader slammed on the brakes and told Mac to make sure it wasn't a feint. He jumped from the SUV before it came to a complete stop and took off at a dead run. "You got any lights and sirens on this tug? If so, you better light'em up." Jimenez watched as the big marshal started flipping switches when suddenly a blaring noise ripped the lunch hour traffic.

The powerful eight-cylinder engine overtook the van with the other marshals in it and was at least five car lengths ahead of the train. Jimenez was pointing out the L station platform up ahead when a Cadillac smashed into O'Sullivan's side of the SUV.

The SUV was sent careening until it came to rest sideways blocking traffic in both directions. "Are you straight?" Jimenez couldn't see any visible signs of injury, but when the marshal unhooked his seatbelt and tried the door, it was jammed. There wasn't any time to waste as she leaped from the damaged vehicle and took off towards the platform. Over the cacophony of traffic noise, O'Sullivan thought he heard her tell him to, "Catch up!"

Jimenez heard fast-moving feet and glanced back. Marshal Eugenia Proctor, aka Genie, was gaining on her. Midway up the stairs the detective sincerely thought that she was loo old far this kind of shit. At the top step, she saw the train's doors sliding shut. If Butterfly was there, she would find her. Her eyes started scanning the crowd when Genie showed up beside her. They decided to split up and hurriedly went in different directions.

She couldn't believe her luck as the bright yellow dress darted smoothly through pedestrian traffic moving to the opposite set of stairs about twenty feet ahead. Jimenez drew her service weapon holding it low at her thigh. "FREEZE! Don't you fucking move! A Chicago patrolman was pointing his gun at her. "Drop the gun or I'll light you up like Sears Tower!" Genie saw the commotion, but Jimenez threw her a head nod in the direction of their fugitive and she stayed on task. "Slowly raise your hands and drop the gun!" She raised her hands while responding calmly, "I'm not dropping my weapon risking an accidental discharge officer. I'm a homicide detective on loan to a federal fugitive recovery team. My ID and badge are in my left jacket pocket."

The young white patrolman's hands were shaking like dice at a crap table. "Bitch! Either drop the gun, or I drop you!" Without warning the officer felt cold, brutal steel pressing into his temple. "I'm U.S. Marshal Terrence Roderick O'Sullivan of a fugitive recovery task force out of the southeastern district of Michigan. Holster your weapon son and we won't have a clusterfuck where I'm explaining to the evening news and my superiors why I had to knock some sense into an overly aggressive cop with a federal hydro shock round." The patrolman slowly lowered his gun.

While Jimenez and O'Sullivan were producing their credentials, Genie walked up with a woman in a yellow dress. She was not their fugitive. Bernadette Holmes was rushing away from the area when leaving her job as a nanny for a family living up the block from the Winthrop building because she was late for a doctor's appointment. Although she shared the same curvaceous frame as Butterfly Baxter, up close the Holmes woman didn't have the other woman's natural beauty.

Even though the old man driving the Cadillac that T-boned O'Sullivan and Jimenez seemed fine, he was taken to Cook County General Hospital as a precautionary measure. By the time things got smoothed over with CPD, Butterfly's trail was colder than a polar bear in the Arctic Circle. Back inside the penthouse, Jimenez tried getting any useful information out of the Nothnagel women she could, but Sommar was obviously still in shock, refusing any medical attention and didn't want to pursue charges. When the detective suggested that the young wife rest she noticed the alarm on her face. "We're still checking some things in the master, how 'bout you use one of your guestrooms. The relief on the woman's face was almost palpable.

Pamela and Jimenez were standing outside of the bedroom where they deposited Sommar. "Don't you think she needs to see a doctor?" Pamela motioned for the detective to follow her. O'Sullivan and most of his team were quartered in the kitchen trying to come up with a lead of any kind when the door to the study closed blocking them out. "Are we speaking off the record or do I need counsel?" Jimenez watched the woman position herself at her desk in an effort to re-establish some sense of control that Butterfly had ripped from her life. "Off the record? Of course. I Just want to find Butterfly Baxter before she hurts anyone else."

"Octavia Winters. That's the name of her alter ego. She's more dangerous than you could ever imagine." Using hypothetical terms, Pamela Nothnagel conveyed a story so dark and twisted that even the hardened homicide detective was thrown. "She's not only super smart, she's also cunning. Butterfly didn't hurt my wife to hurt my wife, she hurt my wife to hurt me and teach me a lesson I'd forgotten."

"What lesson is that Mrs. Nothnagel?"

"Never defy the H-B-l-C. Since our college days, she's either the head bitch in charge or scheming to become it. She's been my lover, friend, madame, and abuser, but throughout the course of our relationship the only thing she has been consistently without fail is my enemy."

Jimenez was anxious for any lead and this conversation was seemingly a bust. "How does this help me capture her?" The wife looked earnestly into Jimenez's eyes before responding. "I've learned over the years that to have a greater chance of defeating an enemy, you must know them better than anyone or anything else on earth."

Jimenez leaned closer. "Okay, give me something." Pamela smoothed her hands over her hair and said, "Whatever you think she's going to do, she won't. Whatever you think she'll never do because it seems too improbable or impossible, she more than likely will. Butterfly is more daring than a Hollywood stunt woman on crystal meth and ten times smarter than anyone I've ever met without even trying. She loves to perform, and the world is all a stage."

The woman could see the impatience growing in the detective. "There are only two things she loves. The first is revenge. In her mind, even the smallest slight must be accounted for. The second is her son. I'm not speaking in any normal sense, no sociopath can really love. But she loves the thought of him as her property." Pamela Nothnagel made it clear to Jimenez that they were in that order. Revenge, then Albany. Just then there was a knock at the study door.

Before Jimenez could respond, O'Sullivan stuck his big redhead in asking to speak with her. He whispered hurriedly in her ear then pulled the door shut on the women. Suspiciously, Pamela asked, "Is there a lead of some kind?" The detective nodded before replying, "They believe she's headed west." Pamela stood from behind her desk. "Only if the opportunity for revenge and Albany are there waiting for her. If not, I sincerely doubt it." Jimenez's gut was in total agreement.

She spoke to the woman a short while longer. "I have to go but I appreciate your cooperation and rest assured my report will reflect that as well as how I believe Butterfly Baxter duped you. You and your wife had no idea she was a fugitive." "What about my past activities?" It looks a second to register before Jimenez spoke. "Not my jurisdiction, and I do believe the statute of limitations has expired. Besides, far as I'm concerned, it was more honorable than your current profession." She placed a comforting hand on the other woman's shoulder and advised her to get her wife some help. On the way out, Pamela reminded the detective to be careful and thanked her for her concern.

Outside of the building, the team was loitering next to the Sprinter van and an identical SUV like the one damaged in the crash. "Where'd the new wheels come from?" Jimenez asked. Genie dangled the key fob in the air before telling her it was a loaner from the CFO of the FBI. Jimenez rolled her eyes, "You guys love your acronyms."

O'Sullivan told her that the Ferret pinged the cellphone supposedly in possession of their fugitive and that it was heading southwest before the signal ended. For a good while, it was at a strip mall near Halstead in the hundreds. "CPD showed up flashing the fugitive's photo around and got a hit with a gypsy cab driver. The locals are trying to pull surveillance video, but they tell us most of the exterior cameras are damaged and a few of the stores only have 'em for show." The illegal cabdriver did recall having a conversation with Butterfly Baxter where she talked about going to Las Vegas after stopping to see the arches in St Louis. Genie recounted this to Jimenez before O'Sullivan asked for a private chat.

"We're going to chase her down. You're welcome to join us. Hell, I can even get you a federal check as a consultant if you want it. She refused the offer and told him that she'd rather run the case from back in Detroit. Although it was technically the truth, in her gut she knew for almost a certainty that Butterfly wasn't headed west. Her conversation with the gypsy cab driver was a fine bit of misdirection. "Where's my go bag?" He pointed to the backseat of the SUV. She pulled it from the truck, quickly checked the contents, and told him that she was on the next Greyhound bus home.

The marshal screwed up his face. "Granted, your city has its problems but don't tell me money is so tight on a local level that you have to take the bus. Shit, I'll buy you a plane ticket, you'll be home in an hour instead of six hours or worse." She politely refused.

"I hate TSA, and a bus ride can be oddly therapeutic after stressing over trying to catch this crazy bitch." She wanted to tell the big redhead that he and his team were on a wild goose chase, but the man was just as stubborn as she was. "I'll find my way to the bus station. You guys just get on Baxter's trail and keep me updated." She shook everyone's hand except for O'Sullivan. Jimenez gave him a hearty hug whispering in his ear, "See you later Hooch." The big man smiled, "Take care Detective Sergeant Jimenez."

The entire team watched her walk off, but it was Genie who broke the silence. "If you didn't tap that, you really should boss. She likes you." He gave her a menacing glare before telling everyone to load up.

9 FLOAT LIKE A BUTTERFLY

Rodney pulled out a large ring of keys, found the correct one, and was using it to unlock the service elevator when he heard a woman's voice ask for a ride downstairs. He said, "No". Without turning all the way around, he looked at the stiletto encased feet and was a little irritated they weren't moving away from him. Rodney hated talking to these rich assholes. They were supposed to be well-bred, but to him, they were just a different breed.

"Dis issa service elevator used for building maintenance only." He looked down and back, and to his dismay the pretty feet were still planted. Ready to tell the woman with the expensive shoes to beat it, he turned all the way around and saw a beautiful woman crying softly. "I'm sorry Miss, this here elevator car ain't for people like you. It's for service people like me."

Rodney could be a bit of a dick, but he was a gentleman first. Octavia let the waterworks flow. "Whassa matta Miss?" She wiped gently at her eyes so as not to smear what little makeup she wore. "Oh, I must look a mess! Please forgive me, this is embarrassing." Octavia inhaled, straining the fabric of her dress with her breasts. "My prick of an ex is stalking me. Right now, he's in the lobby waiting on me to show myself. I can't face the man. He's an absolute abusive jackass."

Placing a manicured finger on his chest, Octavia ran a nail under the man's name tag. He felt stirrings that usually took a pill and at least a half-hour of porn to Ignite. "Rodney, I need your help. I mean, I could call the cops, but who wants the hassle?" The maintenance man was so busy staring at her cleavage, he almost forgot the woman was in distress. At that moment the elevator arrived, and the doors slid open with a welcoming whoosh. She took him by an arm pressing her full firm breasts against his body while guiding him into the elevator car. "Wait a minute Miss!"

She watched cautiously as he quickly scooped up his toolbox and returned to her side. "Do you mind if I call you Rod? Rodney seems so formal." She didn't give him time to answer as she stepped closer and kissed him lightly on his ear. "Listen Rod, I'm very thankful to have finally come across a real man such as yourself." The subsequent throaty, "Thank you" was enough to make him her co-conspirator. "Now tell me how we're going to dodge my ex."

In his fifty-plus years, Rodney Jalisco had dealt with all kinds, past, and present. But when this gorgeous black broad flashed the founding father, Benjamin Franklin then stuffed it in his pant pocket fondling the family jewels in the process, he would've carried her out to O'Hare on his back. "You'll never even have to lay eyes on the bastard. Do you gotta car?" Octavia pursed her full cupid bow lips while shaking her head from side to side. "It's okay cause I'm about to take my lunch break and my van's parked at the rear service dock."

"But won't we be seen on camera by security at the front desk? I don't want you getting into any trouble because of me..." He quickly explained that he knew how to avoid every surveillance camera, in and outside the building. "Don't worry Miss, no one'll see you at all."

Octavia knew that the way to a man's heart was his dick. Hugging him close, she gave him another quick peck. This time on the lips. If there had been an ex stalking her, Rodney was sufficiently primed to snatch a hammer from his toolbox and beat the son of a bitch's brains out.

The van smelled of old corned beef sandwiches, grease, and Ax body wash. She didn't mind as she slipped out of sight in the cargo area where she stayed until they were well away from the building. He dropped her on Michigan Avenue. From there she made it to a strip mall in south Chicago. It was time to blend in.

The authorities probably had a good idea of what she was wearing, so she stopped at a department store. As much as she hated to do it, Octavia traded in the beautiful Alexander McQueen for tight jeans, tee-shirt, jacket, and gym shoes. While in the dressing room, she smoothed back her luxurious mane of dark hair and pulled it into a ponytail but didn't change clothes just yet. At the counter waiting on her items to be rung up, she snagged a pair of cheap paparazzi shades compliments of the five-finger discount. Thanks to handyman Rodney, she not only made it out of the building but safely away.

Oddly, Octavia was still excited from her morning tryst with Sommar and almost called the woman. Then it dawned on her that she'd tossed her phone in the back of that pickup. Can't be too careful with technology being the way that it is. She went to a Walmart and purchased a few disposable phones aptly nicknamed, "burners," and placed one in the secret compartment of her purse, one in her bag, and the other in her bra. It was a beautiful day. Octavia decided to walk. She caught quite a few stares from passerby's and changed her mind and decided to use public transportation, something she hadn't done since her youth. The bus took her north on Stoney Island until crossing 79th street. Octavia wanted to grab a bite to eat but needed to get out of the Windy City. She saw a gas station in the distance and headed for it. Once there she argued with the clerk about using the bathroom. He was an ass, but after she told him that her cousin was a secretary for the feds and would love to pass along information of discrimination and possible federal tax fraud for rigging pumps to her bosses, he grew extremely compliant.

In the John, she dared not sit on the toilet. Just looking at it made her vagina snap shut tighter than a clam. Octavia split open one of her store bags and stood in its center while changing clothes. After doing a precarious balancing act, she was dressed in jeans, gym shoes, and a tee-shirt so tight that her heart could be seen beating. Her final piece of clothing was a pink satin baseball jacket with the word, BEAUTIFUL emblazoned on the back.

A heavy woman in her early forties with a joyful smile said hello while passing Octavia to enter the gas station. The woman had climbed out of an older model minivan with Indiana plates. There looked to be some suitcases piled in the back. She walked closer and saw a teenage boy starting to pump the gas and asked if he was from Chicago or just visiting. The sixteen-year-old obviously liked what he saw judging by the tent in his pants. His name was Harvey. He and his mom were heading back home to Gary which was the direction Octavia was headed.

Harvey was sure to tell the woman that he was a wide receiver for the Roosevelt Crusaders varsity football team. They'd been in Chicago visiting his sick aunt. The young man was a wealth of information, telling her everything. If she gave him some sex, he'd probably be able to tell her the future. Harvey's mother, the joyful round woman returned, and Octavia introduced herself as, Debra Ann Mayes.

Mary Robinson, whom everyone called Miss Mary, listened as Octavia spun her deceitful tale of trying to make it back east. "It'll be great if you guys could take me as far as Gary. I can give you something on the gas." The woman didn't seem too sure about giving a stranger a ride. After all, they are living in dangerous times she thought. The boy tipped the scales when he said, "Moma, didn't you say we should strive to be good Christians." Octavia quickly stuffed a one-hundred-dollar bill into the woman's palm to try and further sway the woman on her side. "Well, I guess It's no harm in giving a pretty girl a lift." Excitedly, Harvey, the wide receiver shook off the gas nozzle and hung it on the pump.

A little over an hour later they were at a truck slop outside of Magic City. Miss Mary had to use the bathroom, so while she was gone Octavia, aka Debra Mayes, treated young Harvey to a quick hand job. Once she placed his hand on her tit and told him to grip it like a football, it took about thirty seconds for him to explode. By the time his mom was walking across the parking lot, Harvey was zipped up with a goofy grin on his face. He wanted her phone number and to be able to contact her on Instagram or Facebook. She told him to just enjoy the memory and held a finger to her lips warning him to be silent because of his approaching mom.

"Thanks, Miss Mary, I really appreciate the ride. You'd take care." The women hugged each other. "I'm gonna pray for you baby. Now you be careful out here." Octavia watched her get behind the wheel, waved at young Mr. Harvey who looked as though he were about to cry, then walked into the truck stop. Talk about hungry, she hadn't eaten anything since Sommar this morning. Being on the run worked up an appetite.

Although it was early evening, the sun still hung in the sky. No longer yellow like the dress she wore earlier, but now it was the color of fresh-squeezed orange juice. She slid into a booth scanning the crowd and spotted a couple of "dump trucks." Low-level whores who allowed the truckers to dump their bodily fluids into them for a small fee. Sitting at the counter was a handsome Indiana state trooper who resembled a young Michael Douglas, right down to the cleft in his chin.

Octavia was thinking of all manner of nasty things he could do with that beautiful chin when a waitress appeared. She gave the overworked underpaid woman a quick once over. Mid-thirties pushing fifty wearing sensible thick rubber-soled shoes with a Copper Fit wrist glove on her right hand. Underneath the black hairnet, her bleach blond dye job showed traces of her natural hair color at the roots. The woman's uniform top was extra tight to bring attention to a pair of full double D's encased in a pushup bra two sizes too small. Her name tag told Octavia all she needed to know.

Smiling brightly, she said, "Hello Amber Lynn. I'm Debra, and I'm looking to eat something really good. What do you recommend?" The tired waitress smiled back showing a gold tooth on her right upper incisor with a diamond embedded in it, then suggested the Breakfast Semi. "Is it as scrumptious as you?"

The waitress perked up, pushed her tits out, and ran her tongue over the gold. "I know it's evening, but it's good. Your choice of pancakes or French toast, four strips of bacon, two sausage links, two patties, two eggs however you want 'em, hash browns, three slices of toast, and a bowl of grits."

Octavia rubbed her stomach and asked playfully, "Only three slices of toast?" She ordered the Breakfast Semi with scrambled eggs and sweet tea. Amber Lynn stopped by several times to check on her and they chatted. Octavia was done eating and now chugging black coffee to stay alert. She observed all the males and a few of the female truckers but didn't quite find what she wanted until her third cup.

He was at the counter talking to Amber Lynn. They spoke as if they've known one another for a while. He looked around fiftyish with the look of a schoolteacher who was always hoping better days were just around the corner.

"Hey, didn't you say you were heading east and needed a ride?" Octavia looked up from her coffee. Amber Lynn's smile was forced, and she seemed a tad bit nervous.

"Sure do, why are you offering after your shift?"

"No, but you see that guy at the counter with the blazer on? Well, he's heading east and looking for some company to break the monotony." Octavia asked if she knew the guy and her answer made up her mind. "Not really. He comes in maybe once a month. Says his name's Art. Seems harmless to me but hey, I'm not the one looking for a ride."

She slid a crisp fifty-dollar bill under the ketchup bottle and stood with her bags. "Tell him I'm interested sweetie, but all that coffee has me having to pee something awful. I need to use the Jane." Octavia pointed to the money and told the waitress to keep the change, then grabbed her ass. She knew it was okay. Women like Amber Lynn crave attention of any kind. In fact, women like her were starving for it. After using the bathroom and freshening up her makeup, she looked for Art. He was gone and the waitress wasn't anywhere in sight. Damn!

Octavia walked towards the entrance and saw Amber Lynn smoking an E-cigarette through the glass. "What's up girl? Where'd my ride go?" Amber Lynn pointed to a mint green Subaru parked a few rows up and left of the door. "He's waiting for you." She thanked the woman who was nervously puffing on the E-cigarette and hurriedly walked over to the car. Leaning down into the open window and seeing Art, Octavia thought of all the trouble she could get into with the little man and how much trouble the little man might be.

10 ALL YOU REALLY NEED IS ART

Arthur Millings sat inside his twelve-year-old Subaru Forester wailing on his chocolate treat. He and Amber Lynn had an arrangement. Anytime there was a promising piece of tail at the Truck Stop Diner, she'd call him up. By promising he meant young women in their late teens to early thirties without a lot of wear and tear. His game was simple. Art would offer the ladies a ride. Usually, they were heading east, but it didn't matter because he had a sex spot covering east and another covering west. That's what he called his motel rooms.

Whatever drugs they were into, he readily supplied along with a little something to make them more pliable. That something was a cocktail of Rohypnol and a strong prescription muscle relaxer. After using them for his sexual enjoyment, he'd leave them in the motel room. When they woke up they'd find a note thanking them for a wild night of sex and fifty dollars. Most of his victims couldn't remember anything that happened, but those who did spend their time trying to forget. Who cares about bad women with questionable reputations? Even in the {Me Too} era, they were afraid to come forward.

Unknown to Art, he and a man named Sanford Tolliver were soulmates. The unexpected sound of the woman's voice startled him. Although he had surreptitiously checked out the woman inside, it was something special to see her up close. He unlocked the door, "Get on in young lady," but she didn't get in. Leaning down through the window she said seductively, "Only if you're going east."

"Sure, the waitress told me you need a lift?"

"I sure do!" She told him before climbing in and tossing her bag in the back then placing her purse in her lap. He motioned for her to put the seatbelt on. "Forgive me for being rude. My name's Debra Mayes."

He extended his hand while introducing himself and thought her hand was uncomfortably hot to the touch. The closeness and heady smell of her perfume and warm breath was arousing.

Art pulled out onto the interstate while telling her his bullshit story. "I'm visiting my sister in Port Huron who's sick. She's been dealing with Lupus, so once a month I spend a few days checking on her and taking care of her needs." Art made sure to tell his new acquaintance that he always stopped at a motel to rest. She offered to help drive, but when he asked about a current driver's license, she smoothly changed the subject. "I'm fine with a little rest up myself. I'm only going as far as the turnoff to Toledo." A Kelly Clarkson song that Art liked came on the radio. Turning up the volume, he mused that tonight was going to be very interesting.

Octavia slipped fully into her role as Debra Ann Mayes. Art wanted to know her story, and Debbie had a doozy. The twenty-seven year-old was a hustler from nowhere, born from the reproductive organs of nobody's. At fifteen she escaped foster care and its many abuses only to plug in with a bad crowd. Before she knew it, Debra was speeding down awful avenues in the world of sex trafficking. She was snorting nose candy to stay up and popping opioid pills to come down. For a while, everything was one big party, but after coming close to being convicted of a felony she decided a change was needed. Waitress, stripper, whore, receptionist. Uber driver and now drifter. Debra Ann was a good person who'd been through some bad shit and thus far survived.

They were just entering the city limits of Ann Arbor, home to the University of Michigan. "Art, I'm sorry to disappoint you if you were thinking I was some decent, young woman."

"Just because you've been through some indecent situations doesn't make you indecent." She twisted towards him as far as her seatbelt would allow.

"Listening to you talk about your job and how you take care of your sister makes me think there are still good people in the world. I'm just not one of them." Art rubbed her thigh. Beautiful with a load of baggage and low self-esteem. This was almost too easy. "I'm not as good as you make me out to be."

Octavia glared at him as If his admission stunned her. "What kind of bad things have you ever done?"

Shrugging he told her, "I've done some drugs and ... I hope this doesn't make you feel uncomfortable, but I've frequented prostitutes in the past." Now it was her turn to run his thigh. "We've all made mistakes. Don't beat yourself up." Her hand crept further up until it was resting on his member, then it was gone.

Checking his mirrors Art took the exit. Ten minutes later they were pulling into the back parking lot of the Pine Crest Motel where his friend Glover was the night manager. In exchange for a free room off the books and a witness if any of the women made a fuss, Art took pictures of his victims in all manner of lewd positions and shared them with the man. "We don't have to check-in or anything?" He grabbed their bags from the back.

"No. I have an arrangement. I call ahead. The key should be right under those pinecones on the door." Sure enough, she watched him lift up the wreath of pinecones on room 109 and a key fell out. He unlocked the door and cut on the light.

11 THE SHORT BUS

Jimenez was texting her partner Gleason which felt kind of weird because she was definitely a soloist. She told him in short to double the patrols around Dr. Daniels's apartment building and when he inquired about what went wrong, she texted; (F-ed up! Butterfly dodged the net). Her bus had just pulled out of Kalamazoo where she was propositioned no less than five times for sex and asked four times if she wanted to buy dime bags of crack or heroin. Politely declining she made her way through the throng of travelers, sex addicts, and drug dealers while noting all the players, even snapping a few discreet photos. As a professional courtesy, she'd drop an email to Kalamazoo PD.

This particular bus ride made her think she was on the short bus. That small yellow school bus which carried the children who had learning disabilities. Somehow that woman got out of the Winthrop building undetected. Chicago PD did a top to bottom search and found neither hide nor hair of Butterfly. O'Sullivan called about twenty minutes ago. His team was headed to East St Louis, Illinois and if there were no signs of their fugitive they'd go as far as St Louis, Missouri. If they didn't catch a whiff of the woman there, they'd be heading back to Detroit. The two promised to keep each other updated and hung up.

The young woman sitting next to Jimenez was awfully nervous. She replaced an older gentleman from Champaign who was visiting his daughter in a suburb of Kalamazoo. He talked about the great jazz trumpeter Miles Davis for most of their ride together. Other than that, he seemed like a nice guy. The detective gave her the once over. Caucasian, anywhere from nineteen to twenty-two, about five foot four, one hundred thirty pounds. Her brunette hair was done in a shoulder-length bob with red highlights. She kept her left hand up to her cheek to cover the burgundy bruise underneath her eye. The young woman cautiously accepted the hand being offered. "Hi, my name's Jaysena. I'm heading back to Detroit from the Windy City."

"Ericka, I'm Ericka".

For the rest of the trip, the two talked and the detective's mind was taken off of her current case. It took Jimenez's considerable interrogation skills to milk the truth from the baby next to her. Really, that's all the young woman was. Although she looked a little older than what she appeared, Ericka had just turned seventeen last month. Jimenez was only off by a few years, but at that stage of life, a few years were monumental.

It seems Ericka was driven to Kalamazoo by her supposed boyfriend, a creep named Battle, under the guise of visiting his cousin. The truth was much more sinister. Once there, he wanted her to turn some tricks to make him some money. When she refused, he let his cousin and two of his boys break her in by raping her while he watched and directed the action. As soon as they left her alone, she was able to steal some money from one of the men's discarded pants pockets, climb out the window, and escape.

"Once he finds out I'm gone he'll probably be waiting at the bus station in Detroit." She turned to Jimenez with tears streaking her cheeks and in almost a whisper added, "I thought he loved me."

Jimenez played it cool for the time being, but if this Battle jerk was waiting, he would get the war he wanted. Her gut was telling her it was going to be a long night. She encouraged Ericka to take a nap. It wasn't long before the young girl's head was resting on Jimenez's shoulder.

The detective stared out the bus window thinking about the case. Dr. Daniels, the strange hitman dying of cancer turned informant and her fugitive, Butterfly Baxter. Something about this entire case was off. Something scratching just beneath the surface of her consciousness trying to break through but not strong enough. Right when she thought she had grasped a thread to unravel the mystery, her phone vibrated against her chest. Reaching into her inside pocket and retrieving it, she pressed send.

"Hello, my lovely Latina!" Jimenez felt as though she'd been hit with a large dose of epinephrine. She jolted alert in her seat. Quickly looking at the caller ID she was crestfallen when it read 'PRIVATE.' "Who is this?" The laughing was beautiful. It almost made the detective smile. "You are so cute! You know exactly who this is. Here I am, balls deep in some tight virgin booty, and all I can think about is you. Stop playing coy."

"Okay, you crazy bitch! Did you really have to assault the Nothnagel woman?"

"Is that what she said? It was consensual. Sommar came so much it was like a spring thaw. She was dehydrated from orgasming. Hell, I had to give her Pedialyte."

"Sick fuck! I'm going to find you and it won't end well." Jimenez could hear someone in the background in obvious distress. "Don't worry about me, Chiquita…"

"What are you doing?"

"You mean, who am I doing? Well, I'm actually admiring a little art and thinking about me and you."

"Turn yourself in. Butterflies don't do so well in jars."

There was that laughter again, but in the background was still that vigorous grunting. "Catch you later detective."

Jimenez's voice was low and deadly. "Not if I catch you first."

12 STING LIKE A BEE ... ITCH!

For all of Octavia's ruthless viciousness, she was green when it came to schemes of this kind. Art was a predator of a different sort. He had already prepared a drink for them that would no doubt knock them out. They'd surely wake up with sore orifices. Back at the Truck Slop Diner, Butterfly sat by silently and watched Amber Lynn and Art interact. They knew each other much better than the bleach blond let on. Octavia could be full of herself and not pay attention to the details. That's where the devil was. Right there in the details.

Art didn't ask enough questions about his passenger before agreeing to give up a ride. Why would he take a waitress's word that he hardly knew? No man would. He thought Octavia or Debra Ann Mayes was prey. She might be, but Butterfly was not. In fact, Butterfly was adept at predatory behavior. That's how she was able to spot the asshole spiking their drink. Right then and there she made an executive decision and took over.

The right hook was powerful as it connected with Art's left ear. He went down like the sack of shit he was. Dizzy to the point of nausea with his equilibrium thrown off, he was virtually helpless as Butterfly opened his goody bag and found a pair of leather restraints. They were better than handcuffs because they left no marks.

After pulling him to the bed she took off his clothes, everything except for his undershirt. She also found a ball gag and put it on him when he started screaming, "Glover!" over and over. He had nipple clamps, butt plugs, vibrators of all sizes, and bottles of oils and ointments. Butterfly's favorite toy was a fat ten-inch strap-on ribbed vibrator. She showed Art.

"We're going to have some fun. If you don't cooperate I'll hurt you." She reached for him and he kicked her in her left breast. "Didn't I just tell you what would happen if you didn't cooperate!" With uncanny speed, she dodged to the side of the queen-sized bed and grabbed the chain tethered to his restraints pulling his arms upward. The pain was so intense that he almost passed out. With her free hand, she grabbed his testicles, squeezing them until the muscles in his thighs and buttocks strained with tension. "Listen, every time you're a bad boy, I'm making lemonade, and the only way to make good lemonade is freshly squeezed lemons." Butterfly gripped his testicles again. Art passed out.

While he was out, she went through his things. The most interesting was the laptop. When he came to, she was sitting naked in a chair next to the bed wearing the massive strap-on. He could feel something wet between his buttocks. "I'm gonna need your password. If I take out that ball gag and you say anything other than your password, I'll hurt you. If I have to, I will drag your scrawny butt into the bathroom and waterboard you like you're a terrorist." She pulled out the gag and he tried negotiating. The gag went back in and she sat on his waist. After squeezing his testicles for a few minutes, she asked again. This time he was compliant. CHERRY POPPA all caps.

Sitting back in the chair, she casually swiped right as she scrolled through the lewd photos. Art had no imagination, but he was hung. There were some videos, but she didn't have the time to watch them. Hell, she was excited enough. Setting aside the laptop she walked close to the bed. "Blow me! If you scream again, I'll do more than hurt you. I'll shred your spirit." She pulled out the gag and replaced it with the latex phallus. Art tentatively took it into his mouth. "Look at me while you suck me off. It turns me on." Wide-eyed with fear he fellated Butterfly.

"See that wasn't so bad." Butterfly replaced the gag. "This is going to probably hurt a little, and you look like a screamer." With his hands still restrained behind his back, she slapped him hard on his buttocks leaving a clear red handprint. "Get up on your knees, arch that back. I want that pink ass pointed up high!" The wetness he felt earlier was an anal lubricant.

"Sodomy is barbaric, in a sexy way. Now relax and just let it glide in." She was pounding his guts like a jackhammer and all he could do was take it. The two times he tried to stop her from impaling him, she hurt him so bad that he wished he were dead.

"Where's my phone?" Butterfly pulled out slowly. "Don't soil yourself or I'll make you eat every drop." Art believed her totally. This bitch was insane!

He watched her got a phone from her purse along with a business card. "I need to orgasm something awful." She dialed and put the phone on speaker, while it was ringing, she told him, "Remember that the more you tense up, the greater the pain."

Art heard the entire conversation. For the first time in his life, he knew what real fear felt like. Her voice was casual, but her thrusts were angry. When she hung up, he felt strong hands gripping his waist. "Back dat ass up Chiquita!" Art was terrified and barely moved. "If you don't back your ass up, I'm going to tie a string around your balls and keep feeding you those erectile enhancement pills until you burst."

He was crying in earnest now as he backed into the huge vibrator. Something was telling him he wouldn't survive the night. "That's right Chiquita, make mommy feel good!" Twenty minutes later, Butterfly turned him onto his back and fed him his fettle stay hard pills then spent some time going through the rest of his things.

"Artie! You've been a really bad boy. From the looks of it you've raped dozens of women." She was fondling his genitals.
"Unfortunately for you, there's always someone worse and we are that someone Art." She went over to the dresser. "I found your coke. It's pretty good." Butterfly scooped a hefty pile onto one of the takeout menus provided by the motel. When she turned around the man was as hard as concrete. "Nice woody! Pretty impressive for a dipshit from Indiana."

Butterfly stuck a fingernail into the powdery narcotic, taking a healthy snort up each nostril then thought, "Fuck it!" and stuck her nose in it inhaling loudly. Imitating Al Pacino's character in the movie Scarface, Butterfly said, "Okay, I reloaded!" Then she shoved about three grams worth of the drug up Art's nostrils before slipping him on a condom.

"I gotta be honest, I'm horny. I've been so tense lately. Guess what? Me and my bestie are going to fuck you to death, and we haven't even been properly introduced. The name's Fly. Butter Fly! Get it? Like Bond, James Bond."

Several hours later Art was still erect and in great pain. Even though the restraints were comfortable, his arms hurt, especially with the nymphomaniac bouncing up and down on him like a trampoline. Before this night he loved sex, now he wished he'd never heard of it. "Artie, that was a real workout, but I have to get going. I really enjoyed myself, thanks." She climbed off of him and slapped his member. "Impressive, but my bestie wants a word with you."

Maybe it was the cocaine coupled with fear which caused him to see what he was now seeing. The woman stood at the foot of the bed in front of him rolling her shoulders and cracking her neck. A metamorphosis seemed to be taking place. She appeared angrier and her facial features were slightly different. Art was scared. He wanted to beg for forgiveness, swear he'd never take advantage of another woman, but the ball gag prevented this. Even if he could talk, he doubted it would matter.

"Hello, Arthur! You were going to drug me, rape me? Then what?" His eyes grew wide as saucers. "Don't act like you don't know who I am!" She slapped him hard across the face then walked over to the dresser where a sandwich bag of coke still sat. She took a couple of snorts and wiped at her nose. "I started to overdose you, but cocaine Isn't your drug of choice. It isn't what you're addicted to is it? Your drug is sex. Well, let's see if you can overdose on it because I'm gonna give you enough to last an eternity."

Octavia mounted his face and just sat on it. Art bucked violently like a bronco for a minute or two but his energy was quickly depleted. With the ball gag already secured in his mouth, he could only breathe through his nose. A nose that was firmly covered with her vagina.

Fear, cocaine, or pure adrenaline, Art wasn't sure which was responsible for his rapidly beating heart. The tingling sensation shot up his left arm and crept into the pectoral muscle causing a sharp spasm. Octavia raised up a little allowing him to catch a few snatches of breath. It wouldn't do for the coroner to find aggressive hemorrhaging in his eyes. The combination of erectile enhancement pills, coke, and fear were far too much for Art as a massive heart attack claimed his life. Arthur Milling's final thought was that he'd been screwed to death.

It was still dark out when they left. Each took turns cleaning the body and the room. Butterfly unhooked the large vibrator from the strap-on harness and left it on the bed, removed the condom, and placed his hand around his member. Octavia emptied most of the coke out of the baggie into the toilet but left some on the dresser. She took his laptop though left his bag of tricks. The scene was set! Middle-aged man parties himself into a heart attack. Butterfly placed some money in his wallet to throw off any possible investigation. If something nefarious was up, surely, they'd taken his money and valuables.

They made sure not to leave a single trace of themselves. They checked the room four more times because you could never be too sure. Octavia turned the latch so the door would automatically lock when she closed it and left the key on the nightstand. Thankfully, the dependable Subaru started right up as they kept their pretty head down until well past the front office. The night manager was nodding at the desk as the Subaru quietly pulled out and made its way to Detroit. Chicago would be surprised to see them.

13 MYSTERY MAN SOLVED

It seemed like it was barely the last shift instead of a couple of days ago that she was right here doing the very same thing. There was almost a feeling of déjà Vu. Lt. Templeton sat with her and Gleason receiving a report on what happened concerning Butterfly Baxter evading arrest again. Jimenez explained to Templeton the conversation she had with Pamela Nothnagel, along with her current theory that their fugitive wasn't running away from them. "She's not afraid of us. It's all a game to her. One she's winning right now. When we spoke, she was sociopathic calm as if she were thoroughly enjoying herself."

Gleason interjected with the reason why he couldn't get a backtrace going. "The call was routed through the internet. Calling 'private' only blocks the number from the called party, not the phone carrier. I was able to trace the number to a burner cellphone, that's now either off or destroyed by now."

"We have no idea where she is, but I discussed things over with Gleason and we're pretty confident she'll make a play for her son, Albany."

Templeton wrung his hands together. "What do you need from me?"

"Round the clock surveillance units on Dr. Daniels' apartment."

The lieutenant grew thoughtful. "I'll give you three people for forty-eight hours and that's it. If nothing comes of the Baxter woman by then we'll have to move on to other matters and just wait for her to screw up."

The detectives were getting ready to leave when Templeton motioned them back in their seats. "Aren't you gonna tell me about the incident at the Greyhound station Detective Sergeant Jimenez?" Sarcastically, he went on, "Like why I've got one asshole at Detroit Receiving Hospital in critical condition with a GSW and another with a broken jaw over at County?" Gleason tried easing out of the office. "Not so fast detective! Where in the hell do you think you're going?

You were on the scene too, weren't you?"

Gleason sat down but didn't answer. Jimenez took this as her cue to take the lead. She began recounting how she met seventeen-year-old Ericka Nichols on the bus leaving Kalamazoo. "When the two of us walked out of the bus station on Howard and 6th street, we were approached by two males. One Shawn Dougherty, Caucasian aka Big Shawn and a Latino, later identified as Benito Battle aka Bobby Battle. Both perps are from southwest Detroit."

She went on to explain how the men tried forcibly taking the minor and when she intervened, the Bobby Battle character slapped her face and told her to mind her own business. She identified herself as DPD and attempted to take him into custody. He threw a haymaker that would've taken her head off had it connected. Jimenez luckily ducked and caught the offender with an overhand left, hence the broken jaw. "While my partner Detective Gleason, who was picking me up was exiting his vehicle and trying to ascertain the situation, the other perp, Big Shawn drew down on me and was shot by a patrolman working the bus station."

Templeton listened intently and waited a few seconds to make sure she was done. "Bulllll... shit! If I were a betting man, and I am, I'm laying a thousand to one odds you provoked this Battle and his buddy, so that you could mete out a little personal Jimenez justice." Before she could respond, he held up a staying hand. "You and the partner you never wanted, get the hell out of my office, and solve some cases." They skulked away before he decided to really chew them out.

Sitting at her desk Jimenez had a couple of things bothering her. The first was where in the world was Butterfly Baxter and how many people will fall prey to her psychotic, sadomasochistic ways before she could be brought to justice? The other was the man in the confession video. Who was he and where is he now? She could do nothing about the first at the moment, but there was something she could do about the second. Jimenez shoved the files on her blotter to the side loading a copy of the confession video to her desktop computer. She watched it several times at various speeds until finally something jumped out at her. "Hey, Gleason!"

The bald man turned from where he was standing talking to a female patrol officer and held up an index finger signaling for Jimenez to hold on, before turning back to the woman. He laughed and whispered something in her ear which made her eyebrows raise. When he finally came over, Jimenez cautioned him about where not to be putting his nightstick, then pointed to the image frozen on the computer monitor. "Do you think you can get that kid who's good with the computers to digitally enhance the prescription bottle in our confessor's hand so we can get a lead on the prescribing doctor's name?"

Gleason asked her to move and took her seat. "We don't need him. Although, I believe he's working on the video already. Last year when the department upgraded our systems and tried to get the city council to pass mandatory facial recognition protocols, we got all types of enhancement software."

She watched as he clicked on the toolbar, then moved the mouse to the proper software icon clicking again. "Oops! I forgot to merge the file with the software program which will only take a sec." She watched patiently until the image of the confessor holding the pill bottle popped on the screen again. He clicked on the bottle several times. Each time the software captured the pixels and rearranged them until the prescribing doctor's name could be seen.

"We should've been on top of this a long time ago," Jimenez told Gleason disgustedly. He moved the cursor up to a set of numbers near the top of the bottle. Curiously, she asked what they were.

"Pharmacy Identification numbers."

"What do we need'em for?"

He gave her a look that said, "You're not so smart after all," just before pointing to the screen and saying, "How many doctors share the surname of Johnson?" Gleason saw the light bulb appear over her head and continued, "Those numbers will lead us to a pharmacy which will lead us to our mystery man or at the very least his doctor."

They ran the pharmacy ID numbers, they tracked back to the

Karmanos Cancer Institute in the Detroit Medical Center. "Let's print up a few good quality stills of our mystery man and hit the DMC."

"Without a subpoena, how far do you think we'll get?"

Jimenez pointed to his head, "Grass sure doesn't grow on a busy street, neither does common sense. A stage four cancer patient has to be known to more than just his doctor."

Thirty minutes later, Gleason turned off of Warren avenue onto Beaubien. The entire DMC complex was within walking distance. Normally he would've pulled right up to the entrance, but Jimenez was snoring and drooling at the mouth so he parked and dropped a dollar in coins into the meter. When he cracked the passenger side door she started awake. "Where are we?"

"The KCI is just a short walk over that way. I didn't want to pull up to the entrance with you slobbering at the mouth like a newborn or have someone think we have an active shooter situation because of your machine gun snoring."

She smiled while wiping away the saliva with the sleeve of her jacket. "I've got some in my pocket."

He looked confused and asked, "Some what?"

"A can of go fuck yourself!"

"I'd suggest you do the same, but your snoring would get in the way." Jimenez tried suppressing her laughter but couldn't. Gleason helped her from the car then handed her a breath mint and a small stack of the confessed killer's photos. "You can use the walk to wake up and get your thoughts in order." She mumbled a sarcastic, "Thanks" while staring at the photo. Distractedly she followed him towards the cancer institute.

Jimenez crossed between two parked cars without looking both ways. The screech of brakes and blaring horn blast woke her up completely. When she looked, she was a foot or so away from the front bumper of an older black woman's subcompact. The detectives saw the window roll down and the grey-haired woman's head appear. "Get yo' skinny ass out the damn street!"

Jimenez held up three fingers, "Pick one grandma!" Gleason stood by as ugly words were exchanged. When things started getting really intense, he flashed his badge waiving the senior citizen on. "Heifer, thirty years ago I'd be out this car, beating your ass up and down this street! Police or no police!" A few more ugly words and she drove off. "Don't you just love Detroit versus Everybody?" Gleason only shook his head.

Inside the Karmanos Cancer Institute, they stopped at the information desk and got directions to the hospital pharmacy. Once there, they showed the mystery man's photo to some of the customers, but no one seemed to know him. They struck paydirt with the pharmacologist. "That's Mr. Kiddick. I haven't seen him for a while. Is he missing or something?" Jimenez looked at the woman and said, "Something." Gleason turned on the charm and they were given the full name of the right Dr. Johnson.

"How do you want to approach the doc?" Jimenez thought about it while they waited on the elevator. The ride up was crowded, so they didn't speak until they got off. In a low tone, she said, "This Kiddick guy is technically missing. We go with that."

Doctor Harriet Johnson was one of the top oncologists in the country and rather young. The detectives introduced themselves and showed the petite woman who could pass for a younger version of supreme court justice Ruth Bader Ginsburg the photo of Mr. Kiddick. "Is this man a patient of yours?"

She studied the face and handed the photo back. "What is this about, exactly?"

Jimenez stayed silent and observed the doctor while Gleason explained that the man was missing. The oncologist was sharp and asked, "Detectives, you introduced yourselves as belonging to homicide. Don't you have a missing person's department? Why is homicide looking for a missing man?"

Gleason smoothed his hand over the front of his tie. "We're not at liberty to divulge any case particulars, but I want to be upfront with you." He looked at Jimenez who gave a slight nod that it was okay to continue.

"We believe this man to be involved in not only murder but the key to closing an open kidnapping and sexual assault case perpetrated by someone else. We believe he has information which can help us."

"You have his name and a database. I'm sure you can track him without my help."

The detective erupted, "Time is of the essence. Lives are at risk!" The doctor's penetrating gaze was locked with Jimenez's when Gleason interrupted. "Computers, 1's and 0's can't give us the measure of a man. Only an observant intelligent mind can do that."

Dr. Johnson smiled. "Are you playing to my ego? Not every doctor will capitulate when you stroke their ego detective."

She rose from her desk walking over to a filing cabinet on the far wall, rifled through the files, extracted one, and placed it on her desk. "Doctor, patient confidentiality precludes me from assisting in your Investigation unless my patient is an imminent threat to himself or others, or you have a subpoena. In this case, I have no knowledge of either." She checked her watch. "I have a consult in exactly five minutes. I'm going to check with my receptionist and walk down to my colleague's office to see if he recorded last week's episode of Grey's Anatomy. When I return, both of you should be gone." She glared at Jimenez for a second before leaving and pulling the door shut behind her.

As soon as the door closed, Gleason pulled out his cellphone and started taking pictures of the first few pages which contained patient information. Closing the file back he said excitedly, "Mr. William Kiddick. We got him!"

On the way to the car, Jimenez asked to see Gleason's phone and pulled up the photos. "His emergency contact it seems is his daughter. Cassandra Kiddick. There's an address in Harper Woods with a phone number listed. We can run a search on them back in the car."

He saw the pep in her step and knew the new info invigorated her. While driving back to homicide Jimenez pulled up Willam Kiddick's last known address then had Gleason make a detour. When they pulled up, there was a team of contractors doing various repairs at the address while an eagle-eyed neighbor south of Kiddick's place watched it all. Jimenez told Gleason to stay in the car approaching the woman alone.

Her name was Ethel Darsky. She was proud to tell the detectives she was seventy-eight and in good health. When Jimenez introduced herself and inquired about Mr. Kiddick, Ethel asked whether or not the dirty bitch finally took him out. It seems the second Mrs. Kiddick was an adulteress.

"She was screwing his friend. Every time Billy left, that cheating bitch came," Ethel said. It seems Kiddick use to confide in the old woman. The ex-wife was from Ethel's account a gold-digging opportunist who tried to knock him off the wagon at every turn. She divorced him, leaving him in debt, Ethel told her.

"Any idea where Mr. Kiddick is?"

"Far away from here. The last time I saw him he told me he was headed overseas."

Jimenez thanked the woman and slid into the seat next to Gleason pulling out her cell phone. She called her first cousin Rosa Quintero who worked for Customs and Border Patrol. After promising to stop by for dinner, Jimenez gave her the name. Several minutes later Rosa said, "William B. Kiddick, his daughter and grandson all flew to New Zealand. I show reentry for the grandson and daughter, none for the primary."

"Can you send me the paperwork? I got a hot case going." They haggled for another three minutes before Rosa negotiated another Sunday dinner out of her hardworking younger relative. Jimenez promised to call her later and hung up.

"Fucking New Zealand! No extradition with the United States."

Gleason shrugged, "At least we got a lead." Jimenez slumped in her seat.

"Drop me at the squad and go relax. Tomorrow, we meet Ms. Kiddick."

14 ALBANY

Morgan sat with Chi on the roof of her apartment. The night was a little chilly, so they were both wearing lightweight jackets. He held a glass of scotch with the half-full bottle resting within easy reach by his feet. Chi needed to be focused and ultra alert. A steaming mug of coffee suited her just fine as she watched sympathetically tracking the tears running slowly down her handsome brother in law's face. The monitor of the laptop resting on the patio couch next to him was casting an eerie glow before she reached over and shut it.

"She's been lying to me this entire time...Our marriage has been nothing but a sham!" "I never would've believed you or anyone else if told my wife was an adulterer, pathological liar, sexual deviant, and garden variety sociopath. But tonight I've seen all the proof I need to see."

She said nothing in response to Morgan's venting. She was well aware of the mash-up of emotions the man was feeling because she'd felt them too. Including the feeling of being betrayed by someone she loved.

He groaned inwardly before asking, "Why even tell me any of this? This is definitely a case of ignorance being bliss. Why not let me continue believing in your sister's innocence?" She tried out one of her fake smiles on him before replying.

"Yes, ignorance is bliss. Yet, in this situation like so many others, it only delays the inevitable." She witnessed the pain crawl across his face like a dying man.

"Oh my God! What I would give not to know any of this."

It's like those public service announcements after those G.I.Joe "cartoons when I was a kid, "Knowing is half the battle."

Her brother in law's face contorted even more displaying the anguish he was feeling. "Chicago! Are you serious? My fucking wife, your sister, has a son by your deceased husband who it seems she had killed because their conspiracy to murder you fell apart." He slapped the palm of his hand against the laptop. "From the look of these videos, she's playing for the entire LBGTQ community and you're quoting from cartoons. This is surreal!" Ignoring his outburst, she told him, "Morgan, it's far better that we know now so that we can move on with rebuilding our lives."

He reached for the bottle of scotch, "I can't stay in Detroit any longer. My business needs my personal attention. I have to get back down south and away from all this. When my soon to be ex-wife is caught, they'll be a trial and I can't afford to come under that type of scrutiny. My business will suffer."

Chicago asked the most important question on her mind. "What about Albany?" Morgan made it clear there was no way he was in any shape to make that work.

"Don't mistake my words Chi. I love him as if he were my own flesh and blood, but I can't give him the stability he'll need to get through this ordeal."

"Morgan, I do understand. Technically I'm his stepmother and biologically his aunt. His mother is on the run for unspeakable crimes. If you'll sign an affidavit forgoing any rights and giving me temporary guardianship, I'll go into probate court and file for custody. Using Butterfly's abandonment as an argument there shouldn't be a problem." Morgan up-ended his glass draining the last of the Amber liquid.

"Thanks, Chi for handling this. Let me know if you need anything from me and it's done."

She dismissed the offer with a wave of her hand. "Morgan there's really nothing you need to do except be there for Albany when he needs you. Make no mistake, he will need you."

They agreed he'd stay on for another day to visit with Chicago's lawyer and render an affidavit then return down south. The boy will be safe with his auntie Chi. She is going to make sure of it. Albany accompanied Chicago to the Coleman A. Young municipal building which housed the Wayne County Probate Court. Her lawyer Zuleika Norwood along with her associate William Hunt met with them outside of Judge Idele Hartwell's courtroom. Attorney Hunt kept Albany company while the two women went in front of the bar. Albany was a little Sullen and withdrawn, but all things considered, holding up well. Chicago woke him up early and made his favorite breakfast with strawberry waffles with a dollop of whipped cream. While they ain't she explained to him what was happening. She thought his first question would be, where's my mom? And she was prepared for it. Instead, his only concern was whether or not he would be able to stay with her.

Later, at the attorney's office, his mood worsened when he found out Morgan would be leaving. Though he calmed visibly when his stepfather promised he would contact him every day and visit regularly when all of this was done. Afterward, Chicago pulled him aside telling him she thought it would be best if he were gone from the apartment before they returned home and he agreed.

The judge was fair and extremely efficient. The honorable Idele Hartwell granted Chicago temporary custody with a six-month review to make sure all is well. If Butterfly is still incarcerated at that time, temporary custody will continue. The judge also stipulated that if the biological mother resolved her legal issues by then, she may petition the court to reestablish her parental rights. The entire process took a few hours because they weren't originally on the court docket. She thanked her attorneys while taking her nephew's hand in her own.

"Are you hungry?" The boy shrugged his shoulders noncommittally. "Well, I am. I sure could use your help eating a meat lover's deluxe Detroit deep dish pizza from Buddy's Pizza. How about it?"

Albany mumbled, "I guess." Chicago squeezed his hand.

161

"Thanks, baby, I hate to eat alone." She knew they were going to be alright. Like her mother, Big Shirley used to say, "In time all problems solve themselves.

It was one o'clock in the morning when the ringing of her cell phone woke her. She felt around until her hand found the device and answered with a sleepy hello.

"Windy City, I'm sorry for waking you up, but I have a few questions." The sound of her sister's voice made her bolt upright on the couch she was sleeping on as though she'd been hit with a jolt of electricity.

"Butterly? Girl, stop this madness and turn yourself in!"

"Sweet sister, sister, sister...Are you crazy. I didn't kill your husband. To be quite honest, I was rather fond of Dorian." Chicago asked her about conspiring with her late husband to kill her.

The silence on the line was deafening. "Windy, he tricked both of us. Your husband was very manipulative." She knew better than to argue.

"Where are you? Please just turn yourself in before you get hurt."

Butterfly brushed her pleas aside. "All I can tell you is that I'm safe. How is my son? Can I speak with him? Let me hear his voice?" Her questions were fired rapidly and filled with emotion, but Chicago's heart at the moment was encased in steel.

"It's after one in the morning for Pete's sake!" Butterfly quickly asked about Morgan and she told her that he was back in Georgia. "I bet he hates me, I know you do."

Chicago rubbed the last vestiges of sleep from her eyes before saying, "Since you were born, I've loved you more than anyone else on this earth, but you're out of control. Baby, you need to turn yourself in and accept responsibility for the things you've done." She waited for a response that never came. The line was dead. Quickly, she scrolled through her call log finding Jimenez's number and thumbed her for a text message. Butterfly's call came from a private number and she sounded as if she were off her meds. The police had no idea who or what they were dealing with. Unfortunately, Chicago knew all too well.

Later the next day, Butterfly's son Albany was in his room at Chicago's apartment playing one of his video games. Morgan had overnighted the boy's gaming system along with some of his other belongings to make him feel more comfortable during his stay in Detroit. Even though he missed his mother, he felt right at home with his Auntie Chi. Albany loved spending time with her. They definitely had a special connection. He just wished all this, whatever this was, wasn't happening.

Jimenez eventually returned Chicago's text with a phone call. She'd just gotten back from out of town and was very busy, but had also admitted to receiving a call from Butterfly. Law enforcement had no idea where the fugitive was. The detective Sergeant believed in her gut that Butterfly Baxter was not only close but possibly responsible for a suspicious death of one, Arthur Millings of Port Huron, Michigan who was found dead in the Pinecrest Motel in Ann Arbor.

Initially, it was thought to be a natural death until another guest gave a description matching Butterfly. Jimenez suggested their department classify it as suspicious until further investigation. In addition, the victim's vehicle was found on the Northeast side of the Motor City in a high crime area known as Beirut. The entire interior was burnt to a crisp.

Chicago listened earnestly, offering her attention and little else when the detective asked, "Dr. Daniels, do you know a William Kiddick?"

She didn't open up to the detective. She said that the name didn't ring any bells but sounded vaguely familiar. When she asked Jimenez about the inquiry, the detective shut things down, playing her cards close to her chest. Chicago couldn't blame her because so was she.

There was round the clock surveillance outside Chicago's apartment, but with no Butterfly, it would be pulled soon. No matter, Chicago didn't fear anyone. Dealing with Sanford Smalls had made her fearless. It didn't hurt that she held a concealed carry permit either. Should Butterfly make an appearance in an attempt to do harm, Chicago's semi-automatic Glock would be the one talking.

One thing the behavioral psychologist noted was the change in Jimenez. Years of education and dealing with the human psyche and plain old woman's intuition was telling her that something was different. The detective was all business and she wanted to know what changed and why.

15 The Present

The detectives went to Cassandra Kiddick's place near Harper Woods over by Kelly Road. She was living with her son in a well-kept three-bedroom brick ranch. Gleason sat next to the woman on her couch as he questioned her. "Ms. Kiddick, your father is in a great deal of trouble. We know he flew out of the country with you and your kid."

"Long as a person has a legal passport, it's not a crime to travel outside of the country. You guys say you're Detroit police detectives, of what exactly?"

Gleason and Jimenez looked at each other before he answered. "Homicide. We're tasked with catching the worst of the worst."

"Is this about my cheating skank of a stepmother? My father had nothing to do with that. He was at a Pistons game with me and my son when that happened."

They told her they were not at liberty to say why they were there. "We already know he flew with you and his grandson to New Zealand and that only you and your son returned. Ms. Kiddick your father is in a great deal of trouble and you could be, too, if you don't cooperate."

The woman looked thoughtful, so Jimenez added, "We'd like to know where he is, if he's using an alias, and if you're in contact with him." Gleason looked at the woman then glanced slightly at his partner who was standing by the picture window. If she was going to spill it, now would be the time.

"What exactly is my father accused of?"

"We can't get into the details of our case, but as my partner told you a minute ago, we're from homicide. Does that clue you in a little?" Jimenez was tired of playing nice.

"Detective Gomez ... "

"It's Detective Sergeant Jimenez!" she clarified with a sharp edge to her voice that didn't seem to faze Ms. Kiddick one bit.

"Whatever! I don't think either of you wants to go where my father is to find him."

Gleason asked, "Did he leave New Zealand? Where is he hiding at now, Ms. Kiddick?" A smirk appeared at the corners of the woman's mouth.

"My father is dead. He died almost a month ago." She went on to tell them that they could check with the state department. He was cremated at the expense of the New Zealand government. They asked for proof and she told them that the state department has a copy of the death certificate. "Do your job detectives. Now if you would be so kind as to leave my home, I need to pick my son up.

"Just to be sure," Jimenez asked, "How did he die?"

Even though the woman was pushing the door closed Jimenez clearly heard the young woman say, "Laughing." Jimenez told Gleason to drive because she needed to think. She explained to her partner that everything seemed to fit but not quite. A blue-collar guy with stage four cancer turns into a contract killer. But how? How is he connected to Butterfly Baxter? These two people rotate in very different circles of life. How did they meet? These questions all needed to be answered, especially the latter. Something was bugging her about this. Something she couldn't quite grasp.

Gleason navigated the early afternoon traffic knowing that his partner was doing her solo investigation thing in her head. He dared not interrupt her. He was about to tell her to answer her cellphone because she had ignored it for the last two incoming calls when she snatched it up on the fourth ring. "Detective Sergeant Jimenez ... Yes, sir ... Jeez! Okay, right away sir. She flicked on the lights and sirens. "Punch it, Gleason! We need to be at headquarters pronto. Gleason saw the excitement mixed with adrenaline dancing in her eyes. "What's up?"

Jimenez yelled for a woman who was pulling slowly to the curb to get the hell out of their way. "Butterfly Baxter just turned herself in!"

Gleason pressed his foot down on the accelerator and concentrated on his driving. Jimenez had closed her eyes and was mumbling something to herself. Gleason thought to himself, she looks as crazy as this case is.

Detroit was a nice place to visit, but Butterfly wouldn't want to live here anymore. Too much violence for her taste. Well, almost. After ditching Art's car, she stood outside a gentlemen's club on East Eight Mile Road and allowed an older man to pick her up. Phil was in good shape and not bad looking. He'd hit the lottery for a few thousand dollars the day before and wanted to treat himself. Butterfly crafted a quick lie telling him she was a stripper named Luscious out of Florida who had just rolled into town. Her old girlfriend London reneged on a place for her to stay. And without a picture ID, Luscious whose real name was Phyllis believe it or not, couldn't check into a hotel.

Phil, who was buzzing off of two-dollar beers and six-dollar tequila shots offered to take her to a motel and get her a room; no strings attached. Butterfly asked if he would mind letting her repay him for his kindness with dinner at this chicken place her girlfriend, London, introduced her to during her last stay in Detroit. Phil was only too happy to be in the presence of this beautiful woman and eagerly accepted.

She directed him to Midtown where Gus's Famous Fried Chicken was located right around the corner from Chicago's apartment building. Luscious, convinced Phil to order take out because it was getting late. The truth was she scoped out a few police surveillance units in the area and wanted to get away from there as soon as possible. There was no need to press her luck. Not only that, but it pays to think everyone is out to get you. During her college years as a madame, she had to be extremely paranoid. The sex trade had become complicated with the media showing criminal organizations enslaving women and children. Whether you were a cultured madame such as she or a Ukrainian mobster, the time in prison would be the same. A girl had to balance risk versus reward. Just like now. As much as she loved Albany, the risk was too great. Anytime you take a gamble you need to be able to Kenny Rogers that shit. "Know when to hold 'em, know when to fold 'em, know when to walk away and know when to run." She knew when to do all of the above.

Butterfly decided to let Phil spend the night, he was sweet. She started dancing for him then one thing led to another and she ended up dancing on him. In the morning after a night of some good sex, she asked Phil if he could get the room for another night. She tried to pay for it, but he wouldn't let her. They parted ways after having a morning "nice to have met you" screw.

The Suez Motel on Eight Mile Road on the Detroit/Warren border was typical of most inner-city motels. Cable, porn, and a check in desk that sold male enhancements and flavored condoms. She went there after Phil left and requested a new room. The clerk was giving her a hard time until she slid him a hundred-dollar bill. Butterfly made it clear to him that she also wanted the registration switched to her name, Alice Inland. No, she didn't have her ID on her. It was in the room and for a hundred dollars she wasn't going back to get it. That shut the clerk up. Her bluff worked. The police obviously knew her Octavia Winters alias, so she could no longer keep that identification on her. She had several more stashed and would get to them soon enough. What she needed now was sleep. Once she switched rooms and showered, she bolted the door then slept like a caterpillar.

When she woke up, she felt refreshed and invigorated. She even took her pills. The night before, while dreaming she had a wild epiphany. The key to her release was in her capture. With that thought in mind, she used her phone to do an internet search for criminal defense attorneys operating out of Wayne County, the county that encompasses Detroit.

She found four who she thought were qualified to represent her. Butterfly took her time and searched each of their individual backgrounds. Only one of the four stood out. Not because they had been reprimanded by the Michigan Bar Association for zealously representing a client and breaking a few rules, but because in a news report the lawyer called the Wayne County Prosecutor's office her arch enemy. That's what Butterfly needed. Someone who wanted to fight and destroy their enemy.

A little after 1:00 p.m. Butterfly left a message with the attorney's secretary. It was late in the evening before she received a callback. Ben Franklin speaks! Money talks while bullshit walks. The lawyer wanted $50,000.00 to take the case, nonrefundable. The entire matter appeared to be circumstantial on its face, but it couldn't be known for sure until the defense received discovery. Discovery is all of the evidence the prosecution has in their possession. It includes but it's not limited to, police reports, witness statements, and physical evidence. More than likely there wouldn't be a bond and she'd have to remain in the county jail.

Expect the best but prepare for the worst. The attorney advised Butterfly to lay low for a few days while she checked with her contacts at the courts and inside the department. If things looked good, they could proceed. If they looked bad, then Butterfly would leave the country.

On Tuesday morning she gathered her belongings and packed her bags, took a taxi to a nearby strip mall where she purchased jeans, gym shoes, a tee-shirt, and a lightweight jacket. Jails were like hospitals, always kept cold to keep germs to a minimum. After changing her clothes in the store's dressing room, she made her way downtown to the Kennedy Building on Griswold and Lafayette. Her lawyer was expecting her arrival. Once there, she found Stephanie Fishman discreetly waiting on her in the empty hallway around the corner from the main entrance.

Stephanie was put together nicely. Her long chestnut hair was pulled up and back into a coiled bun. Her charcoal grey pantsuit was tailored to fit her smallish waist and too wide hips. The peekaboo Louboutin shoes were this year's and her silk blouse had a higher thread count than Butterfly's sheets back home in Georgia. "I didn't want you traipsing through the outer office. No one is to be trusted when your life is on the line. If another lawyer's client recognizes you, they might dime you out for a deal." Butterfly looked around as she was ushered through a door marked with the word, Supplies. "This door leads right into my office."

The pretty lawyer motioned for Butterfly to have a seat in one of three leather chairs positioned in front of her desk. "Why three chairs?" Stephanie Fishman pointed out each seat. "Lawyer loved one and client." Butterfly looked around the office. It was expensively decorated but functional. "You stated on the phone that you were bringing a retainer correct?"

Butterfly sat her Chanel purse on the desk then laid it flat to unscrew the platinum knobs on its bottom. Once the secret compartment was revealed, Butterfly pulled out and deftly counted $50,000.00. "This is your fee in full as agreed upon – nonrefundable. And this is …" she kept counting, "… another $25,000.00 just in case that beautiful bitch Lady Justice needs some glasses to see my innocence."

Attorney Fishman leaned casually forward in her chair. "I hope you aren't suggesting bribery of any kind. As an officer of the court, I can't be a party to …" Butterfly cut her off, "I have no idea what you're talking about. A quality defense isn't cheap. I have vast sums of money at my disposal; so, I'm incentivizing you. Should we avoid a trial I have another 50K for you. Let's skip any other extraneous minutiae and get down to the crux of it. What do they have against me?"

Fishman liked this client. "Everything and the kitchen sink, circumstantially that is. There really is no physical evidence against you at all." She snatched up a manila folder from her desk, opened it, and ran quickly through a litany of charges.

Fishman told Butterfly, "Mrs. Baxter, my source inside of the department tells me the guy you allegedly hired to murder your brother-in law is dead. So, we're going to see if we can get most of these charges thrown out at the probable cause hearing. Some of them we'll have to fight, but if we get rid of the capital murder charge then

170

we can navigate you clear of prison. If not, we go for a quick bench trial."

"Why a bench trial? Why not a jury trial?"

"Taking a bench trial means that only a judge will hear the case; which is good because there's no tangible evidence. A jury will open up the emotional floodgates. The prosecution will leverage facts and try to make the evidence of guilt."

"Please explain this leveraging of facts. What does that mean?"

Attorney Fishman stood up and walked around her desk taking a seat next to her. "In spite of the jeans and gym shoes, your beauty and feminine sexuality are still bursting through. I put you in front of a jury and the prosecution utters one word about you not only screwing your sister's husband but having his child, you'll go directly to jail for a very long time. I'm pretty sure any jury we pick will hate you. Hell, I hate you! You're rich, educated, articulate, and gorgeous. If you want to be back in Georgia picking peaches and baking pecan pies, let me do my job. I have daddy issues and I hate to lose."

"Fine. What's the next step then?"

Fishman looked at her watch, "In 90 minutes or so we'll meet a few local news reporters in front of police headquarters where I'll preach the gospel of your innocence. In turn, you'll depict DPD as being on a witch hunt because they couldn't close a high-profile case. You turned yourself in because you're scared the police might kill you. They already shot up a van with your family in it. You're a wife, mother, and college graduate who's never been in trouble with the law. Are you getting this?" Butterfly nodded.

"Can you cry on cue? It would be wonderful if you could. I hope you can at least act a little."

Butterfly was definitely ready for her closeup. Fox2 News, WDIV Channel 4 representing NBC, and WXYZ Channel 7 of ABC were all huddled together in a 180 degree arc with their microphones poised. In front of them stood Butterfly Baxter flanked by her attorney, Stephanie Fishman, and one of her second-year associates, an African American woman named Brenda Walker. Anyone looking would be moved by the tears cascading down Butterfly's honey brown cheeks like water down a sheet of glass. She stood close to her attorney while the associate gently patted her back to comfort her. "My client is innocent of all charges except perhaps the fleeing and alluding charge. Technically under the law, she may be guilty, but there are mitigating circumstances. Would you stay stagnate when a Detroit police officer is firing a large caliber weapon at you? No!"

Stephanie Fishman continued, "My client is going to read a prepared statement then walk into police headquarters behind us here and voluntarily surrender. I only hope you, the media, are fair in your reporting." She stood to the side and behind Butterfly letting her step up to the bank of microphones.

"My name is Butterfly Baxter. I'm being falsely accused of crimes I didn't commit. I am a law-abiding citizen with no criminal record who has made some moral mistakes, but I've not broken any laws. I only know that I don't want to end up like one of those people who are falsely convicted then released 20 years down the road after being found innocent. I'm asking that no rush judgments be made. Thank you!"

Questions started flying from the reporters but as previously planned, the attorney and client ignored them. Stephanie Fishman linked arms with Butterfly Baxter on her right while the associate did the same on her left. They were the picture of support and innocence as they walked through the doors of police headquarters.

Jimenez stood in the corner of the interrogation room looking like a petulant child. Her demeanor became sullen as she crossed her arms glaring at Butterfly Baxter and her lawyers while Gleason turned off the video showing the confessed killer, William Kiddick. "We know your client had an affair with the deceased Dr. Brooks and gave birth to his son. We also know your client is a sexual deviant just like Sanford Smalls."

Looking at Gleason, Stephanie Fishman asked, "Who are you guys, the morals police? My client enjoys sex and that's not a crime." "It is when you have the person you're screwing murdered," Gleason said.

Butterfly smirked at him and turned towards Jimenez who started to speak. "If she tells us about her involvement in her sister's kidnapping and how she came to hire William Kiddick to kill her brother-in-law, I'll personally speak with the prosecutor."

Fishman guffawed. "Please, don't insult us. I can speak with the prosecutor. That doesn't do shit! We're not looking for leniency or a plea bargain. We're looking to be exonerated."

"I love a delusional lawyer. You make my job a lot easier."

Butterfly sat there unmoving, staring at Jimenez as she finished speaking. "My client isn't telling you shit. In fact, detectives, we're done. My associate, Attorney Walker will remain with Mrs. Baxter throughout the booking process. Remember she's represented by counsel."

Fishman stood collecting her briefcase. Jimenez spoke up before the lawyer could leave. "I don't need a confession for me to know what really happened. Your client is and probably always has been jealous of her big sister. It's the curse of Cain and Able, but your client upped the ante. She doesn't just want her sister dead, she hands her over to a sadist who repeatedly rapes and tortures her. What will little Albany think when he realizes mommy lied to him about daddy and tried to kill his aunt. Hell," Jimenez looked at Butterfly, "… you'll never know because you'll be deep inside a prison cell locked away." She walked over to the door blocking it with her body. "Any juror with half a brain will be able to see through the thin facade you use to mask the monster you really are."

"That'll be enough detective."

Jimenez pointed a finger in the lawyer's face, "Fuck if it is! It'll be enough when I say it's enough! Your sister will raise your son and he'll hate you! Albany will hate you the way you hate everyone and everything!"

At that outburst from Jimenez, Butterfly said something barely audible. "What did you say?" Jimenez asked.

"I said, let me get two tacos, a diet coke, and extra sour cream." Everyone looked confused. "You are the bitch who takes my order at Taco Bell, aren't you?" Stephanie Fishman told her client to be quiet.

"No, it's fine counselor. Your black, psycho, whore client wants to play the race card. I understand when a hoe ain't playing with a full deck that she has to play the only card she has left."

Butterfly wanted to kill Jimenez. "Fuck you! How are you even working? Do have a green card?"

"Keep talking, give that pretty pink tongue of yours some exercise because when you get upstate it's gonna double as a panty liner for the women in your cellblock, you sick bitch."

Butterfly poked her tongue out at Jimenez and said, "Yo momma!" Then she burst into laughter.

The detective quickly turned and walked out. She still heard Butterfly laughing after the door was closed.

Gleason got up opening the door again and motioned for a female officer to accompany the arrestee to booking. Fishman leaned down into her client's ear. "Keep your mouth shut! Clients who talk don't walk. I'll be visiting you first thing in the morning. There are plenty of desperate people where you're going who'll trade you for a get out of jail free card. Remember that!" She nodded to Walker who gave her a thumb's up. The female officer cuffed Butterfly and escorted her out with the associate lawyer following close behind. Butterfly had never been in jail before. She thought to herself, hopefully, it's as advertised. Only the strong survive.

The arraignment was done by video. Bond was set at one million dollars cash or as surety on the kidnapping charges and remanded on Dorian's murder. The prosecutor Felicia Lindsay tried to consolidate the cases, but the judge would not allow it. Combining the cases without enough evidence would be extremely prejudicial.

Right after the arraignment, Attorney Fishman showed up at the jail. The probable cause hearing was set on the court's calendar for two weeks later and they needed to be prepared. "It's a good thing the judge wouldn't allow the kidnapping case of your sister and the murder of her husband to be conjoined. I really think we can get the murder charge kicked."

"What about the kidnapping?" Butterfly asked.

Fishman replied, "That's another story."

Butterfly sat in the tiny room on the hard wooden stool separated from her lawyer by three inches of plexiglass. At the bottom of the plexiglass was an opening about 2-1/2" from the tabletop. It allowed for the passing of legal documents between attorney and client. "Why is the kidnapping charge another story?" She asked.

Fishman was blunt, "You had a child with your brother-in-law, which you hid from your sister for years. It shows you are not only capable of deception, but you're exceptional at it. The prosecution has a strong motive for a circumstantial case; but with Dr. Brooks dead and having an equal motive, we can blame him for everything and create reasonable doubt."

Butterfly asked, "So, if we get the murder charge thrown out, can I make bond on the other charges?"

Fishman looked at her curiously. "Do you have a million dollars to post?"

'Yes, I do; but it would be more prudent for my husband Morgan to post it when the time comes."

175

Fishman wondered how she could get a man whom she lied to and cheated on to pay a million-dollar bond. They talked further about both cases along with possible defense strategies. Not once did the lawyer ever ask if she did it. Fishman didn't ask because she didn't care to know. If she knew and her client took the witness stand and lied, she could be disbarred for suborning perjury. Tell me no secrets and I'll zealously defend your lies, Fishman thought as she left the jail.

Chicago hung up the phone from Morgan. Butterfly had somehow gotten hold of a cellphone and threatened him into paying her bond once the murder charges were thrown out. The call to Chicago was Morgan giving her a heads up. Butterfly had something heavy on Morgan the mogul concerning some shady real estate deals and bribery of local officials in several cities in the South. When and if the time came, he was going to have to bond her out or take the chance she'd expose some of his questionable business practices. That could get him and a few of his closest cronies in very hot water.

Chicago understood his position and didn't begrudge his decision, not one bit. She tried calming him down but to no avail. Her disturbed sister getting out of jail could be more than a serious problem, it could end up being a fatal one. Butterfly would definitely come for her son and Chicago couldn't let that happen. There was no way that she would allow Albany to be influenced any longer by her twisted sister. The Lord alone knows what lies beneath his skin lurking in his gene pool already. Look at his mother, alluringly beautiful on the outside; and hideously ugly on the inside. Butterfly was raised well, provided for, and educated even better. Chicago surmised that her behavior was hereditary. She definitely takes after their father.

It's not like she can recall the bad times. The beatings, cursing, struggling to make ends meet after their father would steal Big Shirley's paycheck. She wasn't even a gleam in his eye when he was killed and yet, she's exactly like him. Mean spirited, selfish, and always wanting. Just like her father Martin Daniels, always wanting what he wasn't supposed to have. Charismatic, handsome, and sweet on the outside. On the inside, he was rotten to his core, just like his daughter.

Musing to herself, Chicago thought again of their father. Martin Daniels was dead and buried long before his youngest child was even known to exist, and the proverbial apple still didn't fall far from the tree. She concluded that it must be in the blood. It has to be hereditary, she thought while walking to Albany's room and cracking the door. Her little man was asleep in his bed snoring softly. Chicago remembered that age. It was before the pain, emotional anguish, and nightmares. Still, she couldn't ignore the thought that it was the pain that made her who she was again.

She closed the bedroom door and walked back into the living area, sitting on the couch in the dark. Her thoughts ran to a time shared with her parents. The childhood innocence which snuggled around Albany like a warm blanket was not even a warm breath fluttering against her hair at that age. All she remembered from childhood was guilt and long-suffering pain.

It was visiting day for Butterfly in the Wayne County jail. Visiting Chicago's earliest memories went back to when she was three or four years old. They weren't pleasant memories like they should have been at that tender age. Screaming, yelling, cursing, crying, all jumbled together with the background noise of crashing dishes and tumbling furniture. She was a smart child comprehending beyond her young years. She quickly caught on to what was happening around her. She'd watch her father come home long enough to have sex with her mother and swindle some money out of her. Always in a drunken stupor, he'd rest up like he was on vacation then leave again. Big Shirley loved her Marty D. Her daughter loved and feared him at the same time. Sometimes her dad was her protector and hero. At other times he was a villain and assaulted her; it just depended on the day.

When Chicago was eleven, her mother took her father's house keys and forbade him to be in the house without her being present. Chicago blamed herself for that. "Mama my bed stinks!" Big Shirley was tired from her double shift at the laundry. Exhausted, she said, "Then go change your sheets. I thought that I told you to change them yesterday."

"I changed them this morning before I left for school," Chicago replied. Chicago went and swapped them out again. She pulled the sheets off her bed rolling them into a ball then carried them to the washroom in the basement. When she came back upstairs her mother told her, "You dropped your underwear, baby." Picking them up between her thumb and forefinger as though they were radioactive, Chicago told her mother, "These are   not mine, Momma, they're see through." When her mom looked at the underwear, she saw that the zebra print sheer front panties were too big for either of them.

Later that night she heard her parents arguing. Evidently, her father had brought a woman into Big Shirley's house and had sex with her in his daughter's bed. From that day on he wasn't supposed to be in the house by himself. Sometimes he would come by while Big Shirley was at work and try to weasel himself in, but Chicago never let him. He would curse and keep up a ruckus until she threatened to call the police or even worse, call her mother at work. But there was one time she had a moment of weakness and let him in. That was the last time Chicago ever saw him in that house again.

It was visiting day for Butterfly in the Wayne County Jail. Visiting days were determined by the first alphabet of an inmate's last name. Personal visits were only allowed Monday through Friday. Each day, four to six alphabets were allowed to see a friend or loved one once either in the morning, noon, or evening. Inmates and visitors talked with each other through a thick slab of plexiglass covered in the last person's spittle like a Jackson Pollack painting. When the sheriff's deputy told Butterfly she had a personal visit, she was surprised, to say the least. Morgan made it clear that he preferred her dead. Albany couldn't come on his own, and Chicago couldn't get past the metal detector with that pole up her ass. So, she was at a loss as to who it could be.

Butterfly was playing cards when the deputy called her over the intercom letting her know she had a visitor. Looking around the rock she laid eyes on Crystal, a twenty-something stud lesbian who liked to be called Chris. "Hey! Play this hand for me."

The young stud was big for a woman. She pushed her locks out of her face making it easy for anyone to see the prominent black eye against her smooth yellow skin. "Yeah, I got you Fly." She and Butterfly had a small misunderstanding when she hit the rock. Chris thought Butterfly was in need of protection and made it clear she was it. That night the stud made her move by attacking Butterfly in their cell. The kick to her vagina was excruciatingly painful, but it was the knee to Chris's jaw that knocked her out cold. From that moment on she was Butterfly's bitch. The black eye was for not properly cleaning their cell the day before. "Hold it down, I'll be back in a few."

The other eight women on the rock were grateful that Butterfly showed up putting a leash on Chris. After using the bathroom and checking her appearance in the mirror she went to the front of the cellblock where the deputy buzzed her out. Another deputy escorted her to the visiting bay next to the floor's control module. The guard in the module told her over the intercom, "Baxter, booth number three!" She walked down to three and sat on the hard wooden stool that was bolted to the floor and stared through the dirty spit covered glass. After five minutes or so, she began growing impatient. Just when her mind was made up to check with the guard in the module, Chicago opened the door and walked into the small booth across the glass from her.

Butterfly watched her big sister brush off the plastic chair on her side and sit down. "How are you doing Caterpillar?" She was a little slow in responding because although she thought her sister incapable of hating her, she didn't expect a visit from her either. "Please don't call me that. Listen, they have it all wrong."

Chicago smoothed invisible wrinkles from the front of her skirt before replying. "Which part Butterfly? The part where you've been screwing my husband for years and had his child or the part where you had him murdered? Oh, wait! I know what part they got wrong," Chicago said sarcastically. "The part where the two people I love most in the world conspired to have me murdered by delivering me into the hands of a violent sexual sadist who used my rectum as a storage facility for all of his kinky toys."

"I had nothing to do with Dorian's murder, but I think you already know that. Your husband manipulated both of us. You have every right to be angry with me, Chicago, but again, I had nothing to do with that maniac who kidnapped you."

She looked at her sister with utter disdain. "I love you more than you'll ever know in this lifetime. Your entire life I've taken care of you and you repay me with treachery and deceit."

Butterfly leaned closer to the glass. "You could have written that in a letter. Why are you here?"

Tears rolled down Chicago's face. "I'm here for my stepson, Albany. Really, I should say our son, shouldn't I?" At the mention of Albany's name, Butterfly became defensive. "What about my son?" "Correction little sister - our son!"

Butterfly was incensed. "Bitch, please! There is no 'our son.' You feel as though I took something from you and now, you're trying to take something from me."

Chicago wiped at her tears while shaking her head vigorously from side to side. "I want you to sign over your parental rights to me. I want Albany to have a real chance at life. He can't have that with you." She could see Butterfly about to interrupt her and hurried on. "You're a great mother, at least you act like one. But you are a lousy person. Do you think that I don't know the things you've done over the years? I've constantly watched out for you, cleaning up your messes. I send you to college and you want to play Heidi Fleiss."

When Chicago mentioned Butterfly's prostitution business, she calmed considerably. Staring at her nails nonchalantly, she asked, "How long have you known about it?"

"Long enough!" Chicago emphasized.

"It's amazing that you knew about me fucking and sucking 1,000 miles away but knew nothing when your dear husband would lift my skirt and drive himself inside me while you were in the next room."

Her words were like a slap in Chicago's face. "Call me naive but considering we're family, I didn't expect that from you. Why do you hate me?"

"Think back, Windy City. Think back!"

"I don't have time for any guessing games, and this isn't about us. This is about what's best for Albany and regardless of what happens with you and your legal woes, I'm going to take him from you. Anyone can tell that you're obviously unfit to be a real mother to Albany because of the reasons you're in jail."

A tempest of pure rage flickered brightly in her smoldering eyes. "Are you trying to help Albany or yourself? After all, that dried up barren sheath you call a vagina can no longer produce a child. That's why your husband preferred this …" Butterfly said and grabbed at her crotch, "… over you! He could see life at the end of this tunnel."

Chicago threw her hands up in surrender. "I'm not going to sit here and listen to this garbage." She stood to leave and so did Butterfly.

"Then say, bye Bitch!"

Smiling, Chicago said, "Bye Bitch!" then turned and walked out of the visiting booth without a backward glance. Her little sister was doing what she does best, acting out! Butterfly's screams vibrated the steel, glass, and concrete as she yelled after her sister. "Never! Never! Never! You'll never take him from me!"

Waiting for an elevator, Chicago thought, Poor Butterfly. I hope she's taking her medication.

Jimenez, Gleason, and assistant prosecutor Lindsay sat in Lindsay's small 9th-floor office in the Frank Murphy Hall of Justice where the Wayne County prosecutor's office is located. Felicia Lindsay looked more like a television actress than an overworked, underpaid civil servant. She stood a little over 6' in her comfortable 3" pumps. Her height came in handy in college where she played forward for the Lady Spartans, Michigan State University's female basketball team. After taking advantage of a full-ride athletic scholarship, she attended law school at the University of Michigan. Unlike most law graduates, she passed the bar exam on her first attempt, then applied for a job as a prosecutor. For eight years she'd been grinding it out with the worst criminal element in Wayne county.

181

Jimenez brought the case to her because Lindsay knew about warfare. She never brought a knife to a gunfight. The assistant prosecutor always brought a bigger gun. "Stephanie Fishman is one to watch. She'd blow the judge like a Miles Davis solo if she thought it would get her client off." Lindsay remarked candidly. The detectives didn't respond because they knew that she would do the same and swallow if it meant getting a conviction. "I don't expect us to get anywhere with the murder of Butterfly Baxter's alleged co-conspirator, Dr. Dorian Brooks. Considering his promiscuity, a third-rate attorney can make the case that there were other people with motives enough to want him dead."

"What about the video confession of William Kiddick?" Gleason asked.

"What about it? A jury will never see it. Fishman already filed a motion to quash, challenging the admissibility of the video. William Kiddick is dead and without corroboration, so is this piece of evidence. However, the kidnapping and conspiracy to commit murder charges have a good circumstantial backbone. Those will stick; I'll make sure of it." She held up the stack of salacious letters with the flash drive of all the lewd and lascivious pictures along with videos. "Once jurors see this, Mrs. Baxter's goose is cooked. If she's smart, she'll cop-out."

Jimenez tossed in her two cents. "She's very smart, but her massive ego won't allow her to take a plea deal. I've interrogated the woman; she'll never admit guilt. It's not in her nature."

"What exactly is Mrs. Baxter's nature?" Lindsay quipped. Jimenez looked her in the eye. "In a word —evil."

Felicia Lindsay started stuffing files into her briefcase. Gleason stared transfixed as she tossed back her thick auburn hair, crinkled her perfect upturned nose, and told them, "Evil or not, I've got an appearance in Judge Evans' courtroom right now. We've got an hour or so to be in front of Judge Talbot for Baxter's first probable cause hearing. Don't expect much. All I can do is give the defense a preview of how difficult their lives will soon be. Any questions?"

Jimenez and Gleason looked at one another. "No questions, just an observation. I believe there are other forces at play here," Jimenez said.

Looking at his partner, Gleason asked, "What do you mean?"

"I mean we spent years without coming up with anything remotely resembling evidence or a suspect, then boom! Everything starts coming together, but not quite. There's evidence but not enough. There's finger-pointing by an unseen hand, but no visible person behind it. Something is off and I just can't figure out what. Just call it a gut feeling."

Felicia Lindsay stood up and opened up her office door bringing their meeting to a close. "Don't ever say that again. If Stephanie Fishman got a whiff of our lead detective having doubts, she'd rip us a new one."

"There's no doubt that Butterfly Baxter is guilty of a lot of shit. I'm just not sure exactly what at this point."

Looking at Detective Jimenez, Lindsay reiterated, "Again detective, keep your thoughts, feelings, or whatever buried. They're not meant for public consumption."

Jimenez gave Lindsay an affirmative nod, but it didn't change her gut feeling that something about this entire case was off.

Two hours later the detectives sat in the witness area next to Judge Talbot's courtroom. They recognized Cassandra Kiddick as soon as they came in. When they spoke to her she ignored them and moved to the furthest corner of the room. They didn't say anything else to her, thinking that she may have been instructed not to speak to them. The detectives huddled quietly and discussed in hushed tones what they thought about the case. At first, they were hopeful that they'd catch their confessed killer, William Kiddick, and strike a deal with him for his testimony. But since he was dead, that wasn't possible.

The door opened and a bailiff ushered in a serious-looking woman in a navy-blue skirt and jacket who kept glancing at her wristwatch. A few minutes later the same bailiff reappeared. "Detective Gleason, you're up." Jimenez watched him leave then let her gaze drift to the other two women in the room who seemed completely absorbed in their thoughts.

Outside in the main hallway Chicago, too, was completely absorbed with her own thoughts. She had been subpoenaed by the defense. Butterfly's attorney had spoken to her briefly and asked her to wait outside the courtroom with her associate, Ms. Walker. The woman was sitting across from Chicago trying hard to keep an eye on her without being obvious. What value she could be to her sister's defense strategy, Chicago couldn't fathom. So, she just sat there patiently hoping all would be revealed in due time. Just as she started to work on a crossword puzzle from the newspaper, she saw Detective Gleason walk out of a door next to the courtroom and into the court itself. He gave her a tight smile before disappearing inside. Chicago still couldn't understand why she was there for the defense; but she remained calm and answered number 13 down. A seven-letter word for a person of interest; 'suspect.'

Judge Talbot's court was very active that morning. His clerk Deborah McKinney, a green-eyed, red-haired middle-aged woman of Irish descent had been calling cases that were on the docket with the efficiency of a seasoned short-order cook. Margot Rodgers, who could only be described as ancient was Talbot's stenographer. Ancient or not her wrinkled brown paper looking fingers were fast. Gleason stepped up to the bench where the Judge swore him in. Then he took a seat in the witness box.

The courtroom was full except for five or so seats in the first row behind the defense. The detective looked at Butterfly Baxter admiring the woman's grace under pressure. He thought, she certainly personifies the term, "Never let 'em see you sweat." She wore a black pantsuit with a red silk blouse and an oversized black bow tie. His eyes wandered from her Tom Ford stilettos back up to her long luxurious hair hanging in loose tendrils. She certainly didn't look like a woman who's been in lockup on serious charges.

Prosecutor Lindsay followed his line of sight, but her thoughts were much different from his. She was thinking that the more women on the jury the better. They would hate her. Judge Talbot ceded the floor to the prosecution for direct examination.

"Prosecutor Lindsay, your witness. "She stood behind the lectern separating the prosecution and defense cutting an imposing figure with her height and flowing auburn hair. There were fourteen empty seats in the jury box, but in her mind, she was playing to twelve jurors and their two alternates. If she could convince them, then one judge shouldn't be a problem. Legally, all she had to do at this stage was prove a prima facie case, which simply meant it was more likely than not that Mrs. Baxter contracted the murder of her lover, Dr. Dorian Brooks. All things considered there was little chance of that happening, but what little there was, Lindsay would take it. She knew there wasn't enough admissible evidence for this case to make it to a jury. Considering Talbot was going to hear the other charges also, this would be a good time for her to muddy the waters in her favor.

"Good morning, sir. Could you please state your name and where you are employed for the record?" The detective pulled the microphone closer to his face before responding. "My name is Donald Gleason. I am a detective for the Detroit Police Department; specifically, their homicide division. Currently, I operate with HTF. That's the Homicide Task Force, a unit comprised of several other local, state, and federal law enforcement agencies."

"How long have you worked as a police officer?"

"I've been with DPD for 15 years. My first nine were spent on patrol, my last six as a detective in homicide."

"How many homicides have you been primary or rather lead detective on?"

Gleason gave a thoughtful pause, "Well over a hundred."

Prosecutor Lindsay flipped through a thin file in front of her before asking, "On December 13th, two years ago were you notified of a homicide having taken place in the 4200 block of West Harper in the City of Detroit, County of Wayne?"

"Yes. In the early morning hours of the aforementioned date, I responded to a homicide of a middle-aged white male from apparent gunshot wounds."

"At some point were you able to ascertain the decedent's name?" Gleason pulled a small notebook from his inside jacket pocket. "Dr. Dorian Xavier Brooks, 48 years old, a lifelong resident of the metropolitan area."

"What did your preliminary investigation uncover?"

Gleason said that they originally thought it was a carjacking until they received a video pointing to the victim's sister-in-law.

Stephanie Fishman shot out of her seat like a rocket. "Objection, Your Honor! The so-called video confession is in question as to admissibility. I believe Your Honor has already made a ruling on a motion filed by the defense to squash."

Judge Talbot covered his microphone while speaking to his clerk. She passed him a cluster of papers that he thumbed through quickly then said, "The court did rule on the defense's motion to quash. The motion was granted, and all parties were notified of such. There was an exception to my ruling. My understanding is that the person confessing in the video is dead. However, if the prosecution finds that someone else was present for example, someone who may have assisted in making the video, the court will allow it. With no corroborating witness, it and anything gleaned from it is out."

Prosecutor Lindsay flipped out and raised several arguments, but in the end, the judge only allowed Gleason's testimony about the video for context. "The prosecution may continue the direct examination of its witness."

Addressing Detective Gleason, Prosecutor Lindsay asked, "Did there come a time when you were able to question the defendant?"

Gleason pointed to Butterfly Baxter. "A team tried to affect the defendant's arrest, but she fled on a 100 mile an hour chase."

"In your experience, do innocent people flee from the police?"

Fishman jumped up yelling, "Objection your Honor! Cause for speculation." The judge sustained the objection.

Lindsay thought for a moment, "Besides being the victim's sister-in-law, did they have another relationship?"
"Objection! Relevance? Fishman asked. Judge Talbot overruled her and told the witness to answer.

"Yes. During our investigation, we found irrefutable evidence that the victim and defendant were having an affair."

"And what was that evidence detective?" "The two had a child together."

Prosecutor Lindsay looked at Butterfly while asking Gleason. "So, she had reason to want him murdered?" Attorney Fishman was halfway out of her seat when Lindsay yelled, "Strike that! No further questions Your Honor!"

The prosecution called Cassandra Kiddick to the witness stand. The bailiff escorted the woman into the courtroom directing her to stand at the bar facing Judge Talbot. Once she was sworn in and seated the prosecutor asked her to say her name for the record. She did and seemed to be eagerly awaiting the next question. "Is your father William Kiddick?"

"Yes, he was my father."

"Was your father? Is he dead Ms. Kiddick?"

The woman pushed a lock of hair away from her face. "Very, yes."

Prosecutor Lindsay paused for effect before asking, "Could you please tell the court, when and where?"

She looked up and away before training her eyes on the prosecutor. "My father fell off a cliff in New Zealand."

"Although your father died from his fall off of a cliff, wasn't he diagnosed with stage four pancreatic cancer before that?" A simple yes flowed into the microphone and out through the court's speaker system. Turning to the right, Lindsay asked the witness, "Have you ever seen the defendant, Butterfly Baxter before today?"

"Only once when she gave my father a large envelope." Attorney Fishman yelled, "Objection your Honor! It's obvious that the prosecution is trying to backdoor your earlier ruling."

Judge Talbot looked down from his perch. "Sustained! Don't test me Ms. Lindsay or you'll fail."

The prosecution had no further questions for the witness, but Attorney Fishman had a few.

"Good morning Ms. Kiddick. Have you ever seen my client and your father engaged in conversation?" The witness answered no. "Did you witness your father and/or the defendant kill Dr. Dorian Brooks?" Another no.

"Were you in any way involved with your father in the murder of Dr. Brooks?" The witness gave an indignant "No!" But Fishman was on a roll.

"Where were you on December 13th between the hours of 2:00 a.m. and 3:00 a.m. almost two years ago?"

Looking at Attorney Fishman Ms. Kiddick replied, "I don't remember. That was a long time ago."

"Is it possible that you were killing Dr. Brooks because your affair went bad?" Before any objection could be made Attorney Fishman smoothly said, "Strike that last question. I believe this witness is done or rather, I'm done with this witness." She turned to Prosecutor Lindsay and smirked.

"The witness may be excused if there's no redirect from the prosecution," the judge stated

Felicia Lindsay stated aloud for the record, "Nothing further." Lindsay then contemplated her next move. The room was silent while everyone stared at the prosecution's table waiting for what was coming next. What they never expected is what actually happened.

"Do you have any more witnesses?" Judge Talbot asked. There was a deep look of consternation on Lindsay's face. Then she said, "Your Honor, we the prosecution would like to dismiss all charges against the defendant, Butterfly Baxter."

Looking up the judge asked, "Are you sure? This seems to have been a waste of the court's time."

"Your Honor, it will be an even greater waste if we were to continue. "She looked at Stephanie Fishman wanting to slap the smirk off her arrogant face. The prosecution will be reviewing the case file to see if future charges are warranted.

Judge Talbot formally dismissed the charges and went into recess. Butterfly turned to her lawyer, "Is that it? Am I free to go?" Fishman saw the joy in her client's face and was brought back to reality herself. There was no way Lindsay would just drop all the charges. The murder charges were never going anywhere, but the conspiracy to kidnap charges have teeth. "Don't get too, excited, Mrs. Baxter. Double jeopardy isn't attached; so, they can refile at any time. I'm going to stick around until you get processed out in case they try any funny business."

They watched as Prosecutor Lindsay gathered her things and hurriedly walked out of the courtroom. The bailiff came over holding handcuffs signaling Butterfly that it was time to go. "Keep your mouth shut and I'll be over to the jail as soon as I can." Butterfly nodded as the deputy secured the cuffs on her wrists.

Out in the hallway, Stephanie Fishman saw all the other players involved in the case. Detective Sargent Jimenez, Detective Gleason, and Prosecutor Lindsay were huddled around Dr. Chicago Daniels. Fishman's associate, Brenda Walker was trying to run interference when she intervened.

"Excuse me, Dr. Daniels don't buy into these people's brand of B.S. Your sister is being released because their case doesn't exist. It never did! They were too lazy to initiate a real investigation, so they found an easy target to pin things on."

The prosecutor and the detectives were all quiet. They didn't make a peep. Alarm bells went off in Fishman's brain. She felt afraid and she only felt afraid when she didn't know what was going on. Fishman took her associate by the arm extricating her from the mix. "Dr. Daniels, when your sister is processed out, I'll give you a call."

Chicago nodded blankly and watched her sister's lawyers disappear down the corridor. "What happened? Is that true? Is my sister really being released?"

Prosecutor Lindsay ignored the waves of hostility emanating off of the detectives, especially Jimenez. "Don't worry Dr. Daniels, your sister won't be going anywhere for at least a few days. It's all by design. Needless to say, I can't divulge any specifics, but I need you to trust the system." She turned to the detectives telling them they would meet later.

She turned back to Chicago and addressed her, "Dr. Daniels, I need to make some moves before the court closes. My office will be in touch soon." All three were throwing questions at the retreating prosecutor. In the end, the detectives walked Chicago out of the Frank Murphy Hall of Justice to the corner of St. Antoine and Beaubien Streets where her car was parked, assuring her that everything would be fine.

Butterfly was feeling giddy. It wouldn't be too much longer before she was released from custody. At the moment she was alone in a holding cell in the registry. Once her fingerprints cleared and it was determined she had no wants or warrants from any other law enforcement agency, Butterfly would be cut loose. Until then, she was pacing slowly from one end of the cell to the other making mental notes of things to do. First, she would divorce Morgan making him pay a one-time settlement. Next, she'd move across the country, because the west coast could use a talking Butterfly. Last but not least, she would need to hire a dependable hard worker who knew how to follow detailed instructions. It would be the only way she could get rid of her sister. If she were to murder Chicago herself the police would be at her door before the body grew cold.

She was thinking of countless ways to dispose of old Windy City and reclaim her son when a deputy unlocked her cell, beckoning for her to follow. Butterfly was taken to a small visitor's room where her lawyer, Stephanie Fishman sat looking pensive. There was no glass partition separating them, just a small metal table with two metal plates attached to it for seats. Butterfly was about to speak when Fishman held a finger to her lips for her to be quiet. When the guard locked the door and walked away the lawyer spoke. "Listen closely to what I have to say. You're not going anywhere today." Butterfly was expressionless. "Did you hear me?"

"I heard you, please continue."

Fishman explained to her that a source inside the prosecutor's office told her they had filed new charges against Butterfly. They were going to release her then arrest her on fleeing and eluding, resisting arrest, and obstruction, but not before doing a precinct bounce. At that, Butterfly asked, "What's a precinct bounce?"

"That's when they move you around keeping you incommunicado." Fishman had a little juice herself, however; and would stop them from shuffling Butterfly around and make sure she would be properly arraigned and bonded out. "The key is remaining patient. My guess is that the prosecutor will try to get a tether condition added to your bond so they can monitor your movements."

"Make sure that doesn't happen." Butterfly stated.

"Don't worry, I will. I knew that there was no way that little opportunistic cock sucking hack Lindsay would drop the charges against you unless she had something else in mind."

Butterfly only nodded throughout the lawyer's conversation. "When will I be out?"

"In about a week or less. Just enough time for the powers that be to devise a plan to try and trick you into incriminating yourself."

"That'll never happen. These people are really trying my patience. Make sure you get me out of here as soon as you can." Butterfly stood up visibly thinking as she walked to the door. "It's okay. I can use the extra time to solidify a place to stay while I'm out on bond."

"I almost forgot. Do you have someone you can stay with?"

"I own property in and around the Detroit area. Trust me, I'll be fine," Butterfly said.

Stephanie Fishman had dealt with all manner of criminals and those accused of all types of crimes. But never had she come across someone calm, cool, dangerous, and together as Butterfly Baxter.

Two weeks later and they were still surveilling Butterfly. It was true. Mrs. Baxter did seem to own plenty of residential property in the Detroit area, including a beautiful brick two-story home on the east side. The magistrate wouldn't go for a tether monitor, so Butterfly Baxter was released on a $100,000.00 cash surety bond and allowed to move into a home she owned on Bliss Street off of Van Dyke Avenue. The neighborhood wasn't as nice as it had been in years past, but there was no doubt that she could handle it.

Jimenez and Gleason were both pissed when Prosecutor Lindsay dropped the charges against Baxter. They wanted to know what the hell she was thinking. If her reasoning wasn't sound, they intended to go over her head to her department supervisor. Gleason vividly recalled that day in the prosecutor's office.

192

He had to restrain his partner, even though the prospect of a good catfight seemed pretty exciting. After everyone had calmed down, Lindsay explained her plan. It wasn't a sure thing, but it was better than taking Baxter to trial and losing. If that happened double jeopardy would be in place and she couldn't be tried again. With the new strategy, if they lost, they would still have another opportunity to get Butterfly. Lindsay would refile on the murder and kidnapping charges and take their chances then.

Both Jimenez and Gleason looked at their watches almost simultaneously. It was after ten in the morning and their suspect was probably still asleep. The past few days had been very busy for Mrs. Baxter. Meeting delivery trucks, shopping for clothes, and buying household items. Jimenez had to pee. It made her angry that she was sitting in an uncomfortable car, while Baxter was sleeping in.

It had been five days since her release from custody. Fishman was right. Butterfly was processed out and arrested again right in the lobby of the jail. It took a week for her to be arraigned on the new charges and almost three days to be bonded out. Fishman was on her job. Butterfly had given her power of attorney and she procured the house keys from the management company, changed the alarm codes, and rented Butterfly a vehicle. With the handcuff marks still visible on her wrists, she was out buying cheap furniture and a couple of television sets. There were multiple undercover police cars following her every time she set foot outside of the house. Her bright red rental car was easy to spot, and she wanted it that way. At least until the time came when she didn't.

She had thought about ordering cable but then imagined the cable guy as an undercover cop sent into plant listening devices. Forget it! She ordered up Wi-Fi from AT&T and bought an Amazon Fire Stick. It took six minutes to find a hacker's chat room and get information on how to illegally encode the Fire Stick. Another eight minutes to logon to a different site and do the deed. In a total of 16 minutes, Butterfly was kicked back, relaxed, and watching a recent episode of the Looming Tower.

That was the previous night. She'd been up since 5:00 in the morning. After a thirty-minute bout of high impact calisthenics, she took an ice-cold shower to keep her skintight and youthful, then ate breakfast. It was a light one, with granola cereal, Greek yogurt, and orange juice. The empty refrigerator reminded her that she needed to go grocery shopping. She thought to herself, A girl could use some eggs, almond milk, and fresh fruit. She pulled out her new laptop and read some of the online newspaper sites, then channel surfed back and forth between the morning news- talk shows while making a mental note that those bad, bad, boys, Matt Lauer and Charlie Rose were missing. It was surprising considering their occupation and that they didn't have the sense to know trouble was spelled S-E-X. Butterfly had just switched from a game show to a talk show when she realized that she was bored out of her mind. Octavia wasn't speaking to her, so she was all alone.

Octavia was upset and not speaking with Butterfly because Butterfly called Chicago groveling like a peasant, apologizing to the old bitch just so she could see her bastard child. Chicago shot her down like a clay pigeon at a skeet shoot. "I'm not sure how it might affect Albany. Let me think about it," she said. Octavia was pissed and began cursing and bringing up the past. Butterfly accepted a great deal of her shit, but when she kept making derogatory remarks about her child, she took the gloves off. Words like slut, whore, and cunt were thrown around like air molecules.

Enough was enough! Butterfly had to remind Miss Southern Belle that it was Octavia who had two abortions and she was just jealous that Butterfly had someone to love other than her phony ass! Octavia asked for an apology. Butterfly refused.

"You practically beg that bitch of a sister of yours to forgive you and me you refuse to apologize to! You ungrateful cunt! After all, I've done for you. Without me, you'd be selling your ass to some man for a bushel of snot-nose kids and a five-year-old minivan!" That last exchange ended in them no longer speaking.

It was true that Chicago was intentionally keeping Albany from her, but there was nothing she could do about it. Butterfly was just about to watch the View on T.V. when her cellphone rang. Only three people had her new number. Morgan, Chicago, and Attorney Fishman. She doubted if it were Morgan the Mogul. He was mad about their proposed divorce settlement.

"I don't think it's right that I should have to give you anything. You're the one out screwing around like a nymphomaniac!" He said.

Her response was childish. "Sticks and stones may break my bones, but my not being silent about your business practices will hurt you." Finally, after some very heated negotiations, she accepted a onetime cash settlement. A messenger would bring the papers next week and she'd sign them but would only give the papers back to the messenger when her offshore account balance changed.

It wouldn't be Chicago calling. Not with that oak tree up her ass. That left the attorney. She was surprised when she heard her sister's voice. "Hello, Windy City. Are you calling because you realize how important the bond between mother and child is?"

Chicago absorbed the slight effortlessly. "Albany wants to see you. We'll make it tomorrow for a late lunch. Let's say 2:00 p.m."

Butterfly could barely contain her excitement. "I'll be there. Do you need me to bring anything?" After several seconds she realized that she was speaking to dead air. It didn't bother her that Chicago had hung up on her. She couldn't care less as long as she was able to see Albany. Butterfly rushed upstairs to her bedroom where there were piles of bags filled with her new clothes. She found a purple silk blouse she'd bought from Neiman Marcus. Standing in front of her dresser mirror, she held the blouse up admiring herself.

"Oh! This bitch calls and you go running."

"I thought you weren't speaking to me, Octavia?"

"You think because you wear purple it'll make you royalty! You'll always be a peasant because you think small. You're a fucking academic genius who doesn't have enough common sense to fit in an ant's ass.

That sister of yours is using that bastard son to keep you off balance and lead you around by the nose. I keep telling you that she's up to something, but you won't listen."

Butterfly threw the blouse aside, "You jealous whore! Don't be mad at me because you vacuum sucked your children out of your vagina and into a biohazard bag." Butterfly regretted what she said before it flew out of her mouth. She looked at the mirror into Octavia's eyes and saw the rage brewing like a dark sky right before a tornado. Butterfly expected screaming and yelling. What she didn't expect was the calm even tone that she got.

"After everything I've done for you. You are selfish Butterfly! Without me, you'd probably be waking up with a wet crack in a random bed or taking DNA tests on daytime TV to establish paternity. You're on your own. Let's see how you do without me."

"Octavia, I'm sorry! Octavia? Octavia?" Butterfly might as well have been talking to herself. She was gone. Butterfly sat on the edge of the bed, closed her eyes, and screamed Octavia's name telepathically for ten minutes and never got an answer. The last time she was this upset was when Butterfly decided to keep Albany. Octavia didn't speak to her until Albany could walk and talk. She kept crying while apologizing profusely. Still, no Octavia. It was like when she was growing up. Butterfly was all alone again. The situation was almost enough to make her want to kill Octavia. Butterfly thought she's such a fucking drama queen. Somewhere in the shallow parts of her mind, the term murder-suicide swam around.

At 1:00 p.m., Butterfly got into her rental car and drove right up the street from her house to the corner of Seven Mile Road and Van Dyke. There was a GameStop store that sold all of the latest videogames and accessories. The night before she used the internet to find out what the hottest new games were, so it took only a few minutes to pull them off the shelves. The salesperson convinced her to buy a new virtual reality visor to act in concert with her son's gaming system. Butterfly was intrigued; so much so that she had lost track of time. Looking at her watch, she saw it was 1:33 p.m.

She hurriedly paid for her things and was fast walking to her car when out of nowhere, Cassandra Kiddick appeared. "My father was a smart man. He found the connection between you and Sanford Smalls. Here's my number." Butterfly stared at the piece of paper as though it were a venomous snake. Cassandra Kiddick shoved the slip of paper into Butterfly's jacket pocket. "Call me by tomorrow morning and we'll discuss money, or I'll have to drop an anonymous tip to the proper authorities."

Butterfly never said a word. She just smiled, pressed the button on the key fob disengaging the car's alarm, and settled into the driver's seat. She watched Cassandra Kiddick in the rearview mirror as she walked across the parking lot. They must think she's stupid. It's obvious the police are involved. Okay, she thought, let the games begin.

She was almost late arriving at Chicago's apartment. She wondered what the police could be up to and who else might be involved. Chicago might have something to do with this setup, she thought to herself. After all, she called out of the blue with an invitation to lunch knowing there was no way Butterfly would refuse the chance to see her Albany. By the time she reached the top floor, her mind was clear, and she began to form a semblance of a plan, which was compartmentalized for later. At that very moment, it was all about Albany.

Chicago was standing at the open door with a stern look on her face. Before Butterfly could speak, she said, "He's in his room. You can't take him outside of this building with the exception of the roof. None of your tricks or manipulations."

Butterfly walked past her into the apartment. "It's great to see you too, Sis!"

Closing the door, Chicago said, "I mean it! Don't try me Butterfly." The two women shared a brief stare down. "Lunch will be served in a minute."

"It smells like corned beef."

"Corned beef sandwiches with Cole slaw to be exact."

Butterfly held up the bag. "I'm going to see my son. Just call when you're ready for us to eat."

Chicago stood in her way. "Keep in mind what I've told you. Albany has a lot of questions that don't need to be answered right now. If he starts in on you, refer him to me."

Butterfly turned sideways edging by her. "You can't help but try and control everyone around you. Is it because your life is so chaotic? Albany is my child and I think as his mother, I know what's best for him." Chicago walked away towards the kitchen.

"If you want to be in his life, you will do as I say or be like Momma's Uncle Alvin."

"I've never heard of Momma having an Uncle Alvin."

Chicago was setting plates on the dining room table when she looked at Butterfly smiling and said, "My point exactly. Tread lightly little sister, lest you tread no more. Now, go see Albany and tell him lunch is ready." Butterfly was about to speak when Chicago cut her off. "Do as I say, little girl, before I make sure you're nothing more than a faded memory in a picture frame on the mantle."

Butterfly swallowed the nasty retort she had planned. She watched as Chicago went back to setting the table with her back turned; then she flipped her off and stomped off to see Albany.

Butterfly hugged and kissed her baby, thrilled to see him. He bombarded her with a slew of questions that made her want to go against Chicago's wishes and answer them. But then thought better of it. She distracted him with the virtual reality visor and videogames she'd bought for him. The two of them had gotten so involved with their play that she forgot all about lunch until Chicago yelled for them both. After lunch, Butterfly and Albany went up on the roof while Chicago cleaned up. They shot pool, played ping pong, and threw horseshoes until they were exhausted.

Butterfly assured Albany that things would work themselves out and mother and son would be back together soon. He asked about Morgan and whether or not they'd be a family again. She told him the truth. "No. We probably won't, but anything is possible." They went down to his room and played one of his new games. It was fast approaching evening by the time they were done. She hugged and kissed him again and left him staring at the television screen. Chicago was sitting at the dining room table drinking some wine when Butterfly sidled up for a little tête-à-tête.

"Thank you for allowing me to see Albany. He really was missing me."

Chicago pushed an empty wineglass towards her little sister. "Would you like some? It's expensive as hell. Your baby's daddy bought it for our fifth wedding anniversary. It was worth only a hundred dollars a bottle back then. Now it retails for eight hundred. Dorian bought two cases saying it was a good investment. We were supposed to open a bottle on each of our future anniversaries."

Butterfly picked up the bottle and drank straight from it. "Boohoo! Are we missing your cheating husband?"

Chicago laughed, "Shouldn't you be on your way home, wherever that is. Don't you have a curfew or something?"

Butterfly took another swig from the wine bottle. "No, I don't have a curfew and you know exactly where I live. You remember Momma's old house on Bliss, the one she left us when she died?"

Chicago jumped up from her seat seemingly to attack her sister; then thought of Albany. "When I sold that house and gave you half the proceeds what did you do? Did you go behind my back and buy it?" Butterfly's face flushed. She was excited by the look of anguish on the old bitch's face. "I told you when you wanted to keep the property, that it held nothing but awful memories for me and our mother. Why would you buy it, let alone want to live there?"

Butterfly held her hands out in front of her while mockingly saying, "Whoa there! You look like you're about to turn violent. Let's back up a little. I bought the house on Bliss several years ago because it belonged to our mother. Owning it made me feel closer to Big Shirley. Knowing that it bothers you is just a bonus."

Chicago sat back down shaking her head in utter disappointment. "How? Where? I don't understand."

"You don't understand what?"

"Where Momma and I went wrong raising you and how you turned out to be so evil and apathetic towards the feelings of others." Butterfly laughed in her face.

"Later for that. Let's get to the good stuff before my baby comes out of his room. Let's talk about my baby daddy, your late husband, Dorian.

"I'm not going there with you!"

Butterfly took a healthy swallow from the bottle swishing it around like mouthwash, gargled, and declared, "This is some good shit! All you have to do is listen, Chicago."

Chicago cocked her head as if to say, 'get on with it.'

She listened as her sister told her that it was understandable for her to believe the lies told by the police. If someone wanted her dead, it was Dorian by himself. "Anyway, I think you had him killed and attempted to frame me for it. The whole two birds with one stone thing. You have your revenge and as a bonus, my son."

She calmly stood up and pulled the wine bottle from Butterfly's grasp. "Leave my home!"

"Do you think I'm stupid? Far from it, Windy City, far from it. I didn't have anything to do with Dorian's murder. I've given it considerable thought and the only thing that makes sense is that someone is playing marionette behind the scenes. The only person close enough to pull any strings in this drama besides me is you. With me in prison and hubby taking a dirt nap, you would have it all. There's just one problem."

They reached the front door and Chicago held it open. "And what's that Caterpillar?"

Butterfly walked to within an inch of her sister's face. "Me!"

The detectives were with Cassandra Kiddick at her home near Harper Woods on the east side of Detroit. "Where's your son Ms. Kiddick?"

She looked out her living room window. "He's with his father. Listen, Sargent Jimenez, I'm not too enthusiastic about this plan. You should have seen how that lady looked at me. You ever watch National Geographic when they show the female lion eyeing a gazelle? That's how that Baxter woman looked at me. She wouldn't even take the number you guys gave me to give her. I had to shove it in her pocket. She never said a word either; just stared at me like I was lunch."

Gleason, too, was concerned about the young woman's role in this affair. "When she calls, you have to be cool, Cassandra. Remember you're the one in control and we have your back. Butterfly Baxter is under 24-hour surveillance and can't get anywhere near you without us knowing about it. It's important when she calls the phone we gave you that you to hit the recording app and follow the script just the way we practiced."

Jimenez joined in. "After the conversation, call us immediately and we'll be right over to wire you up for the meeting with her. Remember, she controls absolutely nothing. You do! Just follow the script."

Gleason added, "Trust us. We've done this before. You'll meet with her, she'll pay you off for the fake info, and we will arrest her." Jimenez thought to herself, I hope Lindsay's plan works. They needed real evidence or some type of leverage to extract a confession from Butterfly Baxter.

Cassandra gave the two detectives an uncertain look. Jimenez recognized the look and told her, "My partner and I are available to you at any time of the day or night. You should be fine; but if you encounter anything out of the ordinary, anything suspicious at all, you contact us or 911 immediately."

"I'll do exactly as I've been told, Cassandra replied. "You guys just make sure and talk to that asshole insurance investigator. After all, my dad did die in an accident."

Cassandra was hesitant to be involved until Prosecutor Lindsay told her that she could make sure the insurance company didn't come after her for fraud. Ms. Kiddick received a visit from an insurance investigator, who told her they had reason to believe her father's accident was really a suicide and that she helped to cover it up. Of course, she denied it emphatically, but when Prosecutor Lindsay told her she could make sure the investigator went away as long as Cassandra cooperated, she agreed. That money was going for her son's education. There was no way she was giving it back.

Jimenez didn't like that Lindsay used a detective posing as an insurance investigator to trick the young woman into helping them, but at times a little deception was necessary. They cautioned her again to be careful and then they left. Once in their car, they expressed their concerns.

"Butterfly Baxter has a string of bad acts under her belt and I damn sure don't want Cassandra Kiddick to be another one." Gleason started driving.

"I know what you mean, Sarge. We've got a good surveillance detail on our suspect. Let's think positive. I mean, hell, they're up her ass so deep that they're making her breakfast and tucking her in. Everything is going to be fine."

"From your mouth to God's ears," Gleason said. Just to be sure she contacted the detail and was told Mrs. Baxter went to her sister's apartment in midtown for several hours, stopped at a gas station, then went back to the residence on Bliss. Jimenez gave strict orders that she be notified if their perp stepped out again for anything. Her gut was clenching and unclenching as if it was trying to tell her something was wrong. She shared her feelings with Gleason. He told her it was probably those you buy-we fry greasy chicken wings she'd eaten for lunch. Shaking her head, no, but saying nothing Jimenez was certain that something was amiss. She just couldn't tell what it was.

She had been back at the house on Bliss for several hours. Butterfly made sure to 'allow' her watchers unencumbered sight to every move she made up until the point when she walked through the front door and discreetly out the back, slipping into the brick two-car garage with its hard-packed dirt floor. In one of the corners were a pickaxe, shovel, and spade. Butterfly inhaled the mustiness of the otherwise clean garage as she pulled on a pair of heavy-duty work gloves and went straight for the pick. The ground near the west wall was a bit softer than the rest.

By the time she finished, it was almost time for the 11:00 news. She shook off specks of loose dirt, checked her immediate surroundings, and stealthily made her way back into the house. Butterfly undressed right inside the backdoor, leaving her clothes and shoes on the landing going into the basement. She would need them again. But right then she pulled on a forest green fleece jogging suit and a good pair of running shoes that she had placed there earlier.

Her house backed onto an abandoned recreation center. The second day she was at the house, she cut a hole in her back fence just in case she needed to boogie on out of there in a hurry. The 8' tall privacy fence behind the house ran the length of the city block. The recreation center's field was a little overgrown but made for a good escape route if the police came knocking. Butterfly left her cellphone in the house with it on a call to an acquaintance in San Francisco who'd swear they were talking the entire time. She gave explicit instructions for them to end the conversation after 1 hour and 36 minutes. It should be more than enough time for her to take care of business. One final check of her watch and she tightened her shoestrings, pulled her hoodie up, and slid through the hole in the fence. When she made it to the other side of the field, she found a gap in the chain-link and wiggled through taking off at the brisk pace of a six-minute mile.

Butterfly got to her destination in 32 minutes. The only light coming from the house came through the front windows and looked as though it was from the glare of the television. The ranch-style house sat on a corner lot with an attached garage that faced a side street. She walked through the rear gate into the backyard as if she belonged there. A side window with a screen in it was open. She picked up a sharp rock and punched a hole in the screen; then slit it all the way across with her finger.

On the ground next to some old lawn furniture and children's toys was a plastic planter with a small fern growing in it. Butterfly flipped it upside down and stood on it. In seconds she was in what looked like a child's bedroom. The incredible Hulk curtains and Ironman night light were a dead giveaway. Butterfly crouched down absolutely still; listening with her eyes closed. All she could hear was a television. Her natural inclination was to head for the sound, but her instincts were telling her to ignore it and check the rooms in the back first.

Across from the room where she entered was another bedroom. It must be hers, Butterfly thought. Pictures of the woman and a cute, impish looking brown-haired little boy were sprinkled on the dresser and nightstand. An economy pack of tampons and a slew of feminine hygiene products were just sitting on top of the wardrobe. Butterfly knew from that and the absence of any male clothes or toiletries that no man was present. Any self-respecting woman with a man likes to keep her feminine products secret. She checked another bedroom that looked like it was being used for storage. She gave a quick check of a bathroom and linen closet. By the time she reached the sound of the television, she was feeling right at home.

Cassandra Kiddick was curled up like a piece of shrimp on her living room couch asleep, while Jimmy Fallon told political jokes. Butterfly took some seconds and watched the rise and fall of her chest; assuring herself that Cassandra Kiddick was, in fact, asleep. On the coffee table in front of her was a small revolver. Butterfly tiptoed over and pocketed the gun while thinking how to appropriately wake the sleeping nobody. Then it came to her.

She looked through a doorway and saw a plastic bag lying on a kitchen table. It fit easily over the young woman's head; then was tightened at the nape of her neck. By the time Cassandra realized what was happening, she was short of breath and disoriented. Butterfly stepped back and watched curiously as Cassandra Kiddick tore at the plastic gulping in deep breaths of air. She wanted to run or scream, but she saw Butterfly holding her own gun aimed at her forehead.

"Hello. Let's get right to it Cassandra. Where's this evidence you're supposed to have against me?"

Rubbing her throat, she answered, "It's somewhere safe."

"Liar, liar house on fire! I don't believe you. This picture is all wrong. Your son is away, you're asleep on the couch with a loaded .38 and lying to me. Let's start over okay?"

"I'm not lying to you. If you don't leave now, I'm going to make your life miserable!"

"Misery loves company."

"I'm the type of company you don't want to keep," Cassandra said.

Just as Butterfly started laughing at that remark, she swung her gun hand forward and slapped Cassandra on the side of the head. The woman shrank deeper into the couch cushions clutching her wound. Almost immediately she could feel the lump rising under the palm of her hand. "You silly little girl with your false display of toughness. I'll give you one more chance to help yourself and unlike the police, I'm going to make your honesty worth your while. Take 60 seconds to think about your predicament then we'll start again."

Cassandra started to speak, but Butterfly held a finger to her lips for silence and glanced at her watch. "58, 59, okay I'll start. Are you working for the police?" Cassandra started to lie but thought better of it looking at Butterfly, who resembled a hungry lioness licking her chops.

"Yeah, I guess."
"You guess? Bitch, you better know for sure!"

Butterfly raised her hand to strike Cassandra. "Wait! I'll tell you what I know."

Butterfly sat in front of the woman on the edge of the coffee table. "Go ahead, you have my undivided attention."

She started with how the prosecutor was going to make the insurance investigator go away if she helped the police.

"Insurance companies don't payout then investigate. The prosecutor knows that you helped your father commit suicide. They just can't prove it. Did you check out the investigator making sure he or she wasn't a cop?" The dumb look on her face said it all. "There's no way your old man can have any incriminating evidence against me because I don't know him and had nothing to do with Dorian's death. So, where's the evidence?"

"There isn't any. The detectives just told me what to say to you." "Someone is setting me up and I think you know who it is. Tell me everything about your father and do it as fast as you can. Your life depends on it." When Butterfly cocked the hammer on the gun, Cassandra told all she could.

She listened, only interrupting to ask a question or two when needed. Butterfly knew all along the police were involved. Now she knew who else was, too.

When Cassandra was all talked out, they sat silently for a few minutes while Butterfly put it all together. "What are you going to do with me?"

"You're a single mother just like me. I'll do anything to protect my son and be with him, as I'm sure you would to be with yours. The only way for me to feel comfortable about letting you go is for you to take the money I'm going to offer you. This way, you're involved with something criminal. I'll have something on you, and we can forget about me sneaking in here holding you at gunpoint."

"How much money are we talking about?" Butterfly did some quick calculations. "How about $32,000.00 cash tonight and in a day or two another $18,000.00? That's $50,000.00 tax-free."

Cassandra Kiddick was all for it. "How will I get the money tonight?"

"You'll have to come with me to my house." The young woman hadn't made her mind up about the money, but either way, she saw it as an opportunity to escape this woman. "I know you're just agreeing to take the money to get away from me, but think about this: If I were a dangerous person like the police claim, why not put a pillow over your head and shoot you with your own gun? I just wanted to find out what in the hell is going on and who's behind it so I can be reunited with my son. They lied to you. There's no insurance investigator. I bet they used an undercover cop to trick you. They're the bad people! If I was a killer, you'd be dead, and that handsome little boy would be growing up without a mother. Please just take the money. I'm sure you could use it."

When it was put like that, it made a lot of sense "But, why are you still holding a gun on me then?"

"Because I'm not sure I can trust you yet. This is your gun. You are working with the police to frame me. By your own admission, there is no evidence. They gave you a script to play out. Think Cassandra!"

"Okay, okay!" The young woman was wearing leggings and a tee shirt. Butterfly let her slip on a pair of sandals then followed her through the kitchen out through a door and into the garage. They were taking Cassandra's ten-year-old minivan. "You drive," Butterfly told her while crouching behind the driver's seat and shoving the gun into the woman's ribs. "Please, don't do anything stupid. I don't want to hurt you but, I don't want to be away from my son either." The garage door opened then closed remotely. Butterfly gave her directions that kept them off of main roads. Ten minutes later they were a block over from her house on the opposite side of the recreation center's field.

She explained their method of entry to her property and that it was necessary because of the police surveillance. Butterfly pushed Cassandra through the hole in the fence bordering her backyard and motioned her into the garage. Once there she told her, "Wait here while I grab your money." The young woman could only see a sliver of moonlight shining through the garage's window." It's almost pitch black in here!"

Butterfly told her to keep her voice down. "Turn around, there's a battery-operated camping lantern hanging on the wall." When the woman turned she felt a powerful blow to the back of her head. After she dropped like a sack of potatoes to the ground Butterfly brought the butt of the gun down several more times. She checked her pulse then pinched her nose while covering her mouth, cutting off her oxygen. When Butterfly was sure Cassandra Kiddick was dead, she grabbed her ankles and drug her over to the grave kicking her in.

Searching the dead woman's pockets for the car keys and rushing back to the minivan, Butterfly made it to Cassandra's house in record time. She wiped down everything she touched including the gun, leaving it under the driver's seat, then she ran back home in almost record time. Her legs were burning from running, but she felt good. After checking to make sure Cassandra was where she left her, Butterfly crept into the house retrieving her phone. Her call log showed a conversation that lasted one hour and 36 minutes. There were no missed calls, but her battery was low. She found her charger, plugged up the phone, and snagged a bottle of water. She drank it slowly thinking about how much she missed Octavia. They were best friends. No one knew her better except maybe Chicago. Windy City could sometimes tell what Butterfly was thinking. It saddened her that Octavia was missing out on all of the fun, but when they made up, she would give her the juicy details.

Back in the garage, she worked as fast as humanly possible. Cassandra, you little nobody, you were foolish to throw in with the police, she thought.

Butterfly knew that she didn't have to kill Cassandra, but she did it to mind fuck that Jimenez bitch; and what better way to do that than making a police lackey disappear? She grabbed a push broom and spread all of the displaced dirt around until the floor felt even. In the morning after the sun came up, Butterfly would check and make sure everything looked as it should.

She was exhausted from the night's activities. She stepped outside the garage pulling the side door shut and went into the house. Before taking a bath, she washed her clothes and shoes. As she relaxed in the tub soaking her aching muscles, she began thinking about the total destruction of Chicago. The sister, not the city.

It was late and Albany was asleep. After his mother left, he bombarded Auntie Chi with questions; but got very few answers. Chicago was able to fend him off for the time being, but she knew that everything had to come to an end. All of the lies, diabolical deceptions and pretending had to stop. She lay on the loveseat in her bedroom staring at the ceiling wondering how different her life would be if Butterfly wasn't in it.

Like a film changing a scene, her thoughts changed to when Dorian brought her home from the hospital after being rescued. He catered to all of her needs like they were newlyweds. They both knew there was an ugly elephant in the room, but they tiptoed around it for fear of being crushed by it.

Chicago hadn't only been kidnapped, she had been sexually assaulted, too. Dorian attempted to address the matter, but how do you approach the subject of your wife being a madman's sex slave? He fumbled at it until Chicago saved him by refusing to discuss it. Their California king-sized bed was large enough to hold them both with plenty of space in between so they didn't have to touch. Any type of physical contact felt repulsive to her. What she needed more than a kind word or a pat on the back, was time; time to heal mentally as well as physically. Dorian didn't get it because he was there 24/7. At first, Chicago thought it was a show of his love and commitment to their marriage vows, for better or for worse. Then, something inside told her it was contrived. It felt wrong like he was acting out a part in a soap opera. Chicago practically begged him to go back to work at the university. Almost a week later when Dorian eventually left to resume teaching, she was thankful. The apartment was peaceful. She needed some solitude more than anything.

Two days after he went back to work, Chicago was going through her things from the hospital. The night before, Dorian had asked the whereabouts of her wedding ring. He had waited to ask because he didn't want to upset her. He wondered if it had been stolen.

Her wedding ring, diamond bracelet, watch, and earrings were all there. But it was odd because she was holding a third earring, which was impossible. The platinum and diamond-encrusted earrings in the shape of two dolphins hugging each other were custom made and very expensive. The jeweler who sold them to Chicago was also the designer. They were four of five and five of five respectively. The other three pairs were purchased a day before Chicago bought hers from a Scandinavian tourist and her twin girls. No one in the western hemisphere should own a pair of those beside Butterfly and Chicago.

She started racking her brain to figure out what was going on when flashes of her rescue and subsequent hospital stay flooded her consciousness. Her body seemed to be pulled down to the floor by some unseen force. Chicago brought her knees to her chest and wrapped her arms around her legs. Her head began to throb as an image of her lying on a plastic-covered floor bleeding profusely rushed to the front of her mind. Chicago thought she must have been hallucinating when she heard her sister's voice cursing her like a sailor and wishing her to die an instant before bullets came crashing through the walls and door striking her in the shoulder and leg. She could almost feel the heroin coursing through her veins making the pain bearable until she passed out.

When she came to, the door was being kicked in. Police were telling her not to move and that she was safe. Men and women wearing bulletproof vests with big guns were asking her who else was involved. Between the heroin and adrenaline rush, she couldn't answer. They were having a problem getting a gurney into the room where she was because of the brain matter and the body of Sanford Smalls blocking the hall.

Finally, the powers that be threw a sheet over him and two EMTs bandaged Chicago's wounds then carried her out. Just before reaching the body, they set her down to adjust their hold on her and that's when she saw what she thought was her earring shining under the officer's flashlight beams. Chicago snatched it up right before they lifted her over Sanford's body placing her on a gurney. When she focused again, she was being brought out of an abandoned building in a rundown neighborhood, and then put in an ambulance. Consciousness was like a game of 'Where's Waldo.' It was here, there, then gone again.

She recalled an emergency room doctor explaining what was happening and what they were going to do to help her. She was severely dehydrated, and she had two gunshot wounds. But even more than those injuries was the fact that he had to have a rape kit done on her. Chicago almost lost it when they started putting her legs in stirrups. A nurse was right near her and calmed her down. She kept telling Chicago, "You're safe. It's okay. You're safe, Dr. Daniels."

After that examination, she was taken to X-ray where that same nurse, a lovely Asian woman with a kind, grandmotherly nature removed her jewelry, even the earring that was clasped in her fist. The woman stroked her hair telling her not to worry and kept repeating over and over that she was safe. "I'll personally hold it for you until you're out of surgery."

Chicago came through her surgery and after leaving the recovery room, was placed in a private suite. Dorian, Morgan, and Butterfly visited briefly along with Detective Sargent Jimenez. At the time, Chicago didn't know who the attractive Hispanic looking woman was in the corner but could see that she was watching her visitors intensely.

Later, the grandmotherly nurse who took her jewelry came in and woke her up. "Hey, there beautiful! I didn't mean to disturb you; I just came to bring your things." Chicago's mouth was so dry she just nodded. The nurse, who introduced herself as Belinda Shea, poured her a cup of water from the pitcher on the bedside table. The woman said, "Here, I know your mouth probably feels like you're chewing on cotton balls. I'm not your duty nurse, but since I'm already here bringing your stuff, I might as well check your vitals."

211

When the woman was done, she leaned over Chicago checking both of her ears. "I thought so. You only have one piercing in each ear. A pretty girl like you doesn't want to stretch her earlobes by putting two of those heavy earrings in one hole." She tucked Chicago in and told her she would pray for her. Chicago hadn't given the moment with Brenda Nguyen any thought until later.

She stared at all three earrings she was holding in the palm of her hand. Her memories of that time must have been subconsciously repressed. Now they were as clear as Baccarat crystal. She wanted to confide in Dorian when he came home from work, but she didn't want him to think she was crazy or overreacting. Besides, lately, her husband wasn't exactly himself. He seemed a little strange and not just because of what happened to her. His false empathy and good husband shtick made her see him as someone else. No. She would keep her own counsel until she found out more.

Thinking back, it didn't take long for more to come. A few days later while she was napping, the home phone rang. Both she and Dorian picked it up almost simultaneously on the third ring. Before she could answer she heard her husband say, "Dr. Brooks speaking." Butterfly's voice responded, "Where's wifey?"

"Taking a siesta. Why?"

In a coquettish voice, Butterfly replied, "I was hoping to speak with Dr. Marvin Gaye. My vagina is in need of some sexual healing."

Just as boldly and in a mock professional tone, Dorian stated, "If you tell me the exact nature of your problem, I'll let you know whether or not I can be of assistance."

"Well, it's constantly wet and very, very tight."

Chicago couldn't believe what she was hearing. She covered the mouthpiece with her free hand and held her breath for fear of making a sound and being discovered. "I think that I can help you little slut. But I told you that we need to keep a low profile." Dorian and Butterfly started to engage in a phone sex session that made Chicago feel as though she were intruding. Carefully she hung up the extension. What in the hell is going on! My husband and Butterfly are having an affair, she thought. Chicago was in shock!

A short time later Dorian walked into their bedroom calling her name. She astutely played sleep. When he went to work the next morning, Chicago searched his things and went through his home computer. She had discovered his password by chance a month before her kidnapping. While looking at the surveillance monitors, she saw him in their apartment office and watched his keystrokes. That was that. Her search yielded nothing. The day after, Chicago searched the entire apartment again more thoroughly. Still nothing! With no place left to search she started thinking maybe she was crazy. Out of desperation to find something, she went up to the roof.

Chicago dug into the sand of the horseshoe pits, checked the pockets of the pool table and searched for any hidden compartments. It wasn't until she looked into the broiler section of Dorian's precious grill that she hit pay dirt. There was a plastic Ziploc bag full of letters and two flash drives. Chicago glanced at her watch. The asshole would be home soon, so she put the bag back where she found it and decided to wait until the next day to discover just what was cooking.

Chicago couldn't sleep and could hardly eat anything at all as she waited for Dorian to leave for work. The son of a bitch acted so concernedly about her welfare. It was all a freaking act! She thought to herself. Then she concluded, Guess what? If he could act, then she could too! The next day he noticed a change in her behavior, but she covered it up telling him that she woke up not feeling well. He offered to stay home until she told him it was just menstrual cramps. Dorian bought it and was off to work. Chicago had the plastic bag in her hands before the asshole reached the end of the block. She took it down into her bedroom.

Chicago never knew correspondence could be so salacious. There were over thirty letters, none of them more than four pages long. She read nineteen of them and stopped for a coffee break. It was a little after 1:00 p.m. when she finished. And even though that asshole Dorian wouldn't be home for another four or five hours, she couldn't bring herself to start watching the flash drive. Curiosity nearly consumed her. However, her mind was already overloaded with the knowledge that her sister and her husband were not only having an affair but that their affair produced a child. After reading the letters there was no doubt that both of them were responsible for placing her in the hands of a madman. The gut-wrenching question was: Would they try again?

When she did watch what was on those flash drives, she discovered that in the more than twenty years of their marriage, Dorian had slept with more than 200 women. Most of them were students who ranged in age from late teens to early thirties of all races, shapes, and hair colors. Their pictures were on one of the drives along with some videos. In most of those, Butterfly and a gorgeous full figured woman were engaged in sexual acts that could only be categorized as hardcore pornography. By the time Chicago was done it was almost time for Dorian to come home. She put the evidence of that asshole's adultery back in the broiler and slipped into the shower letting the water hide her tears.

They would pay for what they had done. Both of them would pay dearly. Chicago started making a quick recovery. It was all part of her plan. She knew who her enemies were. It sickened her to no end sleeping with one and related to the other. What she needed more than anything was a plausible excuse to leave the apartment when she wanted to without raising suspicion. It came by way of Sanford Smalls shooting her up with heroin. Chicago told Dorian that she was having uncontrollable urges to use narcotics and had decided to attend some local NA/AA meetings. He suggested one-on-one therapy, but she dismissed the suggestion.

"You know how the psychology community is. Patient-client confidentiality wouldn't mean anything when a colleague started treating me. If not a loose-lipped doctor, then a secretary might divulge that I'm seeking treatment. I'd rather go about it this way," she told him.

The meetings were held in halls, community centers, and churches all over the Detroit area. Anytime Chicago wanted to get out of the house because she felt the desire to smash Dorian's face in with a hammer or cut out his cheating heart with one of his $400.00 ceramic knives, she would tell him that she needed a meeting. Unbeknownst to him was that most of her time out of the apartment was spent at the gun range or taking classes to acquire a CCW permit. Her compact Glock 23, .40 caliber semiautomatic pistol was her only friend besides her business partner, Freida Goldberg. Though she spoke to Freida at least three times a week, she didn't let her visit, nor did Chicago visit her. Freida was a whiz at reading body language and Chicago couldn't afford to be psychoanalyzed at that moment.

It was at one of those NA/AA meetings that she met Billy the Kidd. Even though he was just as wounded as she was, he was still able to laugh. Billy was funny in that self-deprecating kind of way. They became fast friends after leaving a meeting one night and holding up at a donut shop to trade war stories. Billy's first wife Camille died of a brain aneurysm nine years into their marriage. More than eight years went by with him believing he would never find love again. Then he met Karen. She was a godsend at that time in his life. Alcoholism had him in its painful grip and thoughts of suicide were his happiest moments. But Karen changed all of that. In three years, she had helped him get back on the right track. Life was good, his business was turning a profit, and loving Karen was great.

They married and five years later, divorced. For the life of him, he couldn't understand what went wrong. He begged her to reconcile, maybe go to marriage counseling or do anything else necessary to keep them together. She refused and went ahead with the proceedings. When it was finalized, Billy found out around the time he started to make his first alimony payment that he was almost broke. With the help of his daughter from his first marriage, he discovered that someone forged his name and took out a five year, hundred-thousand dollar loan.

The only persons with access to his financial papers were his former business partner, Brandon, and his ex-wife. Then the real bombshell dropped. Billy went over to Brandon's to confront him and see what the hell was going on, but he had moved. One of his neighbors who knew Billy told him that his best friend and former business partner was living in Brownstown. When he finally tracked him down, he saw his ex-wife Karen, playing grab-ass with Brandon. He confronted both of them. Things got ugly and the police were called. To add further insult to injury, Billy was diagnosed with cancer.

The more Chicago and Billy talked, the more they each realized how much they had in common. Chicago and Billy were both betrayed by the two people they loved and trusted most in the world. Over six months, the two shared intimate details about their spouses and themselves. Together at the donut shop one day Billy said, "Honestly, I would love to kill them both."

Chicago gave him a very serious look. "I know the feeling, but how would you get away with it if you did?"

Billy thought about it for a while. "There's no way for me to get away with it. The police would come and arrest me. If I paid someone, that'd give them leverage over me for blackmail and if they got caught, they'd tell what they knew to bargain for a lesser sentence. Believe me Lakeshore, I've given it a lot of thought."

Chicago pushed their coffee cups aside and took his hands in hers. "What if I told you there was a way?"

That remark captured his interest. "And just what do you propose?" They leaned closer to one another lowering their voices in a conspiracy. Pretty soon a viable plan took shape. But to Billy at first, it was a silly plan. Then to show her sincerity, Chicago acted alone.

Unlike Chicago, her sister didn't spend the night as an insomniac trudging through shitty memories of the past. Butterfly slept like a baby on its mother's breast waking up right before noon. The events of the previous night were a distant, though fond memory. She knew that she didn't have to kill Cassandra Kiddick, although she did hope Octavia would approve of her take-charge attitude and start speaking with her again because of it. Sadly, Butterfly was wrong and didn't hear from her. The reward in killing Cassandra was that she was able to find out who was responsible for setting her up for Dorian's murder; and as a bonus, she'd get to twist the screws tight into that smarty pants detective bitch in the process. Can't really ask for much more than that, she thought with a smile. The lovely 'Latina' is going to flip her fucking lid when she can't find her stool pigeon, Butterfly thought stretching her arms high above her head, then leaning forward touching her toes yawning away last night's exhaustion.

She didn't want to get out of bed, but she had to make an appearance for her surveillance detail. Besides, she needed groceries. She'd be lucky to find a yogurt cup or a spoon of coffee. After a much needed morning pee, she went down into the kitchen. There was no more yogurt or cereal, but thankfully, there was enough coffee for two cups. She sipped slowly while making a to-do list for herself.

Butterfly figured since she was in the inner city she might as well dress the part and go ghetto fabulous. Tight jeans, expensive top, and running shoes. Normally she wouldn't wear running shoes unless she was running, but these shoes were evidence of a crime and needed to be disposed of. A Detroit Tiger's baseball cap pulled low over her brow completed her ensemble. As soon as she stepped outside onto the porch, Butterfly could feel the eyes of her watchers on her and, Damn, it felt good! Who better to be your alibi witness than a bunch of dumbass cops? she thought to herself with a wicked smile.

The big Hemi engine roared to life and Butterfly eased out of the driveway. Her first stop was a shoe store where she purchased two new pairs of running shoes. Politely she asked the clerk to discard the ones she was wearing and wore one of the new pair out of the store. The clerk was a little dumbfounded because they were the same brand of shoe and seemed to be fairly new themselves. What the hey, it was her money. Next was the grocery store where she bought only enough food for a week. Someone in her position never knew when it would be time to hit the road.

She was proud of herself. Not once did she look in her mirrors and try to find the police following her. They were like the sun. Sometimes you can't see it, but you know it's there. Butterfly pulled into her driveway and went to her trunk for her groceries. When she returned to the car for her shoes, Jimenez pulled up behind Butterfly's car. "You're blocking me in detective. I may need to make a quick getaway."

Jimenez got out and leaned against the fender of her unmarked car and said, "I'm just stopping by to talk."

"My lawyer wouldn't appreciate me not taking her advice and speaking to the police without her. What is this anyway, some type of cop courtesy call or did you lose something and believe perhaps you'll find it here?"

Jasenya Jimenez hadn't punched another person in the face in almost five years. Butterfly would be the second and by far the most enjoyable, but she had a job to do. "This is an informal visit. If you didn't do any of the things you're accused of, then maybe you know who did."

"If I knew, I would have served them up the way you serve blow jobs like a McDonald's sign."

Jimenez laughed, "I see you're still upset about the whole black crackwhore thing."

"Not at all detective, I was merely making an observation." Jimenez opened her car door.

"I had no idea you were afraid of me. Forgive me for troubling you, Mrs. Baxter."

A flash of anger clouded Butterfly's face for a fraction of a second. "Detective, I'm not afraid of you. I'm afraid for you. If you keep up this wild goose chase of little ole me, surely you're going to be fired or at the very least demoted." With that remark, Butterfly walked into her house with her groceries.

Boldly, Detective Jimenez followed her into the house. Butterfly didn't protest. She just put away her groceries while Jimenez studied everything around her closely. "Did you go out last night Mrs. Baxter?" Butterfly put away a head of lettuce in the crisper section of the refrigerator.

"Come on jefe, your people are following me. You know my every move. Don't waste my time, detective, ask better questions or respect yourself enough to leave. "Jimenez pulled out a photograph tossing it on the kitchen countertop.

Casually, Butterfly continued putting away her canned goods before she looked down at the photo. "The Blackmailer. Why are you showing me a pic of her?"

Jimenez took a step closer. "You admit that you know her?"

"I admit nothing of the sort. I know of this woman. I've seen her twice in my life. Once in court where I was being falsely prosecuted and again in the parking lot of the strip mall up the street. She approached me and told me to call her if I wanted to buy back some damaging evidence, she supposedly had that could implicate me in a crime."

"Did you call her?"

Butterfly smiled, "For what? It was impossible for her to have any evidence against me because I wasn't involved in anything." Handing the woman her phone she said, "Check my call log. I think you already know I haven't called this person."

Jimenez saw only two calls. One number she recognized as belonging to Dr. Daniels and the other belonged to a California area code. Jimenez handed her phone back. Butterfly took it and walked into the living room where she offered the detective a seat. Jimenez declined. "Is she in trouble or something?"

"I'm not sure, is she?"

"How in the hell would I know? I'm not psychic."

"I think you know more than you're telling me." Jimenez walked slowly around the downstairs.

"Are you looking for something detective?"

The detective sat on the couch next to her prime suspect. "Cassandra Kiddick went missing from her home last night. No one's heard from her." Butterfly looked genuinely concerned and said, "Then shouldn't you be out there looking for her?"

Jimenez stood up and began to pace. "That's why I'm here Mrs. Baxter. I was thinking maybe you could help me."

Butterfly looked confused. "Me? How can I help you?"

"I hear that you are very intelligent. In fact, you have a genius level IQ, I'm told. Help me out and just give me a hypothetical scenario as to what you think may have happened?"

Crossing her legs at the knee, Butterfly said, "I'll take my best shot. Let's see, Ms. Kiddick probably allowed someone to convince her to undertake a foolish pursuit without telling her of the consequences. That person is at this very moment feeling like a real piece of shit for pulling the young woman into their affairs. Now, that's as close as I can get without having firsthand knowledge of what actually happened to her."

Looking into Butterfly's eyes Jimenez thought, I know this evil bitch had a hand in Cassandra Kiddick's disappearance. However, she had to play it smooth just in case there was a chance of saving the young woman. Jimenez decided to try a different tact. "This house is very nice, especially for the area. How long have you owned it?"

"It once belonged to my mother. When she and my father moved from Illinois to Michigan, he bought it for her. After he died my mother couldn't stand the constant reminder of him, so she moved to the west side where I grew up and made this a rental property. Years later my sister sold it. Chicago used to say it was haunted, but I bought it back anyway."

Jimenez kept looking around. "Did you do all of the upgrades?" Butterfly nodded. "Wow, it's really nice. Do you mind if I look around?" The detective asked.

"Of course not. Would you like a guided tour, or would you rather go at it alone? Matter of fact, it's probably better if you take it all in on your own. I'll wait right here."

"Are you giving me permission to search your home, Mrs. Baxter?"

Butterfly laughed. "Not at all. I'm giving you the opportunity to look around for signs of Ms. Kiddick, because I know what you don't."

Jimenez grew instantly curious. "And what's that?"

"Someone's setting me up. If you find out who around me has a connection to the man in that horrific confession video, you'll find out who's responsible for setting these events in motion." Butterfly picked up the remote and started channel surfing. "You should hurry, detective."
"Why?"

"Because if Cassandra Kiddick is missing and not dead, the first 48 hours are crucial in finding her. At least that's what all the cop shows say."

Jimenez quickly went through every room and space big enough to hide a body. There were no signs of blood or a struggle. If Baxter is responsible for Cassandra Kiddick's disappearance, she covered her tracks well. "The finished basement is really nice. If this home were in a different zip code it would be worth a few hundred thousand."

Butterfly set the remote down. "Detective are you through looking around?"

Jimenez was in the doorway when she pulled out one of her business cards. "Call me if you hear from Ms. Kiddick."

"She has no reason to call me detective," taking the business card and turning it over between her fingers. "Besides, in court, she came across as the type of woman who, once gone, would stay gone forever. But do you think I could just call you if I feel the need to unburden my soul? You seem like a very good listener. Almost like you can read between the lines of a situation and see the truth.

"Jimenez gave a tight smile as she wondered how much time they'd give her for shooting this soulless excuse for a human being. Butterfly asked again, "Well can I?"

"Can you what, Mrs. Baxter?"

"You seemed a million miles away. I was asking if I could just call you if I felt the need?"

Jimenez stuck out her hand and said, "Of course, call me if you want."

Butterfly didn't take her hand for a simple shake, she took it and caressed it. "We may have gotten off on the wrong foot. Would you like to come back in and talk about it?"

Jimenez eased her hand away and said, "I have the distinct feeling we will be seeing one another soon enough. Have a good day Mrs. Baxter and thanks for your help."

Outside, the detective looked up the length of the driveway. When Mrs. Baxter closed the front door, Jimenez took the opportunity to look around the backyard. The garage door was up showing a virtually empty space except for a small lawnmower and a few garden tools. She walked back to her car, checking out Baxter's rental from bumper to bumper. Even though the surveillance detail swore by the Pope that their coverage had been skintight, Jimenez still believed Butterfly Baxter was involved in Cassandra Kiddick's disappearance. She had no idea how, but vowing to herself she thought, I don't know how, but I will.

Starting the car and pulling out of the driveway, she saw the blinds move. When she reached the corner, the passenger in a grey panel van waved at her. Jimenez waved back, vaguely familiar with the officer on the daytime surveillance detail. They had Baxter hemmed in from both ends of the block. If she moved, they were going to know about it.

Jimenez texted Gleason, who was still at Cassandra Kiddick's house. When the woman didn't answer her phone, they grew worried and decided to do a safety check. What they found was extremely disturbing. All the doors were locked, but a screen had been cut and pushed out of a back window. Underneath that same window in the dirt was a clear shoe impression. They made a forced entry and searched the entire house. Nothing was missing.

The only sign of foul play was the cut screen until they called in a forensics team. The doors to Cassandra Kiddick's house didn't have any fingerprints on them. They found her van in the garage was with a loaded revolver under the driver's seat, but there were no prints on the van's steering wheel or door handles. Why would Cassandra Kiddick wipe down her own car and house? They initiated a quick canvas of the neighborhood and came up empty. Sometimes the absence of evidence is evidence enough. That train of thought led her to Butterfly Baxter's door. As anger filled her mind, she felt her chest begin to expand as she thought. Some way, somehow, she had a hand in this.

Jimenez pulled her car over and started screaming, swearing, and beating the steering wheel to get her frustration out. She knew the young woman was dead; her gut told her so. After two or three minutes she was exhausted. She was hoarse and breathing raggedly when she started up her car again. But more than ever she vowed to crush Butterfly.

Detective Sargent Jimenez went to her sister's apartment and told her about Cassandra Kiddick. Chicago listened but had little to say. "Dr. Daniels, if you think of anything please contact me." Between them on a table was a picture of the missing woman and another of her father. "Are you sure that you don't know either of them?"

She viewed both photos earnestly before saying, "Not that I can recall."

"Please think back before you were kidnapped."

Chicago looked over the photographs again. "I'm getting nothing detective. Sorry."

Chicago knew an end had to come to Butterfly's machinations. The scheming, lies, pain, and death all had to stop. Jimenez told her that the missing woman had a son about Albany's age. There was no doubt in the detective's mind that Cassandra Kiddick was dead, and that Butterfly was somehow responsible.

Listening intently, Chicago took in all Jimenez had to say then she let the detective leave without the truth. It was a heavy burden to bear, though over the years she had carried worse. She sat at the dining room table thinking about everything that had transpired in the past few years. She began to cry, then quickly admonished herself. The events that were currently taking place had been set in motion years ago.

She gave a sudden start thinking Albany had called her name, but she was all alone. Chicago called her friend Freida Goldberg early that morning and asked her to watch her nephew for a few days. She explained that she had some important matters to take care of and needed the favor. Freida was only too happy to help. The truth was much more complicated. Chicago was worried about everything, especially Butterfly. When she told Albany, he would be staying with her friend for a short time, he only asked if he could take his gaming system. Freida was glad to see Chicago and thought she looked better than ever. The doctor in her was probing for signs of depression or suicidal tendencies, while the friend understood when Chicago asked her to just be her friend.

The evening was fast approaching by the time Chicago had her home cleaned and all of her important papers in order. She tried to handwrite a letter to Albany in an effort to explain things but failed miserably. Chicago was just a few years older than him when she was forced to grow up overnight and she by no means wanted that for him. He needed to remain a child for as long as possible. She crumpled the letter and tossed it into the trash. Butterfly needed to be stopped and there was only one way to do it. She got on her knees and prayed to God that He would guide her in her actions this night. Before leaving the apartment, she chambered a round in her Glock. It was time to bring this deadly drama to a close.

Locking her apartment up, she went to her Mercedes S65 coupe. During the entire drive, all she could think about was Butterfly as a baby. Chicago always wanted the best for her; but no matter what was given to Butterfly, she always wanted more. Her brain seemed to have been set on autopilot because she drove into her sister's driveway behind her rental car without recalling how she'd gotten there. It was dizzying seeing what was once home and knowing it was now a grave.

She blew her horn twice, then got out and went to the front door. Butterfly was waiting with a smile on her face. "My, my, my! As I live and breathe, if it isn't the great Chicago Daniels. To what do I owe this displeasure?"

Chicago ignored her sister's heavy sarcastic wit. "Can I come in?" She waved her inside then peered up and down the block.

After closing and deadbolting the door Butterfly asked, "What do you want thief?" Chicago looked around to see if someone else was present. "Don't look surprised, Windy City! I'm speaking to you."
Chicago unzipped her jacket, then shoved the key fob into her front pocket freeing up her left hand. "You're the only thief I know. You steal husbands and lives."

"Your husband gave himself to me freely. Over, under, from behind, on his knees and over again. I didn't have to steal him, I only had to accept him."

Chicago sidestepped the bait. "What did you do with Cassandra?" Butterfly seemed to glow with triumph. "Answer me Caterpillar!"

"Call me Butterfly or leave!"

As calmly as she could, Chicago asked, "Do you know where that young woman is, Butterfly?"

"Why do you care, she's just another stranger isn't she? Unless…?"

"Unless what?"

"Unless you've been lying this entire time and you know the woman and her father. Either that or you're working with the police."

Chicago turned on her with fire in her eyes. "Don't be absurd! Why would I be cooperating with the police? All I've ever done is try and help you."

"Help me! So, you were helping me when you framed me for your husband's murder and stole my son?"

Disbelief overwhelmed Chicago. "You disturbed, misguided little girl! My husband or should I say, your baby's daddy and you set me up to be killed by a sexual sadist with mommy issues, and here you are with the audacity to make these preposterous accusations. You are insane!" Tears trickled down Chicago's face. "Do you have any idea the things he did to me?

"Stop your whining!" Butterfly yelled. "Dorian used to call you 'Miss Missionary.' Honey, you needed someone to loosen you up and get you in the mood."

The force of the slap caught Butterfly off guard and sent her flying into the dining room table. When she righted herself, she was staring down the very large, dark hole of a Glock pistol!

Chicago made Butterfly sit on the floor with her hands in her pockets so she couldn't make any sudden moves. Then she pulled out a dining room chair and sat down facing her. "What now Windy City? Let me guess, you're going to kill me. Your little sister."

She pointed the gun at her chest. "Spare me! You and Dorian had no problems trying to kill me. After everything I've done for you, you screw my husband and give birth to his child. What did I do to you, to make you hate me so, much?"

As if Chicago hadn't spoken Butterfly said, "Only one of us is leaving here alive Windy City. So, play your cards right and I just might tell you."

Butterfly pulled her legs underneath her hips. "Put your legs straight out in front of you and cross them at the ankles."

"That's reason number one. You're a bossy know-it-all bitch! It's always been Chicago this and Chicago that! Momma was in on it, too. 'Let's check with Chicago first.' But the real reason I can't stand the sight of your stuck-up ass is, David Howard."

Chicago couldn't believe what she was hearing. "You can't be serious!"

It was Butterfly's turn to look in disbelief. "David Howard! Handsome David Howard, my first love! You destroyed our relationship, then he died! I've never forgiven you for that! Her once pretty features were now distorted in rage.

Responding, Chicago said, "Skipping school and having unprotected sex with an eighteen-year-old when you're only sixteen is not appropriate behavior for a teenage girl. I was looking out for you Caterpillar."

Butterfly snatched her hands from her pockets preparing to get up when Chicago pointed the gun freezing her motion. "Don't call me that! Don't ever call me that again! Look at me! I'm not a child anymore!"

Chicago had almost forgotten about how intense Butterfly could be when she became angry. She urged her to calm down. "We're getting off track. Tell me what you know about Cassandra Kiddick?"

Butterfly started to regain control of herself and the situation. "Why do you care? Is it because you and her father were friends?" Chicago stumbled over her denial. "Save it, sister, I know everything. Cassandra didn't know about you and her father being friends, but when I questioned her, she told me her father was an alcoholic who attended NA/AA meetings. Did you know I had Dorian follow you to a few of those meetings just to make sure you were actually attending them? I wanted to be sure you were clueless as to what was really going on. Then when Dorian was murdered you virtually stopped going."

Chicago was becoming annoyed. "What are you insinuating?" Butterfly leaned casually back against the wall.

"I think you met Cassandra's father at one of those meetings and became friends. Friends with deadly benefits."

"You haven't been taking your medication, have you?"

"It dulls my thinking ability, Lakeshore. Isn't that what William Kiddick called you?"

Chicago looked at her as though she were crazy. "What in the hell are you talking about?"

"Oh, that's right, you called him Billy, didn't you?" Butterfly recounted a memory of one day speaking with Chicago over the phone and being told they'd have to speak later because Billy was on the other line. "When I asked who this Billy person was, I distinctly recall you saying a friend. Now it's obvious to me they are one and the same; so, we're not going to waste time debating on the validity of that. It was a smart play. Have him kill Dorian and frame me. Brilliant plan, though like mine, poor execution. Good help is truly … Anyway, you gave the police the letters and flash drive. The police only had half of the total correspondence and one flash drive. When I reviewed the evidence against me, I realized the letters concerning Albany were all missing as was the flash drive with the video of my giving birth and pictures of Albany. Who would exclude that besides ole Auntie Chi? Let's cut the bullshit!"

Chicago just stared at the woman in front of her not knowing who she was. "It's obvious that you're having a psychotic break with reality. Tell me what happened to Cassandra and I promise we'll get you some help."

"Do you really want to know?"

Chicago squatted in front of her, "Yes, please tell me?"

Butterfly studied her nails. "I need a manicure." Chicago didn't say a word, just waited patiently. "All that digging can ruin a girl's nails, you know?"

"What digging Butterfly?"

Butterfly pointed towards the backyard. "Out in the garage. The nosey nobody is out there taking a dirt nap."

Chicago was mortified. "Please tell me you're lying or playing one of your sick, twisted games."

"She was working for the cops. Plus, that hairstyle was enough to want her dead, anyway." Butterfly laughed, "It's all your fault. You brought her into our business. You brought her close to me." Chicago sat back on her haunches emotionally depleted. Her mouth kept opening and closing, but no words came out. "Cat got your tongue?"

When Chicago found her voice she said, "I always knew there was the possibility of you having mental disease or defect. I just never thought you'd be a monster."

Butterfly demanded to know what she meant. "Children of incest often have physical deformities or mental disorders."

Butterfly started to rise off of the floor, but Chicago made it to her feet first and cautioned her against moving again. "Are you saying I am a child of an incestuous relationship?" The nod was almost imperceptible but came across as a scream to Butterfly. "Are you trying to fuck with my mind, Dr. Daniels! You're suggesting Momma and Daddy were brother and sister?"

"That's not what I'm saying. You need to just be quiet and let me tell you some things!"

Butterfly was becoming angrier. "You better hurry up or I'm going to make you use that," referring to the gun in her sister's hand.

Chicago holstered her pistol and sat back down in the chair in front of Butterfly.

"I'm going to tell you the truth about how you came to be in this world and why I think you're so messed up. All you have to do is sit there and listen."

"What if I don't want to buy the shit you're selling? Then what? You pull out your gun and shoot me?"

Chicago looked at her pleadingly. "I just need you to listen. What you do with what you hear is on you."

Despite her education, self-preservation, and what she knew to be right, Chicago still blamed herself for what happened that night. She was almost 13 years old and already bigger than her mother, Big Shirley. Chicago was smart, responsible, and utterly naive. When her father, Martin Daniels begged her to open the door and let him come in, she refused. The man was no longer allowed in the house unless Momma was there, too. When he kept knocking saying it was an emergency her resolve to never let him in, slipped a little. When he said he was hurt and needed his baby's help, Chicago couldn't deny him anymore. She just had to let him in. As soon as she cracked the door, her father bum-rushed through shoving her aside. Chicago got a strong whiff of alcohol seeping from his pores along with the tobacco smoke saturating his clothes.

She wondered if she'd done the right thing as she locked and closed the door. "Girl, where you say your Momma was?"

"She's at work but will be home in a couple of hours." Chicago watched him stagger to the bathroom and push the door shut. She could remember clear as day the sound of the shower running and her turning to look at the clock over the fireplace. It was 3:29 in the morning. If she went back to bed now, she'd be able to get at least two and a half more hours of sleep. Before she was able to fall back into her dreams, she heard the shower turn off. A few minutes later her bedroom door was pushed open. The nightlight plugged into the wall socket gave off enough illumination for her to see her father framed in the doorway naked with a towel draped about his neck. Chicago shut her eyes tight, silently praying he would leave. Then she felt the covers being pulled back. "This is my room! Momma's room is next door," she shouted at her father. A strong hand clamped over her mouth like a vise while another thrust her nightgown up to her waist and tore at her panties. They were her favorite, with little green and purple irises covering them. The screams issuing from her throat were no more than muffled pleas falling on deaf ears.

"You need a man to make you a woman! I made your Momma one and she can't get enough of me. Now it's your turn!"

The pain was so intense that she blacked out. When she came to, her own father was pumping savagely between her thighs. She fought him! Scratching, biting, spitting! Chicago did all that she could to stop him; then he came and stopped himself. "Turnover!" She screamed louder that time and he struck her hard across the face almost knocking her unconscious. She was dizzy and in so much pain down there that when he forcibly turned her onto her stomach Chicago was too weak to stop him.

She tried screaming again, but she could barely breathe with her face pressed roughly into the mattress. Then as viciously and suddenly as it began, it ended. Chicago lay crying, bleeding, and begging for her father to get off of her when his body just rolled away hitting the floor with a loud thud.

"How could you do this to me!" Chicago yelled at him. Slowly opening her eyes, she saw that the overhead light was on. It wasn't until turning her head that she saw all the blood. Big Shirley let go of the kitchen knife clutched in her fist and held her arms open for her only child. They hugged each other for what seemed like forever. Big Shirley never said anything about calling the police. What Chicago remembered most about her mother was how composed she seemed and that not a single tear graced her cheeks.

Big Shirley guided her to the bathroom and told her to shower and douche herself clean down there. When Chicago finished, there were clothes sitting atop the closed toilet seat. She put them on almost robotically and stepped from the bathroom. Looking through the open bedroom door she could see her mother wrapping her father's lifeless body in old sheets and garbage bags.

Next to her were two buckets. One was a dark, murky crimson, the other a frothy light pink. Chicago never asked what was going on, she just went to the hall linen closet and grabbed more towels setting them on the floor next to her mother. Then she took the darkest bucket of water to the bathroom and emptied its contents. The swirl of the toilet water was almost therapeutic for Chicago as she imagined her father, Martin Daniels, being flushed down to hell like that commercial of the Tidy Bowl Man. When his blood was gone, she reached under the vanity for some bleach and soap powder, made freshwater, and went back to her mother's side. After they cleaned up everything and stripped the bed down to the mattress, Big Shirley told her, "Let's go out to the garage Chi." The young girl was emotionally confused as she looked down at her father's body on the floor of the bedroom. Big Shirley took her by the arm leading her through the house to the back. "There's no rest for the weary. We have a woman's work to do."

"Yes, Momma."

It took most of the day with several breaks in between before they were done. Chicago thought Big Shirley had gone a little overboard with the deepness of the hole and told her as much. She responded, "I'm just trying to get him close enough to his final destination." That night Big Shirley called in sick at her job; just as she had called the school earlier and told them that her daughter was sick and would be absent for a few days. It started raining cats and dogs. Mother and daughter loaded husband and father onto a heavy wool blanket and dragged him out the back door and into the garage. When Martin Daniels was laid in what was to be his eternal resting place, they took turns covering him with dirt until the hole was filled. The rest of it was piled into a wheelbarrow to be discarded later. Big Shirley took a small bible from her coat pocket and read the 23rd Psalm. Then as almost an afterthought, she read verses two and three from Proverbs chapter 21: "Every way of a man is right in his own eyes: but the Lord pondereth the hearts. To do justice and judgment is more acceptable to the Lord than sacrifice. Amen!"

Jimenez should've been going home and getting some much needed rest. Instead, she drove aimlessly around; or so she thought. Without realizing it, she found herself parking on a side street and walking around the corner to the surveillance van on Bliss. Jameson who was sitting in the back opened the sliding panel door letting her in. The detective climbed over her knocking over a two-liter plastic bottle filled with urine. She held it up asking Yolanda Jameson, "Officer, is your thing small enough to fit into this bottle or you just got perfect aim?"

The woman laughed, "Naw sarge. I'm wearing an adult diaper.

That's him with the little wee-wee."

Thaddeus who was napping in the driver's seat said, "Hey sarge, sorry you had to hear that. She's always bragging about hers is bigger than mine. What's up?"

Jimenez took the binoculars from Jameson's hand "Not much. I just stopped by to check on our suspect. When did that car pull up?"

"You mean that 12-cylinder, German crafted luxury sports coupe worth over $150,000.00? It got here about 20 minutes ago."

"Who are you? You sound like a commercial for Mercedes Benz."

Blushing, Jameson said, "I love high-end sports cars. Anyway, I couldn't see the woman's face clearly, but I'm pretty sure it was our suspect's sister, Dr. Daniels. I had the guys at the other end of the street circle the block and get the plate number. It's registered to one, Dr. Chicago Alexandria Daniels."

The detective and two officers traded cop talk for a little while, but Jimenez couldn't shake the feeling that something was up. No matter how hard she tried, she didn't see the two sisters having a family reunion. "Officer Jameson let's go for a walk. Thaddeus! Wakeup! We're taking a look to see. Keep your eyes peeled and your radio on." The two women left the van walking on the opposite side of the street from Butterfly's house. They could see the front lights on through the slits in the blinds, but little else. When they reached the corner, Jimenez gave a thumbs up to the other surveillance unit as she and Jameson crossed to the other side making their way back to the van.

Most of the houses were dark with only the dull blue glare of a television's light visible through their windows. When the two were a house away from their suspect's residence they heard an awful scream followed by angry yelling. Jimenez went right into action.

"Jameson, cover the back of the house and if you see or hear anything else, call for backup immediately!"

"Copy that Sarge!"

She watched the other woman take off crouching low into the darkness with a hand placed on the butt of her service weapon. Jimenez crept up on Butterfly's porch peeking through the blinds. What she saw almost made her freeze. Quietly, she went to the front door and tried the knob; it didn't budge. There was a mid-sized clay pot on the porch. She picked it up, looking through the window again. She knew that this was a now or never moment. Jimenez cocked her arm back like she was pitching for the Detroit Tigers and let the pot fly. Three seconds later, all hell broke loose!

"I don't believe you! You're a liar! Liar! You're lying trying to mess with my head!" Butterfly was screaming and crying hysterically.

Chicago tried to calm her, but she wouldn't listen. "Momma and I buried your father in that same garage where you buried Cassandra Kiddick, Billy's daughter." Chicago's heart was ripping into pieces as she watched her daughter curl into a helpless bundle of emotions. "Big Shirley, my mother, thought it would be best if you were raised as my sister. I was only 13 years and 4 months old when you were born. Barely a teenager, let alone woman enough to be raising a child. Your grandmother didn't want the rape to be my curse and you to be my punishment. Though honestly, I've never felt that way. I always loved you. I knew I was pregnant with you and never once thought about having an abortion. I could never kill my child, my flesh, and blood."

Butterfly unfurled herself, wiping at her eyes. "So, you're my biological mother and your father is my father?" Chicago nodded her head up and down. "No wonder Big Shirley would tell me to do whatever you said. Is that why you were always helping me with my homework, concerned about my education, what I wore, where I went, how I talked, and who I talked to?"

"I have always only wanted what was best for you."

Butterfly spat out at Chicago, "So, my entire life has been a lie, hasn't it?"

Chicago told her that it wasn't. "I wanted you to have a chance at life the way your grandmother gave me a chance. Telling you the truth of your genesis would've only robbed you of any hope at having a good life."

Butterfly crawled away from her mother huddling in a far corner. "I hate you!" She screamed to the top of her lungs.

"No, you don't Caterpillar. You just hate the situation. All of this can work out for the best if you are willing to go into treatment and get back on your medications."

Butterfly stared at her wide-eyed like a frightened child. Her frightened child. "You want to put me in some hospital, locked conveniently away on some psych ward drooling at the mouth with grannie panties pulled up to my armpits! You want to hide me, your dirty, shameful little secret and then you'll have Albany all to yourself."

"Don't talk like that! Albany is your son, but he's, my grandson. He's not a piece of property to have. Just do as I say and go into the hospital voluntarily."

Butterfly grew thoughtful. "What about Cassandra and all of the other shit?" Chicago pulled her to her feet, "That'll be our dirty secret. You'll get the best treatment, and the best defense money can buy. No more voices, no more hurting."

Chicago knew better than to turn her back on someone with mental issues. During her residency at the Detroit Medical Center, the chief psychiatrist told her, "Unless you have eyes in the back of your head, never turn away from a patient." As she was turning away from Butterfly an image of that doctor's face instantaneously flooded her mind. She began to spin back around when a blow struck her on the side of the head sending her into the wall. Chicago's back and shoulders were being pummeled with fists, then suddenly it stopped when she fell to one knee.

"Turn around Dr. Daniels!" The voice didn't sound like Butterfly's. It had a southern lilt with hard edges. "Don't do anything stupid Mommy dearest. I'd hate to have to kill you prematurely." Chicago felt at her waist and touched an empty holster. "That stupid bitch, Butterfly is a nut job of the worse kind. Do you know she was buying that good mother, Joan Crawford bullshit you were spewing! She was actually going to go into treatment. What would that mean for me, Dr. Daniel's behavioral psychologist? It means I'm fucking dead or at the very least, locked away in some damp, dark corridor of a mind restrained by a cocktail of anti-this and mood inhibitor that! No thank you! See Doc, you can't "Hey Caterpillar" me because I'm running this show!"

Chicago was facing a virtual stranger. The voice was different, and so was the face. It was Butterfly, but there were just subtle differences. The eyes looked darker and seemed flat. Her mouth usually full and voluptuous now appeared thin and cruel.

"Who are you?"

"I'm Octavia Winters, your late husband's true mistress. We've never met before though I'm sure you've tasted me a time or two on Dorian's lips. Oh! We almost met that time you came back early from some seminar. I made Butterfly tell you she came to Detroit to surprise you when really I was teaching your husband techniques from the Kama Sutra." Chicago tried to get up. "Unh, Unh; not a good idea. I will kill you."

Chicago could tell that whoever the personality was, meant what she was saying. "Why would you want to hurt me when we don't even know each other?"

"Bitch, I know all about you from Dorian and the dummy. Though I must admit, I never saw the whole 'I was raped by my daddy and he's your daddy, too, thing coming.' Kudos, like mother like daughter on the body in the garage deal. I had nothing to do with that at all. Butterfly did it to impress me. Can you believe it? If she really wanted to impress me, she should have murdered you. Nothing like a little matricide to solidify an eternal bond."

Chicago knew her best chance at survival was to keep her talking. "Whose idea was it to kill me? Yours or Dorian?"

Octavia laughed joylessly. "The hardest bone in your husband's body was his penis. The man was a spineless, insecure baby who hated that he couldn't control his wife. He actually wanted you to accept his extramarital activities as par for the course. I knew you'd never go for it and convinced him to erase you all together. The butterfly was a little apprehensive. But once I latched onto the 'Handsome David Howard' situation and stoked the flames with a word here, and an irrational emotion there, Butterfly became a thriving member of the team, Chicago Must Die!"

"Did you know she almost committed suicide? The dummy was so distraught over having that bastard with your husband, she tried to overdose on opioids. I had to make her vomit otherwise, I'd have horns and a pitchfork right now. Don't you get it? Butterfly is a fragile creature who is incapable of handling too much pressure and what do you do? You come in here and drop the MOTHER bomb and expect there to be no fallout! How foolish are you, Dr. Daniels? Don't answer, that was rhetorical."

Chicago held up her hand pleadingly. "Please put the gun down!

There are police already on this street surveilling you and this house! You'll be arrested!"

The crazed woman pointed the gun in her direction. "That's wonderful! It means the police didn't do their job. They weren't in time to save me when you attempted to exact your revenge. You came here under the guise of discussing Albany's future. Once I let you in, you went ballistic and pulled your gun. A struggle ensued, I came away with the weapon then begged you to stop this madness, but you were deranged. You rushed at me and I fired into the wall over your head as a warning, but you kept coming."

A gunshot ripped the air, the bullet smashing into the wall over Chicago's head. "Goodbye, Dr. Daniels!" At the exact moment, Octavia's finger was tensing on the trigger the front living room window exploded, sending flying shards of glass raining everywhere. Octavia turned and fired at a dark silhouette. From her position on the floor, Chicago could see the returning muzzle flashes right before several rounds struck her daughter throwing her backward through the air and crashing into the dining table and chairs. There was an eerie silence when all of the shooting stopped. Chicago looked through the shattered window and saw Detective Sargent Jimenez with her arms extended forward and her gun gripped in both hands.

She was screaming for no one to move, but Chicago ignored the detective's commands scrambling frantically across the floor to Butterfly. "Get an ambulance! Oh Caterpillar, what have you done!" Chicago quickly took off her jacket pressing it to her daughter's chest.

Butterfly's voice was at first child-like. "Mommy, Octavia made me do it. I didn't want to Mommy. She made me." Chicago had to lean down close to her mouth to hear what else she was trying to say. "I'm just playing. Your beautiful Butterfly is going to hell and I'm driving with no brakes. Fuck you! Mommy fucking dearest!" Octavia said.

Chicago watched as a frothy bubble of blood burst at the corner of her daughter's lips. She stroked her face gently while watching Butterfly's eyes go from flat hard reflections of nothingness to soft spheres of sorrow. "I'm sorry Windy ..." Chicago said the only thing she could say in this traumatic situation. "I love you. No matter what, I'll always love you." Chicago not only watched Butterfly breathe her last breath, she felt it depart from her child's body. That same last breath stole a piece of Chicago's soul.

16 THE FUTURE

It had been five months since Butterfly's death. Albany was torn up inside over his mom's passing and had just recently begun to return to his normal self. Chicago also had her moments when she broke down in a torrential outpouring of tears. Thankfully, her friend Freida was there to help counsel her through the initial stages of grief. Both Chicago and Albany no longer wanted to be in Detroit. So, Chicago arranged with Morgan to find them a home down in Georgia. He found a perfect five-bedroom, four and a half bath brick Tudor, with a detached three-car garage sporting a studio apartment above it.

She closed on the house six weeks prior to moving to Georgia and she shipped most of her furniture down south two weeks prior. Camping out in the middle of the apartment wasn't half bad. Albany loved sleeping on an air mattress and watching television on his laptop and eating takeout. They were living out of their suitcases until the next day when Morgan would arrive. He would fly in, then rent a luxury Mercedes Sprinter van as the one Butterfly fled from the police in. The reason they were driving and not flying was to spend some quality time with Albany, trying to create new memories to wash away the old, painful ones. Albany was happy with the move, but Chicago knew better than anyone that a child could be of two minds.

Her friend Freida was a godsend. She agreed with Chicago concerning how to handle the transition and had been instrumental in counseling Albany, too. Frieda also found him a wonderful child psychologist in the Buckhead section of Atlanta to take him on as a patient. The move wasn't difficult for Chicago. With the exception of Freida, she had no attachments to the Motor City. Even though she was financially solid, she still wanted to work. Chicago was sure the Atlanta area could use a good behavioral psychologist. Working would do her a world of good. After all, an idle mind is the devil's workshop.

The very next morning, Chicago and her grandson were packed up and ready to go. Grandson! Just thinking it brought joy to her heart. Never before had she been able to say it aloud for fear her world would implode. Now that the cat was out of the bag Chicago was elated. Albany, too, found out the truth; but still preferred to call her Auntie Chi. "I'm all packed, Auntie Chi! I brushed my teeth and packed my computer and stuff. Let's go!" She hugged him while playfully spinning him around until they were both dizzy. Her cellphone ringing interrupted their fun. She had to search for it and finally found it underneath a pile of clothing slated for donation to the Goodwill.

It was Detective Jimenez calling to let her know they were releasing Butterfly's property. The detective didn't know Chicago and Butterfly were mother and daughter as she continued referring to them as sisters. "Dr. Daniels, your sister's belongings are no longer being held as evidence. You being the next of kin and all, I figured you would like to have her things." Jimenez told her to drop by the department in a couple of hours and retrieve the items, otherwise, Chicago would have to wait until the next day.

Considering she wouldn't be in Detroit the next day, today seemed like a good time to pick up Butterfly's things. "I'll be there in about an hour and a half." She hung up and then made an important call. When she was done, she went to find her grandson.

When everything was loaded up and Albany had his gaming system connected to the van's entertainment console, Chicago turned in her seat facing Morgan. "Well brother, we're ready. We just have one stop to make."

He ran the back of his hand across his forehead in a gesture of wiping away imaginary sweat. "I thought for a moment there you were going to call me son in law." She playfully punched him in the shoulder. In an effort at full disclosure, she sat him down before Butterfly's funeral and told him the truth about everything - almost everything.

The funeral was small. Very small. Morgan, Albany, and her, along with the two detectives, Gleason and Jimenez were the only mourners in attendance, initially. Near the end, right before the casket was closed, two beautiful women came in. One, a statuesque blond with vacant eyes that appeared fearful as her gaze flitted around the funeral home's chapel. It was almost as if she expected a ghost to materialize any second. The other one was a full-figured brunette who seemed to have graduated from the same school of arrogance and upper echelon egotism as Butterfly. She laid a black silk rose on Butterfly's chest.

They didn't stay long. The two stared down into the casket until Chicago stepped up to usher them to their seats before the reading of the eulogy. When she walked up to thank them for coming and asked if they would be going to the internment, it was then that she realized the brunette was one of the porn stars she saw on the flash drive blowing her late husband. Pamela Nothnagel said, "We came to make sure … to see for ourselves." Chicago watched as the blond burst into tears while being led out by the brunette. Whether they were tears of joy or sadness was unknown, but Chicago wouldn't bet that they were the latter.

Surprisingly, Morgan was extremely understanding. Even though he never was so callous as to voice it, he seemed relieved Butterfly was dead instead of alive and on trial. At some point, she may have accepted help for her mental disorders, but Morgan thought that point was a long way off at the time of her death. Chicago never wanted her child dead. She only wanted her contained. "Where is this stop we need to make?" Morgan asked while pulling off. "We need to get Butterfly's property from the police. Detective Jimenez phoned this morning saying it was no longer needed for evidence."

He looked over his shoulder to where his stepson sat tinkering with a videogame. "It won't take long will it?"

"Without my crystal ball I can't tell you for sure, but I'm thinking around an hour or so."

"That long?" He gave an exasperated sigh.

They arrived at police headquarters in no time at all. Morgan refused to go in and hopped in the back with Albany. Chicago stuck out her tongue before saying, "You could've joined me for moral support." When she reached the building, she gave up her purse and walked slowly through a metal detector. The uniformed sergeant at the desk asked her name and who she was there to see. He checked the computer along with her driver's license, then gave her a visitor's badge. Jimenez was waiting on her as soon as she stepped from the elevator. "Dr. Daniels, please follow me." Chicago glanced at her watch before being led into a small windowless room with a two-way mirror on the wall facing her. A 5x3 foot metal table sat in the center with two chairs. Jimenez offered her a seat.

Chicago sat her purse next to a plastic evidence bag with several manila file folders. "Do I have to sign some papers?"

"Maybe later. Right now, I would just like to ask you some questions if you don't mind."

"Questions about what?" Chicago asked with a tinge of apprehension straining her voice.

"Please, indulge me if you will Dr. Daniels. I have some things I want to show you, then you can take your sister's belongings and leave. As a matter of fact, you don't have to speak to me at all and if it'll make you feel more comfortable you can have an attorney present."

Chicago's annoyance came through loud and clear. "Are you interrogating me, detective? Am I under arrest or something?"

Jimenez sat down in front of her, "Why in the world would you ask that? This is an informal conversation to address some loose ends. I would appreciate your assistance." This last request seemed to mollify the doctor somewhat. "How can I help?" Chicago said.

While Jimenez pulled one of the file folders from the stack, Chicago stared at her reflection in the two-way mirror wondering who might be observing her from the other side. If she were Superwoman gifted with the power of X-ray vision, her eyes would be looking directly into the baby blues of Prosecutor Lindsay. If she looked to Felicia Lindsay's left, Chicago would be staring at Detective Donald

Gleason. If she were to look slightly above and to the right of his bald head, she would see Lieutenant Templeton stroking his three-day-old beard growth while jingling loose change in his pocket with his free hand. The trio was intently observing Chicago for any type of physical tell or a cadence change in her voice to see if she were lying. "Butterfly was a very busy bee. During my investigation, I discovered that back in college, she ran a highly profitable illegal escort service through an internet website, SnatchMe.com. Were you aware of it?"

Surprise showed openly on Chicago's face. "If I had been aware detective, I would have notified the proper authorities. However, it doesn't seem farfetched in hindsight. Butterfly needed power and control over people. Sex was the weapon she used to gain those things."

Jimenez opened the folder in front of her. "We're also pretty sure she murdered a man named Arthur Millings at the Pinecrest Motel in Ann Arbor and stole his car. When we searched the house on Bliss the night, she

tried to kill you …"

Chicago interrupted. "It was her alter ego, Octavia Winters who tried to kill me."

Jimenez shrugged her shoulders, "It's sorta like tomato, to-mah-toe, potato, po-tah-toe. Anyway, as I was saying Dr. Daniels, we found a lot of cash at your sister's house and I recalled reading in this file," the detective stabbed her finger into the papers. "… that poor Arthur Millings had a stack of crisp hundred-dollar bills in his wallet at the time of his death. On a hunch, I had the Ann Arbor PD fingerprint the money and send me a photocopy of all the bills. The numbers fit perfectly in sequential order with bills found at the house on Bliss and your sister's fingerprints were on several of them.
A nice thumb and index. We can place that murder in the solved column."

Jimenez extracted another file folder from the stack next to Chicago's purse and spun it around so that it faced the doctor. A photograph of a badly decomposed body resting in a shallow grave stared back at her. "We finally found the whereabouts of Cassandra Kiddick. We believe your sister kidnapped her from her home and murdered her."

Chicago shifted uncomfortably in the hard metal chair. "How is that possible when Butterfly was under constant surveillance by your department? What proof do you have?"

The detective dug through the file pulling out a few more photographs and spread them out. "Being a businesswoman and dabbling in real estate I'm sure you've heard, it's all about location, location, location." One picture showed a wide shot of the house on Bliss. Another showed the garage with crime scene tape cordoning off the area, while another showed people from the coroner's office removing a black body bag. "No one else had access to that house around the time of Ms. Kiddick's disappearance except your sister. As you can see, that is the garage on Bliss at the house you grew up in as an adolescent, isn't it?"

Chicago peered closely at the pictures. "Yes, until I was thirteen. Then my mother moved us to the west side of the city."

Jimenez quickly shuffled the contents of the file together like a deck of cards and replaced it with another. "How old were you when your parents died?"

"My mother died when I was in my early thirties. I was barely a teenager when my father died."

Jimenez looked up and away as though she were recovering a memory. "I recall reading in here somewhere your mother was interned at Woodlawn Cemetery, but I couldn't find a final resting place for your father or a death certificate on him either."

The detective pulled out another photo of a deep grave with a collection of human bones in it. "Did you attend your father's funeral, Dr. Daniels?"

Chicago nervously answered, "No, my mother had him cremated." "It's funny you should say that because …"

Jimenez picked up a small box from underneath the table marked evidence and pulled from it an old well-worn leather wallet. The detective opened the billfold and took out a license. "Would you mind reading the name on this and telling me if you recognize the photo there? "Chicago's fingers grazed the edge of the license then drew back like she had touched a blue flame. "See right here where it says, Martin Michael Daniels. Despite being buried 30 plus years in a fucking garage, this license looks as though it were minted yesterday."

Chicago peered closely at the photo of her father. "This is my daddy! You said this license was buried for over 30 years. Where did you find it?"

"I certainly didn't find it in an urn full of your father's ashes."

Chicago told the detective she didn't have a clue as to what she was implying.

"Let's cut the bullshit, Doc! You no longer have to be clueless. We found a second grave in the garage, which belonged to your father. But you already knew that." Chicago appeared flabbergasted. "I had no idea detective, my mother told me he was cremated."

Jimenez slammed her fist on the table startling the doctor.

"Who in the fuck do you think I am? Some flatfoot beat cop with 20 years in and looking to lay low until I retire! This is my life! I live for this shit! I am a detective! I detect, Dr. Daniels and right now I'm detecting bullshit. If you don't start being honest with me, I can't help you." Chicago placed both her hands on the table and started to stand. "I've had enough of these baseless accusations."

Jimenez stared her down. "You might want to stay for my next question."

With more than a touch of irritation, Chicago asked, "And what might that be?"

Jimenez pointed for her to sit back down. Warily she did so. "Do you and your sister have the same father?" The look on her face when she answered was of pure annoyance. "Yes, of course."

"I knew that already because we were able to recover DNA from some of your father's bones and match it to you and Butterfly."

"Then why ask me?"

"Just crossing my T's and dotting my I's."

Detective Jimenez picked through the files and pulled another from the stack. "This is a DNA report. See, I did some digging into the lives of the Daniels clan. Your birth certificate is standard. However, Butterfly's is a live birth certificate. Shirley Daniels the mother and affiant, swore that Butterfly Octavia Daniels was born at home. It made me even more curious and I decided to run your DNA again." Chicago's facial expression declared she knew exactly where this was going. "I ran it against your sister's, and you could've knocked me over with a feather when the results came in." Chicago stared at her reflection in the two-way mirror. She had grown three shades paler in a fraction of a second. That change didn't escape Jimenez or go unnoticed by the unseen observers behind the glass. Chicago leaned back in her chair.

"You're right! Let's cut the shit. Butterfly is, was, my daughter. We share the same father. Martin Daniels raped me when I was 12 1/2 years old and got me pregnant. My mother raised us as sisters to make my life easier."

"Tell me something I don't know, like how did your father get into that hole in the garage?"

"Maybe he tripped, or karma pushed him in. Hell, if I know. I was only a child."

"Be careful Dr. Daniels, I'm your life preserver in an ocean of pain."

Chicago seemed to instantly regain her composure. "I am the master of my fate. The captain of my soul. I don't need a life preserver, detective."

Detective Jimenez laughed. "Before it's over you'll need the damn coastguard to pull you from the shit you're in." Jimenez took a photograph from a file. "Do you know this woman?"

Chicago scrutinized the woman's picture. "She looks familiar, but I can't place her.

"Her name is Trina Boyd. The picture you're looking at is from an AA/NA meeting. Ms. Boyd was ten years clean and sober in this photo."

Chicago looked nonplussed. "So, what. Everyone knows I attended some meetings."

Jimenez smiled. Chicago did not like that smile. "Look just over Ms. Boyd's shoulder. Her left shoulder. Can you see it? Wait, I have another photo. The boys and girls in computer services enlarged it." The detective hurriedly found the photo she wanted.

Chicago's irritation began to show. "Why are you showing me pictures of people I don't know. I want my sis . . . daughter's property and to leave, that's all."

Jimenez held up the photograph she'd just found. Chicago's mouth hung open for a brief moment then closed with an audible snap. "Can you see who that is?"

"That's a picture of me."

Jimenez moved her finger directly next to Chicago's likeness. "And this man whom you're obviously talking to?" She just stared at the detective. "Let me help you. That there is William Kiddick, the man who confessed to killing your late husband." You could have heard an ant fart from the silence that followed her statement. "Do you deny knowing him, because I have signed witness statements from others attending these meetings who will swear that you two were bosom buddies?"

Chicago took a deep breath easing her nerves and exhaled slowly to calm herself. "I don't recall this picture or ever having met that man. What you have is a group photo. Furthermore, while it may be obvious to you, we're talking, to me, it looks like two people who don't know each other being caught in someone else's camera shot. If memory serves me right this man admitted in that horrible video to stalking my family members. Maybe he saw my kidnapping in the media and decided to insinuate himself in my life."

Jimenez became livid. Her face was flushed, and her breathing deepened. "Bullshit! So, this is the fucking game you want to play? I thought doctors were supposed to be smart!" The detective was out of her seat glowering over Chicago. "We're past the stage of denial, Dr. Daniels. Let me tell you what I know!"

The detective began methodically laying out her case. She told Chicago her sister slash daughter was and always had been mentally disturbed.

"Being she's a child of incest, it isn't hard to fathom. She was breaking the bedsprings with your late husband and had his child. Together this delightful duo decides to get rid of you. Take Chicago off the map so to speak, but our world-famous sadistic asshole decided to keep you as a sex pet rather than complete the contract. In the process of Sanford Smalls turning you into his heroin-addicted queen, someone double taps him in his sweet spot. Are you still with me, because the plot thickens? You are rescued, but not before being shot twice.

We were watching Dr. Brooks like a hawk. My gut told me he was involved. However, no one was watching your daughter. I think she murdered Sanford Smalls and shot you. How am I doing so, far?" Chicago gave a disheartened shrug. Jimenez slapped her palm flat against the table. "Please don't insult my intelligence. Sure, I only graduated from McKenzie High school, but I did so with honors, picking up a couple of degrees from the community college. No Ph.D., but I'm smart, with enough common sense to know you knew."

Chicago glanced at her watch then clasped her hands in her lap. "What is it that I'm supposed to know detective?"

"Not what you know! What you knew! You knew that your sister slash daughter was not only screwing your sorry excuse for a husband, you knew that they were the ones who were responsible for putting you in the path of a psycho."

Chicago shook her head erratically from side to side. "No, that's not true. If I would've known they were trying to kill me, I would have called you guys, the police."

Jimenez paced back and forth while grinning and laughing to herself. Chicago watched her and felt like she should say something. "I learned of their affair from you and your partner right in this very room."

Suddenly the detective stopped and faced her. "I seriously doubt that. The whole Oscar performance you gave at your home on the roof that day was fucking brilliant. Meryl Streep would've kissed your ass and asked for pointers had she seen it. You let me come to you, then handed over those letters and the flash drive putting me right up Butterfly's ass. You played me like a rookie! Moving right along. Your daughter ran high-end whores during her four-year college stint, which was not an easy feat with competition from the Russians, Armenians, etc. I checked with Chicago PD and Northwestern University campus police after I discovered that information. She never came up on anyone's radar. Dr. Daniels, your daughter may have been crazy, but she was crazy like a fox. There's no way Mrs. Butterfly Daniels Baxter left that many breadcrumbs leading back to herself. So, let me ask you: Why'd you kill your husband and frame her?"

Chicago started crying. "Save the croc drops for the jury and answer my question."

"I didn't kill my husband and I resent this entire line of questioning." Detective Jimenez leaned on the table and in a near whisper said, "I believe you, Dr. Daniels. No, you didn't kill him. You just hired William Kiddick to do it for you." Chicago remained silent glancing at her watch again.

"Are you late for something?" Chicago still said nothing. Jimenez sat back down taking the woman's hands in hers and turned on her empathy.

"Confess your sins. I know the burden you carry is a heavy one. Right here, right now, I'm giving you the opportunity to unburden yourself. Lay it all on me. I get it! Butterfly and Dorian betrayed you and you wanted revenge."

She pulled her hands away from the detective's grasp placing them back in her lap. "I have no sins to confess to you. I'm Baptist, not Catholic. My sins are told directly to God but thank you anyway." Chicago wiped at her tears then asked, "Can I have my daughter's property? I would like to go now."

Jimenez stretched her arms above her head yawning rudely without covering her mouth. "You can leave anytime you want; but wouldn't you like to hear how I think you paid William Kiddick to kill your husband?"

"It's impossible for you to do because I didn't pay one red cent towards that end." Jimenez slid her chair back, stood, and grabbed another file. Chicago watched silently as the detective opened the folder and arranged some photographic evidence over the tabletop.

"You see, I believe you and William Kiddick became fast friends. He told you all about his ex-wife and best bud getting it on behind his back and forging his signature to steal over a hundred K. In turn, you told him about your husband and sister who we now know is your daughter, banging like rabbits in a cabbage patch and how they tried to have you murdered. Let's not forget them gifting you to a sexual sadist. After much talk, you guys decide to do something—get revenge. The problem is being too close to the people you want to destroy. Anybody who watches Law & Order reruns knows the spouse or ex is prime suspect numero uno." Jimenez scooted away from the table looking down at Chicago's feet. "What size shoe do you wear?"

"Why detective? What is this all about?" "Indulge me."

Chicago looked down at her feet. "I wear size 6-1/2 and sometimes a size 7 depending on the shoe."

Jimenez pushed a photo towards Chicago. "This is an imprint of a woman's size 6-1/2 Adidas walking shoe. It was made near the curb in some soft dirt at a murder scene in Brownstown."

"That's a little outside of your jurisdiction isn't it, detective?"

"Injustice anywhere is a job for police everywhere, Dr. Daniels. Besides, once I explain things in their totality you'll understand." Jimenez looked down at the photo and feigned surprise. "Que chingados? Forgive me. Sometimes when I get excited, I revert to my native tongue. Do you speak Spanish?" Chicago shook her head. "I said, what the fuck? Did you know the shoe print in the photograph is the same size as yours?"

Chicago looked directly at the two-way mirror behind Jimenez when she spoke. "I don't own a pair of Adidas and plenty of women and perhaps children wear the same size. In fact, Butterfly did." Jimenez shuffled some more reports and photographs. "What does any of this have to do with me?" Chicago asked.

The detective leaned forward casually, "That's just it. It has everything to do with you."

Then she shoved two photographs towards her suspect, one male, and one female, each showing visible gunshot wounds to the head. Chicago flinched at the death depicted in front of her. "Why are you presenting these horrible pictures as if they were greeting cards? Detective, you are way out of line!"

"Mentirosa! Liar!" The detective shouted at the doctor. Chicago looked away from the woman's penetrating gaze.

"You couldn't kill your own child, but you could frame her for killing your husband and get her locked away, maybe get some help for her mental issues. Ingenious plan. Beats the hell out of a drive-by." Chicago hung her head as fat teardrops raced to her chin. "Your payment to William Kiddick for killing your husband and framing your daughter was this!" The detective held up the photos of Brandon Fuller and Karen Kiddick's corpses. "You caught the happy couple and blew their thoughts all over the driveway but left a shoe print behind. I haven't even told Brownstown PD about you yet, and I won't in exchange for your cooperation."

Chicago seemed older sitting in that hard metal chair. "Exactly, what does my cooperation entail?"

"Tell me about your husband's murder and everything surrounding it and I'll make sure you get a fair shake. Prosecutor Lindsay is behind that glass waiting to authorize a deal that will save you from spending the rest of your life in prison." Chicago began wiping her eyes and sat up straighter in her seat. "I need some time to think."

This time, Jimenez glanced at her watch. "I'll give you five minutes and then I'm coming back through that door with the prosecutor and you're going to either make a deal or go directly to jail." Chicago watched as the detective strolled confidently out of the interrogation room. Then she started thinking in earnest.

Brownstown, Michigan was a stone's throw from Detroit. Chicago rented a car from the airport the day before and an hour later she found that same color, make and model in the parking lot of a lowend gentlemen's club. She stole the license plates and used adhesive backing to affix them to her plates. She chose that club because it was small and didn't have any external surveillance cameras. She wore dark clothing with a baseball cap pulled low over her brow. After months of meticulous planning, Chicago was ready.

The target couple had been out to dinner at Salvador's, an authentic Central American restaurant in the small city. Chicago knew the couple's movements because Billy had bought his deceitful ex-wife the iPhone she still carried. Even though Karen changed the number, she neglected to switch the password, which logged her or anyone else on to a GPS tracking site for lost or stolen phones. Chicago was looking at the website on a burner smartphone, Billy provided.

Leaving the restaurant after they took off, she raced to Brandon Fuller's home, where the lovebirds lived together. Chicago parked down the street next to a grassy field behind a large dual cab truck and waited patiently listening to smooth jazz on the radio.

She thought long and hard about her approach to the couple, so she was ready when Brandon's big Chevy Silverado passed her by and swung into the driveway. Chicago pulled up leaving the engine running, the car door opened, and the interior lights off. With a manila envelope in one gloved hand and a Ruger .357 snub-nosed revolver gripped tightly in her right jacket pocket, Chicago walked up, "Process server!" In one fluid motion, she extended her left hand with the envelope letting it drop as she pointed the gun, stood on tiptoe, and shot Brandon once in his face, then again in the center of his chest.

Karen was frozen in shock as Chicago spun and fired into her face at a downward angle. The first bullet punched out the woman's left eye socket and the other copper jacketed hollow point round tunneled through her brain coming to rest lazily at the back of her skull. As Karen slumped to the driveway's pavement her head banged against the big Chevy's tire rim with a sickening thud. Turning, Chicago shot Brandon almost point-blank in the head two more times and let the empty gun slip from her fingers like Michael Corleone in the Godfather movie. She rushed back to the car.

Before getting on the freeway, she pulled onto a dark, dirt road and stripped down to her birthday suit, grabbed a blue jersey dress off the passenger seat, and slipped it on along with a pair of sandals. Next, she exited the vehicle and snatched the stolen plates off, revealing the legitimate one. Quickly, Chicago looked around to make sure she was alone then tossed everything in a ditch. Weather reports for the area predicted heavy rains for the next several days. Any valuable evidence would be washed away. Back in the car, she went through a quick checklist. She used her right hand instead of her natural left and stood on her tiptoes to confuse the angle and entry of the bullets, switched the plates, and got rid of her shoes and clothing. They'd never connect the dots to her.

Back in Detroit she parked the car around the block from her apartment building and let the air out of the rear driver's side tire. She called the rental company's service center explained to them that she caught a flat close to home and while checking things out, mistakenly locked the keys inside the car. Chicago instructed them to retrieve the vehicle, which they were happy to do. Dorian was waiting for her, wanting to know where she'd been. His wife told him that she was at a meeting over at the Methodist church on Seldon, right up the street. Excusing herself she went and took a bath. A part of her was horrified by what she had just done, while the rest of her luxuriated in the knowledge that Dorian and Butterfly would very soon, reap what they have sown.

Jimenez stood looking through the glass at Dr. Daniels as she stared at the photographs showing the bodies of Karen Kiddick and Brandon Fuller. Around her, Lieutenant Templeton was speaking on his cellphone as was Detective Gleason. Prosecutor Lindsay sidled up to her. "She's all but broken. Do you want me to step in for the full court press?"

"Yeah, why not. I'm ready to be done with this." Jimenez looked at her watch's stopwatch as eight seconds wound down. It beeped letting her know the doctor's five minutes were up. "Let's end this," she said as Gleason hung up his phone.

"You're doing great partner."

"When the ink is dry on her confession, I'll be doing great."

He watched as she and Felicia Lindsay entered the room on the opposite side of the glass. Templeton came and stood next to him. "The doctor's about to give it up like my wife after a bottle of white Zinfandel." Gleason laughed.

Chicago looked up as the women entered the room. "Hello Dr. Daniels," Lindsay greeted her. "I'm only going to say this once. You confess all, and I do mean all, and I'll take natural life without the possibility of parole off the table."

Jimenez added. "That includes what you know of your father's death."

Prosecutor Lindsay spoke in harsh tones, "That's the deal. Take it or leave it. To be honest, I'm hoping you will leave it. This is a slam dunk. The media attention alone will guarantee me a promotion."

Chicago openly looked at her watch then picked up her purse and stood. "I'm not taking any deal because I've done nothing wrong. You tricked me down here under the guise of retrieving my child's property whom you shot and killed detective. This is an emotionally trying time for me and rightfully so." They both tried to interrupt her, but she held up a defiant hand to stop them. "I've listened to all I'm going to listen to from any of you. To start from the beginning; my father viciously raped me before I was even a teenager. The last time I saw him alive, he was tearing my hymen and spilling his semen inside me. My mother told me he was dead to us and concocted a story for my 12-year-old mind to regurgitate if anyone asked about him and that's what I've been doing all of these years. From that sexual assault, my daughter Butterfly was born and raised as my sister. I feel immense shame for that deception, but I will not allow either of you to use it to make me confess to crimes I haven't committed."

Jimenez was growing angrier by the second. "You murdered that couple in Brownstown. You're going to prison for a long time. A pretty woman like you is going to make some stud dike really happy."

"You think I'm pretty? Then maybe I should be more concerned about you Sargent. The only place I'm going is home. You have plenty of suppositional theory, but nothing in the way of proof. E-mail, DNA, fingerprints, hair fibers, or eyewitnesses to tie me to anything. So, what, because you have a photograph of me and William Kiddick. I don't know him. Outside of him attending the same AA/NA meeting as me for whatever his reasons were, you'd be hard-pressed to show any jury a connection. As for the horrible murder of that lovely looking couple, I ask you to show me a gun, witness, or any physical evidence putting me at the scene beside a shoe print from a style of shoe I don't own, but I think maybe my daughter did." Prosecutor Lindsay told Jimenez, "Charge her with everything you can think of." The detective chimed in, "If I were you, I'd tell the truth right now before things get tough for you."

Chicago laughed at them. "When I was growing up my father used to tell people he named me after the city he loved. Truth is, my mother, named me Chicago because it was the toughest thing she'd ever known and Alexandria because in antiquity it was said to have been where the smartest people on earth congregated. Simply put, I'm very smart and a thousand times tougher than I look.

Let's see, my considerable bank account, intelligence an ocean of sharks calling themselves lawyers in one hand. The shit you're alleging along with the evidence you don't have in the other. Ladies, the scales of justice are already tipping in my favor."

Arrest me on these trumped-up charges. I'll be exonerated, then sue both your departments and the two of you individually. My lawsuit will also include how the Detroit police shot into a vehicle with my family, a family with no criminal history. That coupled with shoddy police work and your constant harassment should grant me a hefty financial civil judgment. Not that I need the money, but what the hell."

At that very moment, there was a loud commotion outside of the interrogation room door. Suddenly, it burst open with Stephanie Fishman yelling, "Not another word Dr. Daniels! If you people didn't know, now you do. This is my client!" The lawyer turned to face Chicago with an apologetic look on her face. "Sorry, I know when you called, I told you I would meet you here, but I was delayed in court. Please forgive me?"

Chicago nodded slightly. Fishman turned to face the other people who were in the room. Lieutenant Templeton and Gleason tried cock blocking her with their lies, but she had dealt with them often enough to know they were full of crap.

The attorney looked at the stack of files, crime scene photographs, and a plastic evidence bag presumably with her client's, daughter's property. Before leaving her apartment, Dr. Daniels had called and retained Fishman giving her a brief summary of events, including the fact that her former client was not the doctor's sister, but her daughter.

257

It was a lot to swallow, but as one of Michigan's top defense attorneys, she's had to stomach much worse. "If she isn't being charged, she's leaving right now."

Confused, everyone looked around at each other as Chicago made her way to the open door. I didn't think so! Dr. Daniels, I'll recover the property and return it to you. Is that what you'd like for me to do?"

She responded, "You have my permission to act as power of attorney in this matter."

Jiminez caught up to Chicago at the bank of elevators. "How can you live with yourself after killing those people?"

Detective, I can ask you the same thing about the death of my child."

Jiminez told her in a matter-of-fact tone, "That was a public service."

The two women faced each other like mortal enemies, but to anyone else, they looked like two professionals waiting on the elevator.

"Since you aren't going to confess and are now represented by counsel tell me, did you or your mother kill your father? Share. I can't use it against you. How did you know your husband and daughter were behind your abduction? Do you have nightmares about the murders, or do you sleep like a baby? Butterfly couldn't help herself; she was mentally disturbed. But you …" Jimenez pointed a finger at Chicago's chest. "Dr. Daniels you of all people knew better but did your worse anyway. Shame on you!"

Chicago looked at the detective without saying a word. "Eventually new evidence will be uncovered, or a witness will step forward., Then you'll pay."

The elevator doors slid open with a whoosh, Chicago walked in and pressed the lobby button. She spoke in Spanish. "Ya page suficinte. I've paid enough already."

Jimenez responded to her own image cast on the now-closed stainless-steel elevator doors, "No erda todo ensuficiente! You haven't paid enough!" It was when she got back to the interrogation room that she realized Dr. Daniels had spoken to her in near-perfect Spanish.

EPILOGUE

Outside in the van, Albany was asleep buckled into one of the captain's chairs. Morgan was on the phone doing his whole titan of the industry thing but hurriedly finished his call after Chicago slid into the passenger seat raising the privacy partition.

"Is everything alright?"

She exhaled the breath she'd been holding. "Never better." Her voice was tinged with sarcasm before softening. "Lo siento."

"What?" Morgan asked.

Chicago squeezed his knee gently. "I said, I'm sorry." "I didn't know you spoke Spanish?"

"Fluently. There's a lot you don't know. Anyway, the police were giving me a hard time, but thankfully I had the foresight to call a lawyer.

"Where's Butterfly's property? Did they release it?" Chicago strapped on her seatbelt. "The lawyer is handling everything. She's going to expedite matters and send it later. Listen, I'm tired of this ugly, wonderful, beautiful city." Morgan saw a brief shadow of pain creep across her face then vanish. "This place holds too many awful memories for me."

He pressed the engine start button and shifted into gear. "Alright, this is your last chance to say goodbye before we head down the Interstate. I warn you once you reach Georgia you'll never want to return."

She looked forlornly out the window knowing she could never say goodbye to Detroit, only I'll see you again. Every year she would come back to visit her Caterpillar and with every day she'd miss her more and more.

Chicago used to believe Butterfly took after their father, but as Morgan pulled up to a stoplight, she could see a reflection of herself in the glass of a building on the corner. She did a double-take. Butterfly's image was superimposed over hers. Chicago knew then that a person could only be a reflection of who and what they know. Butterfly never knew their father, but she knew Chicago all too well.

The End

Here's an excerpt from Carter Lynn's next book entitled:

"Envy and Jealousy."

ENVY

In a surreal fashion of thinking, when one just can't believe what is happening, Envy thought to herself, Margo told me that it would be fun, an adventure like no other. Why do I always have to listen to her? Envy and Margo were best friends, and it wasn't that Envy was weak or by nature a follower. She just felt deep empathy for her friend who seemed to always get the short end of the stick. It was because of that kind of thinking that Envy was in the position she was in.

Copper, rust, old newspaper, and a hint of urine. Wait! She thought to herself, …and excrement. That's what it smells like. It smells like shit. It certainly wasn't the vacation Envy had imagined. Her mouth was duct-taped shut with her wrist tied to the arms of a thick wooden chair. It was pitch black in front of her, but a shaft of errant light was casting eerily from behind. As she looked up, she saw large metal rafters. It didn't take a genius to know that she was being held in some type of warehouse.

At that moment, an ugly woman with a slight boyish frame approached her from the side forcefully spinning her chair 180°. The mannish looking woman wore a cruel mouth beneath almond-shaped brown eyes. She appeared Asian, but when she spoke it was with a mixture of Spanish, Portuguese, and broken English. It was obvious they had the wrong person. A vicious series of slaps stopped Envy's hysterical thoughts causing her to focus in on the moment. The horrid woman gave a short evil laugh that echoed around the huge cavernous space.

Envy studied the waif-like creature in front of her who resembled a velociraptor. Besides the cruel mouth and almond eyes, the woman sported a pockmarked face with a peach-fuzz mustache. Her short dark hair smelled as did the rest of her, like onions and accumulated filth. The tight yellow tank top showed underarm hair with a flat chest and two protruding thimble-sized points, which Envy assumed were breasts with large nipples. The woman's nipples seemed to grow hard in front of her eyes. Hell no. Envy thought silently. Was this some type of crazy sex slavery deal? If it is, she thought again, this ugly bitch is going to be disappointed. My snatch was drier than sandpaper sitting in the Sahara Desert.

The dinosaur reached into the pocket of her dirty jean skirt pulling out a pair of latex gloves. Reaching into the other pocket her captor extracted a needle and a rubber tourniquet. It was the kind used for drawing blood. Within seconds she had drawn three vials of Envy's blood. The hideous woman then turned and moved aside a plastic curtain, which she held open long enough for Envy to get a good look at what lay beyond. It was terrifying. There was a body on a metal slab; the kind you might see in a morgue. She stared in horror as a person in a surgical mask and scrubs pulled a heart from the body and handed it to someone else who was similarly dressed. That person placed the heart in a cooler. Envy could tell the person who extracted the heart was a man when he barked something to 'Ms. Jurassic' who covered her mouth while holding up the vials of her blood. Then the curtain closed blocking Envy's view. She could hear movement. Feet shuffling. Nothing. It made her soul shake.

The curtain opened again and suddenly five people stood before her. Someone yelled something foreign to her ears and overhead lights came on. Most of the warehouse was still shrouded in darkness, but

Envy could clearly see the people in front of her along with the makeshift operating theater behind them. There were three men and two women including the hideous one who took her blood. Two of the men and a woman wore surgical scrubs. She recognized the only man in street clothes as the cab driver from the airport. The woman wearing scrubs walked up to her and pulled out a stethoscope listened to Envy's heart and lungs, shined a penlight into her eyes while lifting her eyelids, then gave a thumbs-up sign to the tall older man, who was obviously in charge. Envy felt a sense of dread as he shooed everyone away except for Mr. Cabdriver and Ms. Jurassic.

The head man made a motion with his index finger and Mr. Cabdriver ripped the tape from her mouth. Envy took in a deep breath, gagging on the dank humid air. "Why are you doing this? What do you want?" She looked at each of them in turn then let her eyes rest on the leader. "Say something damn it!" Maybe they don't speak English, she thought. That's when Mr. Cabdriver hit her in the side of her head causing her vision to blur. Pain from the impact of his fist shot to her stomach making her vomit airplane chicken all over the front of her travel dress. "You will learn to speak only when asked a direct question or given permission." Envy coughed, then spat on the floor at his feet. "Please, just listen to me." Mr. Cabdriver slapped the duct-taped roughly back over her mouth, wiping vomit off his hand onto her shoulder.

At the same time, Ms. Jurassic came and stood behind the chair she was bound to. Envy heard two discernible clicks and found herself being easily rolled across the warehouse floor. A switch was flipped and the corner where they were was bathed in yellow fluorescent light. Directly in front of her was a machine with huge flies buzzing around it. Envy felt rather than heard the two clicks as her chair was locked back into place. That's when the smell of rotting flesh made the vomit on her breath smell like roses.

"Ms. Eversole my real name is unimportant, but everyone calls me the Surgeon. Unfortunately for you, I'm not the make you a better kind." He stopped talking as Mr. Cabdriver came back pushing the metal gurney with the body on it. "This is an industrial-strength woodchipper. It's capable of turning a human body into soup in under five minutes." He snapped his fingers at Ms. Jurassic, and she disappeared for a moment. When she came back into view, she was pushing a huge metal drum underneath a tube at the end of the woodchipper. Proudly the surgeon said, "This is my own design. This tube allows for the human soup to flow into the drum. Then five gallons of diesel fuel is stirred in. After that, it's just a matter of adding a match and voila, the body disappears into smoke."

He snapped his fingers again and Mr. Cabdriver switched on the machine. Envy could see that the body was female. The Y incision cut into the torso flopped closed as Mr. Cabdriver was feeding it into the machine and a dark nipple breast with a tattoo of an angel was exposed. She tried to close her eyes, but Ms. Jurassic forcefully held them open. "There is no escape for you. Your blood is being checked for disease or abnormalities of any kind. Once we have you typed and matched to a potential donor your major organs will be harvested." Then strong hands turned her head and Envy watched mesmerized as red gunk flowed out of the tube into the barrel. "Until that time you will be treated extremely well, up to a point that is."

He stared at the rapidly filling drum.

"Resign yourself to your fate and you will be better off." The Surgeon stroked her hair as one might a stray puppy. "Take her to the barracks. She needs rest."

MIGUEL

Envy was shoved through a set of double doors at the far end of the warehouse. There were two small windowless corrugated styled barracks adjacent to one another. Ms. Jurassic stood off to one side, pulled a small automatic pistol, and aimed it at her head, while Mr. Cabdriver cut her dress and underwear off. He even took her shoes.

It was then that Ms. Jurassic spoke in broken English, "When cut loose, go in shower. No escape. If you try, chop foot off." She smiled showing broken, brown, and deeply stained teeth. Envy had no doubt these people meant business as her bonds were discarded and she was taken into the first barracks. With an arm folded across her breast and a shaking hand cupping her crotch she found herself being stared at by seven pairs of eyes. Her entire body goose-bumped because it was cooler inside the barracks.

Briefly, the other occupants looked up at her entrance; then nonchalantly went back to what they were doing as though what was happening was normal. Some were watching a television mounted high up in a corner of the room while others played checkers or dominoes. It looked more like a mental ward than a place to die. There were five small twin-sized beds on each side. Two were empty. She heard a toilet flush then saw a door open on her right at the rear. A handsome Latino man in his late twenties walked out. Everyone, male and female alike wore neon green short sleeve coveralls. His were rolled down and tied at the waist showing his bare chest. Ms. Jurassic pushed her in the back and quickly fled as the man yelled at her in his native tongue.

As soon as the door was closed and bolted, a young woman with shocking red hair ran up to Envy. "Are you American? I'm American." Envy nodded while looking around. The scene was surreal. No one cared that she was naked or that they all were literally being warehoused for replacement parts to those who could afford it. "Did you hear me? My name is Julia Byrd. That's with a y, not an I. You seem to be out of it. Let's get you all cleaned up." Envy was led into a small shower in the rear where lukewarm water ran over her in a steady stream. A bar of soap was pushed into her hand. She tried focusing on the moment, looking into the empathetic face of the smiling redhead but couldn't. This must be a nightmare! She thought to herself. Then she started screaming in hopes that someone would wake her up. The impish woman slapped her then shook her roughly until she stopped screaming. "Now clean yourself up! We must be strong. Our survival depends on it."

A half an hour later Envy and an energetic Julia who went by the name Byrd, like Lady Byrd Johnson, who once was the first lady of the United States, sat with her on her newly made bunk. They were the only two Americans in their barracks and probably the only ones who spoke English, besides Miguel. "I've been here for three weeks." She pointed to the handsome man in the bunk across from them. "Miguel's been here even longer."

266

Looking at Julia Envy said, "I get what's going on. What I don't get is why no one has tried to overpower the guards. I only saw the two who brought me in and a few people in scrubs."

Julia waved Miguel over. "I'll let him explain." The young man resembled a young Benjamin Bratt. He was about six feet and lean, but from what she could see of his arms and upper torso his muscles were well defined. Despite Envy's dire predicament, she felt a twinge of attraction. He said hello and introduced himself as Miguel Santos Ruiz. Then he explained that he and his twin sister Maitra were kidnapped by a drug cartel and sold to these mercado negros. "These black marketers deal in life, by way of death. They either kidnapped men, women, and children or bought them from cartels and human trafficking organizations. Some of the people in here were sold to these black marketers by their own families!"

"How could someone sell their own flesh and blood to these animals," Envy raised her voice Miguel cautioned her to keep her voice down. "The poverty level in some places is so low that the money families receive for one member allows the rest of them to live on for years. Believe it or not, some of these people think it's a noble sacrifice to ensure the family they love survives."

Envy was stunned into silence listening to Miguel until she realized these two were waiting on her to respond. She didn't know what to say so, she asked a question instead. "Where is your sister?" Miguel looked sad at that question. "They took her three days ago. Her name is Maitra but we, my family calls her little Angel."

Involuntarily, her hand flew to her mouth then she asked cautiously, "Did she have a tattoo of an angel high up on her breast?"

Miguel grabbed Envy's hands in his strong grip unconsciously hurting her. He saw her wince with pain and let go. "I'm sorry Ms…?"

She rubbed her hands together in a washing motion. "Eversole. My name is Envy Eversole."

"Please, tell me what you know." Miguel cried as she told him what she saw. Byrd's energy seemed to dissipate by the time Envy had finished. Both women tried to console him but to no avail.

"We need to escape this place. Let's try to overpower them." Byrd and Miguel looked at her as though she were insane. Miguel began telling her about what he had seen when they brought him to the compound. Foreigners are usually drugged and taken from their hotel room or during a cab ride from the airport. That realization caused Envy to flashback to her fateful taxi ride.

Envy remembered how hot it was in the cab. Mr. Cabdriver told her there was a cooler on the floor at her feet with ice-cold bottled water. She gulped it thirstily as she admired the sights and sounds of Sao Paulo, Brazil. That must've been how they got her.

Miguel and his sister had been kidnapped by a cartel that their older sister, Mexican Federal prosecutor Salina la Rosa Ruiz was trying to arrest and extradite to the U.S. Most of them were primarily of the Sinaloa drug organization. They kidnapped and sold the younger Ruiz twins as a warning to their older sister. The message was clear: DON'T FUCK WITH US!

ESCAPE

He thought they were being held in an old banana warehouse within the Amazon rainforest. Exactly where he couldn't say because 60 percent of the rainforest was within the borders of Brazil. They weren't far from a city though. Once, he heard the guards talking to each other. One told the other about meeting a whore in an hour. They couldn't be far from civilization if the guards were arranging jungle booty calls.

The exterior of the warehouse had at least six to eight armed guards equipped with cameras and dogs, vicious bull mastiffs who looked like American pit bulls, though are far more dangerous. So, even if they were able to make it out, they would be hunted relentlessly.

"This is a multimillion-dollar operation. People all over the globe are paying big money for hearts, livers, or new a kidney. These people here are flunkies. The real jefes are sitting in their ivory towers safe from exposure. We aren't going anywhere. You might as well say your prayers and make peace with God."

Looking shocked at Miguel, Envy asked, "How can you say such a thing? We have to at least try."

Miguel shook his head as he looked at Envy. She watched in dismay as he walked over to his bunk and stretched out on his back with his hands resting behind his head. She asked Byrd if she had given up, too. The mighty Texan squeezed her hand and walked away to where two Latino men played dominos.

A buzzer sounded startling Envy. Everyone stopped what they were doing and stood at the front of their beds. She looked to Byrd for guidance who told her to do the same. Ms. Jurassic came through the barrack doors and did a quick headcount. She held a laser in her hand, which she pointed and was ready to use, if necessary. Mr. Cabdriver stood in the doorway behind her as backup. He had a small caliber automatic in his hand. He also had a laser in his belt. The ugly woman didn't venture more than three feet inside the door. Envy knew, without being told, that Miguel was responsible for Ms. Jurassic's reticence.

After the quick headcount Envy's ugly captor pointed, beckoning her over. Byrd took her by the arm and stood fast. Envy could feel the tremors in the other woman's hands as she held her tightly. "If you go with them, they'll rape you. Trust me, I know."

Envy looked past the impish face studying the green eyes. They were lifeless. "Won't they just take me anyway?" Miguel came next to them in a show of strength.

"They won't want a struggle of any kind. If they damage the product, their boss will kill them. No. They need you to be compliant in your own victimization."

Miguel had fought with them when they came for his sister, Maitra'. He couldn't help Byrd because they came while he was asleep and tasered him. Since that incident, the prisoners slept in shifts to protect each other. She learned that those bastard monsters videoed their sexual assaults and then sold them on the Darknet. Miguel stared angrily at them. Mr. Cabdriver said something in Portuguese to Ms. Jurassic and they left, but it was clear by their body language they were angry about leaving empty-handed.

Suddenly the lights went out. "What's happening?" Envy asked. Her new friends explained to her that their captors cut the power every night to encourage sleep. "The product needs to be healthy in order to send."

Miguel told Byrd to take Envy to the bathroom and that he would take the first watch. The young women squeezed into the small bathroom together and Envy undid her coveralls sitting unashamedly on the toilet. Byrd turned on the water leaning into Envy's ear whispering very fast. When she was finished, she cut the faucet off. "Come on. My bladder is the size of a pea." After the redhead finished, she told Envy, "Let's get some sleep. I'm sure you could use some." Byrd quickly washed her hands then followed her fellow American to bed.

Even though it was dark in the barracks, there were small nightlights spaced at intervals along the upper walls. Envy could see the handsome Miguel holding a folded blanket in his lap and staring at the door. The thick wool blanket was meant to stop the barbs from the taser. He learned that if they couldn't subdue him cleanly, without injury, they would retreat.

Envy wondered if her best friend, who she was supposed to meet in Sao Paulo a day after her arrival, was looking for her. Did she go to the American Embassy and raise hell? She wondered about that and as she thought about what Byrd had whispered in her ear. They did have an escape plan and she was invited. No one had ever escaped. At least that's what the guards told everyone.

It was logical to assume that their captors have hidden cameras and listening devices so, they needed to be careful. Envy wanted to live, get married, have children, and travel the world. She wanted to see places like Dubai, Italy, the French Riviera, and one day, hopefully, attend the Madi Gras in New Orleans. But where she found herself was strange. In less than 48 hours she'd flown to Brazil, been drugged, kidnapped by black-market organ thieves, and seen a body being fed into a woodchipper. Not to mention she barely escaped being raped.

Her parents didn't attend church, but they acquainted her with the Bible. Silently she prayed. Lord, let me live. I promise to lead a good life, but I ask forgiveness for the things I may have to do to survive. And I can't promise you that I won't hurt the people responsible for bringing me here. But I will show them more mercy than they've shown their victims. Amen!

FAILURE

The plan was set. Envy, Byrd, and Miguel went through everything at least a hundred times over the next week. In the early morning, they would remove the portable air conditioning unit located at the back of the barracks and climb out into the warehouse proper. Inside there are usually two armed guards, but that number falls to only one in the wee hours.

Envy wondered how Miguel could know so much about the routines in that horrid place. He told her that he'd been doing reconnaissance at night before she arrived and more recently while she was asleep. Curious, Envy asked, "What kind of job did you have before all this happened?"

Officer Miguel Ruiz was a member of an incorruptible team inside of Mexico's federal police called, Narco Dolor. Dolor means pain in Spanish. His twelve-person team was handpicked by his sister to bring pain to the drug cartel. Miguel was very skilled with weapons and in hand-to-hand combat. That's why he was sure he could overpower the lone guard, procure his weapon and lead them out of the warehouse into the jungle where they would escape their captors and find a way to contact his sister, the prosecutor. He knew there was a private airstrip because he and his twin sister Maitra' were flown in it from Mexico and walked to the warehouse.

Most people thought the northern borders of his country were the worst, but they are not. The cartel strongholds down south are. The methamphetamine and cocaine super labs along with their army of soldiers and private airstrips are far worse. Even though he would be winging it once they made it out, he still felt confident. Maybe they could fly out. Time would tell.

The women cut pieces of their wool blankets up and used strips of material from sheets to make sandals. Miguel planned on taking the guard's boots for himself. He had fashioned three knives from some loose metal in the shower area. Stealthily, the shower area is where he showed Envy and Byrd how to handle their homemade knives efficiently. He shows them how to incapacitate or kill a guard to get away.

The time came for them to make their escape. When he gave the signal, Byrd would retrieve their homemade knives from their hiding place. Miguel would then remove the air conditioning unit while Envy stood to watch just inside the bathroom door. Once the guard in the warehouse was subdued, Miguel would strip him of his clothing and weapons. Envy would sneak from the toilet and Byrd, after quickly stuffing her bed, would sneak from the toilet, too. Stuffing the bed would make it look as if nothing was out of place if someone was watching a surveillance monitor. Afterward, all three would run from the warehouse into the jungle. From that point on it would be all guesswork and common sense.

Envy was nervous but equally excited about being free. She glanced across at Miguel, but because of the darkness, she couldn't tell if he was looking at her or not. She looked over at Byrd and couldn't see her either but heard her humming softly. Envy figured the redhead was just as nervous as she was, but it wouldn't belong.

The other six captives were fast asleep. Envy was so hyped up that her senses were on high alert. She didn't know how much time had passed, but everyone's breathing seemed heavier. Byrd was no longer humming. Envy had grown so anxious that she had to pee. While standing at the sink she studied her shaking hands and willed them to be still. They wouldn't listen. She gave up and made her way back to her bunk. As soon as her butt touched the thin mattress the lights came on practically blinding her. Simultaneously, the door burst open. Mr. Cabdriver, Ms. Jurassic and two very mean looking men in camouflage pants and tee shirts and carrying automatic weapons rushed in and surrounded Miguel's bunk. Ms. Jurassic fired her taser at him just as he was about to hit her with a vicious right hook. Envy watched the horrid sight unfolding a few feet in front of her in slow motion. Miguel's body instantly froze as the high voltage electricity coursed through his chiseled frame. Mr. Cabdriver and one of the other men quickly trussed him with zip ties and dragged his unconscious body outside the barracks. The fear was palpable. Everyone was hoping it was over and at the same time glad it wasn't them.

Ms. Jurassic stopped at the door and stared at Envy. The ugly mannish looking creature licked her cracked lips with a tongue long enough to make Gene Simmons feel inadequate, then winked in what Envy supposed was a seductive gesture. Then she slammed the barracks door behind her. As soon as the door slammed, Byrd was hugging her whispering in her ear, "They took Miguel for surgery. We have to get the fuck out of here, Sugah, or we'll be next."

She was crying, but her resolve to stay alive had never been surer. The two young men who were always playing dominos came over. Both were short and effeminate looking with a rich light brown complexion. The oldest looking of the two had short hair. The other's hair was longer than both women's hair combined.

"We are with you." Short hair said. Just then the lights went out and they all went back to their bunks.

Envy was surprised that Short hair spoke English; however, at that point, any ally was more than welcomed. No one was able to sleep. There was no heavy rhythmic breathing. There were only the wheels of thought turning in all of their brains. Escaping had just become as important as air.

TRY, TRY AGAIN

Diego ran his slim fingers through his short hair. He and Envy had begun making covert trips together to the bathroom for the last two days as had Byrd and Guyvian. Byrd was miming to get him to understand. The four of them were going to keep the same plan with one exception.

Guyvian's little cousin was either dead or in the barracks next door. They were going to make a detour to find out. Another important fact was that the camera was inside the television. Diego had unplugged it a few nights before; and by the time he counted to 192, their captors had arrived to plug it back in. This night those assholes had a surprise coming.

It was a good night for it. A soccer match was on. Envy changed the channel and Diego changed it back. They argued and she snatched the plug from the outlet. Guyvian and Byrd armed with their makeshift knives hurriedly crawled out of the hole made by the air conditioning unit and waited. There were at least three sets of footsteps. No one patrolled the inner warehouse during the evening, because there was little to no activity.

Byrd peaked out from in between the barracks where they crawled. The same man and woman in street clothes approached the door while a heavily armed guard in camouflage fatigues stood off to the side with his back to them. As soon as the man and woman entered, Guyvian jumped past the redhead burying his sharpened metal into the guard's neck while pulling him between the two structures. The first thing Byrd did was pull the Beretta 9mm from the dead guard's holster and took the safety off. She was a Texas girl who knew good boots, barbeque, and guns.

Inside, Ms. Jurassic and Mr. Cabdriver had their lasers out. There was no way Diego or Envy could get close enough to attack before 50,000 volts sat them on their asses. Ms. Jurassic walked over to Envy grabbing at her breasts while licking her lips. "You come with us or I shock you!"

Without thinking about it Envy brought the knife from behind her back. In her mind, she was stabbing the vicious velociraptor in the eye, not a human being. She heard the snap -pop of a laser but felt only a tingle of electricity run through her. The barbs only penetrated the loose-fitting coveralls and not her nesh. Mr. Cabdriver was aiming for Diego's midsection when a rash of red stepped through the doorway hitting him in the back of his head.

Ms. Jurassic screamed as Envy pulled the knife from her eye socket. Diego punched her in the mouth to shut her up. Within three minutes both were tied and gagged.

Guyvian came in motioning for them to follow him. They were about to leave when the man in the first bunk stood in front of Envy with his hand open, palm up. She didn't understand at first then he pointed to the knife, which she gently laid in his hand. He straddled Ms. Jurassic and stabbed her to death. Envy stepped over Mr. Cabdriver on her way out the door while Diego was busy stripping the body of its clothing and boots.

In the barracks next door, the young Brazilian, Guyvian, had an assault rifle with a bandolier of extra magazines across his chest. He tossed the guard's stolen boots and pants at the foot of Miguel's bed. Miguel was naked except for a hospital gown. Envy rushed over helping him to get dressed. He was alert but in grave pain. Guyvian questioned some of the other people and found out that his cousin was long gone. She was most likely dead.

They needed to move. Byrd took off Miguel's gown rolling it up and wrapping it tightly around his waist to protect the wound in his lower backside and to help hold the staples together. The five of them didn't want to leave the others, but they had no choice.

When they exited the barracks the man who had gotten the makeshift knife from Envy was standing there drenched in blood. He held something out to her. She almost didn't take it until she recognized it as a satellite phone. Her father kept one on his airplane. Diego recovered a small automatic pistol from Mr. Cabdriver. Byrd had the Beretta with two extra magazines and Guyvian carried an ugly looking automatic rifle with a pistol tucked in his waist. It was dark, but shafts of ambient light shining through the warehouse windows revealed a door at the opposite end of the building. The group headed straight for it, half dragging, half carrying Miguel. Before Diego pushed through the door, Miguel stopped him and quickly checked to see if it was alarmed.

Byrd and Guyvian were bringing up the rear when they noticed people starting to drift out of the barracks. "We have to go before the guards figure out what happened," Byrd said in a near whisper. Miguel cracked open the cutter door and looked right out at a parking lot with several vehicles. There was a fifteen-year-old jeep Cherokee with big tires and heavy-duty suspension. It took a couple of minutes, but he got it started. They all quickly piled in like circus clowns. Miguel kept the lights off as he circled the building looking for an exit. Fifty yards ahead was a shack with a single figure standing next to it. Diego was riding shotgun. "Aim for the head. The guard's wearing body armor," Miguel cautioned Diego. Everybody tried to make themselves as small as possible while Diego checked the pistol's chamber and rolled his window down. They were a car's length away from that shack when an alarm started blaring like a tornado siren. Diego leaned out of the window and fired several shots at the guard. The guard fell to the ground but was able to raise his rifle and fire a single shot in retaliation.

Miguel used the big jeep as a weapon to crash through the barricade and run that asshole over. He floored the accelerator expecting more gunfire. When none came the other occupants lifted their heads; everyone except for Diego. A neat hole was tattooed over his left eyebrow with a small teardrop of blood trickling from it. His eyes held a vacant stare at anyone who looked at him. Guyvian started to cry and pray in Portuguese. Miguel knew enough of the language he was praying in to determine that Diego was his uncle. They were Brazilian and had been kidnapped from one of the poor sections of Rio de Janeiro. It was dark, but he was sure they were a long way from his home.

Miguel instructed Envy to dial a number. It was useless. The phone was locked requiring a code to get in. Guyvian turned in his seat speaking to Envy. "What is he saying, Miguel?"

"He said that he overheard the man and woman talking about you when they brought him out to test his blood. "What were they saying?" she asked again.

Guyvian ripped off a rapid string of Portuguese for about three or four minutes. The only thing she understood was go. "He said he overheard them planning to make good videos of you and they hoped someone named, go had more product like you to sell. I've dealt with organizations like this before. The Mexican cartels are heavy into human trafficking. They do their business on the internet on what's called the Dark Web or Darknet. Keep that phone. If we make it out of this alive, law enforcement might be able to get something useful out of it."

Envy was speechless. She was just about to say something when Byrd yelled, "Oh shit!" Three vehicles were coming up fast behind them. There was no doubt what their intentions were when the back window of the jeep shattered from gunfire. Byrd switched weapons with Guyvian and started firing back, and Miguel focused intently on his driving.

Thankfully, the road was so narrow they couldn't be passed up and overtaken. He wanted to open up the big engine on the rough jungle road, but it would be suicide in the dark. Even with his lights now on, without knowing the road they could easily die from a crash before the bullets being shot at them found their mark.

Byrd yelled for a new magazine. Guyvian handed her the bandolier and watched her frantically reload. Envy was covering her ears while trying to avoid the hot expended cartridges bursting from the assault rifle. Their ordeal was definitely a nightmare, but Envy was grappling with what she had just heard. Reality was often more frightening than her wildest dreams or imaginings. She could never concoct what she was experiencing at that very moment.

"Everybody, hang on!" Miguel sped up. "There's a river up ahead to our left. I think I see what looks like a small village with some boats! When we round the bend up ahead all of you make for the water, grab a boat and head with the current in the opposite direction!"

"No!" Byrd yelled. "Just drive through the village to the river's edge. We'll all load up and go. The only way we'll survive is by sticking together!"

"I agree!" Envy added over the gunfire and roaring engine. Byrd laid down a barrage of fire causing the lead truck to stall. That gave them a good head start until Envy peeked her head up and saw the men exit the downed truck and push it off the road. They gained maybe a half-mile lead as Miguel fled through the tiny village.

There was one boat with an outboard motor. The rest were either canoes or small aluminum boats requiring oars. None of them were in any shape to row a fucking boat. Guyvian helped Miguel out of the truck and into the craft while Byrd was frantically cranking the motor. That's when Envy saw the awful men flying down the road into the village.

Thinking quickly, she jumped into the driver's seat turning the truck around and pointing it at the approaching vehicles. Grabbing Diego's pant leg, she struggled to pull his leftover and onto the accelerator. Maybe the dead man could save them all one more time. The engine revved loudly as she straightened the steering wheel and closed the door. Reaching through the window, she slammed the gearshift out of neutral, into drive, and ran. Envy heard a thunderous crash behind her and jumped into the boat. She was just thanking God when a bullet punched through her back knocking her face forward into Miguel's lap as the small craft motored with the current. Envy's last thought was that she had successfully escaped.

PRESENT DAY

His strong European accent made her vulva vibrate uncontrollably. Margo Anderson-Mayes was on her hands and knees being taken from behind by a well-endowed young man several years her junior. His words though heavily laced with his Latvian native tongue were clear. Luka worshipped her posterior. With an ass well crafted by Dr. Gosha, her Beverly Hills plastic surgeon, and kept high, light, and fine from hours of Peloton cycling classes, he should. It wasn't a Kardashian ass, but it held just the right plumpness.

Gripping her small waist Luka started increasing his tempo. He reached places her husband couldn't reach with an eight-figure bank account, detailed instructions, and a team of bloodhounds.

It started at her center, swirling like a whirlpool, and then exploded, shooting pleasure to her brain flooding her with endorphins. Damn! He is good! She thought as she orgasmed. He didn't stop there but kept going like the Energizer Bunny sending her over the precipice of pleasure once more. That time, he came along for the ride. Sated, she collapsed onto his satin sheets, which were slick with their coupling. Smiling at her lover, she requested, "Be a dear and get me a cold compress. I want to be ready for round two and right now, swollen as I am, we can't continue." She shuddered with attraction as she watched him pull off a condom large enough to be confused with a pillowcase.

Almost two hours later Margo was showered, dressed, and tying a Lavorra hand-painted silk tie into a Windsor knot at her slender throat letting it rest comfortably between her cleavage. The autumn beige power linen pantsuit sported drab olive Manolo Blahnik heels that were so high, supermodels would have envied her. The jacket was a three-button single-breasted affair with tight lapels. It had to be, considering she wasn't wearing a bra or top. With her firm breasts, she could do that, thanks again to Dr. Gosha.

Turning, she soaked in one last look of Luka sprawled across the bed with that delicious monster resting lazily on his thigh, blew him a kiss, and said, "Bye darling. Fuck you later."

She swung her purse into the passenger seat of her white Rolls Royce Wraith sports coupe and then slid into the plush burgundy leather seat. Her phone automatically synced to the car when it started ringing. Ignoring it, she reached into her purse for the peas wrapped in paper towels taken from her lover's freezer. Margo lifted and positioned the frozen vegetables so that her crotch rested easily on them. The pain and swelling she endured were definitely worth the pleasure she had experienced.

Her phone started up again. The view screen on the dash identified it as her husband. Casually she answered. "Hello Scott, what's up?"

Without hesitation, her husband asked, "How did things go with Luka? I mean did he sign with us or not?" As he talked, she rifled through her bag for her lipstick container, found it, and said sweetly, "Babe, would you hold?"

She pressed mute before he could respond. Adjusting the rearview mirror, she applied a fresh coat of lipstick then quickly unscrewed the base of the container dumping a little of the white powder on the back of her hand. Afterward, she checked to make sure her nostrils were clear. That done, she unmuted her call with Scott. "Are you there, Honey? Now, where were we?"

Sounding a little exasperated he said, "I asked did you get him to sign or not."

Margo drove out of the soccer star's gated hillside mansion onto Pacific coast highway heading back to Los Angeles. "Currently, we have a tentative agreement. Instead of our usual fifteen percent commission he only wants to give up twelve-five," she told her husband.

Scott didn't like that. "Who in the fuck does this kid think he is? Lebron James?"

"He's the hottest, most marketable soccer players since David Beckham and Renaldo," His wife informed him. "In exchange, he has agreed to a four-year contract instead of two and he will shop us to some of his teammates. That twelve and a half percent isn't looking so shabby now, is it? Give me a minute to work on him."